A Child Far
from Home

BOOKS BY LIZZIE PAGE

The War Nurses

Daughters of War

When I Was Yours

The Forgotten Girls

The Wartime Nanny

SHILLING GRANGE CHILDREN'S HOME SERIES

The Orphanage

A Place to Call Home

An Orphan's Song

The Children Left Behind

An Orphan's Wish

Lizzie Page

A Child Far from Home

Bookouture

Published by Bookouture in 2024

An imprint of Storyfire Ltd.
Carmelite House
50 Victoria Embankment
London EC4Y 0DZ

www.bookouture.com

ISBN: 978-1-83525-287-1
eBook ISBN: 978-1-83525-286-4

To Debs, the best sister a girl could ever have.

On 6 December 1941, Anna Freud, the daughter of psychiatrist and founder of psychoanalysis, Sigmund Freud, reported the results of a twelve-month study on evacuation that she had authorised. Its conclusion was that 'separation from their parents is a worse shock for children than a bombing'.

1

SUMMER 1939

Jean

It was a Tuesday morning in early August and Mrs Hardman, Mrs Salt and Mrs Froud were scrubbing the doorsteps of 67 Romberg Road in the sunshine. Mrs Salt, her husband and her four children lived on the top floor, Mrs Froud, her husband and two children on the ground floor, and Mrs Hardman and her daughter Valerie were in the basement rooms.

It was the kind of sweltering summer's day that made you look forward to the respite autumn would offer, but Mrs Hardman – Jean – had stopped looking forward to anything. There were so many horrid rumours flying about.

'If we go to war, they'll send everyone out of London,' Mrs Salt said.

'Everyone?' Jean asked, shielding her eyes from the sun as she looked at Mrs Salt.

'All the children.'

Jean scrubbed until the water in her bucket was dark grey. She didn't like the sound of this. Surely they wouldn't take her Valerie away?

Mrs Salt was a pessimist but with four children under nine, born one after another, like bowling pins falling, who could blame her? The woman didn't have a moment to think. Last year, she had been fooled by *War of the Worlds* on the wireless. She had listened to the whole thing, then hammered on Jean's door, face as white as her laundered sheets, insisting that aliens from Mars were invading Woking in Surrey. So Jean wasn't inclined to believe Mrs Salt just yet. Jean didn't hold with the wireless either. She wasn't the sort to sit still listening to posh fellas droning on about Mesopotamia or genteel ladies talking about how pointing your pinkie towards the sky when you had your tea was a sign of good breeding. Fortunately, Valerie took after her in that way.

Mrs Salt started weeping into her bucket. Mrs Froud had recently suggested to Jean that maybe they should take Mrs Salt to the doctor's – they had pills for hysteria nowadays – but Jean couldn't bring herself to suggest it.

'But it's true,' Mrs Salt persisted. 'They've been planning it for ages. They call it *evacuation*. They're going to take the city children and put them in institutions.'

'Sounds like nonsense to me,' Jean said. Jean had faith, if not in the government then in the incompetence of the government. This lot couldn't organise a piss-up in a brewery. And anyway, they never did anything for the normal people – why would they start now? 'How would it even work? Institutions? Like prisons or hospitals? No. No way.' Jean continued shaking her head at the idea of Valerie somewhere like that.

'That's not it,' corrected Mrs Froud. 'It isn't institutions. Or rather, not only institutions. The plan is that city children will be sent to people's homes. Homes in the countryside.'

'I don't see how...' began Jean again.

While Jean worked ten-, twelve-hour days, Valerie cleaned their place, got the shopping, made dinner, paid the coalman, organised the milkman and tipped the postman. She looked after other people's babies, she kept an eye on Jean – told her when her heart medicine was running out and went to the doctor's when it did.

It was more than that though: Valerie was Jean's girl, her sweetheart, her best friend, her darling. They were a pair, it was the two of them against the world. No one else came close. The idea of Valerie being without her and in someone else's home just didn't make sense.

'There won't be a single child left in the whole of London,' Mrs Salt said ominously. 'The schools are going to organise it and you'll be sent to prison if you don't send your child away.'

Mrs Froud demurred. 'I don't know about that. My Neville says any evacuation will most likely be voluntary.'

'Fines then,' continued Mrs Salt. 'They'll get us one way or another.'

'There's no use getting wound up,' Jean said. 'You've been listening to the wireless too much.' Jean realised she didn't even sound reassuring to herself.

'It won't not happen just because you cover your ears, Mrs Hardman,' Mrs Salt said before blowing her nose.

'Actually, it's not going to happen at all,' Mrs Froud said.

'Why not?'

'Because there *isn't going to be another war*,' declared Mrs Froud with great confidence, and it was music to Jean's ears.

'My Neville says there will be a last-minute save, like with the Munich Agreement. No one's got the stomach for it. Not even *that Adolf* man.'

'My Neville' worked for *The Times* newspaper, and he knew everything before anyone else.

'I hope you're right,' said Jean, and Mrs Froud smiled weakly. Who in their right minds would put the world through that again?

2

Jean

Two weeks later, Hitler invaded Poland. 'My Neville' was wrong, although Mrs Froud wouldn't hear it.

That evening, Valerie and Jean went up to the Salts', where there were bowls of almond sugars and jellied sweets laid out on plates and doilies. Mrs Froud and Lydia were already there. The younger Salt children were in bed, which was a shame; Jean loved a cuddle with the littlest, five-month-old baby Joe.

Mrs Froud had decided to send nine-year-old Lydia away, but not one-year-old Matthew. She had a relative, an old lady in Coventry, who had offered to put them up, but 'My Neville' claimed it would be better for Lydia to go along with the school.

'And my Neville says you should send Valerie too.'

What business was it of Neville Froud?

Mrs Salt had also chosen to send Francine, also nine years old, away with the school – Mr Salt thought the benefits would outweigh the negatives for Francine apparently – but they were keeping the younger children back.

Fortunately, Mr Salt did not have an opinion on Valerie but

had said, 'Everyone must do what everyone must do,' which was no help. Jean had already decided – no thanks to the husbands.

Some people had friends in the countryside. Or they were pulling out all the stops to *make* friends in the countryside. Mrs Blake, two houses down, had an uncle's sister in Leicester who would take in Billy and Pauline. Mrs Hawkins round the corner had a stepfather's cousin – really? – who was going to take Mary in Derby. The Salts had their cousins in Southampton but there wasn't room for them to live there. Jean had racked her brain for long-lost relatives who might be called upon, but it was dead ends everywhere. Her mum had been an only child and she had died young. Jean remembered that she had a cousin, but who knew how to contact them? Her dad had a brother, but goodness knows where he was. They were more like strangers than family.

The prospect of sending Valerie away to an unknown family was terrible – but would Jean be able to keep her back? Jean felt stuck between a rock and a hard place. It wasn't her nature to disobey the rules. But was this a rule she should obey?

There were no fines or punishments. It was voluntary but it was *expected*. How would it look if Jean didn't send her girl away and everyone else did? What would they think of her at the school or in the community? Jean already stood out – she couldn't bear standing out more. She was a sore thumb, desperate to be just another finger.

Perhaps it would be good for her girl to get to see life outside of London, Jean considered. It's never a bad thing to learn how other people live. And maybe, just maybe, it would be good for Jean too? She had been glued to her daughter's hip for years – she knew some people frowned on it; maybe it was time they came a little unstuck?

What swung it though was the Nazis. They were on the rampage. Jean didn't have to hear them spell it out on the wireless to know that war was inevitable – a declaration was imminent. And if they invaded England next? Gas was the thing that terrified her the most. Gas had taken down her father in Ypres – and ever since she was a child, she had had terrible fears of loved ones flailing in front of her, tugging at their collars, trying to breathe. Dying was awful, but there are ways of dying that are even worse. *Don't believe people when they say there isn't a hierarchy,* she thought, *of course there is.*

She couldn't have that. She'd rather send her girl to the other side of the world than risk that.

When Jean told Valerie she was going to be evacuated, Valerie was horrified.

'What does evacuation mean?' she asked in a tiny voice.

'Just sending people out the city to somewhere safer,' Jean said.

People? Jean thought, *not people – children.* But she smiled, trying to act like it wasn't anything serious so Valerie wouldn't worry.

The girls were doing drawings together, lying on their stomachs on the floor. Mrs Salt never told them off for being unladylike, although Mrs Froud sometimes did.

Jean was ashamed to think it now, but before she had a daughter she used to imagine that, if she had one, she might be like Lydia Froud. Not her personality – Lydia could be a little madam – but in appearance. Lydia had white hair, golden skin and eyelashes dark enough that once she came home crying because the teacher said she mustn't wear make-up to school. Lydia always wore a great big bow in her hair, which gave her the air of an enormous present.

Francine Salt was dark and exuberant. She had thick lips and a toothy smile and twig legs and once she had come home crying because the teacher said she needed to eat more. She was the spit of her father, and she was Lydia's shadow.

And then there was her girl. Valerie Hardman had mousy-brown hair that could look dark or fair depending on the light, black eyebrows and a bulbous nose, and was slow to smile, but when she did, it was blinding. Valerie never came home from school crying. Mrs Salt said Valerie knew her own mind, which was a good thing, although it didn't feel like it all the time!

Valerie wore only plain or tortoiseshell clips in her hair; she claimed she was too big for bows.

'Just a little one,' Jean often tried (Jean would have worn them herself if she could) but Valerie always said no.

Valerie was capable and caring. She was also extremely bright – not just Jean's opinion, most of her teachers thought so too. She was so bright that, sometimes, Jean wondered if she'd taken the right baby home.

No, she knew Valerie was the right baby, of course, because Valerie had her father's nose – no mistaking that – and she had Jean's fine hair too, sadly, but sometimes it felt like the girl was a cuckoo in the nest. Actually, it more often felt like Jean was.

'Are you going up the station to wave them off?' asked Mrs Froud.

'The letter from the school said not to.' Jean had thought that settled it. 'They said we should try to avoid distress.'

The headteacher Mrs Lester was a vicious woman who didn't like that there wasn't a Mr Hardman, even though Jean had told her she was widowed. Jean was not looking for more black marks against her name.

'Avoid distress?' Mrs Salt sniffed. 'They're the ones causing the distress!'

'There's no point waving when you can say goodbye at home,' Jean said stoically.

Mrs Salt talked about another thing Jean found concerning: the payments for the billets. Two lots of rent to find!

'The council will help,' Mrs Froud advised.

'Oh?' Jean was puzzled. 'Is the council paying for your girls?'

No, the council wasn't.

'Then I'll manage too.' Jean didn't want handouts. She didn't want Valerie to know their financial situation was worse than the other girls'.

The neighbours drank their tea, they talked about the hot weather and what a problem Mrs Blake's Billy was, but only briefly. Soon they were drawn back to the subject of the evacuation. Jean couldn't think about anything else.

'Operation Pied Piper?' she mused. 'Why've they called it that?'

'What was the story of the Pied Piper?' Mrs Froud asked, 'Oh I'll ask my Neville. He'll know. He knows ev-'

But Mrs Salt interrupted.

'It's a terrible tale. The village of Hamelin was overrun with rats. The Pied Piper came and played and the rats followed him away, but the mayor refused to pay him. So he played again and this time all the children followed him away and they never came home again.'

'Yes, they did,' Jean protested. 'They must have!' What kind of story would it be if they didn't? – and why would they call the evacuation that if the children didn't return?

'They didn't,' Mrs Salt insisted. 'Three stayed back. One who was deaf, one who was blind and one who was lame – all the others died.'

The women fell silent.

'It's just a name,' Mrs Froud said finally. 'It doesn't mean anything.'

For the previous few days Valerie had had stomach-ache and that night, she complained of one again. Jean told her to sleep, 'feel better in the morning,' but Valerie was wide awake. Uneasily, Jean sat on the side of her bed. When Valerie was little, she used to say it was a boat and pretend the wardrobe was land ahead. Oh, the storms they weathered!

'Tell me about my daddy,' Valerie said in a little voice, fighting the sleep that was overcoming her.

This is why Jean hated talking sometimes. Small talk was fine, but then with Valerie bigger talk like this always had to sneak its way in.

'He was brave, sweetheart, and you will be too,' she mumbled, providing the same answer she always did.

Valerie kept her drawings under her pillow, and she pulled one out now. There he was, Daddy Hardman, up a ladder, rescuing two girls from a fire. She had taken great care over the boots and hands, three-four-five fingers! But the head was over-sized and the mouth a down-turned line.

'Wonderful,' said Jean, her heart racing again. Doctor said she ought to avoid excitement because of her arrhythmia but unfortunately life didn't comply. 'You're getting good at drawing people—'

'Not *people*, Daddy,' Valerie corrected.

'That's what I meant,' Jean said as she stood up from the bed.

'How long will I be away for?' Valerie asked quietly.

She hated not knowing everything. Jean pushed the hair off her forehead so she could see more of her girl's sweet face. She would never get used to the idea that she had made Valerie, that Valerie was hers. She was the best thing in Jean's life.

'Two weeks?' she suggested. 'It'll be like a holiday is all. Just till we know for sure that London is safe.'

Valerie and Jean had never had a holiday but they'd seen plenty of other people go off and come back. The Salts went to their cousins in Southampton and returned with a jellyfish sting, sunburn, nappy rash and earache. The Frouds had gone to Wales two years ago, and it had bucketed down the entire time, and their place smelled of damp towels for ages after.

'Will I be back for my birthday?'

The emphasis Valerie put on birthdays always made Jean anxious. Jean felt she would only disappoint the girl. Christmas was the same. The bigger Valerie's dreams, the more Jean panicked.

'I hope so.'

'And if not?'

'I'll just have to come and celebrate with you…'

Valerie wriggled in the bed, smiling.

'Maybe three weeks. No longer than four. They're just not ready for more than that,' Jean said, more to herself than Valerie. 'They've prepared for the journey and a short stay, like when you stayed at the Frouds' that time I was poorly.'

'What if the Nazis invade?' Valerie asked, her eyes suddenly huge with fear.

'We'll see them off.'

'But how?'

'With our brooms and mops.' Jean tickled her girl under the chin as if she were a cat.

'And we will win?'

'Of course. There's no other option,' Jean answered before switching off the light. As she left the room, she silently prayed she was right.

3

_____

Jean

On the morning of the evacuation, Jean made Valerie some porridge and watched her eat, tears in her eyes. She was reminded of the day she brought Valerie home from the hospital – three long weeks after giving birth. She remembered looking down at that sweet face for hours on end. Those searching eyes! Those chubby cheeks! Jean had felt a connection with another human that at a mere sixteen years old she'd never ever felt before – nor since. Goodness, she was feeling sentimental today. Quite out of character. Valerie pushed half of her porridge away and, when Jean scolded her about waste, she said she wasn't hungry. Then she went back to rearrange the things in her suitcase, while Jean got ready for work.

The day before, Jean had realised with horror that Valerie didn't have half of the things she needed. She had a gas mask, yes, in a sturdy black box, but petticoats and special nightwear? Slippers? Gymslip? Two pairs of stockings? And everything was supposed to have a name tag too. As though Jean had time to sew VALERIE HARDMAN everywhere! And they didn't even

have a sturdy bag for it all. Did those government officials think
they were made of money?

In between cleaning jobs, Jean had dashed to the market. She
didn't want the family who took Valerie in to think they were
tinkers. You could buy anything at Petticoat Lane – the joke was
that it was like Harrods – but most of it was knock-off. Browsing at
the stalls, Jean carefully compared prices, and then she went
through the sixpences in her purse. She bought some brand-new
vests, soft white cotton. Valerie had never had new anything before.

She had asked around, and one of the traders produced a
battered brown leather case. He said it was second-hand but it
looked like it was on its tenth.

'For you, darling?'

'For my little girl.'

'The evacuation, is it?' His tone had softened. He looked at
her with sympathy.

It was so unexpected, Jean felt like weeping into his arms
there and then. 'It is!'

'You're going to miss her, aren't you, sweetheart? Doing the
right thing though. Children first. Yours for a pound?'

Valerie had sniffed the leather like it was something delicious. She was such a funny thing. Now she said, 'Mummy, will
I need four pairs of socks? I'm not a centipede.'

She wanted to take her favourite book, *Pinocchio*, but Jean
convinced her there wasn't enough room. Before she left for
work, Jean gave Valerie a kiss on the forehead, thanking the
Lord she had such a compliant daughter.

She told her she would be there for her birthday, if not
before, to be a good girl again, not to be a problem, always keep
her gas mask with her, remember her manners, eat nicely and
write, for heaven's sake. Valerie hated writing, but she nodded.
She was nose-down in the suitcase, reorganising her vests.

'I promise, and Mummy?'

'Yes.'

'Don't worry, I won't be gone long.'

Jean crept out of the house guiltily. She mustn't dwell on it. Dwelling was a failing of hers. She would try to forget the word 'evacuation'. Val wouldn't be away for long. And if anyone could cope, her girl could.

Jean was cleaning Mrs Foley's dining table; there had been another dinner party last night – even as Nazi jackboots stomped on Warsaw there were dinner parties – when the grandfather clock struck seven, making her jump. The children had to be at the station by half past at the latest. The full force of what was happening came back to her. She pictured Valerie and her new suitcase knocking against her skinny knees. She imagined her bravely gulping back tears. Would she have remembered the gas mask? More importantly, would she remember how to put it on?

Out of the window, Jean could see schoolchildren – *and* their parents – racing past. Mrs Lester had said not to go, Jean repeated to herself under her breath, *Avoid distress.*

More fool her for being the only mother stupid enough to obey the rule.

Sometimes, Jean felt as though the school dunce's hat was still prickling on her forehead, itching in her hair, and she was facing the wall in the corner. She had stared at a crack in the plaster for most of her childhood.

Mrs Foley was still in bed when Jean dashed up to her room, a black silk eye mask over her eyes. Jean debated: should she tell her the truth or not?

'I'm sorry, Mrs Foley, I have to leave. I've come over all dizzy.'

'Can't you just polish the silver before you go?'

Jean leaned against the dressing table and started heaving as though she might throw up.

Mrs Foley peeled off her mask and glared. 'I'll dock your wages.'

Hurrying, Jean changed into her outdoor shoes and galloped towards the railway station.

It was turning into another sultry morning, summer fanning its flames, and Jean grew hotter in her coat and stockings. She still had three houses to clean today. Her bag full of dusters was not heavy but it was cumbersome.

By the time she was near the station, crowds of parents were walking away from it.

'They've gone,' one man without a hat said to her cheerfully. 'Nice to have some peace and quiet!'

She ignored him, but she kept going against the throng. She imagined Valerie's face pressed against a train window, trying to seek her out. She should have been there – it was more than a wave; it was everything. How did she always get things so terribly wrong?

Jean had to pay just to get onto the platform. There was an evacuation train there – she saw children at the fogged-up windows, frantically waving at a few stragglers. Were they distressed? She couldn't tell. She couldn't make any of them out but one of them might be her Valerie. Jean waved until her arm ached and then she waved some more with the other arm and then the train pulled away.

4

Valerie

On the walk up to the station, Lydia was crying about her pillowcase, so Valerie offered to swap it for her suitcase. It was a daft thing to offer, but Valerie had anticipated that Lydia would say no, that it was too much bother to unpack in the street. Instead, Lydia's eyes lit up and she sang out, 'I want it!'

Valerie always underestimated Lydia's ability to get people to put themselves out for her.

'Can I have it? Pinkie promise?' Lydia asked in her sweetest voice.

Valerie's case was brown leather, the clasp was smooth and, when her mum had brought it home from the market, it was love at first sight.

Her mum probably wouldn't have let her swap but the words had just jumped out of Valerie's mouth and now she couldn't take them back. This often happened.

She hoped Mrs Froud would intervene with a 'Lydia, don't be selfish,' but Mrs Froud was crying into her handkerchief, and then damply patting Valerie on the shoulder said, 'You are a good girl.'

Once they reached the station, Valerie transferred all her belongings, including the new vests, onto the pavement. Lydia took her things out of her pillowcase and poured them into Valerie's suitcase. When Lydia saw Valerie's pristine vests, her mouth fell open, but here, Valerie stood firm – the suitcase was more than enough.

A fruit cake, golden and moist, was transferred into Valerie's suitcase. Valerie's eyes grew large at the sight of it.

'Make sure you share, Lydia!' Mrs Froud said, noticing Valerie's interest.

Lydia snapped back, 'Yes, Mummy, I KNOW!'

If Valerie ever talked to her mum the way Lydia talked to Mrs Froud, she'd be toast.

Parents were crying. Even some of the mums you wouldn't expect were.

Mrs Salt, Francine's mum, was wiping her eyes on her sleeve. She was one you *would* expect; her mum called her a depressive. Even so, Mrs Salt was Valerie's favourite mother. She was how you pictured a mum to look. Plump and rosy, she was always bending down for a kiss. She had dark hair in a bun and kind, albeit fearful eyes. She also had a slight moustache, which on anyone else would have been comical but on her it was endearing. Francine's dad was nice too. Francine was lucky. Lydia's mum was nice but always harassed, and her dad was handsome but her mum said he was pompous.

Now Mrs Salt leaned over Valerie, smelling of tears and flowers.

'Please look after Francine and Lydia,' she whispered into Valerie's ear as she hugged her.

Valerie nodded. She would have anyway, but it was flattering to be asked. She knew she was the biggest girl here. She would take care of Lydia and Francine like she always did. 'Please don't worry,' she assured Mrs Salt.

She was rewarded with another warm hug. Mrs Froud was still fussing over the fruit cake.

'Give some to the other children, Lydia!'

Valerie's mum always said it was a wonder Mrs Froud didn't forget her own head. And then Mrs Froud said it too: 'You must look after the girls, Valerie...'

Valerie's favourite teacher, Miss Beedle, hurried over to them, clearly worried that they were going to miss the train if they kept on hugging and swapping cases.

'The children will be well looked after,' she told Mrs Froud, then, smiling at Valerie, she added, 'It's my job – not yours.'

'But Valerie is a family friend,' insisted Mrs Froud.

'Stay together, Valerie,' said Mrs Salt, sobbing.

Valerie nodded again. For two or three weeks? She could do this. She was concerned the break would harm her studies, but was reassured by the presence of Miss Beedle. And whatever was going on, it was bound to be educational. She would surely get to learn some interesting things.

Mrs Lester, the headteacher, always found something to be annoyed about, and now she was annoyed at the influx of parents. Valerie heard her complaining to the other teachers: 'No one turned up at St Graham's County High,' she said. And 'Should be like tearing off a plaster.' And 'This is more upsetting for the children.'

But none of the children seemed upset, not even Francine or Lydia. They were maybe tired or bored, but not distressed; even when the teachers placed luggage labels round their necks, most of them thought it was a whole lot of fun.

'Makes the evacuation harder,' Mrs Lester tsked to Miss Beedle.

Evacuation was a funny word, a new word, although

Valerie remembered the poster at the doctor's where her mum cleaned: 'Evacuate your bowels'.

She had tugged on her mum's hands when she read it, and remembered asking, 'What does evacuate your bowels mean?'

'*Val-e-rie!*' was all her mum had said in return.

It is hard being in a friendship of three. Nothing is built for three. The swings, the ball games, the walking in a crocodile are all made for two. Valerie had hoped she, Lydia and Francine might sit as a three on the train but most of the seats were in twos and the ones that weren't were monopolised by the boys. Derek, Ian and Kevin were burping and farting and making themselves at home. Only Patrick kept himself to himself, reading a comic about soldiers. Some of the boys were becoming obsessed with guns and fighting and bombs, even though the war hadn't started yet and Mum said it might not.

Lydia and Francine sat together and Valerie took the seat opposite, by the window. She put her gas mask in its box next to her and looked over at them. Lydia appeared so wholesome, she thought, like a girl in an underground advertisement for sliced bread. Francine was more mysterious. You never knew what she was thinking. Now, Francine was staring so hard at a pair of dice her dad had given her as a goodbye treat that she was going cross-eyed. Valerie wanted to warn her that Lydia would swipe those too if she had half a chance.

They were off, leaving a cloud of black smoke in their wake – and everyone cheered and the children who had someone on the platform blew kisses.

'Your mummy didn't come,' pointed out Lydia.

'She's working.'

Valerie imagined her mum there, in her Sunday best, which was when she looked most beautiful. Her hat, her dark eyes, her lipstick, calling out like she did on sports day once, 'Go, Vally, go!' even after Valerie's egg had dropped off its spoon.

Valerie understood why her mother could not be there and she was used to it. Some of her friends had families so large you could hardly walk a street without them being related to this shopkeeper or that newspaper seller, but she and Mum had always been family enough. You could be jealous, or you could be happy with what you'd got, and Valerie didn't find it hard to be the latter. Nevertheless, it would have been nice to give Mum one last squeeze goodbye.

Maybe her dad would have been there today waving at her like she was a princess, but he couldn't help being dead. Better to have loved and lost than never to have loved at all, her mum always said that.

Miss Beedle did a sloping walk down the train aisle, counting to herself with her lips moving. Miss Beedle liked doing art with the children. She asked them to bring in fruit to school for drawing and, when no one did, she brought in a basket herself and then at the end of the class, after they had observed the curve of the apple, the texture of the pear, she let them eat it all.

'I want all the older children out at the next station. Ten years and up, children, that's you.'

'What?' Valerie asked, confused.

'You're getting off here.' Miss Beedle smiled at Valerie. 'Hedingway Hall.'

'It's a lovely place,' Mrs Lester joined in. 'There'll be lots of facilities. Better than you're used to,' she added under her breath.

'Off you go, Valerie,' Miss Beedle continued, her eyes misty. And then in a low voice, 'You'll have a wonderful time.'

Valerie was frozen to her seat. 'But I promised I'd stay with Lydia and Francine and look after them.'

She remembered Mrs Salt's pleading eyes and Mrs Froud's limp handshake and Lydia's fruit cake in her suitcase.

It wasn't just a promise, although it was half that. They were her friends. There was something so comforting and familiar about them. And they were just as happy in her company as she was in theirs. Her dad would never have abandoned anyone, especially not two little girls.

The two teachers talked in hushed tones as they considered what to do. Francine kept blowing her snotty nose, which may have helped. Finally, Miss Beedle said, 'Fine. We'll do our best to find a place for the three of you – and if not, we'll try to find a place nearby.'

Valerie beamed, but Francine and Lydia didn't seem to realise they had nearly been separated.

As the other children got off the train, Valerie realised she was the absolute oldest left in the carriage – well, apart from the teachers. She was a foot taller than some of the other children and she was no giant herself.

The boys had been rowdy, but grew more subdued the greater the distance from home. Stanley Dooley had his catapult confiscated although Mona Wilson claimed that he had brought two anyway *and* a small pen knife. The twins, Harry and Michael, had been told off about upsetting everyone with their gas masks. Mary Kittle had wanted to throw up but she didn't, while Sharon Barnet did throw up, unannounced.

Patrick didn't look up from his comic once.

'What a landscape!' Miss Beedle said, kneeling next to Valerie and pointing out of the window.

Valerie smiled, trying to appear keen but she still had a stomach-ache. She hadn't had any fresh air at the last stop because Miss Beedle had asked her to count the children again – you could never count children enough.

The countryside was different. Obviously they had trees in London, but here the trees were everywhere, as though accompanying them along. There were fields as far as Valerie could see, and you could see people working in them; they would rise up to look at the passing trains. Everything was yellow, brown and green. Valerie had expected more colours, for some reason.

And then Mrs Lester was calling, 'Look, children.' She was pointing out of the window on the opposite side to where Valerie was sitting.

They all turned to the windows and those who had the window seats pressed themselves to the glass.

'Horses!' the children chorused.

'Not quite!' Mrs Lester smirked at the other teachers. 'Can you believe this?'

Valerie realised the teachers were laughing at them, and it made her catch her breath.

'What are they?' Francine asked.

'Don't you know?' Mrs Lester continued, gloating.

'They're cows,' said Valerie, aggravated by this game. Just how were little children from London meant to know this?

Later, Miss Beedle asked her to move her gas mask, then plumped down on the seat next to her. One of the things Valerie liked about Miss Beedle was that she talked to everyone like they were grown-ups. While others barked commands, Miss Beedle interacted. Miss Beedle had been trying to get the school to let Valerie write with her left hand, but to no avail.

Once, Miss Beedle had shown them paintings by the Impressionists and the Pre-Raphaelites. Francine looked like Lizzie Siddal, Lydia looked like Botticelli's Virgin Mary, while Valerie looked like no one. And once Miss Beedle had told them that she was engaged to be married and her fiancé liked painting too. They dreamed of having a studio together in the countryside one day.

'Were you thinking you'd like to paint them?' Valerie asked.

'I certainly was,' Miss Beedle said brightly, but then she looked concerned again. 'You'll miss your mum,' she said gently. 'You're close, aren't you?'

'But it won't be for long,' returned Valerie brightly.

'No, right, yes,' agreed Miss Beedle. 'And you can tell her about all the exciting things you get to see.'

Valerie wanted to show that she was taking it all in. 'Like the cows.'

'Exactly.'

Such a long way for a holiday, thought Valerie, but it wasn't a normal holiday, not a seaside trip. This trip was about getting out of harm's way. She suddenly had a pang of worry for her mum, now alone in London, which had become a dangerous place.

She felt more sweaty than usual and thought longingly of her new clothes.

She pushed open the window to let in some air, but Lydia insisted the wind would make her hair fly around. She was particular about her hair and Valerie closed it again. The train was slowing down for another stop, only this time Mrs Lester was clapping her hands.

'We're here...'

5

Jean

Jean went to Mrs Hardy's house from the railway station and was relieved that Mrs Hardy was already out so she wouldn't have to answer any questions about why her face was so puffy or her eyes so red. The key was under the mat; if Jean worked like the clappers she'd catch up with the chores. And at least it would distract her from worrying about Val.

Please God, she would be okay.

Jean's favourite houses were the ones that started off in a mess so that she could leave them shining. Unfortunately, she didn't get to make a huge difference to many of the houses she cleaned – they were already in a lovely condition – but still. It was the race *between* the houses that was the real waste of her time. Jean spent too much of her day galloping from one job to the next, spoiling her shoes, but there was no way around it. She even had to turn jobs down (well-paid jobs too) because they were too far away.

The next house was Mrs Cutler's. 'I've sent my son away to the countryside,' Mrs Cutler said while Jean was going about flicking things with the feather duster. 'I can't stop thinking about his tiny face.'

'I sent my daughter away too,' Jean said in a rush of disclosure.

Mrs Cutler's cup clattered onto her saucer. 'I beg your pardon!'

'My Valerie's gone to the countryside too.'

Mrs Cutler's face was so startled, Jean wanted to give it a flick instead of the tassels on the lampshade. You wouldn't think they'd get dirty, but they do. Dust gets everywhere.

'I didn't even know you had a daughter.'

You could almost see the cogs in Mrs Cutler's brain whirring. *She only looks twenty-one, twenty-three at the most.*

'How is that possible?'

That was a bit much! 'The usual way,' Jean said.

'You don't look old enough.'

'I'm twenty-six.'

Three years she had been working for Mrs Cutler. For three years she had known when Mrs Cutler had relations with her husband and that she kept a diary, that she burned letters from her father but kept the letters from her mother in a red ribbon, and Mrs Cutler didn't know a single thing about her.

But what could you do? Mrs Cutler paid promptly, at good rates. Without her, Jean would be stuffed.

'I didn't know...'

'Shall I do the ironing now?'

'And where is she? Your – little girl?'

'My Valerie? She's going to the West Country.'

When Mrs Froud told her that was where they were going, Jean had wanted to scream, because she thought the West Country was abroad. She'd still be on that train, right now, with the teachers.

'She'll be well looked after there.'

Two minutes ago, Mrs Cutler didn't know she had a daughter. Now she knew that her daughter would be well looked after? Although Jean needed to believe that was true, she couldn't help thinking: *Some people think they know everything...*

And then Mrs Cutler said, 'I'm going to join him next week. He's with my parents. It's not safe here any more.'

'Oh?'

'Which means I don't think I'll be needing you any more. I apologise.'

And so it begins, realised Jean.

That night was the first night Jean dreamed about the rat. She was half-asleep when she heard a scratching or felt a presence of something in the room. When she opened her eyes, it was leaning over her – a great big grey rat, size of a newborn baby, its claws pulled up, its tail long, ready to spring. Jean squealed, but when she next opened her eyes, it was gone.

6

Valerie

Once the train had disappeared in a flurry of whistles and steam-snorts, it was as quiet as night on the station platform, even though it was the middle of the day. They were led outside then put in groups, where Valerie wiped Francine's nose and her cheeks and brushed Lydia's hair. Lydia was unhappy when her hair wasn't brushed, while Francine was unhappy when hers was. Valerie didn't have a moment to tidy herself up.

Miss Beedle reiterated the importance of good behaviour to her mostly uninterested audience: 'As guests, you are to appreciate the hospitality being shown.'

Valerie suspected most of the children didn't know what she meant. Helpfully, she hissed, 'Be polite,' to them and, to Stanley, 'Don't be rude.' She often felt like a translator or a go-between adults and children. It was like she spoke both their languages. Miss Beedle said it was because Valerie was good at listening. Valerie suspected it was because she spent more time with adults than with other children.

When Mum came home late from work, the first thing she

said was always, 'I need five minutes,' before Valerie was allowed to talk. Mum was always gasping for a brew – and a cigarette. Once those five minutes were over, she was all Valerie's, unless she was going out doing more cleaning. Valerie could sometimes beat Jean at snap, gin rummy and poker but she could always thrash her at pairs. Jean complained that it was because she had a terrible memory and Valerie's was brilliant. Valerie said, 'Don't worry, Mum, I remember things so you don't have to.'

The groups all walked up the road to a village hall, up a tree-lined lane with lilac flowers round the door. This was promising since lilac was Valerie's favourite colour. They had been travelling for such a long time so, despite not wanting to be here, Valerie couldn't help feeling the relief of arrival. The walk wasn't long; the children didn't have time to complain. They were in a town called Taunton, in Somerset apparently.

Stanley Dooley had wet his shorts, so he was taken off and changed, but the trousers he was given were enormous. Mary Kittle finally threw up, and it splattered on the ground and over Sharon Barnet's shoes.

'They're new!' she shouted. 'My sister only had them for three months.'

Valerie, Francine and Lydia joined the queue at the outside toilet. After a long wait, it was her turn, and Valerie couldn't believe her eyes.

Blood. She couldn't have been more astonished. It wasn't red wee, it wasn't blackcurrant squash, she hadn't the faintest idea how it got there. An injury? A sting? Her new underwear? An insect bite on her bottom? There was only newspaper in the lav. She could fold it and put it in her knickers, but it might crackle. She didn't know what to do. Someone was knocking on the door. Daft Mary Kittle probably. 'Hurry up,' they called.

Valerie wondered if she should tell Mary Kittle – or whoever it was – to call for a teacher, but what on earth would she say? She would have to manage it another way. It would hopefully – please God – have disappeared by bedtime.

Back in the hall, she could only find Mrs Lester, who scowled. 'What is it, girl?' followed by 'Can't it wait?', which wasn't inviting.

'I need my pillowcase,' Valerie whispered, although they had said no one was to have their luggage yet.

'Not now!' Mrs Lester hissed.

After a few minutes, Valerie decided to defy her teacher. She went outside and found her pillowcase squashed under a load of suitcases on the kerb. She tugged out one of the beautiful vests. It was the only thing small enough. With her face scarlet from embarrassment and shame, she went back to the queue for the lavatory.

She would have confided in Miss Beedle, but she was busy coordinating, and Valerie didn't know which words she'd use anyway.

By the time Miss Beedle noticed her with a, 'You're pale, Valerie,' she was standing with a tall man, a vicar maybe, and Valerie couldn't speak in front of him.

What could have happened? The journey maybe? The seats? Could a train do that to you? If it had, then it would affect other people, not just her. She gazed around. No one was acting differently.

She had had a cold for the last few days, could that be it?

She had a distant memory of seeing blood in a lavatory once before, but it wasn't hers and she hadn't asked.

.   .   .

All the children were given a glass of milk, except Mary Kittle, who was green around the gills, and one of the twins because milk brought him out in hives. Some of the smaller children were on the verge of tears again, and Valerie went over to calm them down, but she was thinking she needed five minutes too.

Lydia still hadn't shared her fruit cake. The thought of it, sitting in her beloved suitcase, made Valerie hungry and she temporarily forget about the blood. This wasn't how she'd imagined evacuation. Everything felt slightly off.

And then grown-ups started arriving at the hall.

They were different from people at home; Valerie tried to work out how or why. They were slower-paced maybe, they even spoke slower, or less, and their accents were different from the London ones she was used to. Valerie could understand them, but she had a feeling she might need to be a translator for them too. They dressed better than people at home but not smarter. Their clothes were good-quality, but they were less dressed up.

Miss Beedle put her hand on her shoulder. 'Smile, Valerie, it hasn't happened yet,' and Valerie was going to ask what that meant but pretended she knew.

Mrs Lester clomped past. 'Don't look miserable, girl.'

The adults were having animated discussions over tea in china cups and saucers that were nicer than the best Mum had at home.

A pretty woman in a white blouse and flared skirt said, 'Twin boys, why not? Would you like to live on a farm?' She had a sweet voice like she was coaxing birds to take crusts.

And a young couple, him in a suit and her in a dress, said, 'A little girl would be ideal – she can share with our Beatrice.' They pointed at Lydia, pretty Lydia, who like a rainbow drew the eye wherever she went, but Lydia froze, clutching Francine's hand. Miss Beedle enquired, 'Is there not room for more?' and then said, 'I'm afraid that's not pos...'

Valerie lost track of them, but she thought the pair ended up taking Sharon Barnet and her sicky shoes instead.

'It's only for a couple of weeks,' she told Lenny, a six-year-old who was weeping for his granddad so much that he was hiccupping.

'We'll be home before the month is over,' she told Stanley, who was sitting with his knees up to his face in the corner.

'We don't know when exactly,' corrected Miss Beedle.

'Until it's safe to go back...' Valerie recited.

'Exactly – and we don't know when that will be.'

'But—' began Valerie.

'What we do know is that these people are kind to offer their homes for us, for however long, aren't they?'

Valerie wondered if she and Jean would open their home to holidaying children if things were the other way round. As it was only for a short while, they might, but they had hardly any space themselves so that would be against them. She and Jean shared a room. They had a divider down the middle for privacy, but at night she could hear Jean snoring and it was a comfort to her.

Valerie had read enough novels to know not everyone lived like she and her mother and that many children had their own bedrooms and some even had maids. She wondered what type of house she would go to and if it would be like in the Agatha Christie books: mansion houses with upstairs and downstairs and butlers that you rang a bell for. She knew from one of her novels, *Cold Comfort Farm*, that some places were uncomfortable for outsiders but, with a smattering of good humour and goodwill, you could get by.

An older man with a grey beard was now talking to Stanley – 'You'll have your own room in the attic, and you'll be able to play in the garden, oh and we have a small dog called Buttons, how does that sound to you?'

Valerie thought it sounded heavenly; he'd want to stay

longer than a few weeks surely! But Stanley had laid his cap on his lap and looked as though he was contemplating his options. Maybe he was holding out for a place with a butler?

'My goodness, they're small,' said a new arrival to the hall.

'That one looks like an angel,' said his wife.

Valerie didn't even have to look up to know where the finger was pointing: straight at Lydia.

Time passed slowly. A few adults looked at them then went away. Miss Beedle was running here and there. Finally, some sandwiches were brought out for them to eat. The bread was different from what they had in London and some of the children cried and Francine worried because she wasn't supposed to have kosher or she *was* supposed to have kosher. Valerie wasn't sure.

'What is kosher?' Valerie asked.

'Jewish bread.'

'Perhaps it's okay, if you pray before you eat,' Valerie advised, and Francine closed her eyes before tucking in.

Lydia left her crusts because she was afraid they would make her hair grow curlier. Valerie's stomach was churning too much to eat, although she did have room for something sweet...

'What about the fruit cake?' she reminded Lydia.

'I'm not hungry,' said Lydia and, although Valerie didn't like to think Lydia was spiteful, she did then.

'Are you sisters?' interrupted a woman with a clipboard. Behind her stood a woman with short curly hair. She had a thin face and some wrinkles round her eyes, yet the way she held herself was jaunty. She was wearing a long beige coat belted at the middle and on the collar was pinned a large brooch of coloured glass in the shape of a frog. Valerie thought the brooch – and its owner – looked fascinating.

'We are,' said Lydia, clutching Francine's hand.

'Not *actual* sisters,' clarified Valerie. 'Although we live in the same house.' She avoided Francine's eyes as they filled with tears. Lydia stared stonily ahead.

'That's good – we'll be able to split you up.'

'Nooo,' the girls chorused, and the woman walked away, shaking her head.

'Look what you did!' said Lydia, crossing her arms.

Some of the children left with their 'holiday families', as the children were now calling them. The adults were using the words 'billets' or 'billeting', which Valerie thought had something to do with tickets. The experience reminded Valerie of waiting for the prefect badge in assembly – that hadn't gone well either. When she'd gone home complaining about it, Jean said it was because they always picked the tall girls, and then, exasperated, 'Who wants to be a prefect anyway? It's better to be free.' Eventually Valerie had agreed but secretly she was desperate to be a prefect.

While they waited, Valerie told stories to Francine and Lydia, who was still sulking. Some of the stories were true, some weren't, but she made sure they were all full of peril before they reached a resolution.

This one was about a boy who ran away from home and encountered all sorts of creatures, from dragons and minotaurs to foxes and squirrels. The girls found them all equally scary.

Watching them, the woman with the frog brooch nodded encouragingly.

Valerie didn't dare get up – she was worried she was leaking. Then the woman walked over to Valerie and knelt by her. 'So? What happened next?'

'I don't know!' admitted Valerie and the woman laughed.

'You're a good storyteller.'

'My teachers say that too!' Valerie said to the brooch, then shut her mouth quickly. She knew the modest thing was to say nothing, but sometimes these things bubbled out of her.

The woman smiled, though. 'I'm going to take the younger two girls, is that all right?'

Valerie nodded. As the hours ticked by, she had accepted that it was unlikely they would all find a place together.

'I can't bring you home as well. That would be asking for trouble, I'm afraid.' She put her hand on Valerie's cheek. 'Especially a young lady as clever and beautiful as you. But you're going to be fine. Sit up straight, put a smile on your face, and a nice family will select you soon.'

Valerie didn't see how she was asking for trouble, she was probably the least trouble of anyone, but she murmured a thank-you and sat up straighter. She couldn't bring herself to smile, though. The journey and the discovery in the lavatory had taken everything out of her. Lydia and Francine would be horrified if she told them.

She considered talking to the clipboard lady, but she didn't know what words she could use without being told off.

She wouldn't tell anyone, she decided. Mum wouldn't want her to. Jean prided herself on being private. 'Don't go telling people our business,' was another thing she said. She would wait till she got home.

Francine hugged Valerie goodbye and Lydia held out her doll to kiss like she was doing her a favour. They were acting younger than they were, but it was working a treat. The woman looked uncertainly at her, as though still contemplating her fate. Valerie kept her eyes on the frog brooch. She checked her gas mask was still on her lap.

'You'll be fine,' the woman repeated as though trying to convince herself. 'I don't think I can manage three.'

Valerie felt her usual compulsion to please the adults. 'It's all right, it's only for a few weeks anyway.'

'I'm not sure if that's the case,' the woman said with concern in her voice.

'My mum promised,' Valerie explained. 'She's coming for my birthday too.'

'Is she?' The woman looked around the room awkwardly. Miss Beedle shrugged her shoulders and Valerie flushed. One of them must have got it wrong. She couldn't work out who.

7

Valerie

The hall was nearly empty.

'There are no families left!' a large man said, plumping himself down next to her.

'Oh,' said Valerie. His thigh was pressed alongside hers.

'Sorry, I can't take you home because it's only me,' he continued as if Valerie were begging him to. 'It wouldn't be right.' He licked his lips. He told her he was twenty-five years old and that he was a piano teacher. Despite that, he was wearing wellington boots; a lot were. She had never seen so many wellington boots in her life. 'They don't think it would be acceptable...' he continued. His breath smelled, although she worried hers might too. It had been a long time since she'd brushed her teeth.

'It would be fine though. You and me, we'd get along nicely.'

She felt like he was sitting on top of her, he was that close.

Miss Beedle strode over, unusually agitated. 'Is everything okay here?'

The man didn't seem to welcome her intervention. He

shrugged, then slowly stood up. 'I was explaining why I can't take her. It wouldn't be proper. Poor mite.'

As he backed off, Valerie could feel her tension drain away. As long as it wasn't him, she'd be all right.

Miss Beedle put her hand on Valerie's arm. For once she didn't smell of turps and oils, but you could still see paint in her fingernails.

'If they don't find you a family, you'll lodge with me.'

That sounded wonderful. Lodge? Like playing grown-ups with the nicest teacher of all? Valerie imagined doing art with Miss Beedle in the morning, and reading Shakespeare with the English teacher in the afternoon...

She was about to say, 'Can't we arrange that now?' when an older woman came into the hall. The woman was flushed from hurrying or from wearing a wool coat on this warm day.

'Where are they then?' she asked no one in particular.

One of the clipboarders greeted her nervously. 'Afternoon, Mrs Woods. Good of you to come.'

'There's hardly anyone here!'

'Most have been taken already.'

'Just the runts of the litter left? I'll have some tea if we're going to do this.'

Clipboarder scurried off and the woman took off her gloves, ready for business. She turned to another official.

'I am busy in the shop all day. You could have saved one – seems unfair that you didn't. Are there no lads? I need an older boy. For the shop, you see.'

Miss Beedle stepped forward. 'I'd like to introduce you to Valerie Hardman.' Smiling at Valerie, she continued, 'There is nothing runt of the litter about her. Valerie is an excellent student – gifted, you might say.'

This woman sized her up and down disapprovingly. And Valerie felt sweaty and ashamed: what if she was giving off a scent of blood? She felt like tugging Miss Beedle's sleeve. 'I'll be fine lodging with you!'

'How old?' the woman said, continuing to eye Valerie.

'Ten,' Miss Beedle said.

'If there's no one else, I suppose I'll have to take her. Are you strong?'

Valerie nodded.

'Any good at adding up?'

Miss Beedle didn't say anything and neither did Valerie.

Lodge, thought Valerie. *Please.*

'She's not mute, is she?'

Miss Beedle pleaded with her eyes for Valerie to say something.

'I'm not mute,' she said finally.

And then Mrs Lester dashed over. She and Mrs Woods knew each other! Valerie didn't get how, but they were old friends. And they were clearly pleased to see each other again.

'You couldn't do better than this lady,' Mrs Lester said to Valerie, before apologising to Mrs Woods: 'If I'd known you were here, I would have sorted something out.'

She turned back to Valerie, eyes penetrating like search-lights. 'Mrs Woods and I go back a long way – so remember, I will hear *everything* that goes on.'

It was another ten-minute walk from the hall, but this time away from the station. Mrs Woods marched ahead; Valerie trailed after, dragging her pillowcase along the ground.

It was a plain, old house with a large front window. There was no electricity. There was a thick layer of dirt everywhere. There was only an outside sink with a pump. Oof, the water was cold! She didn't know where the bath was. The toilet was outside too, but she didn't mind that – she didn't want to go bleeding

inside. She minded more that she didn't have a room. There was
a mattress in the upstairs hall at the top of the stairs. There was a
spare room – there had to be for them to get signed off as hosts –
but it was full to the rafters with cardboard boxes of hammers
and screwdrivers and candles and matches. There was a
bedframe in there too somewhere, but it was submerged, so deep
out of sight it may as well have been at the bottom of the ocean.

'Where shall I put my—'

'As long as it's out my way, I don't care.'

Valerie was used to grumpy people; her mother often
returned home with tales of them. Nevertheless, she was taken
aback by how grumpy this one was. She was like a creature in
one of her made-up stories.

If Valerie wrote to her mum, she would only worry and whereas
some parents might dash in like in 'The Charge of the Light
Brigade', Jean wasn't like that.

'We need to get on with things,' Mum liked to say. Or:
'Everyone has to do their bit,' which she said whenever war was
mentioned.

And it was only two weeks 'billeting' anyway. Valerie could
wait it out.

The worst thing was that she had stained her skirt. 'May I
have a bath?' she asked as politely as she could. The thought
that Mrs Woods would tell Mrs Lester that she was rude was
chilling.

'Demanding thing, aren't you?' snapped Mrs Woods before
telling her she couldn't have a bath until next week. 'What will
you do all day? You can't hang around here,' Mrs Woods went
on as she lit a cigarette.

Valerie did her best not to cough. 'I will go to school,' she
explained, mystified.

'Like school, do you?' Mrs Woods asked, a gleam in her eye.

Valerie nodded.

'What? Speak up.'

'I like school,' Valerie whispered.

'Make sure you're a good girl – or you won't go. Understood?'

Yes, Valerie understood.

Valerie had stayed out of the way on the upstairs landing for most of the weekend, until Mrs Woods screamed at her to get out. Then she had wandered around outdoors, getting lost and worrying about the blood and her vests. She couldn't wait for school on Monday.

The evacuated children were all in their own class in a separate building. It was the old gymnasium, which was technically still on the school grounds. And because they were mostly little children, they were all at least one or two years younger than her, she felt like a giraffe in a field of dormice. Valerie had a feeling that she wasn't going to learn much, but at least it was away from Mrs Woods and she could borrow books and educate herself. School had always been Valerie's saving grace, the place she fitted in best. She loved the lined papers, the cool classrooms and the tippy desks where children from generations back had carved their initials in hearts.

Valerie wasn't great at music or maths, but she enjoyed the structure of the school day and the acquisition of knowledge. She enjoyed history, geography and English, but she was curious about most subjects and she learned quickly, even if her handwriting made teachers despair.

Lydia and Francine didn't turn up to the class and that was another worry. Could the woman with the lovely frog brooch be a bad person? What if she was like the witch in *Hansel and Gretel*?

Stanley was scrunching up his work and throwing it at

Michael's head. Michael was thumping his chest and hollering. His host family had promised to take him to see *Tarzan* as soon as the cinemas opened again.

Everyone said what they'd been doing with their Somerset families.

'Apple-picking,' squealed tiny Moira.

'Climbing trees,' said even tinier Ena.

'I went to paddle in the sea,' whispered shy Percy. His host family had a long sleek car with a metallic lady on the bonnet. Stanley said they had oodles of money and they had driven to Lyme Regis and gone fossil-hunting.

This all sounded marvellous. Valerie looked around incredulously, but most of the other children had had such a good time that weekend too that they weren't even jealous.

She had just been unlucky.

After about four days, though, the bleeding finally stopped, and the relief was immense. She rinsed her clothes under the outdoor tap. A few more days passed and Valerie wondered if it had happened at all. Ghosts and monsters were imaginary, so maybe she had imagined the blood. She wished her mum was here to ask.

8

AUTUMN 1939

Jean

Jean's busiest day was Sunday – the opposite to everyone else's – and she liked that. She cleaned the cinema for three hours after the Saturday-night crowd had left it filthy. Sometimes she took left-over bags of sweets home for Valerie – until she heard that some people sucked off the sugar and then put them back in the bag.

It was as she was leaving the cinema on the way to her next job, two days after Valerie had left, that Jean found out that war had broken out. The newspaper boy was screeching, and it was such a contrast to the quiet of the cinema that it felt like a personal affront.

'Chamberlain says it's definitely war. No going back.'

She paid the boy, scanning the headlines for herself. Her heart was racing – everyone's must have been. She guessed the boy was about sixteen; he'd be first in the firing line. And maybe he read her mind, because he looked her dead in the eye and said, 'I'm joining up tomorrow, Missus. Wish me luck.'

He was going to need it. What did an innocent kid like him know about anything?

Jean was at the doctor's surgery for the next four hours, wiping desks, chairs, the filing cabinet and the fireplace. It felt like the quietest place in East London. It was one of the only places where there wasn't someone supervising her or telling her their hard-luck stories. She always made sure to take back some of the proper toilet roll they kept. Perks of the job. It used to last her and Val all week.

She heard a key in the lock and jumped up – no one usually came when she was there. It was the doctor, carrying two cardboard boxes. He didn't seem surprised to see her, so she carried on sweeping and dusting. Then the doctor said to her that his brother had a practice in Surrey. He was taking his parents there.

'I've sent my daughter away,' Jean said, since they were exchanging confidences.

'Good,' he said, approvingly, as she'd hoped. She had done the right thing. From market traders to doctors, everyone agreed. Everyone was saying it: the bombs would come, the Nazis would invade, they'd divide the country into zones and Southend and then London would be the first to fall.

'City in wartime is no place for children.' It wasn't until after he said that and started packing up the surgery that Jean realised she was out of another job.

The cinema didn't even tell Jean they had closed; she went there as usual the week after and found a padlock on the door and a sign: *Regretfully closed till further notice!*

The exclamation mark seemed out of place.

Then one of the women she cleaned for said she was moving in with her daughter in Suffolk. Then another said she wasn't going away but she might as well be.

'Every spare penny is going to the war-fund and as I'm never home anyway, there's no mess! I'm sorry but I imagine you'll be off to do war work too, won't you?'

Would she? As far as Jean knew, war work was factories and farms, and she had no aptitude for either. She remembered hearing about the poor girls who went yellow making munitions during the Great War. That wasn't for her.

And she found the countryside intimidating; she liked the hard edges and sharp corners of the city – she had hard edges and sharp corners too, and London was where she belonged.

Then another lady whose house Jean cleaned told her that she too was leaving, to join family in the Cotswolds.

So now she didn't have the doctor's or the cinema and she was five houses down. She had to pay for her own rent and Valerie's billet, and she would have to pay to go and visit Valerie if it went on much longer. This was a problem.

In the evening, waiting in the blackout, waiting for the bombs to come, without Valerie, Jean's mood grew darker too. Sometimes Mrs Froud would invite her up, but Mrs Froud and her Neville pawed each other like monkeys picking off fleas. You always were a gooseberry with them. And Mrs Salt was busy with her bunch or her in-laws and everybody else. She sometimes left baby Joe with Jean, who felt a special rapport with him – she loved the way he clutched her finger and made cooing noises – but it felt odd to hold him while she couldn't hold her own child.

Neither Mrs Salt nor Mrs Froud seemed to be suffering as Jean was. Maybe it was because they still had other children with them, whereas her child – her world – was gone.

Jean had lost her appetite and she had never had much of one anyway. Without Valerie, she couldn't be bothered to make anything.

She cut bread and toasted it and that was the only effort she was prepared to go to. 'Valerie,' she whispered, imagining her girl whispering back *miss-yous* and *love-yous*.

It looked like the evacuation was going to last longer than they had first anticipated. Jean found it hard to sit with the emotions that whirred in her head. At night, she woke from nightmares of German soldiers with their armbands and foul moustaches. Resistance was futile. She dreamed of thick choking chlorine in her throat, in her eyes or in her head. She dreamed of more rats. She would wake up screaming and the rats would dissolve, but they still felt utterly and horrifyingly real.

Jean wasn't a single young thing, able to join the effort and do whatever it was all the young girls were doing, and she wasn't a married thing sorting out a brood of children either. She was a neither-here-nor-there. War makes heroes of some: Mrs Froud was fond of saying 'My Neville thought so', but what of the others?

The children had been away for three weeks when Mrs Salt told Jean that Francine constantly begged to come home. *Begged!* Valerie wasn't begging. Valerie gave little away in her short letters. If words were presents, you'd say she was mean. 'How's your health?' she asked in her scrawly hand. (You'd think her writing would be more orderly considering she loved school.) 'Are you managing?'

'Don't worry about me!' Jean wrote back. 'Everything is hunky-dory here!'

Jean was careful how she presented her life. She realised she must not show weakness. Valerie would be on to that in a flash and demand to come home. And who knew what horrors awaited her in London.

There was a poster in the street that Jean passed every day

that gave her the shivers. It was a picture of Hitler whispering, *Take them back!* into a mother's ear as she dreamed of her children: *Don't do it, Mother!* it exhorted underneath. Jean felt like the image was aimed directly at her.

Valerie wrote she saw a deer and its babies. She wrote she got an 8 in English. She wrote she kept her gas mask with her all the time, in case.

Jean learned that Mrs Woods was a shopkeeper, and she was glad Valerie was living in a normal working household. Not too snobby. Not too lazy either. Hopefully she'd brought Valerie up well enough that she wouldn't embarrass them. Jean had always wanted a shop. She could picture herself and Val working side by side at a till – things didn't get any better than that. And a hardware store too! Valerie didn't even write about that, except to say it was called Woods Hardware, which was unimaginative. If Jean had a hardware store she would call it 'Toots and Tools' or at least something with a bit of oomph!

As for saying she would visit Valerie – what had she been thinking? Jean had presumed it would be like the school trip to Madame Tussauds. Up the road and back in an hour. But Valerie was an eight-hour round trip away! A whole day's work lost – and then there was the price of the ticket. Mrs Froud said her Neville said the council might help, but it was yet another bureaucratic nightmare and, without Valerie's assistance, Jean never felt strong enough to tackle those.

It's not normal to be this lost, Jean told herself. *Pull yourself together.* But she had too much time to dwell. Something had to change, she knew that.

9

Valerie

After a few days, Mrs Woods decided Valerie was old enough to look after the shop. She told her she was to come straight home from school to take over, and she would do the whole day Saturday as well.

'Otherwise, what would be the point of you being here?' she asked.

Valerie didn't reply. It would only get her in trouble and she was constantly in trouble with Mrs Woods.

The shop, like the spare room, was full of boxes – but open to the public. If the weather was fine, Valerie would have to hang up the saucepans, the watering cans and the stepladders outside on hooks. There was a jingly-jangly door and a long glass counter that reminded Valerie of where Snow White went to sleep in the Disney film. Mrs Woods removed the stool because she didn't want Valerie to sit: Valerie would stand behind the till.

'If any money goes from that till, I will slipper you until you can't sit down,' Mrs Woods announced on her first shift. A cheeky person might have said she couldn't sit down since there was nowhere to sit any more, but Valerie wasn't cheeky. She might have cheeky thoughts, but she was careful not to say them out loud.

'And don't you be telling tales on me to your parents or I'll tell your headteacher you're lying and she won't let you go to school, and you like it there, don't you?'

Mrs Woods was intimidating enough. The prospect of a Mrs Woods—Mrs Lester alliance was petrifying.

That Saturday, Valerie had never been so bored in her life, as the local people browsed the 'tools and household goods'. They spoke slowly – not because they thought she was deaf or stupid; it was how they spoke to everyone. At least they were friendly though, most of them. They called her 'The Woods Girl'.

This label would have been sweet if she had liked Mrs Woods. Other people seemed to like her though. Or she was one of those people you had to make allowances for. There were a lot of people like that back home. 'Don't mind him' (make sure you're never alone with him) or 'Don't worry about her, she means well'.

There were people you made allowances for and people you didn't, and you didn't know why, you just went along with it.

Valerie waited for Lydia and Francine to show up at school. Finally, when she'd done two weeks at Taunton Middle School and they'd done none, she asked Miss Beedle. Miss Beedle, who was holding books to her chest like a shield over her heart, looked uncomfortable at the question.

'The person they're billeting with sent them to a different school.'

'What? Can you do that?'

'Well' – Miss Beedle pulled a face – 'I didn't think so, but she did...'

'I'm meant to be looking after them,' Valerie said. 'They told me...'

It wasn't only that the adults had told her to, she had wanted to. She liked protecting them. And she had failed. What if they wrote home that they'd been abandoned? What if they were in a desperate house like hers or even worse than hers?

Miss Beedle said, 'Don't worry about them, worry about yourself.'

She meant it kindly, but it made Valerie feel jittery. Had she heard that she was a problem for Mrs Woods?

Miss Beedle had worse news. 'I am going back to London,' she said.

'What about all of us?' Valerie asked, devastated to be losing the one adult she trusted.

'You'll stay here...' Miss Beedle answered with a smile that looked forced.

'There are no Nazis there?'

Miss Beedle paused. Unusually, she was lost for words. 'Not yet, anyway,' she eventually said quietly. 'And hopefully never.'

The Somerset countryside was beautiful though. And Valerie loved the sounds as well as the sights. She could hear the birdsong in the morning, and even distant mooing. She had seen sheep at a proximity she would never have imagined, and there was something joyful about the pigs – a thought she would never have imagined either. There was a church on the way to school and tucked away was an overgrown graveyard and a single bench with tenacious weeds that grew through the slats. Valerie took to sitting there, unseen, on a Sunday; it was the only day she had neither school nor shop, and Mrs Woods wanted her out regardless of the weather. However, the lack of people near her, the lack of people who cared for her, made her lonely. The beauty around her that she had no one to share with only accentuated that.

Valerie assumed Mrs Woods would improve over time – once they got used to each other – like people do in stories, but Mrs Woods did not oblige. More and more, Valerie dreaded going to the house. Mrs Woods wasn't strong and it mostly only smarted when she hit her, but it was frightening and humiliating. Mum had never laid a finger on her. Indeed, when she had accidentally trapped Valerie's toe in the door, it had upset her so much that Valerie had had to comfort *her*, not the other way round.

Valerie decided she could cope with Mrs Woods better than many would. She knew she was resilient. The thought of other children – little Stanley or sicky Mary Kittle! – experiencing something similar made her sad, and the thought that her mum would be upset made her even sadder. So, Valerie filled her letters with happy moments: a ladybird landing on her sleeve, a comic found in the street, a smile from a baby – and she could almost convince herself that these good moments happened all the time and were not rare as hens' teeth. Her mother would visit her for her birthday and then she would take her home. Valerie was counting down the days.

10

Jean

Mrs Penn was rattling the newspaper while Jean was sweeping her fireplace. Jean had been cleaning for Mrs Penn for about ten years and she was a favourite.

'They're letting us out our boxes again.' Mrs Penn sounded more bitter each time Jean went round.

Jean knew that during the Great War Mrs Penn had worked as a nurse and it had been 'the best time of my life'.

'You could become a nurse, Mrs Hardman.'

Jean knelt up. 'Not sure I've got the patience!'

'Patients!' Mrs Penn thought she was making a joke, but Jean was being serious.

Jean hated hospitals. She hated blood and she wasn't great with poorly people. Still, she'd have to do something different, and soon. Mrs Cutler had told her about a friend who needed a cleaner – her housemaid had gone to work at a munitions factory already! – but Jean had to turn it down because of how far away it was – a three-hour round trip. No one took that into account.

Jean was now down to six houses.

'What about the buses? They're looking for people.'

'They'll be looking for men!' Jean dismissed her. The buses had been looking for men for as long as she could remember.

'Not any more. They're taking on women to be conductors again. Like last time round. Men go off to fight, so they need women to take their place. You don't fancy being a clippie?'

'Not really!' Jean laughed and carried on cleaning. When she thought about the Great War, she thought about the dreadful state of her father when he first returned. She didn't know him, and her mother had thrown him out because he was covered in lice. And the coughing... he would only last a year. She remembered a street party and a cake made of cardboard. She was there with an auntie and a man who kept bouncing her on his knee although she was too big to bounce, and, when she struggled to get away, Auntie hissed, 'Be nice to Cousin Harry, he's been through a lot.'

Jean looked up suddenly. Mrs Penn was still speaking.

'Pardon?'

'I said sorry, we have to tighten our belts and...'

Jean knew exactly what was coming next...

At the bus station, a bored-looking man in a furry overcoat asked her lots of questions about her education and her experiences, and she lied.

What had she excelled at? Being a dunce? Jean forced words from her mouth – and perhaps they didn't sound as stupid as they might.

Why would she be good on the buses?

Jean said some people got carsick, but she never had. Obviously, she didn't mention the time Valerie's father drove them to a bed and breakfast near Ally Pally and she'd vomited in the glove compartment.

She said she was good with people, whatever that meant.

She said she was good with money. She smiled, suddenly remembering Valerie learning to count on her fingers – 'But Mummy, what happens when you get to eleven?'

'What about family?' the interviewer asked, picking his teeth. He said the hours were long and unsociable. It wouldn't do to have a husband waiting for his dinner. Jean said that she was single, and her family were all dead, which was half-true. He hadn't directly asked about children – if he had, Jean was ready to deny Valerie's existence. She felt instinctively that if they knew she had a daughter there would be no chance of her getting this job. And she needed this job now she was six houses down and counting.

Jean threw in the slogans everyone liked to hear nowadays: 'the importance of doing my bit'. The man nodded impatiently though, like he'd heard it all before. He was going to tell her to leave, she thought, that she had failed, but instead he looked at what he'd found between his teeth, then muttered, 'So when can you start? Because we need you to "do your bit" from yesterday.'

'Soon as you want me,' she suggested nervously. Did this mean she'd got the job? It was hard to believe. She'd never had a proper job before.

'You start on Monday.'

It was Valerie's birthday on Monday. Jean had hoped finally to make the trip down to Somerset to check that she was settling in all right, and to explain that it was probably going to be more than a couple of weeks now...

'How about Tuesday?'

'We have other keen candidates.'

She knew what he was saying. 'Monday it is.'

Jean hurried from the bus station to find Valerie a pretty card and to send it with a shilling. There was no chance it would get there before her birthday, but Jean told herself, Valerie was having such a delightful time in the countryside or in the shop, she would understand.

11

Valerie

Eleven wasn't a big birthday, it wasn't like ten or twelve or even thirteen, but because it wasn't a big one Valerie liked it even more. Poor eleven was an underdog.

Last year, for Valerie's tenth, they'd gone to the cinema where Mum cleaned. Mum had asked if she wanted to invite friends and, naturally, Valerie had chosen Lydia and Francine, but Francine had religious things to do and Lydia had a dance class. Mum thought Valerie minded but she didn't. She loved it when it was just the two of them. Some people called them Tweedledum and Tweedledee but they were probably jealous they weren't close to their mums.

Mum had got a colleague to leave open a side door so they didn't have to pay and could spend the admission fee on sweets and chocolate ice cream instead. Mum never ate a lot, Mrs Froud said she pecked like a sparrow, but it was nice just watching *Bringing Up Baby*, starring Katharine Hepburn, her mum chuckling next to her.

'I need some time out from the shop on Monday afternoon,'

Valerie said carefully, which was how she said everything to Mrs Woods.

'You can't,' Mrs Woods snapped, and then went off on one of her lectures about how Valerie was bleeding her dry, how the money didn't compensate – no amount of money could *ever* compensate – but more wouldn't go amiss.

'Only for a short while, please, Mrs Woods.' Her mother could stand in the shop with her.

Mrs Woods scowled. 'What for?'

'My mother is coming.'

At this Mrs Woods' demeanour changed dramatically. 'Here? Why didn't you let me know?'

'Uh, I *am* letting you know...' Valerie felt discombobulated. She hadn't expected the word 'mother' to have such a magical effect on Mrs Woods. It was like saying 'abracadabra'. If only she'd known this before.

No birthday card arrived before school but Valerie didn't expect it to. Her mum would deliver it by hand.

She hoped there were sweets and books for her too. She missed trips to the library back home. She missed the soothing story of *Pinocchio*. And she couldn't wait to see her mum's smile, and hear her call her 'Val' or 'Vally'. No one else was allowed to call her those.

It was the small things.

Valerie daydreamed all through the school day. It would be quite like her mother to appear at the window at the last minute and to take her out: she had done that once before. They had bought roasted chestnuts from the street seller and eaten them looking at the Tower and her mum had told her about the ravens while everyone else was still doing algebra.

But she didn't come to the school – how would she know where it was? – so as soon as it was finished, Valerie went to the station. She asked the stationmaster about the times of the trains from London.

He felt his beard. 'None direct.'

'I know,' Valerie said, amazed that he thought her that slow-witted. 'She'll come on an indirect one...'

'One every two hours.'

That narrowed it down.

The stationmaster said she wasn't to get in anyone's way, but he didn't mind if she sat nicely. He even got her tea and a biscuit from his house nearby. It reminded her that not everyone was horrid. She'd just been unlucky with Mrs Woods.

She sat on the platform floor, her gas mask dangling from her shoulder, and imagined her father rushing along to see her. Sometimes she imagined he looked like Lydia's dad, Mr Froud, or sometimes Francine's dad, Mr Salt. Today, he looked like the kindly stationmaster. She didn't know an awful lot about Mr Hardman. She knew he had brought her mum flowers every week when they were courting, just because. Valerie knew she had missed out by not having a dad, but that Mum didn't have anyone growing up either.

She pictured her mum darting for the train; she was often late because she worked so hard. Valerie rehearsed what she'd say to her that would show that she was growing up, but also that she would be better off back in London. She was certain of it.

The stationmaster said there were no more trains.

'Has there been a problem on the line?'

He scratched his head. 'I don't think so, dear.'

'I must have missed her,' she told him confidently. 'She might be at the house.'

He looked pleased. 'That'll be it.'

When she got back, she found Mrs Woods had laid every-thing out: best crockery, a plate of apple dumplings, even a lacy tablecloth but Mum wasn't yet there.

Five o'clock, quarter past, half past...

Still her mum hadn't come.

At a quarter to six, Mrs Woods got up. Valerie had never seen her so cheery.

'She's not coming for you, is she? Too busy having a good time in the city to see her daughter, I suppose.'

Valerie stared at her in astonishment. 'That's not nice,' she said finally.

'True though.' Mrs Woods began stacking the plates away, then the cutlery, then the dumplings.

'Can't we wait a little longer...'

Mrs Woods stood over her. Then she slapped Valerie round the face and laughed at her shock.

'I'm sick of the sight of you.'

Usually, Valerie didn't find it hard to forgive her mum anything. That day was the first time it was more difficult.

12

Jean

When Jean told Mrs Salt and Mrs Froud that she was going to work on the buses, Mrs Salt said: 'You'll look smart,' as if that was the important thing about the job! Jean giggled, but secretly she hoped that looking smart was at least a part of it.

Mrs Froud didn't speak for a bit but contorted her mouth strangely. 'I suppose we're all going to have to do things we didn't think we would,' she eventually said grudgingly.

This was a bitter thing to say – couldn't she simply congratulate her, which was what Jean would have done if things were the other way round?

Things were never the other way round though. My Neville's income slid into the Frouds' account like a well-oiled machine and Mrs Froud's life was easy.

But Mrs Froud came to Jean the next day. She'd had a heart-to-heart with her husband.

'My Neville admires anyone who rolls up their sleeves and gets stuck in. So, what I mean to say is, good for you, Mrs Hardman. Go get 'em!'

. . .

The bus was a 47-seater double-decker with room for standing. Jean had been a passenger enough times to know how that worked. Nevertheless, it was interesting to be on the other side of things, like lifting a curtain and seeing what lay backstage.

She had to shadow a conductor for ten days and then she'd be let loose on her own. Her driver, Perry, was about sixty and his breath smelled of tinned meat. At least he was friendly though. Mr Yardley the conductor couldn't have been less interested if he'd tried.

'Two bells to start, ding-ding. Don't go too early,' said Mr Yardley, 'and don't go too late.'

'A question of timing,' agreed Jean.

'Don't try to be smart, girl,' he responded. So, Jean didn't say much after that.

The next week Jean was allocated the Carringtons, father and son, and this was an improvement. Mr Carrington Snr, the conductor, was counting the days till his retirement. He had expected to move to the South Coast, but with the outbreak of war, who knew?

'Fifty years' service – where's my carriage clock?' he kept grumbling.

Son Richard, Mr Carrington Jnr, was the driver and he was so tall, his knees came up to his chest when he was in the driver's seat. He was ginger and lanky too, the type of skinny that people cruelly laugh at in the schoolyard. Valerie saw him eat though; he wasn't malnourished. Whenever she spoke to him, he blushed.

Jean liked the bus itself. What wasn't to like? There was something playful or toy-like about its bold colours and shape. How she would love to show Valerie around it one day!

Mr Carrington Snr said some of the buses had been used for evacuation. It had been madness – the children were shrieking and one of the boys bit a conductor on the arm. He said the teachers were worse than the kids. This might have been Jean's moment to tell her new colleagues about Valerie – but she didn't. She didn't know how they would react.

And then, after a few days shadowing Mr Carrington Snr, it was decided Jean could be let loose on her own. Since this was two days earlier than arranged, Jean was flattered, but the way it was said made her feel like they were letting the monkeys out of the enclosure at London Zoo.

Anything could happen.

13

Valerie

After the fifth adult in the shop called her 'The Woods Girl', Valerie had had enough. The next person who said it, she would set them straight: 'I am not the Woods Girl. My name is Valerie Hardman.'

Valerie remembered asking her mum about her name once. 'Why did you choose "Valerie"?'

'I liked it!' Mum had answered, 'Why else?'

'Aren't I named after anyone?'

She had paused. 'Not really, no.'

Valerie didn't have a middle name either. It was all rather half-hearted.

The next day, someone else said it. A man with lots of white-blond hair was browsing the tools. When she retorted, he looked up, surprised.

'Course you are,' he said, the edges of his eyes crinkling. 'You're your own person, Miss Valerie Hardman!'

At last, someone who understood.

He wanted candles. Everyone wanted candles and matches

and torches and gas masks. One man had come in with a patch over his eye like a pirate: 'You don't have guns?' (They didn't and Valerie was relieved because he mightn't be a good aim.) Nor did they stock hoses or bullets, other much-requested items.

Eventually, the man with lots of white-blond hair bought a watering can. 'Are you from London?' he asked curiously.

She nodded.

'Me too.'

He'd come here for love though, he told her. Married a Somerset beauty at eighteen, never looked back. He was from Walthamstow.

'We're a long way from home, aren't we?' he said. 'Do you miss the city?'

The question nearly brought tears to her eyes. But it wasn't exactly London she missed. She missed her bed, and she missed the sound of her mum snoring or calling, 'Just five minutes, Val' or the sight of her coat on the hook on the door. She missed the smell of the street after the rain and the strange puddings Mrs Froud made. She didn't like fish and Jean never made her eat it, but she missed a Friday-night saveloy from the fish and chips stand. She missed the vinegary chips.

Mrs Woods gave her apple dumplings for breakfast and apple dumplings for tea. She was now made up of 8/10ths apple, 2/10ths misery.

'I don't know.' Her voice was croaky.

It wasn't that she didn't like Somerset. She *could* have liked it here, even this sardine-tin-sized shop had potential – but Mrs Woods? Never. She had made enough allowances for her.

'I bet you miss your mum,' he said.

'She didn't come for my birthday.' Valerie still couldn't fathom it. It hurt every time she remembered it. It hurt far more than the smacks Mrs Woods now routinely administered to her arms and legs. It hurt more than her empty stomach.

'I bet she wanted to,' he said, 'it's hard to get away sometimes.'

Now Valerie had a lump in her throat. It was agony to be so far from her. She missed everything about Jean.

'What about Dad? Miss him too?'

Valerie nodded but she didn't elaborate. She was thinking of her father more and more. In her mind's eye he wore a white shirt, red breeches and braces. Sometimes she dreamed about him too, and in her dreams his face was scarred and raw from fire. People crossed the road to avoid him, but not her, she didn't mind.

The man took something out of his pocket – chocolate! 'We couldn't have a child staying with us,' he said as he handed it over. 'Wife would have loved to. No room, unfortunately.'

The next time Valerie saw the other girls was not until one month later. Francine and Lydia were wearing purple blazers that were too big for them – you couldn't see their fingers in their sleeves – and their shirts were as white as her vests had once been. Straw boaters with a purple ribbon were like the icing on top of an expensive cake.

They bounced into the shop, and it felt like even the shop bell was ringing out to celebrate them. They were like bunny rabbits, she thought. Lydia was as golden as ever, her hair styled and her skin clear. Francine was serene, watching everything, smelling of grass. And they both seemed so well-nourished, thought Valerie, yearning for something she didn't know what. Or was it innocence? Like they didn't know bad things could happen. Like, if you told them you'd been locked in a cupboard without dinner for the crime of asking for a sliver of soap, they wouldn't believe it.

'What do you think of Paul?' asked Francine.

'I don't know a Paul – who is he?'

'Paul!' Francine was incredulous that Valerie didn't have an opinion. 'He's a...' She struggled for the word. 'A person.'

'He's a boy who lives with us sometimes,' Lydia explained.

Why only sometimes? wondered Valerie.

'What do *you* think of him?' she asked.

'He's like our brother here,' said Francine.

'Our Somerset brother,' Lydia corrected.

Valerie wanted to say, 'Don't be silly, your brothers are at home,' but Francine was being serious and Lydia was nodding.

'You will like him, Valerie, I know you will.'

Valerie shrugged. Goodness, it was like the spinning of the world depended on this unknown boy. And yet, Valerie had a strange intuition that this Paul-person might one day be as meaningful to her as he clearly was to Francine and Lydia.

Then Francine squealed, 'We did cooking at Bumble Cottage!'

Even the name of their house was wonderful, thought Valerie enviously.

'And we made you this.' They had brought her a present! It was a biscuit shaped like a gingerbread man.

'Run, run, as fast as you can,' Francine continued.

'You can't catch us, we're the gingerbread man!' squealed Lydia and they dissolved into fits of laughter.

Valerie ate it up, all at once. She was that hungry. The girls stared at her as if they hadn't expected her to eat it at all.

'Doesn't your lady cook with you, Valerie?' Francine asked, now timidly.

Never. Should she tell them that Mrs Woods slapped her, gave her hardly any food, called her a dirty slum kid and her father a filthy slum man too?

No, she thought, what could they do about it?

'Didn't your mummy bring you anything?'

Valerie looked at her friend's trusting face. 'She hasn't visited yet.' It was painful having to admit it. Worse, Francine was looking at her sympathetically and Valerie hated for anyone to feel sorry for her. 'It's fine...'

'Yes!' Francine said brightly. 'Mummy says she's working on the buses. That must be why.'

Lydia sniffed. '*My* daddy says that women should stay at home.'

After they left, twin ponytails bouncing down the road, Valerie felt lonelier than ever. Last year at school they had studied Shackleton's failed mission to the South Pole. And they had to write an essay as if they were trapped on the ice, waiting to be rescued.

Her teacher was pleased. 'You captured the fear, the pain, the cold, the isolation. Well done, Valerie.'

Now it felt like she had foreseen her own future.

Mrs Woods had two settings: nasty and really nasty. Valerie had never encountered such meanness and it was mystifying to her. Some nights, after she locked up the shop and went into the kitchen, there would be a sandwich out for her. Jam or spam or cress. Other times, and these times were more often, Mrs Woods would growl: 'Nothing for you.'

One time, a customer said to her, 'Of course, you know Mrs Woods had a daughter.' Valerie knew about her greasy-haired son; he came on the occasional Sunday. He was a great oaf – a clomping chap with giant boots that he left outside the back door. The first thing he had said to her was, 'Clean them.' She'd done it too. Mrs Woods didn't seem to be that nice to him either, which might have made her feel better but it didn't.

He called her a 'dirty evacuee', which made Mrs Woods cackle: 'You can talk, you filthy git.'

Valerie wasn't sure if that was taking her side or not.

But she didn't know about a daughter. If this was intended to make Valerie feel kindlier towards Mrs Woods, it soon wore off. For one, she wasn't sure it was true; and for another, Mrs Woods was so unrelentingly foul to Valerie that she swiftly forgot her good intentions anyway.

Mrs Woods always had the windows open, now autumn had arrived, it grew increasingly chilly. And when the rain came in, her bedsheet got wet. Mrs Woods said she should be grateful she even had a sheet.

The next time the man from London came into the shop, he was wearing a khaki uniform, and all his lovely white-blond hair had been shaved off. His head seemed too big for his body now, like a toddler's.

'How do I look?' He stood straight self-consciously, then saluted.

'Dapper,' said Valerie, although he looked like a different man. This one, despite the grin, looked older and less handsome than the one last week. She wondered if he had any chocolate this time. She had had stale bread and margarine for tea but that was ages ago.

'Thought I'd check on you before I left.'

Was everyone abandoning her? Valerie scowled until he thumped a box of fudge on the counter. 'All for me?!'

He chuckled. 'Share it with your friends if you like.'

Valerie was unlikely to see Lydia and Francine and, by God, she was not going to give any of this to Mrs Woods, so she tucked right in.

He wandered around the shop before stopping at the large wireless on the right-hand side of the counter.

'Now this is good.'

'I don't think it's for sale.'

He laughed. 'No, it's hers. I remember she used to have it on.'

Valerie shrugged, distracted. The fudge was marvellous. The unexpectedness of it even more so.

'Let me see if I can turn it on.'

It didn't work at first. He was in the shop for a good half an hour, unscrewing bits of the wireless, humming to himself, borrowing all sorts of tools, promising to put them back where they came from. Then finally he got up, looking at his wrist-watch. 'Done. Right in time for *Children's Hour*.'

I don't know what that is,' said Valerie quietly. Every day, someone said something that made her feel like she wasn't paying enough attention.

'Listen and you'll find out.' He headed towards the door, smiling. 'Good luck, my fellow Londoner – far from home.'

'And you...' She had tears in her eyes. It was silly since she hardly knew him.

'Wait,' he came back towards her and, digging in his pockets, he produced five shillings.

'I can't possibly...' Valerie said, still chewing. 'It's too mu—'

'Emergency fund.' He hesitated. 'If it gets too bad, go back to your mum – I bet she misses you like crazy.'

The fudge stopped Valerie feeling hungry for a while, but the wireless stopped her feeling lonely for days. It made her feel as though she had a friend – dozens of friends! The British Home Service was broadcast from up the road in Bristol and the sound was clear as a bell. They did the weather. They did the time. They did the war. It was like someone was holding her hand. The silence was gone. Back home, it was never silent; there was always a Salt child stomping about, there was door-slamming, vans and bicycle bells in the street, kettles boiling, cats jumping, people laughing.

Now, it felt like all that was back again, but it wasn't merely background noise, it was – and this was the strange part – noise made for her. It felt exclusive. She felt like each speaker, each story, each song was somehow presented for her ears only.

The first few segments she listened to, she had even answered back as though they were there in the shop with her.

Now then, boys and girls, do you know anything about puppets?

Valerie admitted, 'Nooo, I don't!'

Neither did I until I met Mr Ingram here. Mr Ingram makes puppets!

Valerie chanted, 'Hello, Mr Ingram!'

He's going to tell us all about them.

The things they talked about on the wireless! It was better than a lesson at school – it was better than a full day at this school.

They did a singalong, and she sang along.

And when a customer came in and Valerie went to switch it off, sometimes the customer might say, 'Don't on my account, I like this show,' and they would listen and smile together.

There was music, there were concertos, big bands, even operas to listen to... In the morning, for some reason, there was the news in Norwegian. Then the normal news in English. And then a drama – John Betjeman was reading from his book. Wireless voices didn't sound like Valerie or Jean or any of their friends, but they didn't sound like the people in Somerset either. It was the talking voices Valerie loved the most, it was talking voices that were great company. She could listen to them all day long. There was Vera Lynn singing 'Goodnight, children, everywhere.' And each evening when Vera Lynn sang the beautiful line about mothers thinking of their children, Valerie's thoughts turned to her own mother and her eyes filled with tears.

14

Jean

Mrs Peabody, the station manager, did schedules and accounts. She took no nonsense from anyone, although no one would have dared give her nonsense anyway. She was married to one of the drivers, Albert, who treated her like a princess. Jean took to both of them immediately. Two other clippies had started at the same time as Jean: Iris and Maud. They were grand sorts too but they were also inseparable old friends, which didn't leave much room for Jean.

Mrs Salt and Mrs Froud used to say bus drivers, like bobbies, got younger every year, but the truth was the bus drivers were mostly older. The younger men had left or were leaving to join up. The first time Jean heard that phrase, she had thought about Valerie's struggles with joined-up writing but now she understood and she heard it often: they were going to war.

Kenny was young but he had a dicky leg. He'd caught in a carnival float when he was a boy. 'Glad of it now, I am,' he said. It meant he wasn't joining up. Jean didn't think much of him. He said he was better at driving than walking. He was a big handsome lad with brown curly hair and he was popular with the passengers. If they thought they were in unsafe hands with Jean, the scrawny conductress, Kenny, despite his dicky leg, had the build and demeanour that said, 'You'll be all right.'

The drivers all drove differently, so inevitably Jean had her preferences. Old Matthews was a terror for overtaking. Kenny drove too fast, Perry too slow, Albert was just right, but he was a stickler for stopping at a stop even when there was nobody there, which drove Jean crackers. Kenny would never do that. His mission was to get from A to B with as few passengers as possible. Richard Carrington, who was also young, was more careful. He would wait for everyone to get sorted before he pulled away.

Jean got to know her routes, the stops and the regulars like the back of her hand. She knew who would get on and who would get off where. Who refused to ring the bell and expected you to read their mind, and who rang the bell too often.

Kenny was the most confident driver in the fleet, but that didn't mean he was the best – it took Valerie a while to realise confidence and skill weren't the same thing although it could look like they were. He drove too fast up to the vehicle in front, then had to slam on the brakes, whereas she preferred a constant speed.

'I've never had an accident!' he liked to boast, which silenced Perry, who had chipped a headlight and Albert, who, early in his career, had apparently driven a bus into a hedge.

Kenny had no accidents, that was true, but he was the sort who caused accidents and then moved off without realising the havoc he'd wreaked around him. The worst thing was that he didn't look thoroughly behind him. Visibility was poor in the blackout, but that meant you should go slower and look harder, no? Sometimes he didn't see the pedestrian darting out or, more frequently, a cyclist in his slipstream. There were parts of the bus he couldn't see from.

'Blind spot,' he'd say with a disarming wink. 'Ding-ding.'

At the job interview, they hadn't told Jean she had to be welcoming; they hadn't said she had to fawn; fair enough, being a clippie wasn't being a hostess. The number 19 to Stepney East was not the Folies Bergère – but life was rotten. Jean felt like it was her duty to spread a little happiness. Her duty but also her pleasure. These were precarious times and Jean felt like she was the antidote. She smiled and was kind to everyone. If she had it in her power to brighten someone's day – she would do so. She wanted to treat people the way she hoped Valerie was being treated. It was almost a superstitious thing.

'Morning,' she called out loudly as the passengers stepped on. She would have said 'Welcome', but the drivers would complain she was up herself.

'Nice day for frogs,' she'd say (if it was raining).

'And fish!'

'And eels!'

There were the passengers who had never ridden on a bus before – the fuel shortages were pushing them to it. Two well-to-do sisters came from the hair salon.

'We've never been on a bus before.'

'I have!' said the younger sister indignantly. 'Don't you remember the time in Marrakech?'

'It's not half as bad as I imagined,' confided the older one. 'I thought everyone would be drunk or homeless or half-dead.'

Jean smirked. 'What makes you think we're not?'

Another time, an elderly man seemed to think Jean was his footman.

'I say, how long are we waiting at this stop?'

'Until all the passengers get on.'

'But there are several!'

'Yes, well...' Jean answered with a shrug.

This type always wanted the route tailor-made for them – a bespoke bus service. They were puzzled that it wasn't. They couldn't understand the 'public' in public transport.

'Why do we go down this road?' they said. 'The other way is quicker.'

Jean could see her reflection in the metallic edges of the seats, in the poles, in the everywhere. How smart she looked, how purposeful. She felt like she was an adult and the passengers were her children. Or she was Matron and these were her patients. She knew if she told anyone this they'd laugh.

One day, a passenger asked her out dancing. He was a married man. How did she know? He told her, that's how.

'My missus won't mind,' he said with a wink.

'I mind,' said Jean, shocked at his audacity. At least with Tony she hadn't realised for months. It was always the married men who seemed to go for her.

'I'll get you some stockings,' he said.

They said there might be a shortage, but like the bombs, nothing had happened yet.

Some men even proposed to her. Jean politely declined, as she did with any other proposition. It was just a bit of fun. She wrote and told Valerie about it. Hoped it made her laugh.

Twice a day, the bus was overrun with schoolchildren. Kenny, in particular, didn't like the 'ankle-biters'.

'I thought they were meant to be in the countryside,' he grumbled, and Jean was relieved she hadn't told him or anyone at work about Valerie because she was doing well, thank you, and the last thing she wanted was to be given the label 'mummy'. The way Kenny talked about the mummies was even worse than how he talked about the kids.

Half the little sods tried to creep on and off without paying. One would occupy you while the other would try to sneak past. Oh, they had many methods, some impressive, some outlandish. Kenny swore if he caught a fare-dodger he'd give them a good hiding.

'Lawlessness has got worse,' everyone said, and everyone had a theory. Kenny's was that it was because so many mothers were working now. Latchkey kids.

Iris, who was more bolshy than Jean, said, 'You're complaining about the war effort now?' and he smirked.

When Jean caught the ruffians, she whispered, 'I'll pay for you. But only this once.'

It put her out of pocket. But it was not just that she felt sorry for them, it was the principle of the thing.

And sometimes, among the schoolchildren, Jean thought she saw Valerie for an instant or two. A girl with her nose in a book, or another girl with the same coat, would still her for a moment – *Could it be?* she would think, and of course it never was. She dreamed that one day she would find Valerie sitting on her bus, the world would be at peace and Jean would cry out, 'Ding-ding, this is my daughter!'

Jean didn't usually miss having a husband. In the past, if she needed to, she had borrowed Mr Salt or My Neville, like when she needed the sideboard moving from one end of the room to another, or when she had a problem opening a particularly stubborn tin. But as more and more children of Valerie's age returned to London, she felt torn about keeping her girl away. It truly was an impossible decision, and it gave her such anguish, especially at night-time, that for the first time in years she wished she had someone to share it with.

One afternoon, Mrs Froud and Mrs Salt brought their gaggle of younger children on the bus. Fortunately, Percy was driving, so they had plenty of time to get on. They said it was to go to the market but they didn't need a bus to get to the market, so Jean was convinced it was to observe her at work.

She was nervous. It was still early days – her second week out of the shadows – and she wished they'd waited until she was more experienced. Or perhaps not even come at all. What was she – an exhibit in Madame Tussauds, a monkey in the zoo? They'd be throwing peanuts at her next.

'Valerie's mummy.' Maisie Salt tugged her sleeve.

'Yes...'

'Why are you here?'

'Because...' Jean considered. 'I'm working. It's important someone checks your tickets and looks after you and helps you with where to go—'

'Why you though?'

This was an uncomfortable yet fair question. She stared back at the girl, who was a miniature version of Francine. 'Why not me?' she said, and that seemed to satisfy her. Then Jean played peekaboo with baby Joe, which made him howl with laughter. He was a darling.

Little Jacob also put a hand up to ask a question: 'Would you let Nazis on the bus?'

'I would not,' Jean said gravely. She sometimes dreamed the streets of London were overrun with Nazis, and she wondered if she would clip their tickets or not. They'd probably refuse to pay anyway.

'How do you stop them?'

'Well, none have tried yet – but if they did, I'd push them off,' she said, and he nodded eagerly. Mrs Salt rolled her eyes and Mrs Froud said, 'My Neville says it won't come to that.'

A quarter of Jean's shift now took place in the dark. There were fewer cars on the road than before – fuel prices – but more people wandering around. And some of the people were idiots – no other word for it. As winter came, the blackout was blacker than black. They covered the bus headlamps, everything. You could hear other vehicles, but you couldn't see them until you were right on top of them.

'What about deaf people?' Jean asked Kenny. She'd known a deaf boy once and he had surprised her by being fantastically self-sufficient.

'They'll have to get out the way fast,' Kenny retorted. 'Otherwise, they'll feel our wheels on their backsides.'

The drivers didn't seem to worry but Jean did. You'd only glimpse them when they were near, and you can't stop a massive ten-tonne bus in a hurry.

One time, it was so dark and foggy that they could hardly see a thing. Richard was driving and he did worry; he said, 'It's blind leading the blind.'

They were on the number 23 and the route took them past the rubbish dump and the industrial estate. It was mostly lots of noisy workers for the factories although they were slightly less noisy now they were mostly young women instead of young men.

There was talk of getting everyone off, but they didn't want to leave anyone high and dry. Jean didn't know what they should do. She thought of the children, her regulars, and elderly people being stranded, but then maybe they'd cancelled their plans anyway.

'My biggest fear is knocking someone down,' Richard said. His face was white.

'I'll walk it.'

Jean led the bus down the street like she was leading an animal to water but without a rope. Richard edged forward and the passengers waited.

They made a good team.

· · ·

There was a family who stood at the bus stop after the library on the number 15 route, a stop that had no other distinguishing features apart from this family, who were there every day.

Their oldest boy, who always appeared dressed too warmly for the weather, waved. He waved each day, with his whole body, and if Jean waved back – she loved waving back – well, he jumped up and down, up and down, with glee. The mother had two other children in a pram and she would rock the pram backwards and forwards, and Jean remembered doing that with Valerie – she didn't seem to remember it not in her head, but in her body, that motion, that shush, shush, shush. At first the mother looked embarrassed at the boy's waving, but then, as she grew used to Jean waving back, she smiled, and before long she was waving excitedly too.

'What's wrong with that kid?' Kenny bluntly cut into Jean's reverie.

'Nothing...'

'He doesn't look like other children.'

'He's a bit different, isn't he?' muttered Jean. 'But he's no harm.'

'They're not even going anywhere,' pointed out Kenny. 'She just brings them there to wave.'

Jean hated it when he talked like that. He had no idea what it was like to be a parent, Jean thought, and the things you do to keep children happy but she couldn't argue because she didn't want Kenny to know about her life.

One good thing though, by the time she got back from work Jean was that exhausted that she slept like a baby. If the rat did come back in her dreams, she was so tired that she didn't even remember it.

15

WINTER 1939

Jean

Jean was on the number 29 and Perry was driving when Valerie's father got on the bus, wanting a ride to Forest Hill. Jean had told Valerie the story about him dying so many times she had almost come to believe it herself. It was too late to jump off and there was nowhere to hide – she had to go and face him.

Tony Cooper was heavier than he used to be but more handsome than ever. His hair was slicked back and black and he had the confidence of a man who had been and expects to be adored. He had dimples. She used to think nobody bad could possibly have dimples. He was more than double her age when they were together – but, she reminded herself, that didn't mean he was double her age now. Now the gap between them was like a tide, shifting and changing, sixteen years, which meant he was probably forty-three to her twenty-seven, which wasn't so weird.

'Tickets please.'

'Bloody hell,' he said. He smelled of cigars. That had always put her off in the old days but its familiarity felt warming now. 'If it isn't! What a blast from the past.'

'Nice to see you too,' she said, although she had mixed feelings. He was from before – and she had worked hard to get away from there.

'How's the girl?'

The girl – did he not remember her name?

Jean distinctly remembered how Tony used to say he wanted to have a baby with her. All that winter they were courting, when Tony would meet her after school, snow had been threatening, but it never came. He said he wanted Stanley for a boy – for Stanley Baldwin – and Mary for a girl after Mary Pickford. That's what he used to say to her, 'You're like Mary Pickford,' and she had gobbled it up, not recognising the insincerity of it.

But when Jean had told Tony she thought she might be in the family way, he yawned several times in quick succession, showing her the blackness of his mouth. He told her to get rid of it. He knew a doctor who'd see to it. His boys cost him a packet and he didn't want another.

'But you said Stanley for a boy – and Mary for a girl...' Up until now, Jean had always agreed with whatever Tony said, but for once she was too incredulous to. 'You said you'd love another son.'

'I didn't mean it, Jean. It's pillow talk. I'm a married man.'

Realisation of her mistake blew through her like a gust of cold wind. 'What are you saying?'

'I'm saying, you'll still be able to have a kid one day,' he said. 'Just not now.'

'What if it's a little girl? Would you want her then?'

'Even worse,' he had said.

. . .

Now the bus stopped with a jolt outside the library. A regular, an old man with his steam train magazines, stepped on. Then two elderly women mounted the step slowly, wobbly on their feet.

And still Tony was staring at Jean like he used to, licking his lips like she was a slice of Victoria sponge. She'd never understood why a man as attractive as he was could be interested in her, but he had made it clear he was. He used to say what they had was 'magnetic'. Certainly, she did feel like a tiny thing pulled towards him without any hope of resistance. He still looked like a matinee idol. He still was out of her league.

Pulling herself back from the memories that flooded her at the sight of him, Jean finally answered: 'Valerie? Yes, she's good. Growing up lovely.'

Having Valerie wasn't what Jean had expected. She didn't know what she'd expected, but it wasn't Valerie. Or maybe she had expected a blank slate, an empty page on which she could imprint herself and her ways. What she found instead was that Valerie, even as a baby, was a fully formed person, a human being with not only her own ideas and emotions, but ideas and emotions that were often in direct opposition to Jean's own.

Jean didn't remember much about the pregnancy except that she had felt well most of the time. Other women grumbled about the parasite and scavenger in their bellies, but once they were born, they seemed happier. Maybe they got their resentment out before the babies were born? With Jean, it was the other way round. While the baby was safe inside her, all was fine; it was only once she was out that the struggle began.

The birth was terrible. She'd heard awful things about Whitechapel Hospital but naively she decided the rumours were exaggerations. She soon learned that if anything, they had understated the situation. The day the pains started, she walked up there, stopping every few minutes to lean against a lamppost and to let the agony break over her. When she got there, the women at the desk ignored her. Jean wore a ring on her wedding finger, said she was Mrs Hardman instead of Miss and that her husband was working away, but they didn't believe her, or they didn't like her. Maybe it was her youth that unnerved them? It felt like they wanted to cut her down. It felt like they thought she deserved to be in as much pain as possible.

When she woke up after a long post-labour sleep, there was no baby. Jean assumed right away that they'd decided she was no good and given her baby to another mother. She could remember thinking, *she'll be better off with you*, and wondering whether she should make a fuss or should she just get up and go home? What did she know about being a mother?

'She's an independent mite,' a nurse said when Jean, in floods of tears, finally dared ask her for information on Valerie's whereabouts. She was only in the nursery on the ground floor. No, she hadn't been taken off but no, Mrs Hardman couldn't see her, she had to rest.

There was cruelty all around her. That was how it felt. She remembered the woman in the next bed weeping for hours on end. Nothing Jean could say would comfort her.

'He's going to kill me,' the woman kept saying, for the baby's dad wasn't pleased that it was another girl.

Jean was prepared to crawl on her hands and knees to the nursery if she didn't get to see her baby soon, but then a new matron appeared.

'There are lots of families looking for newborns.'

'Uh, yes?' Jean responded.

'Are you not giving her away?'

'No, I'm not!' Jean said, now more determined than ever.

'All right!' The matron's face said, *keep your hair on!* 'But there's no Mr Hardman, is there?'

Jean stuttered. 'Well, there is...'

The matron eyed the woman in the next bed, who was now letting out loud snores, then sat down conspiratorially.

'Are you set on keeping it?'

It?

'I am,' Jean answered, quickly becoming furious at this matron.

'Then if I were you,' Matron said, 'don't ever tell anyone there isn't a Mr Hardman. *Especially* not the baby. It darkens a name.'

'What?'

'That she's a bastard,' she said cheerily. She poured Jean a glass of lukewarm water but Jean shook her head. In a week of shocks, this conversation felt the most shocking of all.

'Make up something instead. No one needs to start off with an albatross round their neck, do they?'

One week passed before Jean made it to the nursery to see her baby. The other babies were howling like werewolves, but Valerie lay there, silent and looking startled. Even when Jean picked her up, she didn't fuss but eyed her uncertainly. They would be a team. Not an equal team, Jean realised, a team with stronger and weaker players, but a team nevertheless.

The word 'daughter' made her all twisty inside, like the woman in the next bed's knitting. A son was easy – 'boys love their ma's,' everyone said – but a daughter? Daughters weren't forgiving. They had a critical eye. But this child? She was everything.

It must have been about three or four days after that when Tony came. Tony the rooster, strutting into the hospital like the conquering hero. If only the matron could have seen it – that would show her.

'I couldn't get away,' he said. She didn't mind – she adored him for being there. He had daffodils for her, sweet yellow signs of life – he was so good with flowers, and she was thrilled he was still interested in her. She hadn't blown it. He plumped himself on the mattress, making it spring up at her end.

'I'm so sorry, Jeanie. I can't see you any more.'

And her world collapsed.

The man responsible for the collapse was grinning at her now.

'She's not stayed in London, has she?'

Jean shook her head and, for the first time in a long while, the tears came. She wiped her eyes quickly and clutched her clipper machine to her.

'She's been evacuated to the countryside. I miss her so.'

Miss didn't begin to encapsulate how she felt. She missed her so much sometimes, she wondered if she might die from it. She felt like something had been amputated.

Tony put his hand on her wrist. 'You did good, darling.'

The rat came back that night.

The following day, Jean was scrubbing the front step when Mrs Froud and Mrs Salt arrived and stood over her. It felt like they had something of consequence to impart, so Jean got up; her first thoughts were that it had something to do with Valerie.

'What is it?'

'We went to see the girls yesterday.'

'In Somerset.'

'We got a day return.'

Jean nearly dropped down like a sack of potatoes. The old familiar sense of exclusion hit her like a punch in the stomach. *Dunce. Good-for-nothing. You can't play with us.*

'I would have come...' she managed to say. Instead, she had been all muddled up by the reappearance of Tony.

'But we thought you were working,' they chorused. They

looked upset that she was upset, but Jean found that even more annoying.

'I was, but even so...'

'It was our second time. The lady whose house they are billeted at gave us a warm welcome.'

'Did you see my Val?'

They didn't, and Jean didn't know if that made things better or worse. Valerie was with different people, they explained patiently. Their girls were with a Mrs Howard, somewhere called 'Bumble Cottage'.

'She's posh.' Mrs Salt giggled.

'She speaks all la-di-dah,' said Mrs Froud. 'Bumble Cottage is bigger than all of our places put together. My Neville says Lydia won't want to come home!' They laughed.

They'd gone all the way to Somerset and couldn't be bothered to find her Valerie? Jean knew she would have made sure to see Lydia and Francine if she'd done that journey. Somehow, even though she'd had no idea about it, Jean felt guilty about Mrs Froud and Mrs Salt's visit to their girls, and it propelled her to dash off another letter to Valerie. She told her about the children getting on the bus and how she had felt like she was at the zoo.

'I hope Mrs Woods is treating you well, my dear,' she wrote. She chewed her finger. She had to say something else, something memorable. 'Be grateful to her and remember your manners!'

That evening, Jean looked at the last picture that Valerie had drawn for her before she was evacuated. The picture of a man rescuing two girls from flames. Valerie had even signed her name in the corner. Jean had grown up mostly without a father, so in a strange way it had always made sense to her that Valerie might experience the same. Like history was repeating itself. It was what Jean knew best. It was how she knew to be.

She remembered clearly the moment Tony's abandoning them at the hospital turned into a fire rescue. It was a story at bedtime a long time ago – Jean had hoped it would stop Valerie thinking about her father so much, but instead Valerie had clung to this tale for dear life. Still, Jean didn't imagine it could do much harm.

16

Valerie

Every day, Valerie got lost in the world of radio dramas. She enjoyed the comedy sketches and the plays, especially crime stories. She nearly always worked out whodunnit and if she didn't, she would kick herself. There were love stories too, but in those there were a lot of goings-on behind people's backs and Valerie couldn't approve, even if they were the 'one and only love of their lives' and even if the husband back at home was insane, crippled or cruel (or all three, as was the case in one particularly schmaltzy offering). The strange thing was, she sometimes knew what the voice actors were going to do or say next. She could guess it – it was almost like she had the scripts in her head. If on the rare occasion they didn't do what Valerie anticipated they would do, she couldn't help feeling *they'd* got it wrong, not her, and that her way would have been better.

When Lydia and Francine next came into the shop, Valerie switched off the wireless. The girls were followed by the lady they billeted with – the lady with the frog brooch, Mrs Howard. At first Valerie was disappointed to see her, since it was harder to talk freely when adults were about. Even with the best will in the world, they tended to squash you. But Mrs Howard wasn't like most adults. She was more like a teacher you didn't mind. An older Miss Beedle type perhaps, but one who did English rather than art.

'Veronica, isn't it?'

'Valerie.'

She apologised. She was wearing low-heeled shoes and a tweed skirt and a pale blue blouse. It was an outfit that seemed both lovely and effortless. In the East End, women her age didn't tend to bother unless they were going to a music hall or something.

'Our theatre group are putting on *The Wind in the Willows*. Would you put up a poster in the shop?'

'We helped make it,' shrieked Francine. And Lydia pointed to the part on the poster that said, *1 d children, 2 d for adults*, and said, 'That was me.'

'From little acorns grow big oaks,' Mrs Howard said humorously. 'You will come, I hope,' she went on, and her expression turned serious as she surveyed Valerie. 'It's an amateur production for charity. Nevertheless, it will be an enjoyable night out.'

Valerie made a face that she hoped said she'd like to but she couldn't commit.

'How is everything here?'

Valerie was used to pretending life at Mrs Woods' was harmonious, but staring this direct woman in the eyes and saying so was a different proposition.

'It's not...'

'It's not what you're used to?' Mrs Howard suggested helpfully.

'That's it,' Valerie said, but because she wanted to be agreeable rather than defend her host. Besides, listening to the wireless gave her joy even on an empty stomach. Lydia and Francine wanted to go outside to skip. Valerie couldn't leave and said so. Mrs Howard let the girls go but then hovered.

'And your parents?'

'My mother is a conductor.'

'How marvellous! Are you musical too?'

'Uh, she is on the buses?'

Two circles of red appeared on Mrs Howard's cheeks. 'Oh, I see. Your mother is not a shirker, is she? Excellent.'

When Mum had first written to say that she was now working on the buses, Valerie hadn't known how to react. Jean had seemed almost surprised by it herself. Everything about the world of adult work seemed mysterious to Valerie. If Jean had announced she was going to become a miner or a mermaid, it would have been no odder.

'How about your father, dear? Has he joined up?'

'He died before I was born,' Valerie said in the rehearsed way she had, and watched Mrs Howard's face fall, as people's faces always did.

'I am sorry.'

'It's all right,' Valerie said comfortingly. She was going to say that he died a hero, but she decided not to. She'd wait until she was asked. It would be more impactful that way.

Mrs Howard moved around the shop, picking up the corkscrews and the scissors and putting them down. Outside, the rope spun, and Lydia and Francine called:

'*Teddy bear, teddy bear, turn around. Teddy bear, teddy bear, touch the ground.*'

'I don't know Mrs Woods very well, but she seems a good person.'

Yesterday, Mrs Woods had sent her upstairs without any tea. She had called her a 'slum kid'. She said if Valerie told anyone the school would kick her out.

'Everyone says so,' Valerie said cautiously, and Mrs Howard looked pleased.

'There we are!'

People, even good people, no, *especially* good people, like to hear what they want to hear. They like to hear that things are well, that people are kind, that people are as good as they are.

'I'm glad you're in safe hands.'

Valerie swallowed.

Things were getting worse as time went on. You can endure anything if you think it's a week, a month, but this was turning out to be for an indefinite duration. Mrs Woods' hands were anything but safe. They were hard and cold and most often slapping the backs of Valerie's legs, or her cheeks.

And now if she wrote to Jean, Jean might just say, 'Why? What changed? You said they gave you a wireless, you said the countryside was glorious?' And then if Mrs Woods found out she had written? Well, it wouldn't be good.

Valerie wanted to turn the conversation away from herself. 'How is it with you?'

'I have to admit, it's been tumultuous,' Mrs Howard said, to Valerie's surprise. 'We lost Cassie, a much-loved dog' – she shot a look outside – 'and I have to admit, it's taken far longer for the girls to settle than I had imagined, but it's rewarding all the same. It's an education, isn't it? And we get on with it.'

Valerie couldn't imagine Mrs Woods saying that Valerie was rewarding in any way, shape or form.

She said, 'Sorry to hear about your dog,' and Mrs Howard nodded, but her face was pained.

'These things happen. We're getting another, as soon as I'm ready. I think young people learn from looking after animals, don't they?'

One of Valerie's tasks back at home in London was sweeping a room clear of spiders, since Lydia would howl at creepy-crawlies. As for Francine, she hated things with more than two legs and things with strange faces. So this was a change.

Lydia and Francine came back in the shop, red-faced and laughing. They took out biscuits from their schoolbags. Valerie's mouth was watering, yet her throat was dry. She stared at them; she felt ashamed of herself, yet she couldn't help herself. Lydia's teeth sank into the biscuit. Then Francine's did with hers. The crunch was louder than thunder. Valerie licked her lips.

'I don't like it,' Lydia said, gazing up at Mrs Howard, wide-eyed.

'Throw it away.' Mrs Howard sighed. She shook her head. 'She's such a picky eater. I've never known anyone like it. Was she like this in London?'

Valerie nodded and then said, 'She only likes bread and cheese.'

'I don't!' persisted Lydia. 'I like porridge now.'

Francine nudged her. 'Only with all the honey.'

'So?'

Mrs Howard sighed again, but despite the exasperation she appeared to be enjoying herself too.

'We'll be off now.'

Don't go, Valerie wanted to cry out.

Mrs Howard still looked concerned. 'Don't forget the show! And if ever you want to see the girls at home you're always welcome. Come for supper soon!'

Valerie nodded. She knew that Mrs Woods, for whatever reason, wouldn't let her, and that made it all the more painful to be invited.

17

___

Jean

Jean was still reeling from her encounter with Tony when Richard Carrington told her that he too was joining up. He told her he didn't particularly want to. He felt he *ought* to.

'That's the same thing, isn't it?'

'I suppose.'

Men were joining the services left, right and centre, or the Home Guard or the fire-watchers, or this and that. You could see the Home Guard marching in the park. If you listened closely, you could hear the ack-ack of the air defence guns practising early in the morning. Everyone was practising something. She wondered how a man whose greatest fear was hurting someone would fare in the armed services. He had nothing brutal or brusque about him – not like Tony or even Kenny, for example. They would both call Mr Carrington soft, she imagined, but he wasn't soft, he was sweet.

Side by side in the bus station, Jean and Richard ate their sandwiches. He said he was worried about his dad.

'What about your mother?' Jean enquired.

He coughed. 'Not around any more...'

'I'm sorry,' she said softly.

Richard told her he'd chosen the navy.

'What made you chose that?' Jean said, leaving her crusts.

'I like the sea,' he said, which seemed as good a reason as any.

'If I were a fella,' contemplated Jean, 'I'd chose the air force.'

'Planes scare me,' he said.

'Worse than driving in the dark?' For some reason that made them both laugh.

Richard had hopped on behind the wheel of the number 3 when Mrs Peabody called her over.

'He's sweet on you,' she hissed. 'But I hear Kenny is going to ask you out first.'

'*Kenny?* Really?'

The idea gave Jean the shivers. Kenny was insensitive. He acted as though he had no feelings and certainly wasn't concerned about anyone else's.

'Goodness,' she said, trying to make light of it. 'Men are like buses. You wait for one and then three come along all at once.' She blushed suddenly, thinking of Tony.

'That shouldn't happen,' said Mrs Peabody severely. 'Not if everyone keeps to their schedules.' Then she laughed. 'Richard is a lovely lad though,' she warned. 'Don't break his heart.'

Richard was the opposite of Kenny, Jean thought. He had too many feelings.

Jean didn't feel she was capable of breaking men's hearts, never had been. Although she often got whistled at, and was asked out frequently, it was never serious. She was the one people asked in jest or as a joke. And anyway, she'd always had Valerie to rush home for.

· · ·

A few days went by and fortunately Kenny didn't say anything and nor did Richard; but then, one evening as Jean finished the late shift, she found Richard waiting for her at the station. He was a vision of awkwardness, hands in pockets, his cap down low. People were raising their eyebrows. Kenny's were right up in his hairline.

'Ding-ding, Miss Hardman,' he said with a wink.

'It's not what you think,' she retorted.

Richard ambled over to the bus, his freckly face in a nervy grimace.

Perhaps if he'd asked her out before she'd seen Tony again Jean would have been more receptive, but she couldn't stop thinking of Tony and the conversation on the bus. Tony had been as surprised to see her as she had been to see him – she realised that now. When he put his hand on her sleeve, electricity had sizzled through her.

Richard asked her to come out with him, but there was nowhere to go – no cinema, no dancing, nothing. Iris and Mavis mentioned underground clubs but Richard wasn't in the know and Jean certainly wasn't. Besides, she was working all the hours God sent.

And now the other besides... *what if Tony came back?*

'Well, if we can't go out tonight, I wondered if you would come and see me off tomorrow?' Richard asked, jiggling from side to side.

Jean faltered. She hadn't successfully seen off her own daughter. Should she learn from that, or was it disloyal?

'I'm working tomorrow, Richard,' she explained.

'They'll give you special dispensation if it's important,' he said.

It was gone ten and she was exhausted. She didn't want to stand about arguing.

'Can I walk you home then?' he asked hopefully, and she relented.

London was black and quiet. They could have been anywhere. They could have been in outer space.

'I worry the old man will die when I'm away and I won't find out,' Richard eventually said.

'He won't.' Jean thought she sounded like her old client Mrs Cutler in her stupid certainty. How could she know this? The odds of old lungs or weak hearts surviving a gas attack were more like zero. This was something she had thought about *a lot*.

'I'll let you know if anything happens,' she assured him.

Suddenly, he said, 'You don't think you would be my girl, do you?'

Jean wondered how to let him down gently. 'We hardly know each other, Richard...' she eventually said. He didn't know about the medication she took. He didn't know about her fears and nightmares. He didn't know she had a daughter!

He looked down. 'I thought maybe we could get to know each other. Is it... is there anyone else?'

'Someone else? No-oo.' Jean tidied away stray thoughts of Tony.

'I thought maybe Kenny?' His voice was wary, as though he didn't really want an answer.

'Kenny?' repeated Jean. 'I'm not interested in Kenny...'

'Then who's stopping us?'

Jean tried to explain. 'You won't even be here.'

'We could write?' he suggested, still hopeful.

'I don't have time to write,' Jean said.

Richard was so innocent – he had no idea of the real Jean. Sometimes, she felt like she was living two lives: the mother versus the clippie. And she hated keeping secrets; yet here she was, accruing more and more of them. For once she was glad of the blackout darkness, since she knew her cheeks were aflame too.

'It's not just that,' he said.

'What is it?'

'Nothing...'

'Spit it out.' Jean didn't mean to sound harsh.

Richard continued anyway. 'I feel untethered,' he said in a small voice. Jean could swear she saw tears in his eyes, but it was too dark to be sure. She didn't know what he meant. He seemed to realise that because he added, 'I don't want to die.'

Jean patted him on the back. She appreciated his honesty. 'Everyone's scared,' she said softly. 'Nothing wrong with admitting that but you'll be fine.'

Unexpectedly, a few days later Mrs Peabody gave Jean a day off. She deserved it for good performance, apparently. Jean thought that phrase 'performance' rang true. She rushed to the railway station and got a day return to Somerset. The price of the fare hurt. She could apply for it back but... Then she sent Valerie a telegram.

She couldn't sleep the night before. She was finally going to see her girl.

18

Valerie

When the telegram arrived to say her mother was coming, Valerie's first thought was: *I'll believe it when I see it!*

Well, now she could see her mother, she had to believe it.

They met at the train station. Her mother was wearing a peculiar grey wool jacket and grey trousers. When the other mothers visited they were dressed in their Sunday best, and that was what Valerie had expected Jean to be wearing.

'It's my uniform,' Jean explained self-consciously. 'Smart, isn't it? It's what I wear on the buses. I thought you'd like to see it.'

Valerie couldn't remember her mother in anything like this before, and something about it stuck in her throat. She always imagined Jean racing home in her clothes for cleaning, a head-scarf knotted under her chin. What else had changed while she had been stuck out here in Somerset? She felt as though she couldn't keep up.

'You look so grown up,' her mum kept saying and 'Let me look at you!'

Valerie felt close to tears. She was hungry all the time and her mother had brought her not food but a book, *Snow White*. Not only had Valerie already read it but evil stepmothers and poisoned apples were much too young for her.

'You look different too, Mum...'

'I feel different!' trilled her mum. 'But what about you, Val? You've got no colour in your cheeks.'

Valerie rubbed her face. 'I'm fine,' she said. She imagined Mrs Lester's fury if she told her the truth: *'You complained? About my friend? Out!'*

'Have you lost weight?' Her mother wouldn't stop peering at her. It was disconcerting.

'The food here is strange,' Valerie said. 'That's all.'

Jean went off on a long-winded story about buses. 'And the driver went straight through a red light!' She peered at Valerie. 'Are you sure you're all right?'

'I said I am.'

'I have something funny to tell you: a passenger asked me to be his sweetheart! I said no, obviously, but it gave me a warm feeling – actually that's twice now, but I don't think the first one was being serious. I told my boss – men are like buses!'

Valerie didn't know how to respond. She chewed her fingernails and thought of her father clinging onto a ladder up, up in the sky. *What was he thinking in those last moments?*

Her mum was expecting to visit Mrs Woods.

'She's too busy,' explained Valerie and Mum looked surprised at that, and then recovered, 'So I've got you all to myself then? That's a relief!'

They went into Valerie's graveyard and sat on her favourite bench – the only bench. Her mum said it was a funny place to sit and was there nowhere less spooky? Valerie said she liked the gravestones and imagining what had killed the people under them. Mum made a face and then asked what Valerie had spent her birthday money on. Valerie told her that a card had eventually come but there was no shilling. Mum looked surprised and said, 'How queer. The postal service must have lost it.'

Valerie nodded doubtfully. She wondered if her mother had put the money in at all. She felt weary suddenly – this day that she had looked forward to didn't seem to be the day she had planned.

'Do you still like reading?' Mum asked, as though it were an ailment you grew out of.

'I mostly listen to the shows on the wireless now,' Valerie said, perking up. She was excited to share this with her mother. 'Do you?'

'I don't have time,' said her mum with a weak smile, and Valerie felt empty again. 'I am flat-out. Where's your gas mask?'

'I don't have it with me,' Valerie said and, seeing her mum now look aghast, she added, 'I guess it's different here, Mummy,' she went on quickly, even though she was eleven years old now, 'I really want to come home.'

She hadn't planned to say it, it just came out. Had she planned it, it might have come out in the right order or with more compelling reasons, but it was like grabbing something floating by – why not?

She thought of all the things she hadn't told her mother: the constant hunger. The spiders. The damp. The cold. Freezing in the yard – that would only get worse as winter moved in.

She could see her mum was shocked. She fiddled with a button on her uniform.

'Why?'

'I want to be in London with you,' Valerie said. And when that didn't seem to hit the wicket, she added, 'We should go through this awful war together.'

Her mum didn't say anything.

'I can look after every—'

'I don't need help,' her mum interrupted, 'from you.'

'I can cook and clean and hang up the blackout curtains.'

'I did those ages ago, Val,' her mum replied wearily.

'I can do all the stuff you don't want to do.'

Her mum's eyes welled up. 'Is she no good? Your Mrs Woods?'

'She's all right,' Valerie lied. She remembered Mrs Woods' threats. *I'll tell Mrs Lester of you.* She couldn't not go to school. That would ruin everything. 'But it's not home.'

'Home is not what it was,' Mum said. 'There are hardly any schools, it's dark all the time, everyone's waiting for the—'

'But I need to look after you,' Valerie pleaded.

'You don't,' her mum said harshly. 'I look after myself perfectly well.'

'Loads of children have gone back.'

Jean looked at her with sadness in her eyes. 'They're making a mistake.'

Valerie's temper flared. The thought that her mother of all people knew who was making a mistake and who wasn't was absurd.

'You told me it was a holiday!'

'I *hoped* it was like a holiday.'

'It's not though. And it's been so long!'

'It's only been two months...'

'It feels longer,' Valerie insisted.

'You have to stay here,' her mum said firmly. 'London is dangerous. It's a target – you know that. As soon as it's safe we'll be back together, I promise.' She attempted to squeeze Valerie's shoulder, but Valerie shook her off.

'But there's no Nazis, no bombs.'

'Not *yet*. Anyway, it's not just that, it's black, it's cold, it's dangerous... You're safer here, darling,' her mum said, craning her neck to see the hands of the church clock. 'I'd better go.'

Valerie opened her mouth to argue again but her mum quickly kissed the top of her head, letting her know this conversation was over.

19

Valerie

Over the next few weeks, Mrs Woods continued to give Valerie very little food and demand she spent any time she wasn't at school in the shop.

'Slum child,' she muttered under her breath, and 'Filthy Londoner.'

Valerie tried to think of the positives in her situation. At least she wasn't living with that creepy man in the village hall, that was one. Her mum had finally visited, that was another. And even though the visit had left Valerie disappointed, she hoped that the next one would be better – and come round quicker too. Another positive was the wireless. The difference that made to her life was monumental!

Her life had been divided into pre-evacuation and post-evacuation, but now there was a different axis. Pre-wireless and post-wireless. Post-wireless was infinitely better. She had a permanent companion – she had something to listen to. She had a connection to the world. With the radio there were no complications. It was there, it wasn't there. She got to decide.

And then *It's That Man Again* came on the wireless. It was the second series apparently. It was a story about a man who broadcast his own radio show and was in a constant fight with bureaucracy.

Valerie had heard the thrillers; she had heard the romances – but this was an altogether different order of fun. This was comedy. And it wasn't simply funny, it was hilarious. It was perfection in a box. And it was original too, and different – she couldn't anticipate the lines, and this thrilled her. For once, she didn't know where it was going – and how fantastic was that?

The line 'This is Funf speaking' made her roar. 'I don't mind if I do' nearly brought tears of laughter to her eyes. Once a week, seven o'clock on a Tuesday, she belly-laughed. She howled. She escaped.

Shortly after Jean's visit, Valerie was moved out of the evacuee class and put into a class with local children of her own age, and this also was a great improvement.

'Pair up,' said the teacher, putting her next to a girl with red-red hair and a face full of freckles. 'Help each other.'

Morwenna wore her hair in two plaits that started the day neat and ended the day wild. She had a gap between her two front teeth, which she said made her a good singer. She stuck her tongue out when she wrote and she asked 'Why?' a lot – to the point where it got irritating; but that was the only irritating thing about her. Morwenna was good at arithmetic, whereas Valerie was weaker. Valerie was one of the best in the class at interpreting a text, while Morwenna was weak at English but her handwriting was impeccable. The teacher often held up her work as an example of how to write – and she often held up Valerie's as an example of how not to.

Every day, without fail, as they left the classroom Morwenna begged Valerie to 'come play'.

And every day, Valerie had to explain she couldn't.

'Why?'

'I have to work in the shop.'

'I'll get my mum to ask Mrs Woods if you can come for tea,' Morwenna said. That was another thing about Morwenna. She had a solution to everything.

Valerie told her not to, desperately, but there was no stopping her. Morwenna's parents asked, and this made Mrs Woods furious.

'What the hell did you tell the girl? I don't want you seeing her again.'

So, Valerie couldn't get to play with Morwenna after school, but that wasn't too terrible because at least she had her during the day. At school, they were inseparable. Morwenna taught Valerie old folk songs and bawdy rhymes but she could never sing them as soulfully as Morwenna could.

They talked about their families and after they had been friends for a while, and Valerie was certain Morwenna was someone to be trusted, she told her about her father.

'Did he get a medal? For saving them girls?' Morwenna asked with wide eyes.

'I don't think so – I'll ask my mother next time.'

'Wow. I wish my father did something special.'

Morwenna's father worked on a farm.

'It's okay,' said Valerie magnanimously. 'You're a good person, it doesn't matter about anyone else.'

'True,' agreed Morwenna, who wasn't afflicted with low self-esteem.

Morwenna's parents took her to the charity production of *The Wind in the Willows* at the local theatre and she said it was hilarious. The cheeky mole! That funny Mr Toad! They couldn't believe the actors weren't professionals, it was *that* polished!

Valerie had lots of questions about it: were there evacuees

there? What was the set design like? But another thing about Morwenna was that she got bored with things quickly. She was clearly bored with the subject now and didn't say any more. But finally, Valerie had a friend in Taunton, and that was all that mattered to her.

20

Jean

A couple of weeks after her visit to Somerset, Jean had agreed to meet Tony at the Lyons Tea Rooms after work. What harm was there meeting a married man in public? On the way there, the pavements were covered in leaves, and you could slip and hurt yourself. Peril was all around.

Tony was working as a bookkeeper. 'Essential services,' he told her, slightly pink at admitting it. He, Pauline and the boys lived in Victoria Park. She told him about her visit to Valerie and he said again, 'You sent her to safety – you did the right thing.'

'I miss her though,' Jean admitted glumly. Valerie's scowl when she'd said it wasn't a holiday! And the begging to come back! There was a lot of resentment there – it wasn't like her sweet, soft girl at all. And there weren't many people she could talk about this with. Certainly no one at work. But if she couldn't tell the child's father, who could she tell?

'Those people she is staying with...' Tony enquired. 'Are they any good?'

'She,' corrected Jean. 'I imagine so. She would have to be to have offered to put her up, wouldn't she?'

He pulled a face.

'She has a hardware shop,' she added. 'It sells all sorts.' She sipped her tea but it was too hot. 'Thing is, Valerie didn't seem... she didn't seem her usual chirpy self. She was annoyed with me. She wanted to come home. And she looked awfully pale.'

Tony suddenly pushed back his chair and jumped up. 'Let's go get her.'

'I can't!'

'Yes, you can. I can't have you in this state.'

This was a side to Tony she hadn't seen before. A caring, protective side.

'People change!' he said defensively when she pointed that out to him. Hmm, and none had changed more than her, she thought. She persuaded him to sit down.

'I'm not bringing her home. She's settled there. And there's nothing here for her. She needs a good education. She deserves a chance.'

God knows, with a mother like me, she doesn't have much going for her...

'And remember what happened to my father?' Tony was one of the few people she'd told about the gas.

'He was at war, Jeanie!' Tony said. 'It's different.'

'We're at war,' Jean snapped back. 'It's the same!'

She thought of the poster she passed at least three or four times every day. *Don't do it, Mother!* Jean promised herself she wouldn't – she wouldn't be that selfish.

After he called for the bill, Tony lent over the table and tried to kiss her on the lips – would he be Tony if he didn't try? – but Jean dodged him.

'Please agree to come out with me again.'

'As friends,' she told him firmly. 'I'm not after any funny business.' He laughed. He knew he was winning. The young women on the next table looked over at him and then raised eyebrows at each other.

'All right, but a man can hope.'

They went out again two weeks later. In the meantime, Jean imagined she saw Tony's wife and his boys everywhere she went. She'd rather face Nazis than them.

She could feel herself weakening to Tony's charms. It wasn't only that he was attractive. Although she loved the buses, it was nice to have a break from them; equally, it was pleasant to be with someone she had history with, who knew her from before this ghastly war. It was being seen, being known. You didn't get that a lot in the anonymous city and although she loved being dashing Miss Hardman-on-the-buses, ding-ding, there was something easy about being just Jean.

This second time, he walked her home, and of course he wanted to come in.

'My feet are aching,' he pleaded.

He was a terrible one for blisters, she remembered. He used to soak them in mustard.

'Only for a minute,' she said, giving in.

What was the matter with her? She wasn't normally so gullible. He kept saying he'd changed, he cared now – but he was still a married man. She would always just be his bit on the side.

But it felt safe to have someone there, looking out for her.

He moved closer to her. 'So...' he said, wrapping his arms round her waist.

'So...' Jean answered, unsmiling.

'We used to be good together,' Tony said, his eyes sparkling like they always did.

'Have you left your wife yet?' she asked, remembering why

she couldn't do this again. She knew his wife's name but she didn't feel comfortable saying it.

He gave her a sorry smile. 'It's difficult, sweetheart.'

'How many children do you have now?' Jean asked as she moved his hands from her waist, stepping away.

'Three. What can I say?' he said, hands up in the air – 'I like children.'

Not all of them, she thought. How much easier things would be if he did. If they lived in a house with roses over the door. If she was a real Mrs Hardman, rather than a fake Mrs Hardman in her private life and a Miss Hardman at work. If he was a true father, and Valerie had a man who loved her.

He cleared his throat. 'If I left Pauline, do you think I'd be in with a chance with you, Jeanie?'

Goodness, she thought. She'd never expected him to say that, not in a million years. Once upon a time, it was the thing she most yearned for in the world. Jean knew the odds of him leaving his wife were infinitesimally low.

But it seemed Tony had a knack of saying exactly what she wanted to hear. 'Jeanie, we could be a family. You, me, Valerie...'

That was all she had ever wanted for the girl. A proper family. Like the Frouds and the Salts. You'd think she'd be able to arrange that!

But Valerie didn't know her father was still alive, and Tony didn't know she had told Valerie he was dead. These two secrets filled her with a terrible dread. What on earth had she done? Ruined everything probably.

'Maybe,' she said cautiously, and then, glancing at his face, 'Yes, of course. But could you?'

'I could,' he said.

She thought he was going to kiss her but he said he had to go. Relieved, she led him to the door.

21

Valerie

In the middle of December, Valerie saw Francine and Lydia ambling along near the shop, not in their purple school blazers this time but in pinafores and shiny lace-up shoes. The sight of them made her feel tired. But then they shrieked and galloped towards her, and she got the feeling of home probably more even than she did with Jean.

'What are you doing for Christmas?' yelped Francine.

'We're going back to London!' screeched Lydia.

Valerie was so shocked her legs nearly gave way. The girls grinned at her.

'Not for good?'

Weren't they worried about the gas? Weren't they frightened of the jackboots?

'We don't know yet,' said Lydia.

'So, we're celebrating early, aren't we?' said Francine.

'We're going to hang up socks.'

'Stockings!'

'She's not.'

'I am.'

These two could argue about anything.

'Paul's coming back from boarding school.'

'We're going to a party and then we're going to go on an egg hunt.'

Francine poked her. 'That's Easter, silly billy!'

Lydia laughed. 'Oh, yes, we're going to see Father Christmas.'

'It all sounds jolly,' Valerie said. She felt like they were lying. Or it was one of the stories she used to make up for them? No one could be doing all those fun things. They were supposed to be having a miserable time. Mrs Howard couldn't have understood her mission correctly.

The girls skipped ahead while Valerie stood still. She remembered how she had given up the chance to go to Hedingway Hall with its 'facilities' to look after them.

Mrs Howard reached her. She was lugging a large bag full of papers and books, and she looked puffed out. This time, the brooch pinned on her coat was a perky-looking strawberry. It was almost as cute as the frog one.

'Valerie, dear! How are you?'

'Very well, thank you, Mrs Howard.'

'And your mother?'

'She's staying in London,' Valerie responded grimly.

Her mother's last letter had been a sad affair, full of fears of a gas attack and how important it was that Valerie did not come back. Valerie knew it was in response to her pleading. She thought of the character in her wireless show whose joke was, 'It's being so cheerful that keeps me going!'

'Yes,' said Mrs Howard, a little impatiently. 'Is she well?'

'I suppose,' said Valerie.

'You're not going back for the holidays?'

'No,' Valerie responded sharply. 'It's not safe, my mother says.'

The news that Lydia and Francine were getting back home to their families had pulverised her. She had accepted her fate when she thought it was everyone. To learn that it *wasn't* everyone – that in fact it might be only her who was left – was painful.

'I better go...' she said gloomily. If she didn't get back to the shop, Mrs Woods would scold her. Although the words tended to slide off her now, their powers blunted by repetition, she wanted to eat tonight.

'Keep your chin up,' Mrs Howard instructed her. 'And if we don't see you before, Merry Christmas.'

'Merry Christmas,' Valerie recited automatically.

Mrs Woods was going to see her son in Dorset on Christmas Day, and Valerie would stay at home. Although it meant 'nothing for you' apart from the usual crackers and apples, which increasingly were soft and maggoty, Valerie was pleased with this arrangement; until Mrs Woods said that the shop was shut – obviously – but that Valerie wasn't allowed to go in there.

Which would mean no wireless.

For once, Valerie didn't obey Mrs Woods. She knew where Mrs Woods kept the spare key, so as soon as the woman left on Christmas morning she snuck in with her blanket and sat in there with the wireless for company. There were worse places in the world.

There were prayers and sermons in the morning – it was like being in church – and then there was news and a quiz.

Later, there was a Royal Broadcast. As the King began his speech, Valerie pictured him with his family, warm by the fire, the two princesses with their presents.

> *I said to the man who stood at the Gate of the*
> *   Year,*
> *'Give me a light that I may tread safely into the*
> *   unknown.'*
> *And he replied, 'Go out into the darkness, and*
> *   put your hand into the hand of God.*
> *That shall be to you better than light, and safer*
> *   than a known way.'*

Everyone knew the King had a stutter, and Valerie heard the effort it took him to speak. She heard it like he was talking directly to her, from his mouth to her ear. It was almost like he was another father to her, letting her know that he was there. She wasn't alone. And she knew she had to be strong and that she would be strong.

And then Mrs Woods was in the shop, screaming at her.

22

___

Jean

As soon as she saw them Jean asked Lydia and Francine for news of Valerie, but neither child was particularly communicative, and they didn't have a lot to tell. Jean felt like an overbearing aunt. An aunt who twists your cheeks too hard. How unused to young girls she was now. She had forgotten the way they shrank away from you and giggled.

'Are you looking forward to going back to Somerset?' Jean asked next, but they merely looked at each other and shrugged.

When Mrs Salt explained she had changed her mind and Francine was staying in London, Jean couldn't believe it. Of all the things to do. What about the threat of gas? And most of the local schools weren't even open – there weren't enough teachers!

The evacuation posters that had worked so effectively on Jean had failed to impress Mrs Salt. Jean had to repeat to herself, 'Our situations are different. Our lives are different,' but she couldn't help thinking Mrs Salt was making the wrong decision in keeping Francine home. Not terrible, not ridiculous – as some people insisted – but certainly foolhardy.

Mrs Salt shook her head. 'I'll leave it in God's hands,' she said, which was odd because usually she was proactive and certainly not all of her choices had God's hands over them – but still Jean swallowed her opinions and let little Joe blow raspberries at her.

With Mrs Froud, it wasn't God, it was My Neville's hands she was leaving it in, and My Neville said, 'On no account should the children stay in London after Christmas – an attack was imminent.'

Mrs Salt wasn't standing for that. 'Mr Froud's been saying that since September...'

'That doesn't make it less true now,' argued Mrs Froud. She was sending Lydia back to the countryside.

Jean liked Lydia but Francine was a strange child. Whenever Jean went to see Mrs Salt – mostly to have a cuddle with baby Joe – she was always there like a ghost, behind you, waiting and watching. Jean tried to engage with her but she didn't like meeting your eye.

'What was it like? In the countryside?'

'There were sheep.'

'Oh. And the lady of the house? What is she like?'

Francine considered. 'She is funny.'

'Did you miss your family?'

She had Jacob, the second youngest, on her knee. 'Always.'

'You don't want to go back? You're not scared of all the bombs here?'

Francine shook her head and her dark curls bounced. 'I want to be with Mummy.'

Jean wondered if she'd been told to say that.

'If we go, I want us all to go together,' Mrs Salt insisted.

Jean knew she shouldn't get het up about this, but she felt

Mrs Salt's decision reflected badly on her somehow. Certainly, Valerie wouldn't like it.

Mrs Peabody hummed and hawed before deciding that, never mind the war, they would go ahead and hold their annual bus company Christmas dance. They needed some fun. Jean, Iris and Mavis danced with old Mr Carrington, who told Jean, 'My boy would have loved to ask you out.'

Jean winced. Richard obviously hadn't told his father that she'd turned him down.

Then Jean danced with Kenny, who pressed himself too close to her in front of everyone. It was difficult to push him off without making a scene. She pretended she was enjoying it, but she wasn't. Next, she danced with Mrs Peabody, who warned her about Kenny again, 'a rascal', and 'don't encourage him'.

'I'm not!'

'He thinks you're after him.'

'Good grief.'

Kenny danced with Mavis, who seemed to respond although you never could tell, and it probably wasn't sisterly of Jean, but she thought at least if he got with Mavis he wouldn't be her problem.

Everyone was calling Perry Comrade Stalin because he'd grown a moustache, and this displeased him no end. He and Iris danced for ages but the next morning Iris insisted nothing would come of it; it was just drivers and clippies getting along exactly as they should.

Jean anticipated that Tony would get in touch with a plea for goodwill to all men at Christmas or some such, but he must have been busy with his Pauline and the boys. She imagined them standing side by side at midnight mass or smooching under the mistletoe...

Thank goodness he stayed away. Jean was so lonely, she might have let something happen.

She missed Valerie and now she missed Tony too. It was a mess.

She was invited to Mrs Peabody's for Christmas Day, or upstairs to the Salts, but she didn't think it appropriate. It was a family day and she wasn't family. She was tired after all the long days at work, and if she couldn't be with Valerie, she wanted to be alone.

She told herself that Valerie would be having a marvellous time and that was the important thing.

But on Christmas Eve, Jean couldn't sleep. Each time she closed her eyes, she could hear rats. When she opened her eyes, she saw one, now rubbing its claws, now chewing its own tail. 'Go away,' she hissed, but it just stared at her.

And then in the morning, she saw a mist coming towards them over the streets, dulling the lights, muting the colours, white, white. White Christmas. But it wasn't snow.

Quick.

Fumbling, Jean put on her gas mask. And waited. And waited and waited until the sun came up.

23

Valerie

The misery of Christmas evening stayed with Valerie for a long while. Mrs Woods had returned from her son's raging that money was missing from the till. She accused Valerie of stealing it. She whacked her round the face. Usually she was cautious not to leave a mark, but since it was the school holidays now she showed no such restraint.

Even when Mrs Woods realised the money was still there, she didn't apologise. That was how it was. Valerie worked in the shop every day straight from school and all day Saturday throughout January, February and March. It was better than sitting upstairs, hungry and alone on the damp mattress in the hall. She recommended and sold all sorts in the shop and she escaped into her shows on the wireless. If it weren't for hateful Mrs Woods, who disapproved of everything she did, she might have enjoyed it.

Francine had stayed back in London and Valerie didn't know if she envied her or not. Lydia was back in Somerset, but Valerie rarely saw her. When she did, she was mostly skipping along with a dog with its tail up in the air. One time, she came with Mrs Howard to the shop, but Valerie had the distinct impression that it was Mrs Howard's idea to come and not Lydia's. Valerie asked Lydia if she missed Francine and she shrugged and said, 'I suppose.'

'Is that all?' asked Valerie, who missed Francine's smiley face and uncomplicated ways.

'We have to make the most of it,' Lydia said.

'Out of the mouths of babes,' added Mrs Howard mysti-fyingly.

On *Children's Hour*, they talked about London Zoo. Most of the animals had been evacuated to other zoos outside London and Valerie was pleased to hear it. Sometimes, they went to visit factories or farms. Valerie learned about cows, tapestries, Burma and knitting.

She could say 'Where is the train station?' in Norwegian and also, 'How do you do?' and 'My aunt lives near the library'. Valerie wanted people from Norway to come into the shop so she might show off her fledging language skills. Some customers did come in with a foreign accent, but when she asked, they laughed, and explained, the accent was Scottish.

On the education programmes for schools they were doing long division, and in history, they were talking about Stone-henge, which was not that far away. She started imitating their voices. But the best moment of the week was what she thought of as her show, when the voices were speaking just for her: *It's That Man Again.* Thirty minutes of sheer joy. Thirty minutes when she wasn't desperate to get back home. Thirty minutes when she wasn't furious at her mother.

24

SPRING 1940

Jean

There was still no invasion and still no gas or bombs. Valerie remained in Somerset, although she didn't sound any happier. Lydia was in Somerset too, while Francine still hadn't gone back. Jean paid her two lots of rent diligently and she worked hard. She loved her routes and she loved (some of) the customers. She helped one man who thought he was having a heart attack – it was indigestion. And she traced the owner of a missing wallet with a photo of a beloved in it. The woman had thanked her with a hug and a shilling. She kissed babies and promised that tomorrow would be better – it was like being a politician!

A couple of times Jean went to the cinema after work with Mrs Peabody, but the secret of Valerie weighed heavily – it felt like she had left it too late to come clean even to her closest colleague. And she couldn't bring anyone from the bus company home because Mrs Froud or Mrs Salt might tell.

And still Jean doubted she was doing the right thing for Valerie. The Hitler in the posters – *Take Me Home* –

confirmed she was but still in her dreams the gunmetal rat appeared at the end of her bed. Sometimes, she wondered if she was going mad. There were more and more children on the buses – children who came back from evacuation joining those who'd never gone – and they made Jean's head hurt. They told stories: getting drunk on scrumpy, presents coming out of their ears. Cats, dogs and rabbits in their rooms, scaring bats or bats scaring them. And Jean had to listen to them and had to tell herself she was doing the right thing. One day there would be nothing to fear any longer and Valerie would be sitting happily on her bus – but until that day she was safer in Somerset.

When Valerie was tiny, an old lady in the street had looked after her so that Jean could work. Mrs Hudson would put whisky in Valerie's milk and sugar on her finger, and she was besotted with Valerie, which was what Jean needed.

It was strange; Valerie had started coming out with words and phrases that were not Jean's. It felt like she was not only growing up but growing away from her. 'I could murder a cuppa!' was the first one.

Jean knew where she was getting it from and it wasn't that she didn't like it, it just made her aware of time she wasn't spending with her daughter.

Mrs Hudson always said, 'She'll go far,' and that phrase irritated Jean more than it should have. One day, she couldn't keep it in.

'What do you mean "she'll go far"?'

'She'll go far,' repeated the old woman like Jean was an idiot. 'You won't see her for dust. She won't look back.'

Jean had felt hurt. 'Why do you say that?'

'I know it,' Mrs Hudson said. It felt like she was a witch putting a curse on her beautiful child. As though Valerie would prick her finger on a spinning wheel. As though Jean was destined to lose her.

Jean adjusted to not hearing from Tony, but then one day in March he got on her bus again. Although spring was coming, and there was a lightness in the air, he was all wrapped up in a heavy coat and scarf and leather gloves like he was expecting snow.

'The girl still away?'

Why did he have to speak like that? She felt guilty enough as it was. 'Here is no place for children.' She scowled. 'The government said. Ticket?'

Kenny was driving and he was glaring at Tony, his eyes appraising in the rear-view mirror.

'Wales, is it?'

Did he listen to a word she said?

'Somerset.'

'No, yes, I mean, good – sensible. I was thinking I'll take you for a visit if you like.'

A visit with Tony? A visit though – that was probably what she needed. A reunion with her darling to get her through the long, lonely days. Reunion, reassurance, rekindling. All the R's. It had been six months now – she had no idea how time went by so fast, but she did know it was too long for a mother and young daughter to be apart.

Tony's eyes were upon her. He had surprisingly long eyelashes, for a man.

'No strings though, Tony, you can't...'

She couldn't explain to him why he couldn't meet her – but she didn't have to.

'I'll take you as a friend. It's the least I can do. I won't even meet the girl if you don't want me to.'

'Really?'

'Course.' He made a face. 'Pauline would do her nut if she knew.'

The spectre of his wife *doing her nut*, shaking her chains, was not a nice one.

'I owe you too, don't I?'

Perhaps. Perhaps. Perhaps.

After he'd got off, Kenny called her up to the front. 'If anyone gives you any trouble, Miss Hardman,' he said, emphasising the 'Miss', 'make sure you let me know.'

Jean blushed. 'Appreciated, Kenny, thank you.'

She'd ask Mrs Peabody if she could have Perry or Arthur as her driver next week.

Jean wanted to take Valerie a present, but she had no idea what she might like now. Six months was a long time apart and especially at Valerie's age when they were changing all the time. Valerie's letters were stilted, but then neither of them was the world's greatest correspondent. All Val wrote about nowadays was the wireless. Not toys, not games, not friends, not even school.

Jean got her a little tin bus for sentimental reasons, but had second thoughts and gave it to Mrs Froud's Matthew instead. He was probably the right age; and indeed he was delighted with it – he started vroom, vrooming across the carpet straight away. Mrs Froud was in a funny mood though and the gift didn't soften her one bit.

'My Neville says you're probably vulnerable right now, Mrs Hardman.'

'Pardon me!' responded Jean. 'What's that supposed to mean?'

'You're a career woman, and all alone, that's all. Some men might sniff around, taking advantage...'

'That's what your Neville says, is it?'

'He's only trying to help,' Mrs Froud said, snootily.

Tony had borrowed a car and some fuel.

'I wouldn't do this for just anyone,' he said when he picked her up. Jean could imagine Mrs Froud's sour face pressed against the flat upstairs' window.

'Neville, she's out again!'

Despite having told him no strings, already the trip seemed to come with unspoken conditions. But Tony had bought mints for the journey, and he was all dimpled smiles and promises of cake, so she ignored the voice in her head that was suggesting caution.

She told Tony she had wanted to see Stonehedge since she was a girl but Tony laughed at her– 'It's not called that!' – and anyway *his* route – which didn't go by Stonehedge – was quicker and when someone is doing you a favour and fuel is rarer than hens' teeth, what can you do?

The deal was Tony would drop her off and go and do his business in Lynmouth. He'd be around six hours, so in theory it would work out brilliantly. Jean still didn't trust him not to intrude, not until he parked up about ten minutes' walk from the village, and even then, she wondered if he was going to spring a surprise on them. But he didn't. Thank goodness.

Valerie greeted Jean warmly and was delighted with the liquorice she had brought her. Jean had been anxious about this reunion, so this was a huge relief. They went to the graveyard, which Jean still thought was a weird choice, but this time she knew not to say anything. Maybe she had been wrong about her last visit. Maybe Valerie wasn't resentful, perhaps it had been a bad day.

When Jean told Valerie about her life on the buses, she

didn't seem interested, but when she told her about thumb-sucking Joe and Francine and the rest of the Salt children she perked up.

She kept her hand in the bag of sweets. Jean told her not to eat everything at once, save some for later maybe? Her mouth full, Valerie agreed she would.

Valerie did say she wanted to come home again, but she said it quietly, as though she was saying it out of habit more than anything. Jean explained that the situation was, if possible, even worse than before, so no, she had to stay in Somerset.

Valerie said that the orangutans had been moved to Whip-snade Zoo and Jean laughed and said, 'You see! Everyone's being evacuated now – even the monkeys.' Valerie said they weren't monkeys but she got the point.

'Is Mrs Woods still treating you all right, darling?' Jean asked. Valerie mumbled that everything was fine.

'What about food? Have you grown used to it yet?'

'There's a lot of apple dumplings,' Valerie said, which made Jean laugh. They sounded delicious.

Valerie did ask, 'Have you any photos of my father?' but for once Jean didn't think she handled it too badly. It wasn't only on the buses that diplomacy was important. She said, 'I don't think so,' then 'I'll have a look,' which Valerie seemed to accept. She closed her eyes and leaned her head on Jean's shoulder and, for once, let Jean pet her, and it was heavenly.

Tony had the hump on the way home.

'I thought you were going to introduce us.'

'No!' Jean couldn't help sighing. *Why was he being like this?* 'We agreed we wouldn't.'

Tony didn't mean introduce him as her father, he insisted, he wasn't *that* stupid, but couldn't he at least have come to say hello? As an old friend?

Jean cringed. This was getting too complicated to navigate. It would be impossible to keep them apart. 'Another time.'

'I hope you appreciate what I did,' he said.

'I do...'

'Bit of gratitude is in order.'

'I am grateful,' Jean said. Her whole body was tense.

'I did it though, I did it for you and Valerie, because I wanted to.'

'Thank you,' she said. She felt exhausted. But he was Valerie's father, she reminded herself. They would always be connected. And at least Tony was interested in her as Jean – a person; not many were.

When they got back to hers, he asked to come in.

'Just for a cup of tea, Jean! I drove all that way!' He had a neck ache, a backache and indigestion from the pork pie she'd got him. She felt like these things were all her fault. She said sorry, hoping he would tell her they weren't. These eggshells were difficult to walk on.

Both the Frouds' flat and the Salts' were in darkness, so she had no excuse not to allow him in again.

This time, they did share a kiss, for old times' sake, and if her thoughts, oddly, turned to Richard Carrington, who didn't smell of cigar smoke, she ignored it. Good grief, this war could drive a woman insane.

And then Tony told her something else.

'Pauline's left me,' he said. 'She's taken the kids to Morecambe Bay.'

'Really?' The timing seemed suspicious. Everything seemed suspicious. Where was Morecambe Bay anyway?

'Why don't you come and live with me, sweetheart?' he asked softly. 'You must get lonely, like I do.'

'I can't.'

'Why?'

'Because it's complicated.'

She would have to tell Valerie about him. Yet she didn't see how she could. They had gone too far for that. Too many stories. Too many lies.

'Take your time,' he said. 'Think about it.'

'I will.'

'We can be a proper family.'

She *was* vulnerable to him. The Frouds weren't entirely mistaken. And she hated it about herself.

Once he'd gone, the flat felt emptier than ever. He was right about it: this place was too big for little old her. She felt like a pea wobbling on the edge of a dinner plate. But he was wrong too – he wasn't the answer, she knew that.

25

AUTUMN 1940

Jean

If it weren't for the passengers and the drivers, and Mrs Peabody, Jean would have been lost the summer of 1940. They kept her mind busy and her body exhausted. It was war, war, war – bus, bus, bus. Tony hadn't appeared again and she didn't have another chance to visit Valerie, but Valerie wrote to say she was still busy with the shop during the holidays.

'Don't let Mrs Woods work you too hard!' Jean responded gaily. She thought it was wonderful that with this experience Valerie would be able to walk into any shop-floor job when she was ready.

It was darker than usual, or perhaps darker earlier. Winter was coming – the smell of roasted chestnuts filled the streets and she'd been hunting for gloves. Jean was chatting with a regular about pickling. Another passenger had told her his plans for that evening: a game of backgammon. Someone else was waiting to tell her about *Gone with the Wind*.

And then suddenly – planes. They filled the sky, you could hear them, smell them. Like great, savage birds soaring overhead. 'Are they ours?' she heard someone say. Then someone else said, 'I don't like this...'

Everyone waited. And then there was the wretched sound of an explosion, a hit. They weren't ours.

'Shit,' said Kenny, who never usually swore. He steered the bus to the side of the road. Jean made her way towards him, from pole to pole.

'Should we keep on?' he said.

She turned round. Everyone looked frightened. 'May as well. We've got to get people home – the nearest shelters are a long way from here.'

They kept on. People jumped on the bus all along the route, and for once Kenny let them, without complaint.

'It's started,' one man said, in a jolly voice, but his face was ashen.

'Looks that way!' Jean said quietly.

Jean held onto her pole. It was the only thing that would stop her hands shaking. Her heart was thumping and it was like a beat behind her ears. The fear was like nothing she'd known before. And yet she was the clippie; she had to have a brave face, a brave everything.

It's not gas, it's not, Jean told herself. *Please God, it's not that.*

'There are no public shelters here,' Kenny said, consulting his map. 'Keep with the route or...?'

'Yes please, mister,' said a young girl – not much older than Valerie – who'd overheard. She'd been to see her grandmother in Kilburn.

'If you wouldn't mind awfully,' added another passenger. He was on leave and needed to pick up his car.

Another woman said she needed to fetch her husband's suit for a funeral and 'what a day for it!'

The noise was horrendous. Sounds of a boom and then

things falling down. You couldn't see actual fires but smoke was everywhere. A couple of people were coughing.

'Is it gas?' Jean whispered.

'It's smoke,' said the woman worried about the suit. She patted Jean's shoulder. 'We'll be all right, clippie.'

They finished the route and found the bus station was empty. Kenny directed the remaining passengers to the shelter then said he'd run off to see what he could do. Jean didn't know what she could do; she was all wound up and had nowhere to go.

'Good luck,' he said and they looked at each other, and it was like something meaningful passed between them; then he hurried off in his lopsided way.

She got home in exceptionally fast time; the streets were quiet, the only people out the ARP, and they yelled at her to hurry, hurry, for the nearest shelter.

She had the Morrison shelter in the house, a table with a cage underneath in the kitchen, or the Anderson shelter dug down at the end of their yard. She ran to that one. It was dominated by Frouds and Salts but they called out that there was room for a little one. They were all in there huddled up, white faces, big eyes. For some reason, she wanted to giggle.

'So here it is,' she said.

Mrs Salt sat, her head in her hands like one of those sculptures at the National Gallery.

'There, there,' said Mrs Froud to no one and everyone. 'My Neville says the shelters are safe as houses...'

'*The Germans dropped over 100 tonnes of explosives in one night,*' read Mrs Peabody from the newspaper the next morning. 'We've got to keep going. Anyone want out? Go now.'

Of course no one wanted out.

'We'll finish before dark. If there is a next time, and let's pray there isn't, you stop the bus, find the nearest shelter and get in there straight away. You'll be sitting ducks otherwise.'

Kenny scowled. 'Nearest shelter, my arse! Some areas are better served than others!'

Of course there was a next time. The Germans had just been warming up. There was a next and a next and a next. Sometimes, Jean used the shelter nearest the bus station rather than do the precarious race home.

She got used to existing on less sleep and the cacophony of noise. The dust in the streets that made your eyes dry. 'Here they come' – and then up at six as usual, quick wash, ready to face the day. She kept her conductress clothes on all night for speed. Lipstick without a mirror. Hairbrush without a clue. Show up. Get going.

'Keep London moving,' everyone agreed, 'now more than ever.'

People had been preparing for this, anticipating this, worrying about this for so long, yet still it was a shock that it happened. People were talking to strangers, which they never usually did. And sometimes, people were extraordinarily kind.

Jean had people on the bus in the morning who'd lost everything in the night. She had people wanting the bus to take them to the hospital. She had people clutching their cats or dogs in boxes. She had Girl Guides and tea ladies attending to the injured.

Thank God Valerie was out of it. That was one good thing – Jean didn't have to worry about her girl. Yes, she did feel vindicated, but privately, she wouldn't tell anyone that – she wouldn't tempt fate.

She didn't hear from Tony again. She knew she shouldn't be surprised. He had a habit of turning up when he wasn't needed and not being there when he was, but still. She pictured him fondly, sitting in the Lyons Tea Rooms, fending off the admiring glances from the staff. How generous it was of him to take her to see Valerie.

She did like him, the idea of being a family with him interested her no end, but she wouldn't be his bit on the side again, no way. She wondered if he was deliberately keeping away to keep her interested. If so, it was working.

It made her laugh to think that it was only the darn rat in her nightmares that wanted to spend time with her.

One morning, a woman in a long raincoat was chasing the bus, her belt swinging wildly. Jean rang the bell but Kenny ignored her. He did that lately.

'Ding-ding,' Jean shouted furiously, and when that didn't work, 'Oy, Kenny! Stop!'

Kenny did eventually bring the bus to a halt further down the road.

'Look at her,' Kenny called from the cab, 'she's drunk as a skunk!'

'So?' She helped the woman up the step.

'My husband is dead,' she said, gripping Jean's hands, and then she wailed. Jean had never heard anything like it before in her life.

'Shut her up,' Kenny said. 'She's bad for morale.'

Valerie stared at him. 'You don't have to be so cruel.'

'War *is* cruel.'

Later, she thought, *all the more reason to be nice then!* But at the time, she just put her arm round the woman and sat with her. She didn't take her fare. She let her cry. And then she rang the bell. The whole bus was looking at her. They were aggrieved – a whole one-minute wait! – but the older women in headscarves called her over: 'You did the right thing there, clippie.' And 'If you can't be humane now, when can you be?'

Kenny said nothing. Then put his foot down so hard that the bus jerked forward and Valerie had to hang on or fall down.

26

Jean

Jean's usual markers along the route were disappearing. Now, they had different distinguishing features on the bus route. Not the house with the thatched roof, but the house with no roof. Not the house with the red door but the house with no windows.

The overdressed boy who waved and jumped still waved and jumped and the nice man at the library still got on with his steam train magazines but now they had obstacles and sandbags, roadblocks and chaos to contend with too.

Jean, the Frouds and the Salts were squashed into the shelter. They'd got a pack of playing cards but there were a few missing and no one was in a mind for Old Maid anyway.

Bombs were pounding.

Mrs Salt, surprisingly, was in better spirits than usual. She had been fearing this for so long, there was almost a sense of relief about her that at last it was happening. That the anticipation was the worst bit about it. But then she burst into tears. 'I should have sent Francine away again,' she said.

Francine patted her back ineffectually. 'It's all right, Mummy. I prefer it here.'

'I should have sent away the little ones,' Mrs Salt moaned.

What could you say to that? thought Jean. She didn't want to make Mrs Salt feel worse. Plus, she was unconvinced Mrs Salt meant it.

The children were quiet, like underground creatures. She cuddled little Joe until he fell asleep nuzzled against her. Sometimes he'd open his eyes, see it was her, smile, then close his eyes again. The rest of them hardly slept.

'Do you think we'll ever get used to it?' said Mrs Salt with a sigh.

'It's not going to last,' said Mrs Froud authoritatively. 'My Neville says the Nazis will invade soon and that'll be it.'

Jean, who had found out recently that Neville worked in the accounts department and not on the news desk as she had assumed, thought, *My Neville has been wrong about many things*, but she didn't say that. Mrs Froud was on tenterhooks anyway, and liable to start a fight when she was like this.

Jean still hadn't forgiven them for the 'vulnerable' remark either.

A few days after the bombing started, Mrs Froud announced she was going to evacuate to the countryside. Jean didn't know where exactly, but it wasn't Somerset. She was going on a scheme for mothers of young children. Jean thought she'd insist on being near Lydia. Mrs Froud said she'd tried but she couldn't get a place and where she was going had a whole community set up for people in the same boat as her and little Matthew.

Before Mrs Froud had left, she and Jean had exchanged words.

'You don't have anyone else to worry about, do you?' Mrs

Froud had said crudely. 'Valerie is independent – and you've got your life on the buses. I bet you're having a whale of a time.'

It was the worst possible thing she could have said and it hurt – it felt to Jean as though it came out of nowhere but who knew, maybe Mrs Froud had, like the Nazis, been building up to this all year.

It wasn't true. The Nazis were obliterating London and Jean had a billion things to worry about. And actually, she would have loved a husband and more children to worry about too.

Jean was at work when Mrs Froud left, and she was glad she didn't have to say goodbye or pretend that she cared.

A few days after Mrs Froud went, My Neville moved out too. Jean didn't know where he went; one moment he was there, the next he was gone and there was a note saying, *please help yourself to the vegetables.*

More room in the shelter, Jean thought. She wasn't going to mourn his leaving.

'Won't you go away too, Mrs Salt?' What was keeping the poor woman and her children here? It was like she was glued to the spot. Jean had her work, her responsibilities, her income, all here in London, but Mrs Salt could go anywhere, couldn't she?

'I'm not running away,' Mrs Salt said stubbornly. 'This is my home.'

'Let me take him,' said Jean, gesturing at little Joe, and Mrs Salt relinquished him. His heavy head against her felt like balm to the soul.

Jean, Mrs Salt and Mrs Salt's children spent their nights in the shelter. One time when they emerged, blinking like bats, they saw through the clouds of dust that the house three doors down had been bombed out.

The family weren't there, thank goodness, but it was still a shock to see the masonry, the bricks, the smashed tiles. Everyone was spluttering or muttering it was a 'lucky escape'.

The next day a policeman and a man with a clipboard knocked at Jean's door as she was getting ready for work.

'You have to leave – this house is uninhabitable.'

'Well, that's not true – I am *habitabing* it, obviously,' Jean tried to argue.

'Stay somewhere else,' the policeman said. This was nonsense, she thought. Where would she go?

'Until we tell you it's safe.'

'For goodness' sake. The house is not the problem,' Jean said, she pointed at the sky. It looked the most innocent blue. 'It's the Luftwaffe that is.'

'Orders is as orders does,' the policeman responded cryptically. They were all jobsworths now, Jean thought bitterly. All the good ones had joined up, leaving the pen-pushers and the number-crunchers in charge.

'Where am I meant to go?'

'There are people at St Augustine's Church. Or' – he eyed her uniform – 'you're a clippie, what's wrong with the bus?'

'I'm not living on a bus!' Jean exclaimed.

The other man said, 'We need you to evacuate the building until we let you know you can return.'

Evacuate. Evacuate. Story of their lives.

Mrs Salt and the children took the train to Southampton. She was *not* happy about it. At first Jean thought it was fine, perfectly doable – she spent most nights in the shelter after all – but then Sunday came round and she had nothing to do and nowhere to go. She needed a base. She did three nights in the underground – they'd opened up the tube stations even though the government had said they wouldn't.

At least Val was safe.

· · ·

In the early mornings she crept back to the bus station, washed and tidied herself up there, until the day Mrs Peabody found her.

'We've got my mum, Arthur's cousin and his family were bombed out on Tuesday – otherwise I'd offer you some floorspace.'

Valerie wanted to sob.

'I can't stay in the house. Even Mrs Salt and the children have gone away...' It stung to admit she had nowhere else to go.

While she was on the bus, with Old Matthews humming 'Run, Rabbit Run!' as he drove, she thought about Tony's offer. She pictured his dimples too and his jet-black hair. *'We can be a proper family.'* After all, it was the only offer she had.

That night after work, she knocked on his door.

He swept open his arms like an impresario, a number-crunching king. 'I knew you'd come in the end.'

27

Valerie

One afternoon, while Valerie was replenishing the shelves and listening to *Music While You Work*, three boys came in the shop. They were about her age or a little older. They told her they were building a go-cart – one of them kept calling it a tank – and they had three shillings to spend. She turned off the wireless and got them some of the things they needed, including rope and elastic bands, and suggested others, including wheels and a saddle.

'When we've done it, do you want to have a go?' the smallest boy said.

The third boy screwed up his face. 'No girls in our tank – that's the rule.'

'Yeah,' agreed the small boy, but the third boy looked over at Valerie and smiled. He was a head taller than her and stocky and broad. His skin was nut-brown, although his hair was fair, and he had pushed it away from his forehead so some bits stood up on end.

'Are you one of the children from London?' he asked. It was

funny the way he said 'children' when he wasn't much older than her. 'The evacuated ones...'

She nodded.

'Thought so. Have you ever been fishing?'

This was unexpected.

'No...'

'Would you like to? I'm pretty good.' He reminded her of someone, but she didn't know who. 'You have to be patient.'

'I can't,' she said, gesturing around her. 'I have to look after the shop.'

'All the time?' he said, as his eyebrows reached his forehead.

'Most of the time.'

He thought about that for a moment and then said, 'Bad luck.'

They were at the door when Mrs Woods came in via the back entrance. Valerie tensed, more so when she saw she was followed by the headteacher, Mrs Lester.

Mrs Lester had never – to Valerie's knowledge – visited the shop before. The two were deep in conversation but Mrs Lester stopped talking when she noticed Valerie.

'So, this is where you've been hiding!' she exclaimed.

Valerie didn't know what to say. She had hardly been hiding; this was where she had to work.

'Flirting with the boys, is it?' Mrs Lester continued. 'I'd expect nothing more from a child like you.' She met Mrs Woods' eye and sniggered but the third boy, the one with the nut-brown skin, scowled at her.

'She's not been flirting – she's been helping.'

They both turned round, and Valerie held her breath. Would they be furious at him now?

But instead of being annoyed, Mrs Lester's voice went sickly-soft. 'Oh, hello there!' she said. 'Are you enjoying your holidays?'

'Yes, thank you,' he said.

'Good.' For the first time ever, both women looked a tiny bit abashed. 'Please convey my best wishes to your mother.'

The friends left, but the nice-looking boy looked back. He seemed about to challenge the women on something else, but then obviously decided not to. Valerie would remember that encounter for a long time.

28

Jean

Tony wasn't a bad man. And he was certainly thrilled to put Jean up. The house was compact, smaller than she'd imagined, but it was in a convenient location – it was a thirty-minute walk at most to the bus station.

'What will the neighbours think?'

'I'll tell them I've got a lodger. A hard-working clippie. Who would dare suggest otherwise?'

Who indeed?

Every night he tried to slip into the bed next to her.

'We could be blown to kingdom come tomorrow!' he said, which wasn't a great aphrodisiac.

Or 'We've got a daughter together!'

Sometimes she let him stay.

She thought, *Why am I doing this? I don't feel the way I used to*, but the other part of her thought, *He is Valerie's father*. And it was true that 'we could be dead tomorrow'. The fact was, when Jean was with him it was possibly the only time – other than on the bus – when she could forget her fears.

He understood that he wasn't to meet Valerie but he still wanted to. When he said this, a deep apprehension took over her. It felt like her entire body became encased in dread.

'You've got to tell her about me sooner or later,' he would chirp cheerfully, and Jean would think, *later, later, LATER*.

Tony liked the wireless. He switched it on as soon as he got home, and he wouldn't let Jean talk when it was playing. Sometimes when it was a music show they danced around the table. Tony was light on his feet, and he liked to swing her around, and when he did she laughed like a young girl.

One time he said, 'There's this show you must listen to, you'll love it...'

And Jean knew, she knew which show he was going to say: *It's That Man Again*. She told him, 'That's Valerie's favourite,' and he laughed.

'You see!' he said.

'See what?'

'The apple doesn't fall far from the tree.'

Poor apple, thought Jean. She listened to the show, but she could never hear what was so funny about it. Tony said she had no sense of humour.

Jean thought her situation – of having to evacuate – was like Valerie's, in an odd way, and this experience gave her some insight into how Valerie might be feeling, and maybe, she hoped, one day it would bring them closer. It was hard to imagine they could be any further apart.

29

Valerie

Mrs Woods' greasy-haired, sullen-faced son came in the shop when Valerie was listening to *It's That Man Again*, the worst possible time for an interruption.

Can I do you now, sir? said Mrs Mopp the office char, and the audience and Valerie laughed. She wasn't sure why it was so funny, only that it was.

'Turn that down, will you?'

Couldn't he wait?

Valerie was tempted to call him 'Funf' to see how he'd react. Instead, she turned the wireless off. It was painful but it was better to turn it completely off rather than to hear it as a tinny squawk for attention in the background, out of reach.

He wandered around the shop, inspecting it. He gawped in the till and took the money out of the drawer into his squidgy palm. He told her that some of the goods needed new price tags. He fiddled with the plant pot displays.

'Are we done yet?' she asked, putting the wireless back on to hear the last few minutes.

Don't forget the diver, sir. Every penny makes the water warmer, said one of the characters, making Valerie laugh again.

'I want that.' He was pointing at the wireless.

'You can't. It belongs to the shop.'

'Mu-um!' he called, keeping his eyes on her. Minutes later, Mrs Woods rushed in.

'What's she done now?'

'She said I can't take the wireless...'

'Course he can,' Mrs Woods barked protectively.

Valerie gathered herself. 'I mean, *how* will he take it?'

'Easy,' he said. He tried to pick it up, but it was too heavy for him. He scowled at her like it was her fault. She hoped he'd trap his fingers underneath. Then he braced himself, with a comical expression, and managed to carry it this time.

'Careful!' Mrs Woods shrieked.

He staggered three or four steps, then dropped it smack onto the floor, where it made a weird clunking sound. There was a slight smell of smoke. Valerie covered her mouth. This was the one thing she liked here...

'That's how I'll take it.'

'Ohh!' Even Mrs Woods didn't like that. 'Destructive, that is. Pick it up.'

He tried but now he couldn't get it off the floor. It was well and truly broken.

Mrs Woods turned round. 'Look what you made him do,' she hissed. 'No tea for you, girl.'

That cheered him up. 'Ha, you lost, you little bastard.'

Mrs Woods gave him a stern look. Valerie didn't know this word nor what the look meant, but she could tell it wasn't nice.

The next morning, instead of going to school Valerie stuffed her pillowcase with her things – she didn't have much, so it was light – and then crept to the railway station.

She had the emergency money the man from London had given her and she wasn't going to put up with this any longer. She felt what had happened with Mrs Woods and her son had stirred her out of her stupor. The broken wireless had brought her situation to a head.

She wished she had time to say goodbye to her friend Morwenna, but she'd write to her. She wondered what to do about Lydia and then decided she would send her a telegram from London. Lydia wasn't her responsibility any more.

The sky was strange, that morning. It was blissful blue in one part and then overhead, creating a new horizon, were grey storm clouds.

Valerie bought a ticket.

'Return?'

'No. Single, please.'

She was proud of herself for taking the initiative. Her dad would have wanted that.

She tried to buy a bar of chocolate from the kiosk on the platform.

'Ration book?' the elderly man said without looking up.

'I don't have one...'

Now he looked up. 'Everyone's got one.'

Another thing Mrs Woods had taken from her? Valerie shrugged. Not for long.

She hoped to strike up conversation with other passengers on the train but there was not a person in her carriage. There were hardly any passengers going her way at all. By contrast, the trains heading towards Somerset, which shot past every now and again, were crammed to the rafters.

For the first time in a long while, Valerie felt thirsty for life. She knew that her city was being pounded by the Luftwaffe, that they were sending hundreds of planes – bombs – to beat them into submission.

But she was going home.

30

Jean

Tony was fast asleep when Jean went out to work. She was allocated Old Matthews on the number 3. She was glad she didn't have Kenny. She could feel a fight or something brewing between them. Old Matthews was humming 'We'll Meet Again', and this was better than 'Run, Rabbit Run!'; that tune always made her feel panicky.

One of Jean's favourite parts of this route was the drive down the hill. The driver took their foot off the accelerator and let it go and each time Jean was reminded of sledging down a hill on her mother's tea tray.

The first sign something was wrong was a creaking sound, a kind of noise like something was snapping. This was followed quickly by a yawning, twisting chasm of a sound. Like the sound on the underground, brakes screeching, metal breaking, but multiplied. It was a sound you'd never want to hear.

The bus tilted, one way and then the other, and then like a wild animal it bucked, then bolted, and jerked before collapsing: sinking, sinking, sunk.

The ground had opened up its jaws and they were tumbling in.

Jean was holding on as usual to her clipper machine in one hand and the metal bar in the other. She couldn't hold on, she had to grip the pole tightly, she had to let go of her machine so she could hold on with both hands. If she hadn't held on, she would have been sucked, pushed, forced to the back of the bus, like some of the other passengers were.

It all happened so fast.

The pull of gravity, the swell as some seats seemed to be coming towards her, people slamming at her, and the noise, and the smell. They dropped. One foot, two, three. And then it stopped. It was like a shipwreck, only they weren't at sea, they weren't going to drown. When was it going to end?

Bloodied people were groaning and crying.

'Is everyone all right?'

They were clutching their heads or their arms or their chests. 'Am I alive?' one passenger said. 'Or is this hell?'

'Will someone rescue us?' another passenger called.

I am the clippie, Jean realised. *I am going to have to rescue us.*

She shouted out to Old Matthews: 'All right up in the cab?'

'What the hell happened?'

And then there was more noise, crying and screaming as people realised their predicament. The bus had fallen down a hole – no, not exactly, the hole hadn't been there before. The bus had made a hole and fallen down it. And who was to say that they wouldn't fall deeper – all the way to the centre of the earth?

They got in a human chain.

'Hurry!' urged Jean, surprised that her voice sounded normal. A pregnant woman was weeping, and bleeding from the nose.

'I hit it,' she said, astonished. 'On the pole.' They got her out and then the elderly ladies, then the others.

'My shopping!' one said. She had a bloodied lip.

'Go!' said Jean. She didn't know where she found the authority from, but she took it. 'Keep moving.' Didn't the old dear know they might sink further? They might be lost.

And then it was only her and Old Matthews stuck inside and the bus was still creaking. A noise a bus should never make, a noise nothing should make.

'Ladies first,' he said.

But Old Matthews had been brought out of retirement for this.

'Age before beauty,' she said as he hesitated. 'Go – please.'

'Sorry,' he said.

And she was alone – and the creaking continued. And then it was her turn. She climbed up to the door and hands were stretching down to take hers: heavenly hands, and just as she was pulled firmly onto the pavement, with a horrendous crunching noise, the bus thumped another three feet or so down.

'I've never seen anything like that before,' the man whose hands she was still holding said.

Jean couldn't speak. It was that close.

Someone had got blankets. Old Matthews was holding his arm, his face ashen. There were ambulances and fire engines there.

'Anything wrong with you?'

'All good,' said Old Matthews. Jean knew what he was thinking – no work equals no money. There was no way he was going to admit to being hurt.

'Check you over?' one of the ambulance workers said to her.

'No need,' she said briskly.

'You'll be in shock,' he said. 'Make sure you look after yourself.'

Fat chance of that.

'You can't help anyone else if you're in a state.'

'I know.' Who did he think she was? Some ingénue?

She would report back at the bus station and then get back on the buses for the afternoon until late evening. Spend most of the night in a shelter and then hopefully get a couple of hours' sleep in the morning. Let Tony have his way. Forever. Repeat.

She was shaking as she walked, and her heart was beating fast. She had blood on her hands and she felt like she'd been beaten black and blue. She had nearly died! They all had. It was sheer luck they'd made it out alive. The thought was a dead end though. What could she do with it? She had nearly died. So what?

She was half in a dream as she made her way back to the bus station. Yes, she was in shock. The earth had collapsed! It felt like there was nothing sacred any more. Later, she would struggle to recall anything about the journey back to the station, but then there was Valerie, perched on a stool, awkward smile.

'Hello, Mum...'

31

Valerie

It wasn't the reception Valerie had hoped for. For a few moments, her mum was too astonished to speak. Her hair, her coat, her uniform... everything about her was dusty. Valerie hated to think it but her mum looked like a tramp. A gobs-macked tramp.

They hugged but it was more like Mum was trying to see if Valerie was real and not an illusion.

'Val?' she kept saying. 'How did you...'

'I went to the house first, but no one was there and it was all shut up, so I thought I'd find you here.'

'What the...?' Jean washed her hands and then her face. 'I look... What's happened? What did they do?'

'Nothing,' Valerie said, still mindful of Mrs Woods' connection with Mrs Lester and her school. 'I don't want to live there any more. What happened to you?'

'We fell in a hole,' her mum said and Valerie couldn't make sense of it. A hole? What kind of hole? And who did? Who was this 'we'?

'But how? Why are you here, Valerie?' She was as jittery as a bird.

'I got the train,' Valerie said, deciding to answer the how rather than the why.

'How did you find the money?'

'A man gave it to me,' she said.

Her mum looked horrified again. 'A man?!'

Valerie hadn't expected a big welcome, not a choral ensemble, but she had expected more than this.

'And where's your suitcase?'

Valerie had forgotten her mum didn't know about that. 'I gave it to Lydia.'

'Why?'

'I just did.'

'Don't give away your things,' Jean said. Her voice was steadier now but her hands were trembling. Her nails were bitten to the quick. 'Was the journey all right?'

'Great...' Valerie wanted to say more, but her mother seemed dazed. 'You *are* happy to see me, aren't you?'

Now her mum was scratching her neck. 'I love *seeing* you but we've got nowhere to stay.'

'What?'

'Our house is uninhabitable.'

'So where are *you* living?'

'At a friend's, darling,' said Jean. 'But there's no room. You've got to go back. Please. It's dreadful here.'

Nothing was how she expected. Mum had warned her everything was different in London now, but even so. She went back to the sink. This time, she dabbed at her uniform with a sponge, while Valerie watched.

'Are you going back on the bus?'

Mum looked at her in surprise. 'Course. I have to. Otherwise I don't get paid.'

'Can't we...'

'Val, you have to get away. This is no place for children.' Her mum stared unhappily in the mirror and tried to flatten her wild hair into submission. She wasn't the mummy Valerie knew and loved. Valerie hardly recognised this person.

'I'm not a child, I'm nearly twelve...'

'That's a child,' she snapped.

'Francine's here,' she said.

'She's in Southampton.'

'Other children then.'

'That's... that's up to their parents. I've paid in advance...' Jean covered her face with trembling hands. 'I can't do it, Vally, you've got to get away from here.'

Valerie stared at her incredulously. She didn't know whether to mention the nasty name Mrs Woods' son had called her or not. She decided not. No good would come of it.

She could see this was unwinnable. For once, her mum was immoveable. Valerie would never have expected her to be so determined. The shelters worked, there were other children about, and the Nazis would surely, have to, run out of bombs, but her mum, who could be so flaky about everything, was not flaky on this issue. Not flaky at all.

32

Jean

A few days later and Valerie's brief appearance felt to Jean like nothing more than a fever dream.

That dreadful afternoon, Jean had accompanied Valerie back to the train station, still feeling light-headed and disconnected from everything. If Jean was quiet, Valerie was quieter. Jean had given her money for the journey – and Valerie accepted, but docilely, like she too was in shock.

'I need you to be safe,' Jean had insisted. 'That's all I want. The only thing that's important to me.'

She made sure Valerie got on the train. She hugged her goodbye, but Val was stiff as a poker in her arms.

Jean didn't see Tony that evening or the next day. Saturday night was another bad one and it felt like the whole city was being blown into a thousand pieces. She thought she saw rats everywhere. Tony said she cried out about creatures in her sleep. The big one was clawing its way ever closer. Its long tail was swishing victoriously. The thing that kept her going was the knowledge that at least Val wasn't part of this: her life was better.

Jean didn't see Tony properly until the next Sunday morning. She made him a fried egg on toast. She stared at the out-of-place beauty of the yolk. Its sunshine colour reminded her of Valerie somehow. He wolfed it down.

She still remembered that feeling of the ground breaking up beneath her. And she didn't only remember it in her head, she seemed to remember it with all her body. The way they flew into different corners of the bus. The blood on the seats. That feeling she didn't know what to do with: I was lucky not to die. Was it luck? Should I have died?

'I'd like to have seen her,' Tony said when eventually Jean told him about Valerie's brief visit.

I know you would, thought Jean.

'You should tell her about me,' he said. 'I'll tell her if you won't.'

Jean was so tired she could have slept standing.

'If you do, I'll go straight and tell Pauline and the boys,' she said. Tony knew she meant business and he shut up. It was the only thing she had over him.

Back on the buses, she went over her options in between issuing tickets and welcoming smiles.

She could tell Valerie about Tony and say that she'd thought he'd died. She'd swear he did. And then, bolt from the blue, he'd turned up!

This didn't sound convincing.

Or she could admit the truth: *I told you he was dead* (ouch) *but here he is.*

It was good news, wasn't it? Valerie could hardly complain he wasn't dead. She could send that in a letter.

Or her final option – she could avoid the subject entirely. Not as courageous as Churchill, yet not so cowardly as Chamberlain. What with everything going on, this was Jean's preference right now.

33

Valerie

Valerie tried to fix the wireless, but it was no use. The silence seemed bigger, more ominous without the voices and she missed the last few episodes of *It's That Man Again*. The silence gave her too much space to think about her mum.

Occasionally, Valerie wondered if Jean was her mother at all. For one, Jean hated the wireless, and she didn't like books, and she was scrawny, like a scarecrow, and nervous of everything. And if she were her mother, wouldn't she have let her stay home in London? Both Mrs Salt and Mrs Froud acted as though separation from their children was sheer torture, while Jean went blithely on: 'Did I tell you about one of the passengers on the bus – he said I smelled of heaven!' She knew her mother had to work hard but this was ridiculous.

If her dad was alive, Valerie decided, he would have insisted she come home. He would have walked on burning coals for someone in trouble.

To make everything worse, she and Morwenna had a falling-out.

What happened was that Valerie was hungry and Morwenna had an iced bun. Valerie did not take the iced bun, but she did take the sticky wrapper out of the bin and run her finger along the icing. And it was hard to stop at one finger...

Maybe Morwenna wouldn't mind, but she was more eagle-eyed than Valerie had realised, and she'd noticed other things. She'd noticed Valerie had 'stolen' a bit of sandwich – Morwenna's mother cut them into quarters, which Valerie found strangely moving – and also the left-over bits of a bread pudding.

'For goodness' sake,' she grumbled, looking into her paper bag. 'Did you take some?'

'Sorry,' Valerie mumbled. 'We all do that in London.'

Morwenna had looked at her sceptically. 'I don't like thieves.'

A few days later, there was a poetry contest at the school. There was a poem Valerie liked, that she'd heard on the wireless.

> *Between the dark and the daylight,*
> *When the night is beginning to lower,*
> *Comes a pause in the day's occupations,*
> *That is known as the Children's Hour.*

Valerie changed the words a little and it was done, voilà!

> *Between winter and summer*
> *When the days grow longer*
> *Comes a moment's reflection*
> *I want to go home.*

The problem was the teacher loved it. And the more she extolled its virtues, the more wretched Valerie felt. She tried to explain several times: 'Miss, it's based on something else...' and 'It's kind of copied...' but to her surprise the teacher dismissed her.

'That's fine. We're all standing on the shoulders of giants, Valerie. It works.'

Morwenna hadn't expected Valerie to do well with her poem. Songs and poetry were her thing, she said, guarding her territory.

'That is not original, is it?' she asked. She was, as Jean might have said, sharp as a tack.

Valerie bit her lip. 'I told Miss and she said it was all right.'

Morwenna squinted at her then shook her head.

The blood came back nearly each month, and with it an aching heaviness. Valerie washed then wrung out her vests under the outdoor tap and hung them in secret places in the shop or over rocks in the garden – it took forever for them to dry and sometimes they didn't and were damper than when they started. If Mrs Woods knew what she was doing, she didn't say. The practicalities were dreadful, yet the fear of terrible diseases was even worse. Valerie knew she should have told her mother when she saw her in London – but that horrible day was all so muddled and frantic, it hadn't occurred to her. Would her mother have done anything anyway?

On the day of the poetry prize-giving, at break-time, they played skipping games, but Valerie was now bleeding so profusely, she was sure she could feel blood coursing down her legs. She should have told her mother. She should have told her about being called a bastard. There were many things she should have told her, but all she could think about was the way Jean had pushed for her to be gone. If Jean could have waved a magic wand for Valerie to disappear, she would have.

Valerie wrapped her jumper round her waist.

'I know why you wear that,' Morwenna said coldly. 'You think you've got a big bottom, but everyone says you're too skinny.'

At lunchtime, Valerie asked if Morwenna would share her last cracker; she was famished. Morwenna had shoved it back into her bag – Valerie wouldn't have asked otherwise – but this sent Morwenna into another fury.

'I wish you'd go back home. I've been a friend to you and you've been nothing but pain.'

Nothing but pain sounded like something the adults would say, not her sweet Morwenna. Valerie flushed. Morwenna was one of the few people who kept her going in Somerset. She could put up with Mrs Woods, she could even cope without the wireless, but to be on the wrong side of Morwenna was agony.

In the afternoon, Valerie had to go up on the school stage to collect an award for her poem. She wished more than anything that it was Morwenna, not her. She worried that Morwenna would declare her a fraud. The hall was full of children and invited local guests – she wasn't sure, but she thought she had seen Lydia's host mother, Mrs Howard, queuing to come in. The smell of all the people and the polish – plus the bleeding – was making her feel sick.

'Miss Hardman is one of our London girls and she has reflected on her experiences in this poem,' the teacher said. Mrs Lester was glaring. Morwenna was glaring. 'Put your hands together for Miss Hardman.'

Was Morwenna going to publicly denounce her? Valerie felt she would die if she did. The guilt was tremendous. It felt like five hundred miles in the snow. Pulling a sledge. At the South Pole. Valerie trudged up to the stage. The sound of her feet echoed around the hall. And then she fainted.

· · ·

When she opened her eyes, there were all sorts gathered around her. Morwenna's freckly face, and other faces as well, too close, too worried.

'She's skin and bone.'

'That's a malnourished child.'

'She wanted my food,' Morwenna said, and Valerie could have cried with shame. But then she understood that Morwenna was sobbing and that her dear friend was the one who was ashamed.

'I didn't realise she was hungry. I'm sorry, Val, will you ever forgive me?'

The clinic next to the school smelled of TCP. The lady with a bun and red cheeks and a watch pinned to her chest was a nurse and Valerie had been unceremoniously deposited on her. She seemed far too young to be a nurse. When Valerie pointed that out, she beamed.

The nurse was writing in a notepad. When she'd finished, she looked up and said, 'My husband helped fix your wireless.'

'The man from London?'

'That's him.' She smiled again, and instantly, Valerie felt she could be trusted. 'That's my Stan. Now, Valerie, you've not been eating enough. Why is that?'

Valerie didn't want to say anything, couldn't say anything. She mustn't get Mrs Woods in trouble. She mustn't get her mum in trouble. Mrs Lester was far too powerful. And if she said how hungry she was, mightn't they take Mrs Woods' side? They might even think she was a lunatic. Maybe she *was* a lunatic?

'Valerie, is Mrs Woods not feeding you?'

Valerie thought of Mrs Woods' expression: 'dirty evacuee. Slum kids. Slum parents.' The whack round the face, the slaps on the hand and the backs of her legs. The way Mrs Lester had said, 'Mrs Woods and I go back a long way.'

Mrs Woods would kill her. And that would not even be the worst outcome. 'It's all right,' Valerie whispered.

The nurse's expression didn't change. 'I think we ought to have a chat with your mother.'

Valerie felt like spilt milk. She felt like water dripping between the cracks. She said no, she didn't want to worry her. She said her mother was busy, working.

Again, the nurse wrote in her notepad. 'Is there anything else you want to tell me?' She waited. 'Anything at all...'

Valerie closed her eyes and took a deep breath. 'I think... I might be dying.'

'We won't let her hurt you.'

'It's not just that.'

'My dear girl.' The nurse sounded so concerned that tears prickled Valerie's eyes. No one spoke to her like that any more. 'We're going to make sure you're getting fed.'

Valerie shook her head.

'What is it?' the nurse asked. 'I can't help unless I know what it is.'

For the first time, Valerie talked about the blood. It was hard to find the right words. The nurse listened solemnly as Valerie sniffed. She had the gentlest eyes and she blinked slowly. Then, with the help of a leaflet, she told Valerie everything about her monthlies or menses, and Valerie could have kicked herself – she should have known there was a rational explanation.

She would have them until she was much older. Or pregnant, the nurse explained. She had them, and Valerie's mum had them, and, yes, Morwenna would one day have them, Francine and Lydia too. All the girls would. And the nurse rummaged in her drawers and gave Valerie something she called 'sanitary' products and told her she could throw those old vests away. And everything was going to be all right.

. . .

It took forever for Mrs Woods to let them in, and Valerie feared the nurse would give up waiting, but she stood firm on the step, readying herself for confrontation.

Valerie was sent away to the shop – out of hearing. She strained to listen to the conversation, but it wasn't distinct enough. There were no raised voices; they sounded polite. When she went in, Mrs Woods said in a cloying, unfamiliar tone, 'It seems there's been a misunderstanding.'

'That's right,' said the nurse.

Valerie said, 'Sorry,' because she didn't know what else to say, but she was thinking, *It was no misunderstanding.*

'Anyway, we've arranged alternative accommodation.'

Valerie looked up, shocked.

'Go pack your things,' the nurse said. Valerie didn't give her a moment to change her mind. She took the stairs two at a time. She didn't hear what Mrs Woods said next – she didn't care.

She waited until she was out the house, pillowcase between her arms, before saying, 'But my mummy doesn't want me home...'

'You're not going home. But you're a lucky girl. Mrs Howard has agreed to take you at Bumble Cottage.'

34

Jean

The buses kept Jean busy during the Blitz. Bombs and buses.
Buses and bombs.

A fight broke out on Iris's bus – her route, past three public
houses, picked up a disproportionate number of drunkards –
and she begged to swap shifts. No one wanted to, especially not
Mavis, who loved her route past three churches and one allot-
ment; the passengers were always giving her a lettuce or a
prayer for her trouble. Jean offered – how much worse could it
be? – but Mrs Peabody insisted she stay where she was.

Jean had a regular passenger – ex-army – with a thousand-
yard stare. There were more and more men like him. One baby
made a mess with her bottle of milk and her mother made a
commotion and the soldier said, 'Don't blame the poor mite!'
The mother burst into tears. 'I can't cope with her no more.' So
he rocked the baby the rest of the way.

People were stressed, everyone was petrified. No one was
getting enough sleep. And for the second year running, Jean
couldn't get away for Valerie's birthday – she hoped Valerie

understood. Jean sent a nice card, but she didn't hear if it had arrived or not.

Sometimes, Jean was frightened that her drivers would nod off at the wheel. God knew, she would have. Kenny said his coffees kept him awake, Perry mumbled that he didn't need a lot of shut-eye, Albert said he needed the bell ringing, while Old Matthews said, 'How do you know I don't?' No one laughed.

Jean looked out for her usual route landmarks. She noticed that the family with the boy who waved and jumped were gone.

Thank goodness, she thought. They had been evacuated! Finally, they were safe.

It was Kenny who, a couple of days later, told her the truth.

'Boy's dead.'

As soon as he said it, Jean didn't think she could take any more of this. She held onto the pole. Her legs felt like jelly. The joyful boy?

'Bombings?'

'Measles. Couldn't get seen, hospital was too full.'

'No!'

'It's true,' Kenny insisted. 'Perry knows the family. They're heartbroken.'

She felt heartbroken too: that lovely eager face wouldn't be waving at her any more. As they drove along, Jean was thinking, *How many?*

'How many what?' asked Kenny.

She startled. She hadn't realised she had said it aloud. 'Just thinking...'

'You seem preoccupied.'

'It's awful, isn't it?'

'We have to keep London moving.'

Jean wondered if she might vomit. She wondered if this was her final straw. She had to keep herself going. She attended to the passengers, but inside her mind was like a grasshopper flitting from one image of devastation to another. All this death and destruction and a small boy dead from measles. *And you know what,* she thought, *if instead of killing everyone people worked together to find cures to help, what a world it could be.*

Humanity was wild.

As she got off the bus that evening, feet aching, Kenny asked if she wanted to go with him to the cinema, and her first thought was, *In what capacity'? Co-workers, friends, lovers?* She had a bad feeling it was the latter. There had been no sly glances in the driver's mirror, no jokes back at the station, though; it came from nowhere. Jean found that confusing. *We're not even friends,* she thought. Followed by – *Tony would murder me.*

'Seven thirty,' he said. '*Crimes at the Dark House.*'

It sounded like those were his intentions.

'It'll cheer you up.'

It wasn't a film she wanted to see – the newspaper had given it three stars, she didn't like melodrama, she had no affection for the actor Tod Slaughter... it just didn't feel relevant, not with everything going on.

'I don't think...'

'Come on, Miss Hardman, let's have some fun.'

In the end, the only thing that satisfied Kenny was when she said she was already involved with someone.

'I don't believe you.'

Exasperated, she blurted out, 'I do have someone, and actually I have a daughter with him. Enough now, Kenny.'

That soon shut him up.

He was the first person at work Jean had told and she regretted it instantly.

35

Valerie

Lydia was at the door, holding a bunch of wildflowers, with a dopey expression on her face.

'Give them to her then,' Mrs Howard, behind her, instructed.

At first it looked like Lydia was going to refuse, but when Valerie was about to give up, Lydia finally shot out her arm.

Valerie thought to herself, *Dad used to give Mum flowers every week.*

'We must stop meeting like this!' Mrs Howard said, laughing to show it was a joke. Valerie was going to say that they had never met like this before but instead chuckled along.

'Thank you for taking me in, Mrs Howard,' she added. 'It's good of you.'

She remembered what Mrs Howard had said in the village hall that taking in Valerie would be *asking for trouble*. What had changed?

'I don't believe in shirking, Valerie, do you?'

'No, Mrs Howard.'

Valerie wondered what job Mrs Howard would have for her.

Bumble Cottage was the kind of house you dream about. There was an arch and a gate and a curving path that led to the front door. Actually, there were two front doors, both lovely, and the house was surrounded by garden. In one bit there was a bench, another a table and chairs, and there were flowers; although Mrs Howard said the garden wasn't at its best at the moment, it was wonderful. There were beds of vegetables: potatoes, onions.

'We do try, don't we, Lydia?' Mrs Howard sighed cheerfully. 'It's not my forte.'

Lydia grinned in agreement.

'Lydia wants chickens but I'm not sure.' Mrs Howard went on. 'We have too many fox friends.'

Inside the house, the ceilings were low and there were trinkets and pictures and beams. It wasn't tidy – Jean would have had a fit – but it was light and smelled cosy. There had been a housekeeper, apparently, and a maid, but both were gone to help the war effort. Mrs Howard said, 'It's the laundry that is my biggest bête noire – but we manage.'

And there was the dog, who somehow looked like he had a constant smile on his face. His name was Rex, and it was clear he thought Lydia was his master and that Lydia thought so too, for he followed her everywhere. But he allowed Valerie to stroke him. She was unused to dogs, but she knew she better had get used to it.

Valerie had her own room! She had assumed she and Lydia would share, but no; although the house was called a 'cottage', it was large and there were several large bright bedrooms. It was a huge contrast to staying on Mrs Woods' landing – or even the flat in London.

There was a desk, a cupboard and a chest, and some photos

of people in costumes including one man dressed as a bear, and several people wearing Elizabethan ruffs.

Later, Lydia came in and said, 'You haven't got much.'

Valerie shrugged.

'Mrs Howard will get you new things – you have to tell her what.'

After Valerie had unpacked, she stood in the hall, unsure where to go. Mrs Woods used to go mad if she wasn't either in the shop or in bed.

Lydia came up the stairs, then pointed: 'That's Paul's room.'

'What's he like?'

Lydia ran a finger along the door handle. 'He paints.'

Valerie imagined a boy on a ladder at the side of the house. Maybe she could hold the ladder steady for him? She wanted to be helpful. She did agree with Mrs Howard that shirking was unacceptable.

'The walls?'

Lydia laughed some more. 'Fish.'

'Fish?'

'He paints fish.'

Miss Beedle would approve of that, Valerie thought.

Lydia wanted to show Valerie Paul's room. Valerie knew that Mrs Howard wouldn't like it, but it was always hard to say no to Lydia – she never expected people to resist her.

There were fish pictures on the walls, in bronze ornate frames, and there was pottery too, on the shelves. It took Valerie by surprise – she didn't know what she had been expecting but it wasn't this. It wasn't the room of a boy; it was the room of an artist.

'Girls!' Mrs Howard's voice cut through her thoughts. If she was anything like Mrs Woods, they were in for a beating. 'What's going on? Lydia, you know we don't snoop.'

'She asked me to,' Lydia said, as Valerie looked at her in amazement.

'I'll lock it,' Mrs Howard said as though suggesting they didn't get their knickers in a twist about this.

Mrs Howard didn't seem to mind – she was not like Mrs Woods! – but Valerie still felt terrible at letting her down. But she also wanted to know more about this Paul.

___

36

Valerie

There were so many wonderful things about living at Mrs Howard's, you'd need more than ten fingers to count them on. Wonderful not to have to race back after school to take over in the shop. Instead, Valerie and Morwenna could dawdle, or pick berries until their fingers were purple. Valerie told her that she was eating better now, but Morwenna looked tearful when the issue came up, so Valerie avoided mentioning it again.

Morwenna disliked Mrs Woods almost as much as Valerie did and they enjoyed calling her nicknames together; 'Beastly Woods' was Valerie's favourite.

Morwenna was allowed to play in Mrs Howard's garden and Valerie was allowed to play in Morwenna's. Morwenna did have chickens, and they fed them, playing farmers, and sometimes they sang songs to them too. The chickens were an uncritical audience.

'Your mother is welcome to come and visit,' Mrs Howard said a few days after Valerie moved in. 'In fact, I'm sure we could find room if she wanted to stay. The situation is diabolical in the cities.'

Valerie said that her mother was determined to see the war out in London, which was true, and that she appreciated the offer, which wasn't true because Valerie hadn't told her.

The food at Bumble Cottage was not extravagant but abundant and delicious. There was an elderly housekeeper who came, but she kept irregular hours and no one knew what was happening from one day to the next. On the first evening, Mrs Howard made her tea and some scrambled egg made from powder, with toast and carrot marmalade. She didn't like Valerie picking at things with her fingers, and insisted on knives and forks in the correct hands.

Valerie didn't tell Mrs Howard it was her birthday, but she found out and invited Morwenna around as a surprise, and some friends of her own, and they sang 'Happy Birthday', and other songs. 'If you can't push the boat out on your birthday, when can you?' asked Mrs Howard. Then she explained what a rhetorical question was. There were presents to open too – a notepad for writing and pencils with different leads and a little homemade case to put them in. Valerie felt very special.

There were different names for things in Bumble Cottage. The front room was the drawing room and the living room was the salon. On the wall were framed prints of theatre posters, and when Valerie got up close she could see that it said Miss Wilderspoon, which was Mrs Howard's maiden name. Some of these were in French, German, and other languages that Valerie didn't recognise.

The drawing room was full of books from floor to ceiling, every wall except for the window. Valerie gazed around in awe.

'You're welcome to take any!' explained Mrs Howard. She laughed. 'I don't think there are any that are inappropriate.'

It was overwhelming. Valerie would have hugged her, only she wasn't the huggy sort. 'I will work hard and become good at books!' she promised instead.

'We don't have to be *good at* books,' Mrs Howard corrected briskly. 'They're for enjoyment!' Then she smiled at Valerie. 'It's marvellous you want to better yourself.'

Mrs Howard was a director by profession, a director of plays. When she was a young woman she had lived in Paris and Berlin, and had made a name for herself there. She had stopped directing when Paul was born but she helped a local theatre group put on charity performances.

'It keeps me busy,' she said.

'Did you act?'

'Never.' She raised one eyebrow. 'But I did like actors.'

Valerie wasn't sure what this meant.

When Valerie told her she had never been to the theatre Mrs Howard couldn't believe it. 'I must take you,' she declared. 'You, especially, will adore it.'

She said her theatre group were deliberating over what they should put on this year. They put on Shakespeare every other year, and this year was an every other year.

'I don't know if it will be any good,' she pondered.

And Valerie smiled at her. 'It doesn't have to be good. It's for enjoyment.'

'Touché!' Mrs Howard said delightedly. 'You are a quick learner!'

Valerie didn't imagine it would happen. She was used to adults promising more than they could deliver. Still, the prospect was exciting.

She loved these conversations with Mrs Howard. After a couple more misunderstandings, both involving Lydia, they got on fine. More than fine. Mrs Howard was somehow a kindred spirit. She understood Valerie in a way no one else did.

She didn't directly address what she meant by the thing she

had said in the hall that first day, '*That would be asking for trouble*', but she did say she should have selected Valerie at the start.

Valerie wrote to Francine. 'I still haven't met Paul yet,' she wrote. And Francine wrote back that she was with her mummy and brothers and sisters in Southampton and even though they were living in one small room she liked being with them, but she hoped Valerie would be having a jolly good time. Big kisses.

After she had been at Bumble Cottage for about two weeks, Valerie went back to thank the nurse who had helped her. But the door to the clinic was locked and it looked like everyone had gone away. A woman who was pushing a big Silver Cross pram and holding the hand of a grumpy toddler with only one shoe came over and asked if she might help. After Valerie enquired about the nurse's whereabouts though, her face fell.

'Nurse Eldridge has moved away to be with her parents.'

'Oh.'

'I'm sorry to say her husband is missing presumed... well, you know.'

That lovely man who fixed the wireless and brought strawberries and the emergency money was missing?

'Anything I can do?'

Valerie shook her head.

He was the first person she knew who was dead, apart from her father. He was the first person she knew who had been lost in this stupid war.

The garden smelled of honeysuckle, there was space, there was company, there was ball-throwing and bone-hiding with Rex the dog. The weather was kind to them too that autumn; Valerie learned the phrase Indian summer. The leaves fell and crackled dry and golden everywhere she walked, and it felt like she was shedding something too.

Mrs Howard encouraged them to look at the newspapers every day to understand what was going on in the world. Lydia only pretended though. The stories and the photographs were shocking. You might see a policeman wiping his eyes of tears. Or a man holding a rescued cat. Or a woman sitting on top of a pile of rubble with a cup of tea, or sometimes a bus leaning precariously...

It was hard to imagine that her mother was there, working in the middle of this. Morwenna asked her one time if she was worried, and Valerie was surprised because it hadn't occurred to her that something bad might happen to Jean. That made her feel ashamed of herself and for a short while she prayed to God to keep her mother safe. But after a few weeks of that, she forgot her prayers, and Mrs Howard never insisted.

Another thing she did – or rather *didn't* do – was tell her mum that she had moved. There was something delicious in not telling her and Valerie couldn't work out why. Eventually, she did write and let her know, but for the two whole months she didn't it was a strange and oddly blissful secret.

The only thing Valerie missed from her before life was the wireless, but there was one in the parlour, and one day Mrs Howard noticed her gazing at it and said: 'Valerie, you can listen, if you like. As long as I have my favourites, I don't mind.'

This time, Valerie threw herself at her for a hug.

Then they started talking about what they liked and what they didn't. And even Lydia wandered in from the garden wanting to hear what was going on, but she got bored, and skipped off with Rex. Valerie tuned in to new shows and old favourites. *It's That Man Again* was coming back for its third series.

She had never been so happy in her life.

And that was shameful too, because she was an evacuated child, and she was only here because of war and all the terrible things happening to her hometown; but it was true.

37

WINTER 1940

Valerie

Mrs Howard brought Paul home for the Christmas holidays. That was one thing: when Mrs Howard was talking about Paul, her voice went low and peculiar. Perhaps it was just that she was protective of him. She said, 'I'm a lioness when it comes to threats to my cubs.' Valerie wasn't sure if she was a cub or a threat.

Twice, Mrs Howard made comments on how the girls were not to interfere.

'He won't get in your way. You have your friends, and he has his.'

Valerie didn't mind. This sounded sensible. She was now twelve. He was fourteen. They probably wouldn't have a lot in common.

He was the boy who had come into the shop and offered to take her fishing. She remembered his freckles, the big smile, the way he held your eyes for longer than most people. He didn't seem to recognise her though, or at least he didn't remark on it.

Despite that initial interaction, she didn't much like Paul in the early days. He was arrogant. He was always throwing things or coming and going. He never sat still. Now with a tennis racquet off to the park, now with a cricket bat off to the cricket club.

He didn't like the name of the new dog. 'Boring! All dogs are called Rex!' he complained.

'Well,' said Mrs Howard, exasperated, 'that's what he answers to now.'

'I'll call him Tyrannosaurus Rex,' Paul insisted.

Valerie giggled. And he gave her a look. 'What do you think?'

'How about T.Rex?' she suggested nervously.

He considered her, then the dog, and then put out his hand. 'Deal.'

Valerie didn't realise the hand was for her to shake at first.

'He didn't want to have people here,' Mrs Howard explained once Paul had gone out to teach T.Rex skills in the garden. 'He spends term-time with people fighting for attention. You could say home is his sanctuary.'

Valerie wanted to know more – why did Mrs Howard agree on having them to stay then? But she had screwed her lips tight, which Valerie now understood to mean that she wouldn't get anything else out of her.

Then Paul came in, proclaiming that he had taught T.Rex how to sit, how to offer a paw and how to fetch, and he was so excited no one had the heart to tell him that T.Rex already knew all those.

Paul wasn't home much anyway. He made water bombs and sand bombs with his friends and they played endless game of convoys and concentration camps. He said that most of his friends were miles away at boarding school, but he was one of those easy-going fellas who made friends wherever he went.

Boys on bicycles knocked for him. Boys holding jars of tadpoles waited on the wall for him. Boys out in the street yelled, 'Over here!'

And he didn't treat the house like a sanctuary, whatever Mrs Howard said. He treated it like a playground, a hotel, a springboard for a billion adventures or a place to develop his madcap ideas.

Paul was vociferous about Hitler. Valerie, who had been brought up to never talk about money, religion or politics, found this shocking. Whenever Paul said he'd like to drop bombs on Hitler, Mrs Howard smiled indulgently. But when he said he would take Hitler out at dawn and shoot him and his stupid side parting until you couldn't recognise him, Mrs Howard snapped, 'You're talking like a fool! Go up to your room.'

Paul hardly talked about school, where it was apparent he was popular and successful, although he frequently complained about air raid practice.

He talked about his father and when he did, Valerie listened closely. Paul's father had died young in an accident. That was something they had in common.

'You should be proud of him, Paul,' Mrs Howard always said.

There was a lot of pride flying around Bumble Cottage.

38

Jean

Early December, while the Blitz was still raging, Jean made her way to the house at Romberg Road to check the post. She found a typed letter from the government. It wasn't until the last line that she understood: there had been a mistake – number 67 was habitable and had been all along.

Jean stormed to the council office and leaned over the counter, letter in hand, fire in her belly.

'It has been habitable all this time?'

The woman on the other side of the counter shrugged.

'It's been months. Why didn't anyone tell us?'

'I'm telling you now!'

'But—'

'There's a war on,' counter woman said impatiently.

'I know!'

'Next!'

After work, Jean rustled up an omelette with some leeks a passenger had given her. Tony talked about one of his clients and she told him about a passenger who had hair curlers stuck to her coat. They were like an old married couple, but Jean kept reminding herself they weren't, not really. She didn't know what they were – it was not even a wartime romance; perhaps it was a Blitz-fling.

She told him she was going back home.

'Does that mean we're over?' Tony asked gloomily. He'd put all his leeks to one side. He wasn't big on vegetables.

'Not at all,' she said. She didn't want to upset Tony. 'It means I'll have my house again. Oh, Tony, I need my space – and you need yours.'

She didn't mention Valerie but that was what she was thinking. Valerie would be home soon. *She* was her priority. She had to tell Valerie about Tony. The conversation filled her with terror, but as long as Tony was in her life she couldn't imagine a way round it.

Tony looked unconvinced. 'We'll still see each other?'

'Of course!'

'How often?'

'Often as you like!' Jean pacified him with a big kiss on the lips. He was off to see his boys for Christmas anyway and wouldn't be back until the end of January. Jean wondered if he and Pauline would be sharing a bed, but she didn't ask. She didn't want to know the ins and outs and Tony wasn't likely to tell the truth either.

She told Mrs Salt, who returned from Southampton the next day with her four children in tow.

'They couldn't have told us earlier?'

'It's a disgrace, that's what.'

Jean sent Valerie a Christmas card explaining that the house was habitable now. It was a mix-up! How daft! And Valerie must come back as soon as the dreadful Blitz was over. And it would be soon.

'Fine,' replied Valerie. 'Happy New Year.'

Valerie didn't sound half so keen about joining Jean as she

had been a few months earlier, but Mrs Salt's optimism was contagious, and despite her cynicism Jean felt irrepressible suddenly: she had her home back – everything was going to come together in the end.

It turned out to be an unexpectedly merry Christmas. Jean got a bonus at work and presents from her regulars including hand-knitted gloves, a hip flask and lots of drawings. Her favourite was a children's picture of her, holding onto the pole. She had rosy cheeks and a big smile. It was like the ones Valerie used to do.

Mrs Salt strung up paper chains and had a small Christmas tree with a paper star on the top. Despite not being a Christian, Mrs Salt was a huge lover of Christmas traditions. She cleaned, she cooked, and played marbles with Joe and paper-folding with Maisie and Jacob and all the things Valerie had enjoyed when she was little.

Only once did they have to troop down to the Anderson shelter. Jean had her Morrison shelter too, but she preferred being with them. The children knew what to expect and were obedient.

Jean joked that even the Luftwaffe were having a break for Christmas.

Mrs Salt said, 'I think they are tiring of it. War will be over soon.'

Jean disagreed. She thought people shouldn't confuse what they wished for with what was. Reality wasn't palatable so they pretended otherwise. You couldn't blame them for it, but Jean didn't consider it to be a sensible approach.

Valerie had changed her address and at first Jean thought that Mrs Woods had moved. Then she gathered that Valerie had changed billets. Jean assumed Mrs Woods had got too old or something to care for a child, then she worried Valerie had upset someone. She couldn't understand why Valerie hadn't told her sooner, but she was probably just happy to be back with Lydia. 'What a shame you had to move on,' she wrote. 'Please give Mrs Woods my deepest gratitude.'

Jean got each of the Salt children a snow-globe; she sent one to Valerie as well. The children loved seeing the tiny flakes flutter over the snowman and, although the globes didn't work as well as they did in the films, Jean loved watching them too.

The day after Boxing Day, Jean went back to work, filled with hope that the year ahead might be the one her girl finally came home.

39

Valerie

The chap on the wireless said that, for many, Christmas 1940 would be one of their worst Christmases. The war had been grinding on for over a year now – the rationing and the food shortages were stinging. Many men who had joined up were now overseas, while many women were involved in the war effort at home.

For Valerie, it was one of her best. Maybe it was the contrast with the fear and loneliness of her time with Mrs Woods the year before, or maybe it was being with Mrs Howard, Lydia and Paul.

She was happy, happy, happy. She knew this joy would come to an end soon – as soon as the bombing stopped – but for now, she was content. Perhaps it was knowing she was on borrowed time that made it sweeter.

Mrs Howard had a barn at the end of the garden and two land girls who worked on a nearby farm came to live in it. Prue and Minnie were eighteen and glorious. They seemed to bring drama wherever they went. There were always dogs barking, cats, deliveries from the postman. Another of Mrs Howard's mottos turned out to be 'The more the merrier'.

Valerie had her first theatre trip. Mrs Howard was, she realised, that rare grown-up who delivered on her promises. The Shakespeare play they had finally decided on was *The Tempest*. Valerie had never sat in a theatre, and it was like the cinema except maybe not as exciting and when they ate sweets, people turned round angrily. Valerie didn't understand it all, nor did Lydia and nor did Paul, but she knew she liked it.

Afterwards, Mrs Howard went on a long explanation about it being Shakespeare's last play and about Caliban and Miranda.

'Next year will be more fun,' she admitted. 'It was rather dry, wasn't it?'

Valerie didn't know what dry meant in this sense, but she nodded.

'I liked the relationship between the father and the daughter,' she said, and Mrs Howard's eyes suddenly filled with tears.

'Dear girl,' she said, 'you are wise.'

Paul was also a wireless fan. Valerie had asked him, 'Do you like *It's That Man Again?*' and he had looked at her incredulously. 'Do I like *It's That Man Again?*! I don't like it! I love it!'

From that moment on, the pair of them never stopped listening together. And when they weren't listening together, they were laughing together about their favourite shows. They started doing the catchphrases of the actors, to the frustration of the uncomprehending Mrs Howard and Lydia.

'After you, Claude – no, after you, Cecil.'

'I'll have to ask me dad.'

'But I'm all right now.'

'TTFN.'

They slapped hands. Mrs Howard looked flummoxed. 'When on earth do you listen to all this?'

Lydia looked up from T.Rex. *'I* don't.'

'It's hilarious,' Paul said.

Valerie wasn't sure what Mrs Howard objected to. Maybe it was not educational, or appropriate. She pulled herself together. 'I listen to other things as well,' she explained. *'Children's Hour. In Town Tonight,* and all the dramas.'

'So do I!' yelped Paul. 'I love the dramas!'

'But you never can work out who is going to end up with who!' Valerie shrieked back.

'Marvellous,' Mrs Howard said. There was something in her face though when Valerie looked at her. It wasn't surprise like on her mother's; it certainly wasn't revulsion as with Mrs Woods. It was more like something was crystallising for her and she wasn't entirely sure how she felt about it.

40

Jean

Jean had just got back from work when Mrs Salt knocked. Jean thought she was deciding to leave again, but it wasn't that – Mrs Salt suspected Francine had chickenpox.

'I can't have them all sick at once!' she said, hand on her forehead.

Jean sympathised. She couldn't bear the thought of pink-faced baby Joe covered in spots either. His cheeks were so smooth! And they'd go down like dominoes if they weren't careful.

'Francine can stay in my Morrison shelter at night,' Jean offered. She was growing fond of Francine and that surprised her. 'For a couple of days, until she's not contagious.'

'What about you?' asked Mrs Salt doubtfully, but Jean could see she liked the idea.

'Been there, done that with Valerie last year,' Jean said, stealing a last-minute snuggle with Joe. 'Who's becoming a big boy?'

He replied, 'Cat!'

It was his favourite and only word apparently.

'Better than Blitz, I suppose,' Jean said, but to both of their astonishment, he repeated this: 'Bits, bits!'

Mrs Salt joked that Joe slept so soundly through the bombings that she wondered if he'd be able to sleep when it was all over!

Francine looked all right to Jean that evening, and Jean wondered if it was a false alarm. She got the girl comfortable in the shelter in the kitchen. Francine was reading a comic, so Jean waited until she'd put it down before she asked.

'Do you think Valerie will be happy with Mrs Howard?'

Francine tilted her head, thoughtfully. 'I think she will like Paul.'

Paul? thought Jean. She assumed he was another evacuee maybe, or a helper.

Now she had Francine on her own, Jean had a million questions, but she didn't want to overwhelm her. 'What about her room at the Bumble Cottage?'

'It's cosy.'

'And the food?'

'Yummy!' Francine smiled, rubbing her tummy.

This was all well and good, thought Jean, but she was so anxious about the Tony-shaped secret that she might soon have to divulge that it was of little comfort.

She would simply announce it: *Ta-da... Remember I said your dad was dead? Well, he's not...*

Francine said she didn't mind being apart from her brothers and sister – she was probably used to it by now – however, once she was all snuggled up, she asked, 'Will they be all right?'

'They're in the proper shelter, love!' Jean reminded her. 'They'll be right as rain.' She thought, *It's us you want to worry about!*

Francine fell asleep quickly. She was the same size as Valerie and, in the dark, Jean could almost believe it was her.

The Luftwaffe might have rested over Christmas but Jean was right, unfortunately; there was no respite from them now. They kept coming, relentless. They were pounding the city, and one time they obviously set something off nearby because doorbells kept ringing. At least it wasn't gas, thought Jean. And Francine slept through it all.

In the morning, she woke up, yawned, then put her hands to her face.

'Don't scratch,' said Jean, impressed at Mrs Salt, who clearly had a mother's instinct for illness. Francine's spots had come out.

Jean had been on the bus all day long with her driver, Albert, and her feet were aching when the Nazis started up again. It would have been impossible to get home safely even if she wanted to. Francine would be all right – she'd have to be.

Jean went to the shelter near the bus station and settled in for the night there; she probably got three hours' sleep, which wasn't bad going.

Day broke with a pink and purple bruised sky. Jean decided she'd walk back home, check on Francine and freshen up before work. She turned a corner – and saw that there were fire engines in her street.

Jean ran. She ran as fast as she ever had.

The house was still standing – thank God, thank GOD, she would never leave it again – but there was a kerfuffle out the back, a crowd, a frantic crowd, around where the Anderson shelter was.

'What happened?' she asked. She asked everyone, but no

one knew how to answer. It was their yard, but it didn't look like their yard. And there were people everywhere.

'It took a direct hit,' said a man, wiping sweat off his forehead.

'What?'

'The shelter did...'

Someone blew a whistle and there was silence. Then digging.

Jean joined in, clawing at mud, holding her breath. She pulled and scraped. *This can't be happening*, she told herself. *This must be a bad dream*. A firemen told her to leave off.

'I'm not leaving off,' bellowed Jean in tears, mud smeared over her face. 'These are my people.'

'Is it your Val?' shouted someone.

Thank God it wasn't her Val.

'It's the Salts,' she said. 'It's my neighbours.'

And then there was Francine emerging from the back door, in her nightie, barefoot and shivering. Her lips were blue and her skin was pale. She was holding the snow-globe Jean had got her.

'Where's my mama?' she asked, looking desperately at Jean to tell her everything was okay. 'Mama?'

Jean hurried over to her, took her in her arms. The girl was stiff as a board.

'They're trying, love...'

Again, the fireman blew the whistle for silence. Perhaps they'd heard something.

'Anyone?' he called. 'Give us a sign.'

But it was nothing, it was only the creaking of the wood or the movement of bricks, or the crumbling of the broken world.

'I need names.' Even the fireman had tears in his eyes.

'Mrs Salt. Maisie. Jacob and' – Jean howled – 'little Joe.'

Little Joe. That lovely child who'd stolen her heart – was down there.

41

Valerie

The girls were called into Mrs Howard's drawing room on New Year's Day. The clock on the mantlepiece said eleven o'clock. Mrs Froud stood in front of it, a handkerchief held to her nose. She could hardly get the words out. Matthew Froud rolled a tin bus around on the floor.

'All of them?' Valerie asked incredulously.

'Not Francine,' repeated Mrs Froud. 'She wasn't in the shelter.'

'The others?'

'I'm afraid so.'

Lydia cried, hugging T.Rex, while Valerie stared at the hands of the clock. She had wanted to stay in London just a few months before... She might have been... It was impossible to take in. But while her mother had proved to be right to keep her out of the city, Valerie also couldn't help wondering why Jean had left it to Mrs Froud to break this news. Couldn't she have come too? Yes, there were the bombings, yes, London had to keep moving, but her mother had not once visited her at Bumble Cottage, and if this didn't warrant a trip, what did?

Mrs Froud proposed a walk. She asked Valerie if she wanted to come along, but Valerie could tell she wanted time alone with her children. There were a lot of emotions to process.

Valerie tried to think of Francine and what she might be going through, but she had no idea and it felt too big even to imagine.

When she next saw them, Lydia and Mrs Froud were in the middle of a quarrel and Matthew had his hands over his ears. Mrs Froud wanted to take Lydia back with her to the place where she was staying, and Lydia was refusing. There was something funny about the way she stood, arms folded, her lower lip out, but it wasn't funny really. Mrs Froud was dabbing her red eyes, Lydia was insisting she wouldn't leave the dog, not now, not ever. No dogs were allowed at the new place, Mrs Froud explained, and was pleading with her.

'It's not even your dog, Lydia,' she said, which didn't go down well.

'It's not right,' Mrs Froud said. Lydia tossed her hair and then, with a snarly look, said, 'It's right for me, so...'

Mrs Froud never stood up to Lydia and she wasn't going to make an exception today. She plucked up her handbag and then pulled Matthew off the carpet: 'We're going now.'

Lydia kept her arms folded until Mrs Froud opened the front door, then she ran to her and hugged her. Valerie had a lump in her throat too. She desperately missed Jean, and the feeling that Jean was not missing her hurt her deeply.

42

Jean

For the next few days, Francine lay in Valerie's old bed with her eyes squeezed shut.

Jean showed her some of Valerie's old bits – a music box and a Pinocchio puppet – to try to make her smile, but Francine rolled onto her side and wouldn't look at her.

'You can stay with me; I am out most of the day at work though...'

But it didn't come to that. A couple of days later a woman came from the school, a Miss Beedle, and after greetings and commiserations she said Francine would be evacuated in the short term.

'And in the long term?'

Miss Beedle shrugged helplessly.

'Where will she go? There is family in Southampton, apparently...'

'They've had to evacuate from there as well, I heard.'

The sensible thing would be to send her back to Somerset, thought Jean, with Valerie and Lydia, but when did they do the

sensible thing? And maybe two girls were enough for Mrs
Howard – Jean couldn't blame her for that. She was already
going over and above the call of duty.

'She'll miss the funeral,' Jean said. Her voice had been
croaky for days. Everyone on the bus – who didn't know what
had brought it on – was making fun of her.

'That's for the best, I imagine,' Miss Beedle said.

Jean got Francine ready to leave. She kept trying to reassure
her, but Francine remained silent. It was perhaps silly of Jean to
expect a hug. Francine floated away like she was a ghost.

Jean remembered Richard Carrington telling her about special
dispensation, and she asked for it for the Salts' funeral. She
hadn't had a day off since the Blitz started, and maybe she
should have, to spend time with Valerie, she thought. Maybe
she would still.

Her mind was fizzy with visions of the last few weeks and
the noises, the sounds and the smells. She sometimes wanted to
thump her head to get them out. Sometimes, she felt astonished
at how quickly her world had changed. One minute she was
cleaning, her daughter was safe at home, and the next, her
neighbours were dead, her daughter was far away and rats with
fur the colour of ashtrays filled her dreams.

Mrs Peabody was also exhausted.

'We have to keep London moving.'

'Mm,' said Jean. She didn't dare stop moving or she would
fall asleep. She didn't dare speak or she might cry.

'Is it your family?' Mrs Peabody asked.

'Kind of,' said Jean. She almost wanted her to say no
because actually she didn't want to go to the funeral. All she
could think of was that lovely child in the rubble, the hand that
had clutched hers, and his massive eyes like a baby owl.

She'd rather be distracted by the bus.

Mrs Peabody stamped a paper: 'Half-day.'

The funeral was held in the Jewish cemetery at East Ham and it was like nothing Jean had ever seen. She felt like she had stepped back in time, into Poland or Russia. The service was in a small building like an outhouse. There were many people there. Men and women were on opposite sides of the room, both sides were weeping.

She would never have associated Mrs Salt, who liked dancing and lipstick and puddings with currants and sultanas, with this anachronistic place.

Mrs Froud came back from wherever it was she was staying, and it was like her and Jean's argument had never happened. They fell into each other's arms, clutching each other tightly, and then they went outside, following the coffins as they trundled along on wonky wheels.

The sight of those half-sized boxes being lowered into the ground would never leave Jean. Nor would the image of the aged father of Mrs Salt trying to throw himself into the hole in the ground. He had to be held back.

43

SPRING 1941

Valerie

When Mrs Howard had heard about Francine's family, she too had been upset. She'd said she'd wire London right away and tell them Francine could come back.

Valerie shivered. She knew the rule: *Last in, first out*. And then what would her mother do? But Mrs Howard noticed. 'You are a pleasure to host, dear,' she said. 'You're not going anywhere.'

It turned out it was too late anyway. By the time the offer was made, Francine had already been sent elsewhere.

Paul was kind when he heard too. So kind that Valerie looked at him with new eyes. She knew he was fun, but now she saw he was sympathetic as well.

'Any news from Francine?' he asked a few days later.

'Not yet. I'd write but I don't know where to send it.'

'Well, she knows where you are,' he said.

'Yes, I'll wait to hear from her.'

Somehow, Valerie didn't expect she would.

She didn't hear from Jean either, which was hurtful. Valerie wrote her a long letter about how upset she was about the Salts, and nothing came back. Her mother was too busy on the buses. Fending off the ridiculous men who wanted to take her out or buy her stockings. Was it three or four so far? That was what interested her nowadays.

And then three letters arrived at once. It turned out it was the postal service. And her mum wrote that it was so sad, and she was so upset; yet for some reason it didn't soften Valerie but made her heart harden.

Recently, Valerie had been having more wicked thoughts. She wished Mr Hardman had been the parent who survived and raised her – not Jean. He wouldn't have left her at the mercy of Beastly Woods, that was for sure. She imagined him climbing up to a smoke-filled room. She didn't know if he went in the house or the outside of the house. If he went up the outside of the house, he would have had to have acquired a ladder. He probably thought of her as he helped them out of the window.

How did the children survive yet he did not? Smoke inhalation probably. She read about that in the newspapers. The Blitz had taught them things children shouldn't need to be taught. Poor Dad. He had loved her very much, that was what her mum always said.

And then Valerie imagined that not only did she have a dad, but he fell in love and married Mrs Howard. They would be a family, she and Paul would be brother and sister, they would listen to the wireless together and go to the theatre and she would never have to leave.

When he was next home from school, Paul took Valerie fishing. At first, she sat on the riverbank, watching and keeping quiet, but then he taught her how to cast off, how to reel in, and she enjoyed it.

'Patience is key,' he told her. 'There might be false alarms but when the real thing tugs, you'll know it.'

Valerie enjoyed their conversations (probably more than the fishing!).

'I like artists,' she told him once.

His lip was curved, not in a sneer, more of a question mark. 'How many do you know?' he lightly challenged.

'Two – you and my old schoolteacher, Miss Beedle. Oh, and her fiancé.'

His face twitched. 'I'm not a real artist though.'

'You will be,' she said. That made him smile. His natural expression was earnest so, when he did smile, it was like sunshine breaking through clouds. He wanted to go to New York after the war, he said. They had incredible studios and galleries there.

That day, they caught nothing except for a Lydia on the way home.

'I want to come next time.' Lydia always wanted to join them but when Lydia was there, the mood changed. The balance shifted. Instead of the easy back and forth between them, Lydia became the centre and they were on the sidelines. Valerie knew it wasn't just her. Paul thought so too. With Lydia, you had to mind your Ps and Qs.

Valerie ignored her request, but Paul was generous.

'There's a lot of waiting around for something to happen, and even then, it sometimes doesn't.'

'I'm used to that,' Lydia said, sounding much older than her years, which made Paul laugh. He looked at Valerie for direction. Valerie felt unable to say what she thought.

Next time, Lydia did indeed come along, and they caught three fish. Not tiddlers either – they were five, six inches. A roach and a gudgeon. They put their hands together to measure the difference and Valerie felt a strange sensation run through her when she put her hand against Paul's. She whipped her hand away.

'You're lucky for us, Lydia,' Paul said, and even Valerie had to admit she was.

Lydia laughed gleefully and then said, 'It is boring though, I don't think I will bother again.'

There were parties and picnics, the Goose Fair and Easter egg hunts. There were school recitals, tests and sports days. Valerie loved listening to the wireless or reading in the drawing room or scrumping or climbing a tree or chasing after T.Rex.

She knew how awful her city was having it – and not only her city, other parts of the country too – but she felt distanced; she *was* distanced.

Her mother sent toffee and a hair bow that Valerie gave to Lydia, and a blouse that was too grown-up that Valerie gave to land girl Prue, who had been bemoaning a lack of clothes. It felt nice to do a good deed.

Jean's letters were shorter than ever, written hurriedly in shelters; but they were filled with mistakes – one time she asked about Mrs Woods! She had crossed it out but still. She had no idea. They were emotional too, thought Valerie. Full of *Thank God Valerie was safe*, and *as soon as the Blitz was over, she was to come home*. She couldn't wait. Their being together was the only thing seeing Jean through. And did Valerie like that shirt she sent? – she got it from the market. And what about the pretty bow?

Valerie composed measured responses. She was not looking forward to returning to London but she knew not to say that. She wrote that she was glad that Jean was enjoying herself. She wrote that she understood it was difficult to visit and yes, she had received the toffee. She did not like toffee anymore (it hurt her teeth) but Lydia did.

Valerie wrote that she and Lydia still got on reasonably well, and her friendship with Morwenna was wonderful. Her mother replied, 'Morwenna can visit us in London after the war.' Valerie never once mentioned Paul.

She had known Paul for about half a year when he asked her about her father.

'He died saving people – some children in a house fire.'

'During the war?'

'No, before I was born.'

They both had lost fathers young, both had been brought up by mothers. All right, their mothers couldn't have been more different, but still.

Paul didn't say anything for a while and then he looked straight at her. He was paler in winter, almost sallow, but still freckly. She stared back at him. Then he gave her the biggest smile ever.

'Let's go fishing.'

They had a great day. Valerie caught something first – a pike apparently – but then Paul caught three, including a tench, in a short space of time.

As they were packing up, Paul asked, 'Will you stay in touch after you've gone?'

'How do you mean?' The question took her by surprise. She felt like she had been suddenly hooked.

'They're saying evacuated children will go home soon.'

'I haven't heard that,' she said shortly, hoping it wasn't true. As far as Valerie was concerned now, the Blitz could go on forever.

44

SUMMER 1941

Jean

Mrs Peabody said a journalist from the *Star* magazine wanted to do an article about the rise of the lady-clippie and they'd selected Jean to be in it.

'Me? Why not Iris or Mavis?'

For some reason, Iris or Mavis wouldn't be great faces of the East London Bus service but Jean would be.

Jean was flattered. She wondered what Valerie would say to this.

'What do I have to do?'

She was to think of her highs and lows of conductress life. Jean knew she wouldn't tell them the real highs and certainly not the real lows, but she had answers in place.

They took her photograph. Self-consciously posing with her leg in the air (their idea), her cap in hand (ditto): 'I can't imagine doing any other job!'

That was true.

. . .

They went one night, two nights, three nights – and then a whole week without bombing.

The Blitz is finally over the headlines roared, but it took a while before Jean would let herself believe it.

At least she had done the right thing by Valerie. Thank God she hadn't let Valerie stay at home. If she had done one thing right in her life, it was sending her away.

But now was the time to get her daughter home. This was a promise she would keep.

Now it came to it, Tony didn't seem to like the idea.

'You'll still visit me?' he said. 'And I'll still be able to visit you?'

'Absolutely!' she promised. 'Once I've... you know... explained everything.'

They had a routine of four nights together, three nights off. Since Mrs Salt and her children had gone, Jean had leaned on Tony. Being with him was better than being alone... To a point.

She tried not to sound too excited about Valerie because Tony was sticking his lower lip out again, but she could hardly wait. She sent a letter of her intentions to Mrs Howard, who replied by return of post.

I was expecting this. If the situation in London deteriorates once again, and I pray it doesn't, please be assured, Valerie is always welcome to return.

Hmm, thought Jean. *I'm not sure how I feel about that.*

On the train down to Somerset, Jean felt like it was the first time in a while she'd had time to think – and all she could think about was a series of images like in a film: the bus plummeting down a hole, seeing the Anderson shelter in the backyard destroyed, Francine's devastated face.

Think about Valerie, she reminded herself. *The two of them back together again.*

She had it planned. She wasn't going to tell Valerie about Tony as soon as she was home. There was no rush. She would let her girl know gradually, after a few days of togetherness. 'I have some news...' she would say.

And then, if all went well, she and Tony could get married this time round. (Pauline would have to be out the picture, of course, but it sounded like she would agree to a divorce.) Valerie could even be the bridesmaid. Valerie wasn't necessarily going to be angry, Jean told herself. Heaven knows, she might be entirely unbothered by it. Not everyone was obsessed with their parentage, Jean knew that.

Bumble Cottage was not what Jean had expected. It was large, but it was also flowery and somehow cosy-looking. The arch over the gate was a nice touch. It was a world away from their flat in London, that was obvious. After knocking hesitantly, Jean heard footsteps, then the front door swung open and there was a woman – not Valerie – full of welcome and bonhomie. She introduced herself as Mrs Howard, none other! And Jean wanted to say, 'Where's my Val? I want my girl!' but told herself to calm down and, within seconds, Mrs Howard said, 'Come! The children are preparing a picnic in the garden.'

Mrs Howard was much older than Jean – that was the first surprise – and had a jolly-hockey sticks look about her. She looked like the type of woman who'd never been on a bus before.

Mrs Howard led her through the house, which was not half as tidy as Jean had expected – if it were the other way round, she'd have been cleaning for weeks. There were newspapers, books and dog hair everywhere.

Jean handed over some apples she had picked up at the market and now wished she hadn't. It was coals to Newcastle.

'How marvellous,' Mrs Howard said, striding ahead to the back door, and there she was. Her beautiful girl, her Val was setting things up on a table. A checked tablecloth, plates of sandwiches, the buzz of bees. Her girl, sunshine in a dress. The last time Jean had seen her baby was after the bus landed in a hole and she could hardly look at anyone. The contrast with this peaceful scene was painful. Lydia looked up and waved.

It took Mrs Howard calling, 'Valerie. VALERIE, look who's here!' before she came over.

Val, her girl, brushed her hands down her front. Jean didn't know that dress or those shoes, but she knew that face, that impossible, gorgeous face. The most beautiful face in the world. Now she saw her, she realised it had been too long. Val looked all grown up. It was like it wasn't Valerie any more, it was like she had become her older sister.

Jean didn't know how to express it; she didn't know what to say.

'Hello, we've made bread and butter pudding. Well, crusts and marg pudding...'

'Not for me,' Jean said automatically. When she saw the hurt in Valerie's eyes, she said, 'Go on then.'

Then Lydia came over and cheerfully said, 'Nice to see you again, Mrs Hardman,' like a proper young lady, and Jean laughed because Lydia used to have the worst manners. 'Nice to see you too, Lydia!'

'There's no staff, so we do it ourselves,' Lydia added.

'There is staff!' Valerie exclaimed.

'Only old Mrs Hardcastle, the housekeeper.'

'And Neils, the gardener!'

'There aren't *many* staff... Mrs Howard says it's good for us to be self-fishant,' Lydia said.

'Self-sufficient,' corrected Valerie.

Staff? We never had staff, thought Jean. What were they talking about?

'I do eggs,' Valerie continued. 'Lydia does the bacon.'

'I'm a whizz with a frying pan!'

'In the evening, we throw something together,' Mrs Howard joined in, smiling.

Two glowing young women in boots and trousers appeared from a building beyond and Lydia jumped up.

'Can I offer them some?'

And Mrs Howard said, 'Of course,' and then she explained to Jean, 'They're our land girls. They're at work most of the time or out with the farmers. Oh, to be young again!'

Jean smiled vaguely in response. She was wondering if one of the girls was wearing the blouse she had sent Valerie. Surely not?

It seemed tranquil, sociable and a little magical compared to London. It was like the bus in the crater, the boy with measles and the Salts buried underground had happened to a different Jean in a different life. But they had happened, and it made her think she didn't belong there. It was intimidating and she couldn't understand why Valerie wasn't as intimidated as she was. Didn't she realise this was not their world? And she had never got to the bottom of why Val had moved here anyway. It seemed cheeky. Was Mrs Woods very upset?

They were eating lettuce and cheese when a boy appeared – he was, at a guess, thirteen or fourteen, and Jean realised he must be Mrs Howard's son although to her mind she was old enough to be his grandmother. Jean watched the interaction between them. Val and the boy seemed to be great friends, while Lydia was more interested in petting the dog. After they finished the food and cleared up, Mrs Howard said, 'I expect Mrs Hardman will want to stretch her legs before the train!'

Mrs Hardman didn't, particularly, but she said, 'That's an idea.'

They had two hours or so before they had to be at the railway station. Val said she had packed everything, and Jean said, 'By yourself?' and Val, looking like that was a daft question, muttered, 'Of course.'

'He's a nice boy,' Jean said when they were away from the house.

This was a subject Valerie seemed to prefer. 'We have lots in common!' she trilled. 'His daddy also died when he was small!'

'Did he?' asked Jean, mortified. 'Oh.'

'A loss like that shapes a person, doesn't it? It makes me feel apart from other people – and Paul's the same,' Valerie said, gazing into the distance.

'Right.'

'Although Paul's father died in a car accident, I think, so not the same.'

'No.'

They did a circuit round some country lanes and Jean wanted to change the subject, but nothing animated Valerie so much as talking about Paul or her father did.

'You'll miss it here,' Jean said, and Val shrugged.

'Mrs Howard says I can visit as often as I like.'

That sounded ominous. Surely Val realised the expense.

And then Val said, 'It's nearly four,' and Jean was going to say, 'We don't have to go until five!' but she was glad she didn't, because Valerie wasn't talking about the train, she was talking about a show on the wireless. Again, Jean felt like she couldn't catch up with what was going on.

They trooped back and went into the living room, another densely packed place, books, pictures on the walls and cardboard boxes on the floor labelled HATS or SOCKS or WATER BOTTLES.

They all sat together. Paul, Lydia, the dog, Mrs Howard and even the land girl who might be wearing Valerie's blouse.

'You will enjoy this,' Mrs Howard said in her posh voice. It was like she was talking to horses.

I will not! thought Jean. She saw her daughter's eyes shining. It wasn't just the radio, was it? It was the communal life. It was the country life. She was thriving here.

Jean thought of their cold flat, where Valerie would be alone all day while she was out at work. She thought of the Tony-bombshell she would have to drop on her one day. She thought of the school that was without its best teachers, the libraries that had gone underground or been destroyed or were shuttered shut. Valerie wouldn't fit in in London.

When the show finished, Mrs Howard was the first to get up. 'Better get going, ladies...'

Valerie went upstairs for her bag and the other children went with her and Jean knew it was now or never.

'Mrs Howard,' she said quickly. 'Might I have a word? Do you think Valerie could stay?'

Mrs Howard looked surprised but not astonished.

'She is doing so well and London is still on its knees and...'

The woman clasped her hands. 'You are brave, Mrs Hardman,' she said. 'You're working hard and fighting to keep the capital moving. I can provide sanctuary for Valerie while you do whatever it is you have to do.'

And she didn't say it like it was a negative thing but as though she respected her. Jean *was* working hard. They *were* keeping London moving.

'I'll happily support her for as long as necessary.'

Jean felt tearful. She should be grateful, she was grateful, but at the same time she felt like a gnarly old root, while her girl was blossoming.

Valerie had come back downstairs.

Jean couldn't find the words. Thank goodness for Mrs Howard, who realised and strode over to her.

'Actually, Valerie, there's been a change of plan.'

Valerie looked up and, painfully, Jean saw that her eyes were hopeful: she *wanted* to stay.

'Stay here, darling,' Jean said quickly. 'For a little longer. I think it's right for you...'

Valerie nodded unemotionally, but Jean was sure she saw the hint of a smile.

Paul and Lydia bounded down the stairs, and when they told them, Paul whooped and picked up Valerie and twirled her round, and the dog barked at the excitement.

'I must dash,' Jean said.

'Ta-ta for now,' called out Paul and everyone laughed. It was a catchphrase from that radio show, even Jean cottoned on to that, but something about the casual disregard still hurt.

Finally, Valerie said something. She looked at the rest of them: 'This is Funf speaking.'

'Valerie,' said Mrs Howard more severely, 'address your mother, properly,' and Valerie walked Jean to the door and let Jean hug her, but she was wooden as a corpse and Jean didn't know what she'd done now. Whatever she did was wrong.

'I'll visit every month,' Jean promised.

Valerie sniffed. 'Fine.'

Out of the train window, Jean watched the fields and the trees wave her away. She kept her stiff upper lip as she knew she should. *We need to get on with things*, she told herself as the train rattled along noisily. And *everyone has to do their bit*.

Only once she was back in the flat, safely alone, did Jean let herself cry. Somehow, it felt worse than that warm September day of 1939 when Val had first left her. Indeed, that day was child's play compared to this. This day, Jean felt, was more momentous; it felt like their unravelling was complete.

45

Valerie

That evening, Mrs Howard stood in the doorway of Valerie's room. She didn't often come in; she always insisted the girls needed privacy. Valerie was unpacking her pillowcase and putting her clothes away.

'You are sure you want to stay, Valerie?'

'I am,' said Valerie. 'I think it will be better for me.'

Valerie was delighted and relieved to be staying on at Bumble Cottage; nevertheless, she was hurt that she hadn't been involved in the decision-making. That her mother had blithely handed her over for more weeks – months – years maybe, no one knew – as easily as if she were a punnet of strawberries.

It should have been harder for her mother. She would have liked to see more of a struggle.

It wasn't that she felt she belonged in Somerset instead of London. She didn't particularly; the explanation was simpler – she preferred it.

She no longer cared to go back to London with its beeping

cars, with the black choking smoke and the smog; the sky wasn't the colours it was here – it was mostly tobacco-grey. It was grimy walls and traffic wardens and shouting late at night. Life felt uncoloured-in. If she left now, it would be like leaving partway through a story – she'd never get to know the end.

And then there was Paul.

And Mrs Howard and Lydia and Morwenna and T.Rex.

But especially Paul.

Why would she want to go back?

The purple-blazer school where Lydia went did not have a local high school, so Valerie was continuing at the same school as before. When Lydia was twelve, she would join her too.

Mrs Howard had some reservations about this, though. Valerie heard her talking to her volunteer group as they packed items to send to the armed forces.

'Valerie has been poorly educated.'

This seemed harsh. Although Valerie did not like the head-teacher Mrs Lester, school was otherwise wonderful. There was Miss Beedle and the teacher who made them recite times tables for fudge. The one who let Lizzie Carter, who wasn't right in the head, swing her chair all day long, and never shouted or slapped her hand.

But when she heard Mrs Howard say, 'Valerie is gifted. I knew it from the moment I saw her and I want to make sure she has opportunities,' Valerie forgave her. Because why wouldn't she? That was a lovely thing to overhear. One of the women said Valerie had 'landed on her feet' at Bumble Cottage. Valerie could have found offence at that, but she would happily admit she'd landed on her feet too.

She was also relieved not to have to change schools since she didn't want to leave her lovely Morwenna again.

.   .   .

Through the volunteer group, Valerie also found out more about the mysterious Mr Howard – Paul's late father. One time, Mrs Howard had gone to make coffee, and the group were talking in quick, low voices that immediately made Valerie's ears prick up.

'Do you remember him?' one asked. 'He was such a handsome man!'

'And didn't he know it!'

'He wouldn't like her not having a maid.'

'He was probably having it off with the maid.'

They all laughed. And then, to leave Valerie in no doubt, the same woman muttered, 'Randy old hound.'

And Valerie realised that, although she *thought* she knew them well, there was a whole part of Mrs Howard's and Paul's lives that she was not a part of.

46

AUTUMN 1941

Valerie

Jean had said she would visit Valerie every month, but it was a whole three months before she came for her next visit and she seemed distracted the entire time.

Mrs Howard was out for the whole day with her volunteer group. Valerie wondered if she was staying away on purpose, and she wanted to tell her that she didn't have to. She didn't stay away when Mrs Froud visited Lydia.

Jean wanted to look around the town, 'not the graveyard, please, Val!', so they walked down the quiet high street. When she saw Woods Hardware Store, Jean grew animated and said, 'Was that the one? Shouldn't we pop in and say hello?'

Valerie felt a sudden fury. Didn't Jean realise how rotten it had been for her there? Couldn't she read between the lines? But before she could say anything, they had bumped into Lydia with T.Rex and T.Rex jumped up and Jean looked both delighted to see Lydia, who was 'prettier than ever!', and disconcerted by T.Rex.

At least her mother wasn't wearing her ridiculous bus

uniform for once. She was in a long tweed skirt and a pale jumper. She looked young, thought Valerie. She looked too young to be the mother of a thirteen-year-old. No one would believe it – they'd assume they were sisters.

That day with Jean felt long. They couldn't do normal things together because they didn't have a normal, and Valerie missed her favourite wireless shows. Jean had said she'd give them a listen, but she still didn't know what Valerie was talking about. Jean talked a lot about the passengers on her bus. Half of them seemed to be missing legs, the other half seemed to be drunkards. Many needed to be helped on and off the bus. And none of them seemed to have any money. It sounded as though Jean was subsidising the lot of them.

Valerie had wanted to talk about the war. Mrs Howard had got a map of Europe out and they looked at that. Then she had got a globe and they looked at that. Then T.Rex attempted to chew the globe so they had to put it back on the high shelf and go back to the map.

'Do we have to talk about it? It's over now,' Jean said as they sat in the park.

Valerie yelped at this stupidity: 'It's not over.'

'I mean, the Blitz is over, thank goodness.'

'It's not like you're a soldier,' Valerie said spikily. 'You're a clippie.'

Jean didn't say anything. She had brought plums that a passenger had given her the day before, and she offered one to Valerie. When Valerie refused, Jean shrugged and sank her teeth into it and the juice dripped onto her skirt.

'What do you want to talk about?'

'Do you have a boyfriend?' Valerie squinted at her mother, who had gone red.

'Not... no,' Jean finally responded, and that was apparently the end of the conversation.

Back at the house, Valerie made sandwiches and wished

Jean wouldn't talk with her mouth open. She had no manners. And when she wasn't smoking, she was hiccupping.

'When are you going to visit me in London?' Jean asked brightly, wiping her mouth on her sleeve.

'Soon,' said Valerie, being as vague as she possibly could be. She didn't want to miss school and, even if Paul wasn't home, she liked her weekends here, mooching and helping and doing chores.

'You could see your old room, the places we used to go...'

The Salts' and the Frouds'? And the cinema occasionally? Seriously, what was there to see?

When Valerie entered the new school year, her marks dropped. It was Morwenna who remarked on it first. When they did a maths test from the blackboard, usually Morwenna would be three or four points ahead – now she was a full ten clear.

'Maybe you're just better,' suggested Valerie.

'Doubt it,' said Morwenna. It was the same in science and English. Any subject where there was copying from the board.

Valerie was concerned about the drop, but she couldn't work out the reason. The numbers and letters on the board danced somewhat, but she assumed they'd be dancing for everyone. But when she explained this to Mrs Howard, Mrs Howard was so alarmed that, the next day, she took her to the optometrist and Valerie did an eye test, which confirmed that she was significantly short-sighted.

Valerie tried on three pairs of glasses and couldn't choose. Finally, Mrs Howard said, 'Eenie, meenie, minee, mo...' and her finger landed on the tortoiseshell pair.

Valerie wondered what her mother would think. She'd probably feel sorry for her or say that she looked clever.

Lydia had said to her: 'Boys don't make passes at girls who wear glasses!' but what did Lydia know? – she was ten to

Valerie's thirteen (and had excellent vison; Mrs Howard took her to the optometrist too, the day after she took Valerie).

When Paul came back for the holidays, he did giggle. 'Did you choose them?'

'Your mum did.' She felt foolish.

'She's got good taste,' he said. Valerie waited for the joke – 'usually' or 'what happened?' – but none came.

'I hate them!'

'They make your eyes look smaller!' Paul admitted. 'But your eyes are so big anyway, now they are just normal-sized.'

Valerie couldn't decide if normal-sized eyes was a good thing or not. Probably not.

47

Jean

Some time after her interview with the *Star*, Jean bought a copy of the magazine in the corner shop, flicked through it, saw her photo – which was surprisingly flattering – then bought two more copies.

When the newspaper man said, 'It's not often I meet famous people!' he meant her!

At home, Jean obsessed over it. *Did I really say that? Do I really look like that?* Tony got grumpy, said that she should have mentioned him. It irritated her and she asked him why.

He shrugged. 'That would have been the decent thing to do.'

Jean was going to send a cutting to Valerie but decided not to. It wouldn't impress her. Nothing Jean did was right at the moment. Tony said it was a phase, but what did he know about their daughter? He still came round every Friday night, expecting his 'favours'.

'I can't help myself,' he always said, 'we could be dead tomorrow.'

Jean knew that *Would that be so terrible?* would *not* be the right answer.

Valerie was coming to stay for the first time since she had been evacuated, and Jean was beside herself with excitement. At last they would be together in London again! Valerie was old enough to get the train on her own now. Mrs Howard would pay the fare that end, but Jean would insist on paying her back. Jean had asked for special dispensation from work, and Mrs Peabody had grumbled at first, which was how Jean ended up telling her she had a daughter.

'Why didn't you tell me?' Mrs Peabody said, her face drained of colour.

'I don't know.'

Valerie had half-expected Kenny to divulge but he never had.

'It's lovely,' Mrs Peabody continued and then, hesitantly, she asked, 'Is there... has she... what about Dad?'

'It's complicated,' Jean admitted, and Mrs Peabody mumbled, 'That's one word for it!'

If it was anyone else, Jean would have taken them to the bingo, or shopping or to the cinema, but she knew Valerie. They would go to Highgate Cemetery.

'And you think she'll enjoy that?' Mrs Peabody asked tentatively. Jean couldn't think of anywhere she'd rather go less, but when she had suggested it to Valerie she had been pleased.

But then on the day, instead of Valerie, a telegram arrived that said she was 'too nauseous to travel'.

Jean didn't know the word 'nauseous', but she guessed it meant sick. Why didn't she just say sick? There was no way she would go up to Highgate Cemetery on her own, and she was not on the rota for work, so for the first day since the war had broken out Jean stayed in bed.

. . .

Perry was her driver the next day, Perry who was in love. Yes, there was a twenty-year difference between him and Iris – which reminded Jean of her and Tony – but if you overlooked that, it was a match made in heaven.

Perry already had an engagement ring; he was waiting for the right moment to propose.

'The right moment, eh,' repeated Jean, mystified. 'Just ask her!'

The bus picked up speed. This was where the waving boy used to stand and today, Jean was pleased to see the mother. The valiant woman still managed to get herself up and out after all. Jean prepared to smile and wave back. There was something about her Jean had always identified with.

Down the hill, faster and faster. Picking up speed. Jean raised her arm ready.

It happened so quickly. The woman ran in front of the bus. The bus ran into her and there was a terrible boom-thud of a noise.

The horror.

The bus came to a screeching halt, but not fast enough.

Jean jumped off and ran over to the woman. She got there before anyone else, even the people on the pavement who were closer.

The woman was crumpled on the road. She wasn't yet dead, but Jean knew there was nothing to be done, and she held her hand and after it happened – it happened quickly – she closed her eyes.

Poor Perry was in an absolute state, gibbering to the police officers: 'It wasn't my fault! She came out of nowhere.'

Kenny – for all his brutality – would have been better placed to deal with this.

'She met my eye,' Perry cried.

The police cleared the crowd and Kenny was sent to bring the bus back later. And to clean the blood off.

Jean and Iris sat with trembling Perry in the bus station. The engagement ring stayed in his pocket.

That evening, Jean felt suddenly desperate to speak to Valerie, to tell her she loved her; the Blitz might be over, but the war wasn't, the repercussions weren't – these were terrible times. She wanted to tell her about the awful, awful thing she saw today: a heartbroken mother; a devastated family; a man who might never work again.

But when the telephone call finally connected, Mrs Howard told Jean Valerie was nauseous no longer and had gone off cycling.

Cycling? Since when did Valerie ride a bicycle?

Mrs Howard gave her horsey laugh. 'Fresh air does wonders!'

Jean stared around the condensation-filled telephone box and the misted-up windows. She could almost be back on the bus. Maybe it was good she didn't get to tell Valerie. It would only have upset her.

'Doesn't it?' Jean acted cheerful as though her life depended on it. 'Please tell her I called!' she managed to say before hanging up, feeling the tears start to roll down her cheeks.

48

WINTER 1941

Valerie

Valerie dreamed of Hitler bombing Mrs Woods, and that was shameful, because although Mrs Woods was evil, she was not the enemy. Valerie tried to be forgiving, as they told her she ought to be in school assemblies, but it was hard to let go of the grudge.

She admitted it to Mrs Howard, who said, 'It would be for the best if you could forgive her.' Valerie nodded, shamefaced, but then Mrs Howard said, 'Yet it would be entirely understandable if you couldn't...' and everything felt better.

Valerie was doing well at school, although she often took time off since her menses were still a problem. Sometimes she felt so sick all she could do was curl up into a ball in bed, other times she threw up. T.Rex would stand guard nearby. It was her monthlies which prevented her trip to London – they did seem to spoil everything.

One month, she felt so bad that she asked Morwenna how she coped. Morwenna looked blank and then said, 'I don't mind so long as I can have a baby some day.'

Not long after, Valerie tentatively brought up the subject with Mrs Howard. Mrs Howard prided herself on 'you can talk about anything with me,' and never looking shocked, no matter what the situation was. Now though she looked shocked and said, 'This is what we do.'

Valerie was surprised yet also a little upset. Her host-mother was not usually dismissive.

Later, though, Mrs Howard came to her room to find her and apologised – 'If it's that bad, maybe we could talk to the doctor' – but by now Valerie had got the message and she smiled, said it wasn't necessary. She'd cope.

Mrs Howard's theatre group were putting on *Pygmalion*.

'I don't know it,' admitted Valerie. She hated not knowing stuff – at least, she hated revealing not knowing stuff to Mrs Howard. Not that Mrs Howard ever reacted negatively in any way, but Valerie wanted to impress her at all times. They were kindred spirits in a way. Mrs Howard always had her nose in a book, but she also was practical, down to earth. Valerie had always thought those were opposing things; Mrs Howard made them look complementary.

'I didn't until recently,' Mrs Howard said, although Valerie wasn't sure that was true. 'It's a terrific story. I wonder what you'll make of it.'

The show gave Valerie an uneasy feeling. She was too far back in the theatre to see the expressions on the actors' faces, so had to go on their voices alone, but the voices alone weren't great. The actress playing Eliza was trying to talk like a cockney – like Lydia and herself – yet it was like no accent Valerie had ever heard. However, the rest of the audience seemed to lap it up.

'Honest opinions please,' Mrs Howard said on the way home.

Lydia said it was better than *The Tempest*.

'I see that, yes.'

'The Eliza didn't feel real,' Valerie said.

Mrs Howard's expression changed. 'Would you say it verged on the caricature-esque?'

'Mm,' agreed Valerie, although she didn't know that word and was mostly relieved that she hadn't made a faux pas.

The next day, she heard Mrs Howard talking about it with her friends the volunteers.

'Maybe too close to home,' one suggested, and they laughed.

The best times were when Paul came back. It wasn't like Valerie's life was empty without him, it was just everything was more vivid or colourful when he was there. He ran in, throwing off his coat and shoes: 'Home for the holidays!' Mrs Howard yelled that he created a mess wherever he went, but she never really seemed to mind.

If he was annoyed about all these girls in his house – and the land girls in the barn – occupying his mother's attention while he was away, he didn't express it. He was probably content that they distracted her from him.

One time, he told Valerie, 'You're the one I miss most when I'm at school.'

'Even more than T.Rex?' Valerie said playfully, though she was thrilled.

'He's Lydia's now, isn't he?'

'Oh...' Valerie faltered. 'Does that make you sad?'

'Not at all' – he winked at her – 'there's enough love to go around.'

Paul wouldn't leave the riverbank until he had caught something – it was that important. It could be freezing, the sky could darken, their stomachs might be rumbling, but still they stayed. Sometimes she packed up before him, but not often, because between them, they usually did catch something. And then he brought home the fish. And this was what had surprised her at first. The fish was not for eating, instead, he painted the fish!

Valerie thought if he could see beauty in such plain creatures, there must be something very beautiful in Paul too.

Valerie wondered if Paul would say to her: 'I'm glad you're staying back here after all,' but he never did. She suspected he had been warned not to.

Paul and Mrs Howard had a lot to catch up on. They chatted endlessly about art and radio shows, Paris and New York and how Mrs Howard had once directed a play on Broadway. Yet Mrs Howard was as interested in Valerie as ever, even when Paul was there and Valerie appreciated this. Mrs Howard still encouraged her and Paul to spend plenty of time apart though. Whenever Valerie said they were going fishing, she asked, 'Again?' every single time.

49

SPRING 1942

Valerie

Mrs Howard had to go to London on errands and she asked Valerie if she would like to go with her. Whether these errands were concocted or not, Val was grateful for the chance. It was nearly six months since she'd last seen her mother. Although she would never admit it, not to anyone, she did sometimes yearn for her. She had been sad to miss her chance last time.

Lydia would remain in Somerset – the land girls would keep an eye on her. Mrs Froud did not live in London any more. Apparently, she was having a dismal time of it in the country.

Valerie supposed Paul was coming too, but Mrs Howard said he was going to stay with his friends in Devon. After Mrs Howard said that there was an awkward silence.

Getting off the train in London at midday was like being caught in a whirlwind of people. It was grey, smoky and smoggy. Straight away, Valerie rubbed her eyes and sneezed. The glass of the station clock was cracked; it was wrong too – it was stuck at nine thirty. And there were men in military uniform everywhere. All different colours. Troops sometimes drove through the Somerset countryside, but she had never seen a concentration of them like this. They had loud voices and strange accents. This wasn't how she remembered London.

One of them said, 'Limey, do you want some gum?' but Mrs Howard sprang in: 'Thank you, no.'

'Canadians,' she told Valerie. 'Or Americans. Or Australians. I'm not entirely sure…'

'What's gum?'

'A filthy chewing thing,' Mrs Howard explained, but then she laughed at herself. 'Shall we try some?'

The next time someone offered it, Mrs Howard and Valerie said yes, please. Mrs Howard said it was as disgusting as she had suspected but Valerie enjoyed it.

Mrs Howard was uncertain about letting her go off on her own. 'And your mother is expecting you?'

'Oh yes,' lied Valerie, who – she didn't know why – had deliberately not let her mother know. Aside from Christmas and birthday cards, they now hardly ever wrote; maybe that was why.

'You can ask her to come and join us at the hotel tonight.'

Mrs Howard thought it was too much to return to Somerset on the same day, so they were staying at The Ritz. Valerie was excited about staying in a hotel for her first time.

'I will ask,' Valerie said, thinking she would do no such thing. The thought of Jean, hiccupping in public, putting on her artificial posh voice, which was worse than her normal voice, was mortifying.

About one-quarter of her old street, Romberg Road, was gone. Evaporated. They'd tidied the rubble and masonry where once stood houses into mounds next to the intact houses, and some small children were playing in them. When she walked past, one of them called, 'Got any sweets, missus?' She recognised him – Monty, a boy from her old school – but he didn't recognise her.

Their house had boards up at the higher windows and tarpaulin on the downstairs ones. It looked uninhabited. She was about to knock when a man opened the front door.

He had too much Brylcreem in his hair. For a silly moment she wondered if it was another of the Americans with their gum, although he wasn't in uniform, he was wearing a three-piece suit and brown shoes.

'Hello?' she said. For a moment she wondered if she was at the wrong house.

He startled, flustered. 'Afternoon. Uh, don't mind me...' And he left the building. He was in such a hurry, he almost ran out into the street – and then her mother came up behind her, and her hand flew to her mouth.

'Val!' she said. 'Vally...'

Valerie had planned to hug her, but she was too confused now. 'Who was that man?'

'A neighbour!' said Jean, her palms upwards. 'Come in!'

Valerie followed her in docilely. She felt like a stranger in her own home. Jean was talking, talking.

'I wish you'd said you were coming, I would have arranged something nice for us. Val, how long are you here for?'

'The afternoon...'

'Or at least, baked a cake or a rice pudding.'

'I don't like rice pudding any more,' Valerie said.

'I would have made something you like,' her mother persisted.

The doorbell went, but before Jean could get up to open it, there was the sound of keys and the man shot into the room again, apologising as he did.

'My briefcase,' he said to no one, before scurrying away like a cockroach. 'Nice to meet you, Valerie.'

Jean made tea. In the kitchen, Valerie couldn't help marvelling at how everything was in the same place – nothing had changed, and yet everything had. They went into the sitting room. It was cold and Jean still looked bewildered, twisting her fingers and not drinking her drink.

'Where's the wireless?' Valerie said. That had changed.

'I got rid of it. I never listened anyway... Since when have you worn spectacles, Val?'

Valerie took off her glasses and wiped the lenses on her skirt. Everything had a softness about it, fuzzy-edged, without them.

'Since someone bothered to take me to the opticians.'

'Oh,' said Jean.

Valerie nodded sagely. She could see clearly now.

'Why didn't you tell me you were coming?' Jean kept asking and then apologising that there was nothing to go with the tea unless Valerie fancied bread.

'I sent a letter,' lied Valerie.

'Do you want a slice or not?'

By the fire there was a drying line, and there were big man pants and big man shirts dangling accusingly from it. That man's, she guessed.

'I'm taking in washing,' her mother said as she followed Valerie's eyes, and hurriedly unpegged the bits. She smoothed them down, folded them, then piled them up. Valerie wished she could stack away her confusion just as easily.

'Don't the buses pay enough?'

'It's... we all help each other.'

'Are you sure that wasn't your boyfriend?' asked Valerie.

'No!' her mother retorted promptly. 'You don't want to eat?
We could go out – to a cemetery if you want.'

Valerie shook her head. She was filled with something
halfway between curiosity and rage. 'It looked like he knew you
well. Is it one of the men who ask you dancing?'

Her mother drew on her cigarette. 'What did I tell you
about them?' She blew out smoke.

Valerie winced. 'There was the redhead from the bus?'

Jean blushed. 'He's long gone. He's fighting in Egypt.'

'The passenger on the bus – with the stockings?'

'That was a joke—'

'What do you think Dad would think?' Valerie interrupted.

'What do you mean?' asked Jean. If she was flushed before,
she was shiny now, to the tip of her nose.

'About you meeting someone else?'

'I would guess he'd want me to get on with my life. It's been
a long time. But I haven't!'

Children don't know what's normal and what's not. Or
rather, everything about your life seems normal because you've
got nothing to compare it to. It's only once you start comparing
it to others' that you find out it isn't.

Jean wiped her forehead with a handkerchief. 'You don't
want some bread?'

'I'll take you to your mother,' said the man at the front desk in
the short red jacket and white – *white!* – trousers. Valerie did
not disclose that she had left her mother behind in East London
and that Mrs Howard, the woman waiting for her, was her
evacuee host – what would be the point?

There were plants and mirrors everywhere, which was
disorientating. You couldn't tell what was room and what was
reflection.

'She is waiting in the dining area.'

They were sitting in the poshest room of her life and yet Valerie knew she did not look out of place. Not any longer. There was a large gilt-edged mirror over Mrs Howard's left shoulder and a sophisticated girl reflected back at her. Had she changed that much in three years? It was incredible that she should feel so at home here, and yet she did. She was the youngest person in the room by a good thirty years too, but even that didn't daunt her.

Mrs Howard was asking about Jean.

'She is well, considering.'

Valerie said that a lot now – 'considering' or 'under the circumstances'.

Mrs Howard handed her the menu that the waiter had handed her. It was in a plastic wrapper, handwritten.

'She didn't want to join us this evening?'

'She has plans.'

'I can imagine it's hard.'

Valerie wasn't sure what she was referring to, so she examined the menu. In the background there was chamber music – Valerie knew about chamber music from the wireless. The windows opened onto the gardens and, although you could mostly smell the food and drink being prepared in the kitchens, there was also the faint scent of lavender. The hotel had been hit during the Blitz and several areas destroyed; one side was still in ruins, but there was no hint of bomb damage here. The war, her mother and that 'neighbour' felt like half a world away.

'So hard,' continued Mrs Howard, spearing the asparagus.

'It's harder for some than others,' Valerie said. They talked about Shakespeare plays and radio plays, and Valerie felt better. This was her world now.

50

Jean

Jean couldn't believe she'd been so stupid. Not only had Valerie bumped into Tony, and then there was all that business with the briefcase, but she'd only gone and seen his great big pants.

She had weighed things up in her mind. Valerie had been colder than she ought to be – would the information that he was her father make her feel better?

Jean had decided not.

At least she didn't know anything else. For now. Being with Valerie these days felt like a job interview and she the least favourite candidate. There was no way Jean would have got a job on today's performance.

Why, oh, why, had Jean told Valerie about her stupid suitors, too? It was meant to be a joke, but Jean should have realised – nothing was a joke with Valerie. Everything had to have a deeper meaning and she remembered everything.

Her mouth ran away with her – not with anyone else though, only with Valerie. She was that desperate for connection. Yet whatever she said, whatever she tried, Valerie could be so intimidating.

Jean sometimes forgot that Valerie was growing up and was now a young woman. She wished she was the same little girl she had sent away. Jean liked to imagine Valerie was still a little girl, sitting on her bus, staring out of the window. She had told Valerie this once and Valerie had snorted, 'Why would I be on your bus?'

Over the next few months, Jean tried to get in touch with Valerie more often. She wrote long meandering letters and she tried calling on the telephone. Mostly no one at Bumble Cottage answered. Lydia sometimes did, but she was about as useful as a chocolate teapot. Occasionally Mrs Howard did, and she had this sort of sigh that always prefaced another convoluted excuse for why Valerie couldn't come to the phone.

Jean felt like she was holding on to a kite that was tugging away. The tighter she gripped, the more it tugged, yet she couldn't bring herself to let it go.

51

SUMMER 1943

Jean

Iris from the buses was getting married. Not to Perry – poor nerve-riddled Perry had been discarded shortly after the bus crash – but to a man she had met at her parents' Rotary club. This man was fifty-six!

'She certainly likes the older man,' said Mrs Peabody.

'That's fortunate,' said Jean. 'Since the younger ones are either fighting or dead.'

Jean was invited to the wedding and Tony asked if he could accompany her. Good grief!

Jean asked Iris because there was nothing worse than turning up at a wedding on your own, and Iris said she'd ask Fred. And it turned out Iris's Fred was a generous-minded chap – on his third marriage he'd have to be – and he said, 'Everyone's welcome.'

But on the day, Tony had a head-cold and Jean decided to stay at home with him. And she was glad she didn't go out, because that was the night that the doodlebugs came.

The doodlebugs were deadly and vicious and couldn't be

avoided. With the Blitz you had some advance warning, you could run for shelter, you could protect yourself – even if, as Jean knew too well, much protection was an illusion. But with these you had no time; you were vulnerable and exposed. As soon as the noise stopped, they were about to drop. This was an even worse terror. It made you despair. Jean would never have thought she'd look back at the Blitz fondly.

But as Valerie and Tony read the newspapers the next morning, it proved something: Jean *was* right to keep Valerie away. Whatever harm was being done to their relationship, she was keeping her safe from this latest and most dire threat.

'You won't get the girl back now?' Tony asked.

'No way...' Jean wasn't stupid. She saw the way the land lay: Valerie was in Somerset for the duration of the war now. And maybe that was for the best.

Valerie had stopped writing. At first, Jean could convince herself it was the erratic postal service. Because weren't they going crazy with the letters from the boys overseas, and the worried girlfriends, mothers and grandmothers?

Then she told herself it was schoolwork. School had always been more important than home for Valerie and her teachers more important than Jean. From the moment they had told her way back when that she was gifted, Valerie hadn't looked back. Jean sometimes wished the teachers had never mentioned it. Certainly, Jean herself had done her utmost to forget it. If they hadn't given Valerie false ideas, she would have been happy to be a shopkeeper or a clippie. It wasn't like the job was boring – there were a zillion things to remember, a zillion challenges, AND you had to be friendly to the passengers. You had to be gifted, but in a different way.

Or maybe it was something to do with Mrs Howard?

Jean had tried to be well disposed to Mrs Howard, but she had reminded her of the matron at the hospital when Valerie was born. Full of good advice, but no idea how it would pan out in the real world, in *her* world.

Mrs Peabody's sister was caught up in a doodlebug, and her leg got crushed by a wall, but Mrs Peabody said she was surprised she got away with that. Kenny's father-in-law was killed in the street, along with his dog.

'Send your children away,' the newspaper boy shouted.

'I have, I have,' Jean wanted to shout back.

They kept the buses going. They kept London moving. Sometimes there was that jolt – you'd look up at the sky, heart ticking like crazy. And then the silence. The clicking noise. Then the horror of the explosion.

Did it have your name on it? If it did, the last thing that Jean would think would be: *Valerie, I know you don't believe it, but I really do love you.*

52

Valerie

Paul and Valerie were sitting in the graveyard. Paul had just got back from school. He always asked how her mother was – he had such good manners.

'She doesn't care what I'm doing...' Valerie snipped. She didn't know if that was true, but it *felt* true. The neighbour in the suit with the shiny hair was stuck in her head. There was something going on there, she knew it, but she didn't know what. When she'd asked her mother again, on the telephone, Jean had said, 'Can't women have friends?' And Valerie had thought to herself, Women *can, but you can't*.

They were sitting by the grave of a William Jacob Feather, who had died in 1844. Paul said it was his favourite. Valerie preferred the one next to it: Edna Feather's had a carving of a cherub blowing a trumpet.

'How do you mean?' Paul offered her some marzipan.

Valerie didn't know what she meant. 'She's having a good time in London. She's got her "friends". She has lots of men chasing her, she doesn't want me there.'

She didn't say that she didn't want to be there either, since that wasn't the point.

'It's still dangerous there, isn't that why?'

'She carries on as normal...' Valerie said airily. When she compared her mother to Lydia's or Francine's or even Morwenna's, Jean did not come out favourably.

'Is she still on the buses?'

'I suppose,' Valerie said. 'She likes it. God knows why!'

Paul took his sketchbook out of his bag. Valerie held still like he might draw her, but he didn't draw people. She'd asked him for a bee once too, and he'd refused – he only did fish or landscapes, that was it.

'I like *your* mum,' she said presently. Mrs Howard was her favourite of all.

His pencil scratched the paper like an itch. 'Yeah, she's not bad.'

After a while, he tore a page from his book. He *had* done her a bee – a squiggly little one – just for her.

The next time Paul was back from school was some three months later, and they went to the river. They took a picnic of Scotch egg, liquorice and carrots. The evening before, Lydia had asked to come and Mrs Howard had said they should take her, but they connived to leave early, when she was still asleep. Valerie felt bad about this, but not bad enough to wake her up.

Paul took off his clothes and went swimming in his pants. Valerie got out her *Radio Times* magazine, but, even though she loved to read the wireless listings, she kept reading the same sentence over again.

He stood over her, his head dripping water crystals, and she didn't know where to look.

'Won't you come in? It's fantastic!'

Valerie had her monthlies and, even if she hadn't, she didn't have a bathing suit, and, even if she had, she couldn't imagine stripping off in front of Paul. He had grown up recently.

He threw out his arms like Jesus on the cross and droplets of water spilled from him. The sun glinted in his face, and he looked perfect. 'We could swim out to that fallen tree?'

'I'm trying to read,' she said primly.

It was so hot; he went back into the water a second time. Valerie watched him walk away from her, the protruding bones of his shoulders, the fair hairs on his arms, and she bit her lip. She had to stop herself from calling out, 'Come back...'

This wasn't right. She wouldn't, couldn't think like this. What would Mrs Howard think? It would be letting her down. It would be letting *everyone* down. She went back to picking out wireless shows in her magazine, ignoring both the splashes and Paul shrieking how glorious it was.

When they got back home, Lydia didn't say anything, but Mrs Howard scolded Paul loudly – and Valerie knew it was intended for her too: 'Don't leave people out... How would you like it?'

Valerie had a new favourite wireless show. It was called *The Brains Trust*, it had a jaunty theme tune and it consisted of a panel of clever-clogs who answered questions sent in by the public. The clever-clogs were professors and all of them were men.

She would listen to it with Mrs Howard, who, even when there had been a detailed explanation, would invariably scrunch up her face and complain, 'I wish they would tell us more.' Valerie laughed; she wished they would tell less!

Mrs Howard encouraged Valerie to write in, so they composed questions about bees, dogs and chemical elements. None were broadcast; they couldn't work out why.

Unbeknown to Mrs Howard, Valerie also sent off two more

questions – 'How do you know if a boy loves you?' and 'How do you know if you are in love?'

Yet both of these were also never aired. Valerie was half relieved, half infuriated.

53

AUTUMN 1944

Jean

Jean's life was busy. There was Tony. There were the buses. There were health check-ups, there were letters and occasional visits to Valerie.

Jean had missed out on some of Valerie's childhood years, but she told herself it was right she had missed out. She had got used to Valerie being in Somerset. She had a lot to be grateful for, she kept reminding herself. Some children had been evacuated as far away as Australia, and they *definitely* wouldn't be back until the end of the war and there were no visits or telephone calls.

'Somerset is nothing,' people said, 'you try Canada!'

Other times though, it didn't feel like nothing, and Bumble Cottage felt like a world away in many ways, not only in distance.

She should have got her home, she would think in the middle of the night. That had been her biggest mistake. Her greatest regret. No, she knew, there were other mistakes and regrets too. And the case wasn't cut and dried – she was right to keep Valerie away.

One Friday evening, Tony came to the house at 67 Romberg Road with a sheepish expression on his face. He looked so down in the dumps, Jean wondered if he was ill. He handed her some stockings that he'd managed to get from God knows where.

'Don't say I never get you anything,' he said, but he didn't laugh like he usually did.

'I'd never say that.' She kissed him but he was too preoccupied to kiss her back.

Tony was so peculiar that evening she wondered if he was having a stroke. What would she do if he was? Probably run into the street and call for help. And who would be able to help? There weren't many left who would. It wasn't the community it used to be. Everyone was flung far and wide like sheets of newspaper in the wind.

Tony denied anything was wrong until he next came round, a week later.

'What is it?' she asked, heart in mouth.

'Pauline and the children are coming back.'

'Now?! What about the doodlebugs?'

'Pauline seems to think it's nearly over...'

Jean trembled. 'And so... do you want to reconcile with her?'

'It's not like that,' he said suddenly.

She spun round. 'How do you mean?'

'We didn't split up,' he admitted. 'They were evacuated.' For once, he blushed, and she recoiled from him.

He'd made her believe they'd left him. He'd made her think that Pauline didn't want to be married to him any more. And yet, maybe she had chosen to ignore the truth. She knew he still got letters from Pauline but preferred to believe they were just about the boys. She knew he visited her, but she'd assumed again it was for the boys. He'd lied to her, but she'd let herself be lied to. She'd gone along with it.

'So...'

'So... I'll still pop in and see you now and then,' Tony said huskily.

'I'm not sure that's a good idea,' Jean said, and then, after he didn't say anything, she said, 'When are they coming home?'

'Tonight.'

'Tonight?!' *Good grief!* 'How long have you known?'

Tony grimaced. 'A while,' he said.

Jean collected herself. 'So... it's over.'

'It doesn't have to be...' he said in his wheedling voice.

'I'm not doing that again,' she said, but as she said it she saw that was exactly what she had been doing for the past couple of years. Mistress. Bit on the side. Whatever you wanted to call it. The only one she had been kidding was herself.

Yet, there was another aspect to this. If – and it was a big if – the war was over soon, then she would have Valerie back, and she would have had to split with Tony anyway. She didn't imagine Valerie would sit well with Tony. They had gone past that stage. This was the best possible outcome, she suddenly knew it.

'It's goodbye then,' he said, and Jean nodded. She realised she wasn't a complete doormat. She was merely half a doormat. *Perhaps a doorstopper?* she smirked to herself. *A doorknob?*

'What are you smiling at?' he asked abruptly. And she automatically changed her expression to one of sadness.

'I will miss you,' she said. And she suddenly thought, *please, Valerie, I hope your life and your relationships are better than mine. I'm sorry I didn't set you a good example.*

Now the surprise was wearing off it was replaced by a tremendous relief. Tony had been there when she was at her loneliest but there was no future in it.

And now she didn't have to tell Valerie anything about him.

For a while, the feeling of relief about that obliterated anything else. She and Valerie could get on with their lives. Tony might not be dead, but he was dead to them, and perhaps that was exactly how it should be.

Jean had got away with it, just.

Tony asked her to pack the few bits he kept at her house, and she did. It wasn't like Pauline was going to.

He put on his hat before he kissed her on the cheek. She was shaking.

'Thanks for everything, Jean.'

54

Valerie

Lydia never talked much about her family. When she was with Valerie, all she wanted to talk about was the boyfriends she had at school: Seth or Dennis or Patrick. Valerie couldn't keep up. It reminded her of Jean, but then Lydia was only young. It was excusable at her age.

'They're not really boyfriends,' Lydia said sheepishly. 'They're boys who are friends.'

'I'm sure they're in love with you,' Valerie teased. How couldn't they be? Lydia was a doll, an absolute doll. She was so shiny; it was hard to look at her sometimes.

Lydia lifted her shoulders and then dropped them. 'Maybe, some of them.'

Recently, there was a lot of talk on the wireless about how the generations didn't understand each other. Valerie and Lydia were only two years apart, yet they were like two parallel lines, never finding things to agree on.

Valerie always remembered that moment in the church hall

when she was asked, 'Are you sisters?' and she'd replied, 'Not *actual* sisters.'

That phrase sometimes haunted her. The precociousness. The heartlessness. She felt like Peter denying Jesus. Was that what had damaged them? A throwaway remark like that? She had always got on better with Francine. She should try harder with Lydia, she thought, but it never felt like a priority.

It was Valerie's sixteenth birthday soon, and she sent a card inviting her mother to afternoon tea. Paul wouldn't be there – inter-schools tennis tournament – but Morwenna would. Valerie didn't expect her mother would make it – it was far away simply for a tea-party – but her mother replied that 'Wild horses won't keep me away...'.

But on the afternoon of the tea-party, she didn't come. Valerie pretended she didn't care but she was incandescent. Morwenna and Mrs Howard exchanged worried glances.

She had her monthlies and that made her feel worse. Once again, they were so heavy and painful she felt as though she was being pulled into the earth. She had planned to ask her mother about them – *are they always this awful?* – but where was she?

Swinging around the pole of the number 19, that was where.

The next day, Valerie still hadn't cooled down. Her mother had let her down again. She couldn't believe it and yet she could. She was playing snakes and ladders by herself – and it was every bit as frustrating as her mother was.

There was only chamber music on the wireless. Paul was still away, probably charming lady tennis players, and Lydia was out somewhere with the dog. Valerie played both the blue counter and the red counter. The red counter was winning by seven squares.

She went over her mother's behaviour in her mind. She had always been so happy to send Valerie away – unlike the Frouds and the Salts. She was always 'having a good time' in London, full of the joys.

Bastard, remembered Valerie. She had recently found out what it meant, although she still hadn't found out why Mrs Woods' son had said it to her.

When she had finished with her volunteer group, Mrs Howard tried to placate her. She used the same tone she used with T.Rex if he was whining to go outside at night: 'I'm sure there was a good reason, Valerie.' And 'It's a pity about the distance and the expense...'

But there wasn't a good reason, there was never a good reason.

A telegram came, but it didn't arrive until three days after her birthday and if anything, it made Valerie even more annoyed.

So sorry. Poorly. Will explain soon.

More excuses. More slipping down snakes, thought Valerie. *It's the Brylcreem man in the suit*, she deduced, anger surging through her. Whoever he was, he was the reason Mum didn't want to see her – he was probably the reason she hadn't taken her back to London that time. It was nothing to do with her 'doing so well in Somerset', it was all about this fella.

Mrs Howard gave her a list of jobs that needed doing, since she was in such a funk.

Valerie checked on the chickens. She fed the ducks. She

mowed the lawn. The physical activity helped change her mood but not her resolve. She wouldn't call Jean 'Mum' any more. She would only call her Jean. *Jean* had let her down again.

55

Jean

Jean never got away with anything – what on earth had she been thinking, tempting fate like that? She had the rottenest luck in the world. There was no other explanation for it. If you added up the number of calamities that befell her, she'd be way ahead of the pack. Everything went from bad to worse; yet, this time, it was the speed of the descent that made it remarkable.

Her menses were late.

She couldn't give up work now. Cleaning was a living, but buses could be a career. It wasn't only the salary either. She'd miss the aisle, the stairs, the passengers, the road, the smell of the diesel, the spring in her step. She'd miss the feeling that she – dunce Jean Hardman – was keeping London moving.

And then there was Valerie. As if she'd ever forgive her if she suddenly produced a bundle: 'Ta da, it's your baby brother/sister!' They'd never be close again.

. . .

Thank heavens for Mrs Peabody. Not only had she found a brain doctor for Perry who, after the accident, was too shaky to drive any more, but now she found a telephone number for Jean; a friend of a friend of a friend had used her.

'It's not pleasant,' Mrs Peabody whispered and, a few seconds later, 'Is there no alternative?'

The next day, she even said, 'There are women out there who would love to take care of a baby...'

Jean shivered. She couldn't disappear for nine months. The bus company wouldn't keep her job open. She had no savings, nothing. Everything went on the lodgings, or train fare, or the extras. Even if at best she was only two or three months out of work, it was impossible. She had nothing to fall back on.

Jean's fingers were trembling as she dialled the telephone number from the phone box. What if someone overheard? What if the switchboard operator suspected – could she be reported? But the person who answered spoke in code worthy of the War Office. They knew what she meant without her spelling it out.

She was told an address and given a date, but it was a full month away. Jean wanted to claw at the waistband of her skirt. Get it out of her. NOW. She'd show soon, they said that about the second one.

The second one? It made her mouth dry.

'I need to come sooner.' She would walk there now if they'd let her.

'We're rushed off our feet. Everyone is living like there's no tomorrow,' the voice on the telephone said bitterly. 'But there *is* a tomorrow and we're left picking up the pieces.'

'Please,' Jean said, ignoring her tone. 'I need help sooner. Today.'

She kept having visions of baby Joe. His tiny hand. The way he laughed with his eyes on you, and you wondered if he'd ever stop. The tiny curl of hair that, however much you smoothed it, would not go down.

But there was no budging. Jean knew it. She was a woman who never got away with anything.

She still had two weeks to wait. Two weeks and she wanted the time to fly. She wanted Nazis to invade and put an end to her. She wanted to be gassed or shot or exploded. She wanted to be put out of her misery so that no one would know what a stupid thing she'd done. It had been five minutes of madness. Less than five. Dear God.

She tried to think of options, only it was hard to think; she felt fuzzy and overtired and blurry. Her body was rebelling against her, her body had its own ideas.

She clipped tickets and each clip seemed to take her closer to her doom. Her regular passengers got on and off. One waved a hand in front of her face and said to his friend: 'Our clippie is away with the fairies.'

Mrs Peabody said she looked peaky and recommended sugary tea. 'Are you sure?' she kept saying. 'And he won't help you, Valerie's dad?'

Tony? She wouldn't see him ever again, she resolved.

One of the passengers said she looked like she needed feeding up. Another said she looked like she'd eaten something that disagreed with her.

Another was reading a newspaper and he ignored her, and it gave her such a fury that she nearly punched through the sheet.

One afternoon the bus got a flat tyre, and everyone trooped off laughing and making fun of Albert the driver. It would have been jolly, only Jean was thinking, *God help me*.

If only she could get a puncture and it all be over.

Everything she worked so hard for gone in an instant.

She stood on the top deck of the bus wondering if she had the courage to throw herself down the stairs. She didn't want to die, she didn't. She just wanted this over.

'What's the matter with you?' Kenny asked suspiciously. And in front of everyone. 'You're not in the family way, are you, Miss Hardman?'

'Don't be so ridiculous, Kenny!'

He kept going on about it. So much so, she asked Mrs Peabody if she could go with another driver.

'He's only having fun,' Mrs Peabody said, but Jean remembered how he caused accidents and then moved off without caring about the havoc he'd wreaked. It seemed she was surrounded by men like that.

56

Jean

They called it a procedure. And then afterwards, they told her to go home to rest. If anything felt wrong, Jean was to go to the hospital – but, of course, she wasn't to mention what had happened or how it happened, or where or anything that would give them away.

How will I know if it feels especially wrong? wondered Jean, because everything felt wrong. And there was no way she would go to the hospital again, not unless she was at death's door and probably not even then.

She hadn't thought she'd need the rest, but she did. She was exhausted, aching, relieved. Disgusted.

The blood kept coming. She put the old rags in a bowl by her bed to soak and went to sleep but fitfully. God, she wished Valerie were here. She imagined her sleeping next to her, curled up. Her hair askew. Or giggling: 'Mummy, you were snoring again. I thought someone was playing the trumpet.' Or 'Teacher said we're like Tweedledum and Tweedledee – is that good or bad?'

'Very good! What would a Tweedledum be without a Tweedledee?'

Valerie had liked that.

The rest of the rooms in the house were empty, eerily so. It was never like this before the war. She missed that life – the three families. It wasn't perfect at the time but what was? Looking back, it was idyllic. She had never felt so alone. Even the rat of her nightmares had abandoned her. Now she dreamed of screaming babies and bomb craters and the woman who jumped in front of buses.

Some time later, her temperature spiked. And night became day, and the pain grew and all she could think about was the agony that was her body fighting itself. And she worried her heart would give out. She dreamed she and Valerie were on the same bus and Valerie kept wanting to get off and Jean was shouting at her to wait, wait for the bell.

A face swam in front of her. Jean beamed at it. At last she was back home. 'Valerie, darling? How are you?'

The war was over and they would be mother and daughter again. Finally.

No. It was Mrs Froud and she was talking in a slow voice. Jean felt like she was underwater or floating through the air. That was it, she was untethered again. Why hadn't she stuck to that nice Richard Carrington? He treated people with respect.

Mrs Froud was talking about getting her to hospital.

'A cup of tea will do me,' Jean protested. 'I'll be right as rain.'

There were a billion reasons not to go into the hospital – what could they do anyway? The deed was done – her guilt was sealed; but Mrs Froud didn't hear. Her words were awfully dramatic, like Jean was in an emergency in a film, not real life. Mrs Froud wrapped a coat around her and supported her outside. Jean tried to tell her she needed outdoor shoes not house slippers but Mrs Froud didn't hear that either.

The taxi driver didn't make them pay. He wanted them out of his cab. There was a lot of blood now. They staggered forward, a losing three-legged team. Jean kept apologising and apologising as they went, Mrs Froud telling her she had nothing to apologise for.

A nurse with tidy hair met them at the hospital entrance. How did she get her hair like that, Jean wanted to ask?

'What's she done?' the nurse snapped.

Jean tried to speak but no words came. She was doubled over again, useless as a raggy doll.

'Nothing!' said Mrs Froud.

The nurse gave them both a withering look. 'You're lucky it's me you're talking to, not the doctor, not the matron.'

Jean heard Mrs Froud protesting and the nurse snap back: 'Don't play funny with me.'

Funny, thought Jean before she blacked out.

She was operated on and days and nights passed. Was she treated worse than the other women on the ward? Maybe. But a sense of disbelief shielded her from what was going on around her. Jean was separated from her body. She was not in the bed; in the echoey Edwardian ward, she was far away. She was apart. She was severed. Untethered.

'I need to get back to work,' she told anyone who paused at the end of the bed.

'You'll wait until you're better,' said one.

'Lady of the night, are you?' said another.

She had a vague feeling that she had to be somewhere – not only work, but somewhere she couldn't remember.

They told her to go home eventually. She no longer had a womb.

She sat on her bed, slowly dressing herself. She felt useless. She could have done with Mrs Froud, somebody, anybody, to help her but Mrs Froud had gone off again, and no one else even looked at her. She couldn't put her own shoes on, how the hell would she ever get to Somerset?

'You've got to keep going, you have your daughter to live for,' Mrs Peabody said, not unkindly, when Jean made it to the bus station.

Did she have her daughter though? Really? Suddenly, Jean recalled the somewhere she was meant to be and felt her heart break all over again. Valerie's birthday, of course. She had missed it again.

57

Valerie

Mrs Howard said she'd take Valerie to look around a radio station as a post-birthday treat. Lydia became pouty, so Mrs Howard said she would take Lydia somewhere she liked too. Kennels probably.

Valerie was still feeling cross. Her mother had abandoned her, she kept telling herself. She had made up some cock and bull story about being ill, but it was more likely she was gallivanting around on the number 16 or whatever number it was now. So Valerie was distracted when an upright man greeted them formally at the entrance of a red-brick building in Bristol city centre. His name was Mr Fairweather and, like a lot of men nowadays, he walked with the help of a stick. Mrs Howard bowed out, saying, 'I'll leave you to it.'

After she'd gone, Mr Fairweather relaxed a little. 'Your mother used to be a theatre director before the war. Everyone has heard of her.'

'She still does, small plays and stuff for the war effort.'

'Wow, I must come along.'

'It's only amateurish.'

Valerie should have explained that Mrs Howard wasn't her mum, and she spent the rest of the visit wishing she had. In the studio, they were recording an interview with a local cricket team. And then a local talked about his stamp collection and then it was the news. Mr Fairweather gave her some liquorice left behind by the stamp collector and a stack of old copies of her favourite magazine, the *Radio Times*.

And then it was *It's That Man Again*. Mr Fairweather grinned at her – 'twerps' – and she returned the smile. This was a language she understood.

He was impressed. 'You know it?'

She said, 'Know it? I love it!'

And he told her, incredibly, that he'd worked on series two and what a show it was, what a cast.

'You can't imagine the creative talent in the studio!'

Valerie nodded eagerly and would have talked about it all afternoon, only she was advised Mrs Howard had returned and was waiting for her in the lobby.

But something special had already happened, even before that conversation. Until then, she hadn't considered the show-makers, the producers, the editors, and all the people who had gone into making her favourite shows, but that was the day she saw for the first time that not only was working in wireless a job, but it might be the job for her.

58

SPRING 1945

Jean

Unfortunately, it was several months before Jean felt strong enough to take the train to the West Country. She had managed to get back to work, to raise a faint smile at the 'ding-dings' and the passengers – the nurses, the nuns and the men with injuries – but in the evenings she went straight to bed. It was hard to get up in the mornings too.

All the way there, she hoped Valerie would be affectionate with her. She wished Valerie was the ten-year-old girl she had been before she left, a child full of questions for her mother and wonder at the world. Jean remembered Valerie sharing stories of the naughty children at school and how she always had a wise interpretation: This boy was sad because he was cold. This child was angry because they were tired. Could Valerie not have a wise interpretation for her? Jean knew she wasn't a bad mother. Her heart was in the right place. She'd heard of loads of mothers far worse than she was, yet still their children seemed to love them. It was a puzzle.

Valerie met her at the railway station, but she was grim-faced and her voice clipped. Jean was being punished; she realised this and she apologised, but Valerie insisted there was nothing to apologise for – although her manner said the opposite.

Jean had gifts: a copy of *Gone with the Wind*, a pair of stockings and a small Victoria sponge made with help from Mrs Peabody's ration. Valerie looked over them coldly and then said, 'Thank you,' in a dead voice. 'What do you want to do?' she added.

'Whatever you like!' Jean said. She wanted to be amenable, she wanted to be no trouble.

'Don't care.'

'How about the churchyard?' Jean suggested. 'You like it there...'

On the way, they found Lydia lying next to her dog. The dog was chewing a piece of wood.

'The dog shouldn't have that,' said Jean, but as both girls stared blankly at her, she backed down. 'What do I know?'

Valerie leafed through her book. It made Jean feel excluded and she regretted bringing it. She chatted about the buses but she sounded inane even to herself. Valerie's responses were mostly monosyllabic.

'Now, shall we find Mrs Howard and thank her for looking after you?' Jean eventually asked, trying to feign a brightness she wasn't feeling.

'She doesn't need thanking,' Valerie answered, still in a sulk.

'Of course, she does,' Jean insisted. She may not be perfect, but she would never let her manners slide.

At Bumble Cottage, Jean was convinced Mrs Howard felt sorry for her. She could see it in her eyes. She, Jean, was a failure of a parent and Jean hated it. Who was this lady, who had everything, to make her feel like that?

After some conversation about the weather and the war – both considered to be 'on the turn' – Mrs Howard excused herself. Valerie made tea. Suddenly she scowled at Jean and out it poured.

'You said you'd come for my birthday.'

'I wasn't well, Valerie,' Jean said, staring at her cup. 'Did Lydia say anything?'

'Lydia, no, why?' Valerie's eyes were huge.

'No reason.'

'You said you would visit every few weeks, you haven't kept a single promise.'

They weren't promise-promises, thought Jean desperately, they were hopes. They weren't fixed, they were targets. She knew this wouldn't go down well though.

'Sorry, Valerie,' she whispered.

Her daughter stared at her for what felt like a long time, and then she softened.

'I suppose you're here now.'

I am...'

After her tea Valerie seemed to relax and, when she relaxed, she talked. She talked about Morwenna. She talked about school. She talked about Paul, who was away at a different school – and that was when Jean made another mistake.

'You like this boy, don't you?' she teased. It was a throwaway observation, to show that she was listening.

'We're not all like you, you know,' Valerie said coldly.

'I don't know what you mean,' answered Jean.

If she was at home, she might have put Valerie over her knee or chased her around with a tea towel, but she was here in this countryside cottage where she didn't know how anything worked. And Val was so much older now. Sixteen! And an old sixteen at that. Jean hadn't disciplined her for years. She had missed out on so much. She had no idea how to parent her now. Did Valerie even need Jean any more?

Valerie walked her back to the station. At the ticket office, she said, 'I'm not sure where I want to be – you know, once the war is over,' and it was like a dagger to Jean's heart.

'You can't stay here,' Jean said, laughing, before realising that might be exactly what Valerie was thinking. 'You'll need to work and...'

'I know that!' Valerie said so loudly the stationmaster looked up, surprised. Jean chewed her lip. At least she hadn't told Valerie about Tony. She realised that would probably have sent her over the edge.

Jean wanted to say something affectionate, but the words wouldn't come. She didn't know how. Finally, she managed. 'I will miss you, Vally,' and her girl looked at her with tears in her eyes, or it might have been the wind, and said, 'Same.'

The doodlebug attacks turned out to be short-lived – they were a terrible last hurrah, like a death rattle, Jean supposed, like her and Tony. You could take nothing for granted, but the feeling was widespread – the war was finally coming to a close, the Nazis were defeated.

Everyone was making plans, plans for the first time in years!

Maybe not everyone. The ones with family dead, or missing, or in some camp somewhere, they were still focusing on surviving each day. But most people were starting to look forward.

Jean had kept Valerie away in safety for six years. Six Christmases, six birthdays? Surely she deserved *something*?

Other parents had got their children home – what was wrong with her that she hadn't? No one got what they deserved any more.

She couldn't understand it. She had kept to the rules. She had done everything she was told. She had done her best to avoid distress. She had recognised that Valerie would be better off at Bumble Cottage. She had put her first. She had thrown herself into the war effort. She had protected her child. She had kept her safe.

She had done it all right; yet somehow it had all turned to dust.

It occurred to Jean that she had been in competition with this other woman, this Mrs Howard all along, yet she didn't even know it. Had she realised earlier, perhaps she would have been able to pull out all the stops, done anything to win the prize of her daughter. No, Jean knew, even if she had been aware earlier, she would never have been able to compete. She had been out-done.

She saw some other returned children from when Valerie was at school; Mary Kittle, reunited with her mother, now wore high heels and earrings; Stanley was back with his granddad and even had the beginning of a moustache just like him.

But of their three, the children from 67 Romberg Road; three went away in Operation Pied Piper, Lydia, Francine and her Valerie, and, as yet, none of them had come home.

59

SUMMER 1945

Valerie

The land girls left, jiggling about on the back of the farmer's truck. The village was planning a victory party, but the land girls had decided to leave before. Red-haired Prue was raring to start her job in her father's window firm. 'He's done awfully well out of the war,' she said, biting her lip guiltily.

Tall Minnie was going to secretarial college – 'It was that or be a nurse.' She shrugged her narrow shoulders. Valerie could imagine her being a nurse because she was comforting, but Minnie explained she'd tossed a coin; heads was secretarial college and heads won three out of five times.

Lydia clutched T.Rex to her and the girls made a big fuss of both of them. Lydia was perhaps closer to the land girls than Valerie had realised, or maybe she was just enjoying being the centre of things.

Valerie was surprised when Prue took her by the shoulders and said, 'You're going to go on to do great things, Miss Hardman.'

'Leave her alone,' Minnie said but in a friendly way. 'You do what you like, Val.'

Paul was always away at school, or doing his sports, or at his friends', or preparing for university. To go straight from school to university despite the war was lucky – now if he could get out of national service, he said, he'd be a happy man!

He would come back for the victory party though, and Valerie felt this party was going to be special. It would be. It had to be. She used to dream about them being a family, but that wasn't what she imagined any more. She didn't want him to be her brother...

She sensed he was going to declare himself to her. She imagined him getting down on one knee. Paul had always been the romantic sort. When they listened to love stories on the wireless, he wasn't scornful like Valerie and sometimes she caught him wiping away tears.

And if he didn't declare himself soon, Valerie told herself, she would have to say something herself.

The evening after the land girls left, Mrs Howard said she wanted to talk to Valerie about her future. Valerie went into the drawing room, that favourite room with its swishy curtains, shelves of books and coffee tables that you had to dodge.

The land girls had given Mrs Howard a tapestry they'd made saying 'Home Sweet Home', and it was hanging off one of the shelves. Valerie knew from the way Mrs Howard kept saying, 'How considerate' that she didn't like it, but it was thoughtful and Valerie realised she should get something for Mrs Howard and maybe Paul too and she started wondering what.

Mrs Howard patted next to her on the sofa. 'What are your plans for work, Valerie?'

Valerie flushed. She had longed to speak about this for a while now, longed to be asked, yet now it was her chance a cat had stolen her tongue.

'It sounds stupid...' she began shyly.

'Go on,' Mrs Howard encouraged her.

'Maybe I would like to work in wireless.'

Mrs Howard thumped the nearest table, and the three books and one shepherdess ornament on it jumped. Valerie felt like jumping too.

'Mrs Howard?'

'As I thought!'

'Oh?' Valerie couldn't stop smiling. This wasn't stupid? This was actually a possibility?

'So I had an idea...' Mrs Howard said, bubbling over with enthusiasm. 'I discussed it with Mr Fairweather – do you remember, you met him?'

The man from the studio in Bristol who had worked on *It's That Man Again*? Yes, of course she did.

'And he said they'd be happy to have you on the front desk there. You'd be a receptionist!'

'Gosh!' said Valerie.

Mrs Howard hesitated for one moment and then added, 'There's more! He told me about a scheme for young people at the BBC – in London. He thinks you should apply there.'

'Golly – in London?'

'It could be interesting.'

'This is amazing,' said Valerie.

'We may as well use our connections for the best,' Mrs Howard said, smiling.

'And the other good thing about that is – you'd be able to live with your mother again,' she continued. 'I imagine Mrs Hardman would be over the moon to have you back.'

Valerie nodded. 'Yes, I expect she would.'

Valerie knew her mother wanted her back in London. She made it obvious when she wrote things like: 'When you're home, we'll go to the cinema again. Do you remember we used to go?'

Jean made it sound like it was a regular occurrence!

Or: 'I'm going to bake cakes and we can buy some material from the market and I'll make you a nice dress!'

As if Valerie was interested in clothes!

Or: 'Perhaps we could get you a little job on the buses?'

It was probably that line that did it for Valerie. How little her mother knew her! *Get a little job on the buses? Good grief!*

It wasn't that Valerie didn't think being a clippie wasn't a good job – all right, she didn't; but it wasn't only that – it wasn't Valerie's world. Surely Jean had worked that out by now?

But this... This opportunity was different. This was a chance in a million.

Later that evening, as Valerie was going to her room, Lydia called out for her to come into hers. She was brushing her hair at the dressing table. Three Lydias reflected at her. T.Rex was snoozing at her feet.

'Have you had "the conversation" with Mrs H yet?' Lydia asked.

There was something about the way Lydia said this that made Valerie feel less special than she had earlier on. But naturally Mrs Howard had had a chat with Lydia too – why wouldn't she?

'About?'

'The future. One's future. We are not shirkers!' Lydia said in a poor imitation of Mrs Howard that made Valerie's head hurt.

'I did.'

'What did you say?' Lydia asked.

'I told her I want to work in wireless. What did you say?'

'I said I want to marry a nice man and have lots of children...'

'Ah,' Valerie said, not sure what the correct response to that was.

Lydia chuckled. 'I didn't really. I said I'd like to work at the kennels.'

'That's great,' Valerie said. This she hadn't known. She should have known. O-kay, she wasn't an *actual* sister to Lydia but she should have known that about her at least. Recently she had realised how little she knew about Lydia's inner world.

She had been pleased when she first arrived that they didn't have to share a bedroom. Now she wondered if that had pushed them further apart.

'Of course, I don't really want to work in kennels,' Lydia said, still laughing at Valerie's confusion. 'But I had to say something. If I said I wanted to marry and have children, it would have gone down like a bag of cold sick.'

'Oh?' said Valerie. 'I don't think so...'

'She wouldn't approve. You know that. She wants us all to be "trailblazers" like her. Like you.'

Valerie pulled a face, but she loved the idea of being a trailblazer. She dearly hoped she could make Mrs Howard proud. She would go for the job at the BBC – of course she would. And although she wouldn't take it simply to make her mother happy, the fact that it would was a nice side-effect of the proposition too.

A few days later, Valerie asked Lydia to join her for a walk. Recent events had made her feel she ought to make more of an effort with her old friend – especially since she might be moving away soon. Lydia looked mystified but agreed.

She was accompanied not only by T.Rex but by another dog, Nellie, who she was looking after. They walked on the coastal path.

Valerie remembered how even a walk in the countryside used to make her nervous; now it was one of her happy places. Of course, there were animals in London – foxes and rats, cockroaches and mice – but you seemed to spend your days trying to get rid of them or trying to control them. Here, you lived among them. Lydia was probably better at living among them than she was. She wandered ahead after the dogs. Occasionally she circled back and said things like, 'Maurice keeps asking me to be his girl but he's far too immature— NELLIE! Stop sniffing, he doesn't want to play!'

A man walked past them but then, a few seconds later, doubled back: 'I'm sorry to disturb but do I know you?'

Valerie squinted at him. The sun was behind him so it was hard to see. She couldn't place him but then, as his face came into focus, she did.

'It's you! You fixed the wireless for me!'

The man was thinner than he used to be; he was all cheekbones, raw features, and his coat hung off him. The demob suit wasn't a great fit, but he had the same kind eyes. They shook hands and he wouldn't let go.

'You look the same, older of course, but the same,' he said with a wry smile.

'You too.' Valerie couldn't help but think he looked like he'd had a terrible war. 'I met your wife...'

'Did you?' he asked. 'I didn't know.'

'She was also very kind to me.'

What a dear couple they were. Tears sprang to her eyes at the memory.

'I always wondered how you were...' he continued.

She didn't know what to say to that.

'I should have done more,' he said. 'I knew you were unhappy. I should have reported it to someone, I regret it.'

'No,' she said. 'You did the greatest thing. I couldn't bear the silence and you helped me.'

'What happened? Why are you here? You didn't stay all these years with Mrs Woods?' He looked horrified at the idea.

'No!' Valerie laughed. 'I moved into Bumble Cottage with Mrs Howard.'

He was visibly relieved and squeezed her arm again. 'A child far from home. That's what I called you when my wife asked where the fudge had gone! She told me off for that! Apparently she was saving it for a party.'

Valerie laughed, imagining the rosy-cheeked nurse giving him a talking-to.

'And your mum? – I remember you missed her terribly.'

Valerie felt emotional again, remembering how she missed home and her mum in those early days. What had happened between her and her mother? They used to be so close. Tweedledum and Tweedledee. Nothing that couldn't be fixed, she told herself. She thought of how meekly Jean behaved whenever she visited. It made her contemptuous – but it shouldn't have.

'She's well. She stayed in London throughout...'

'Throughout the Blitz? She must have nerves of steel. Bus work, wasn't it?'

What a memory. Whatever else had been affected, that hadn't. 'That's right.'

'Gruelling stuff, that,' he said. 'Not everybody's cup of tea during a war.'

'Maybe,' admitted Valerie.

Lydia had rejoined them and was gazing at him, biting her lip. The conversation was over anyway. It felt good – like a circle had been joined up – but there was no need for anything else. They said goodbye, a little awkwardly, and he walked off.

'Thank you,' she called after him. 'For everything!' He saluted her and winked.

She could feel Lydia's cool, appraising eyes on her.

'Who *was* that?' she asked breathlessly.

'An old friend,' said Valerie. She didn't want to tell the story of that period of desperation, certainly not to Lydia, who was never good at sympathy.

'He's good-looking. Like a character from a novel with dark secrets. Heathcliff, maybe'

'Heathcliff?' Valerie snorted. Lydia certainly noticed men a lot lately. 'He was generous to me.' *When no one else was*, she thought.

Lydia was pulling a face. 'He *likes* you.'

Sometimes, lovely Lydia – with her entourage of admirers – 'they're not all boyfriends' – made Valerie feel like the plainest woman in the West Country with her frumpy shoes, her functional spectacles and her obsession with the wireless.

Lydia continued, 'Valerie, I didn't know you had it in you!'

Valerie shrugged. She could have told Lydia about his equally compassionate wife, but she decided not to. Let Lydia think what she liked. She knew there was only one man she wanted to be interested in her like that.

60

Valerie

Valerie had decisions to make. Job decisions and love decisions. The job decision was the easier one. Receptionist in Bristol or BBC training scheme in London. If she got an offer from London, she would take it. And the love decision? Did Paul feel about her the way she felt about him – and should she say anything? He *seemed* to like her. Nowadays, when they unexpectedly crossed paths on the stairs, he pinkened, and it was like they were suddenly lost for words around each other. He would push irritably at his hair, swing his racket, or his jar of water, or whatever he was holding. He was painting a lot. He was fishing a lot. When he met her eye, he held it, and when he smiled, it was like she was the only person in the world.

Valerie finally had an inkling why that time, long ago in the church hall, Mrs Howard might not have wanted her to stay.

When Valerie next saw Paul, though, a couple of days after the walk with Lydia, he was in a terrible mood. Mrs Howard noticed: 'He's such a grouch sometimes,' she sighed. 'Don't let him get you down, Valerie.'

He had been fishing and Valerie enquired whether any fish had bitten, and he snapped at her: 'That's not the point...'

What other point of fishing was there?

Even Lydia raised her eyebrows at his attitude.

The day Valerie was going to London for her interview at the BBC, she, Mrs Howard and Lydia had a breakfast of boiled eggs and soldiers together – Paul's favourite; but he stayed upstairs.

When it was time to go, Mrs Howard called and called, then sent Lydia up to fetch him, but she thumped back down the stairs and said, 'He's not there, I don't know where he is.'

'I'll be back soon, anyway,' said Valerie, determined to be cheerful. She was not going to let her trip be ruined. He might be sulking because she was planning on leaving. She couldn't think of another explanation.

She had decided to see her mother first. It was time they became friends again.

61

SUMMER 1945

Jean

Jean had started calling Valerie, once a week or so. After she dialled, she kept her fingers tightly crossed that Valerie might say she was coming home finally. But she never did and Jean couldn't deny how happy her daughter was in Somerset, how she was thriving.

'How is everything?' she always asked brightly during their calls, biting back all the things she wanted to ask, and then one time Valerie said, 'Actually, there's a chance of a position in London.'

Jean could have fainted. This was perfect. She crossed the fingers of the hand not holding the phone. She'd have crossed her toes too if she could.

'That's wonderful! A shop? Or a bank, or a—?' she asked, but Valerie cut her off.

'In wireless. That's what I want to be doing. You must know that?' she asked incredulously.

'Of course,' Jean said quickly. She didn't know wireless was a job. There was so much she didn't know. There was so much she had to catch up on if she was ever going to keep up with her grown-up daughter. 'What does this mean?' she asked, full of hope. She couldn't help it.

'I have an interview, and if it works out, I'll come back to live with you – if you'll have me.'

'Of course I'll have you!' Jean yelped. She wanted to say, *I want nothing more! I'd give anything for that,* but instead she told herself, *be cool, be calm, Valerie doesn't like it when you lose your head.*

'You'll let me know when? I want to get things ready for you.'

'I will,' Valerie agreed, before telling Jean she had to run to help Mrs Howard with something.

As Jean put the telephone down she did a happy jig, ignoring the queue of people behind her.

My girl is coming home!

Back where she should be. Just the two of them again. Valerie, back in her house, back in her room, back in her life.

They had made it.

62

Valerie

On the train to Paddington, Valerie buried her face in her *Radio Times*. The war wasn't yet over, but it was only a matter of days. Mrs Howard said it was the storm before the calm.

In her carriage were two elderly women talking about their afflictions – hips, knees and shoulders – and food – rhubarb and plums, and how they were making the most of it.

At Reading, the women got off and soldiers got on. They didn't seem any older than her. They were talking about a mutual friend. They had thought he was unsuited to the army – one called him 'a nervy bugger' – but it turned out he was born to it. He was a sniper, and took out over twenty-five Nazi bastards. They asked her where she was going and when she told them a job interview, they wished her luck.

Valerie wasn't going straight to the BBC though. Jean had always said that she dreamed of finding Valerie on her bus, so Valerie had decided to surprise her. She felt surprisingly emotional about it. The conversation with the man who had fixed her wireless and given her hope had reminded her of how she'd once missed her mother, and that her work had been gruelling. She understood that, for all her silly stories, Jean had probably been making the best of it – and actually she'd done something remarkable.

But Valerie didn't know which number bus Jean was working on. Maybe she'd forgotten, or maybe she hadn't been told. She knew Jean was switched around a lot. She decided to go to the bus station first, since she was nearer to there than the house at Romberg Road anyway. She'd ask the number and then on it she would get. The last time she met her mother there unexpectedly, it hadn't been a success. This time would be different.

At the bus station, a man with dark curly hair was talking about women's legs to a young, uninterested woman smoking a cigarette. Instantly, Valerie didn't like him. He felt like someone Mrs Howard would call 'bad news'. Nevertheless, they were the only people there to ask.

'Do you know Mrs Hardman – the clippie?'

'I do,' he said, slowly looking her up and down. 'I know her intimately.'

The woman marched off like she was glad of the chance to go.

'Would you happen to know what number bus she's on today?'

'Here, have this while I think about it,' he said, holding out a flaccid sandwich.

'No, thank you,' Valerie said, but she smiled so he didn't think she was being nasty. You had to tread cautiously around men like him. Valerie might be a country bumpkin nowadays, but she remembered that. 'I'll find someone else...'

He surveyed her for a moment. 'Wait. You don't look like your mum. Or maybe you have the same hair?'

Valerie touched her flyaway hair self-consciously. 'People say that.'

A man and an older woman arrived, thank goodness. The man took off his hat and overcoat, hung it up, then scowled at them. 'She's too young for you.'

The first man laughed. A cat jumped up onto a bench and Valerie stroked it, glad of something to do.

'It's Mrs Hardman's daughter.'

'What the hell?' the second man said. 'I didn't know she had a daughter!'

Great, thought Valerie. *She didn't tell people about me. Only this fella.*

'I did,' said the first man, baring his teeth. 'There's a lot I know. You've been away in Dorset, haven't you?' he asked her.

'Somerset.'

'Beautiful part of the world.'

The woman shook her hand warmly. At least *she* seemed to know who Valerie was. 'Does Mum know you're coming?'

'Uh yes – I'm hoping to hop on her bus.'

The first man wouldn't leave her alone. 'How old are you now?'

'Sixteen.'

'Proper big girl...' The way he said it made her uneasy.

'Leave her alone, Kenny,' warned the woman.

'I'm a married man, Chief,' he said smugly. 'Just saying, she's growing up...'

'Do *you* know what bus Mrs Hardman is on?' Valerie persisted.

'Your mum will be on the 19.' He looked from the woman to her, then did a knowing smile at them both. 'Unless she's with your dad.'

The cat dropped down to the ground and slunk off.

'What?' Valerie's head was spinning.

The woman muttered a single warning – 'Kenny!' – under her breath, but he laughed.

Valerie persisted. 'What do you mean, "my dad"?'

The woman was shaking her head frantically. 'It's nothing.' She growled at Kenny, 'It's none of your business.'

Again, Kenny chuckled. 'I'm only trying to help. Mrs Hardman might be with Mr Hardman, that's all I'm saying.'

Her *dad*?

'She lived with him, didn't she, Mrs Peabody? Help me out here.'

Valerie was frozen to the spot. It wasn't possible; this was a ridiculous mistake by a ridiculous man. Yet deep down in some forgotten place, back in her ribs, in her sternum, or somewhere, Valerie had the rumbling knowledge it was true. It felt like rocks falling, starting off light and then smashing down.

Brylcreem man. The way he was so awkward. He had had left his pants in her house. Of course. Of bloody course.

She had been blind.

'What's the address?'

And the woman – Mrs Peabody presumably – said, 'I don't think she'll be there. It's not ongoing.'

Ongoing?

Valerie stared at her. She felt bold now. Bold or raging. 'Give me his address...'

Mrs Peabody fished around in a desk drawer and then gave it her on a piece of paper. Valerie knew the road – it wasn't far.

She left the bus station, but he – Kenny – was calling after her sarcastically, 'You're welcome' – she hadn't said thank you – and Mrs Peabody said, 'What did you go and do that for?' She was sure she heard him say in that nauseating faux-innocent voice, 'It's about time, Chief.'

She had been waiting for explanations, and here they were. Valerie felt like the wind had swept her off her feet. She told herself it still mightn't be true, but she knew it was, it was. She still didn't know which was worse, though – that that man was her father or that her mother had lied about him for all those years.

All her life.

63

Valerie

It was a terraced house with boarded-up windows. The door was maybe once racing green but now, like most of the doors, like most of the city, it was peeling and faded. Valerie counted to three, then knocked.

The man she had met in her house that one time before answered. He didn't look surprised to see her, but his face fell, and his hands shook. He shouted out to someone in the house, 'I'm popping out.' He walked her down the road, fast. He was good-looking in a way, but, like the door, faded and peeling. He also had surprisingly small feet, she thought, turned out like a duck's. He was *nothing* like her. They stopped at a bench outside a public house that had Union Jacks hung wonkily outside and a woman with one curler in the front of her hair tying up signs saying, VE Day Celebrations Here. She nodded and the curler bobbed up and down at Tony and she snapped, 'Usual?' like she was forbidden from using too many words, and he said, 'Please, and something for her.'

He lit a cigar. Through the pub doors Valerie could see a

large, framed picture of Winston Churchill, also smoking a cigar but that was probably the only thing they had in common.

'At last we meet properly!'

He was charming but she didn't like him one bit.

The woman brought out a pint of beer, and a shandy for her. She gripped it tightly, waiting until the woman had disappeared through the double doors before saying, 'I thought you were dead.'

'Your mum's a liar,' he said, supping up the foam.

Valerie didn't like that. She could call her mum a liar – but this man? No.

There was no avoiding his cigar smoke. It dominated. Everything about this seemed squalid and wrong. She wished she were in the countryside, or riverside with Paul, or at a performance with Mrs Howard, anywhere but here. What had her mother seen in him? It was hard to understand.

'So, now you know. Have you got anything you want to ask?'

'I don't suppose you were ever in a fire?'

He smirked. ''Fraid not.'

It got worse and worse.

'Were you ever married?' she persisted. At this he hesitated. Valerie understood.

'To each other, I mean?'

'It's a no to that too,' he said, smiling wryly.

Bastard, she thought. That's what they labelled children like her – and anyone they didn't like. The Nazis were bastards. Her life, her legitimacy was all a big joke to him. She didn't feel differently about herself upon this revelation – why should she? – but she did feel differently about her mother. And father. And the fact that the whole world had seemed to get it before she did.

'Did you know about me?'

'I did,' he admitted. 'But your mum and I agreed it was best I kept away.'

'It was her idea?' Valerie found this unconvincing.

'I thought it was for the best too,' he added.

She looked at the man she had thought was dead. The suit was smart yet shabby, and strained over his middle. His shoes were old yet polished. She realised she had no interest in him. None at all. He wasn't for her. She didn't want to find out his when his birthday was or his favourite pudding. She didn't care what he was like at school or what he had been doing throughout the war – she could guess it was nothing to shout about.

She had been tricked and she had been lied to. The family she thought she had, the stories she'd been told, all were built on a platform of deceit. The foundation of who she was had turned out to be not what she thought it was. There was no heroic dead father. There was a chap chomping on his cigar outside a run-down pub.

And who was to blame for this?

Valerie didn't know what to do next. The plan had been to stay at her mother's place, but now Jean was the last person she wanted to see. Even the thought of her made her shiver.

She walked up to her old school, her happy place. And there, by good fortune, was her old favourite teacher, Miss Beedle, slightly thinner and her face slightly more tired but otherwise looking the same. She was letting children out of the gates. There weren't many children but they were noisy, and they were small – Valerie couldn't remember being that small. Miss Beedle peered warily at Valerie, then, once all the chattering children had left, she rushed over.

'Look who's all grown up!'

Valerie let out a sob.

Thirty minutes later, they were in Miss Beedle's tiny flat – everywhere felt small after Bumble Cottage – and Valerie was

on a patterned settee, a mug of cocoa in one hand and a mono-
grammed handkerchief in the other. There were paintings
everywhere, some oil, some watercolour. Some were hung on
the walls or leant against the walls, some were even lying on the
floor. They were different sizes and on different surfaces and
they were mostly portraits, and they were nearly all of Miss
Beedle's fiancé. There he was: a close-up of a young man's face,
a face in profile, him in cricket jumper, him in uniform. It was
like she was trying to find him in the paintings.

'He died fighting in Italy.' She spoke about it bravely,
matter-of-factly, the way someone does when they've relayed
the same thing many times over.

'I'm sorry,' said Valerie, remembering Miss Beedle had been
looking forward to their lives together, the studio in the countryside.

'Thank you,' Miss Beedle said. 'Tell me, what happened to
you?'

Miss Beedle thought she should still go to the job interview.

'Opportunities like this don't come along often,' she said.
'You've done well to get it.'

'It's connections,' Valerie said flatly, but Miss Beedle
shushed her: 'I'm sure it's more than that.'

*How would you feel if you found out your fiancé was not
really dead and you had been lied to all along?* Valerie was going
to say, but realised that was too raw, not analogous, and
certainly not kind.

She spent the night on Miss Beedle's sofa, trying to think of
good things. She told Miss Beedle about Paul – 'He is an artist
too' – and of course Miss Beedle was well-disposed to another
artist! 'It sounds like he's a lovely young man, Valerie,' she said.

'He is!' Valerie responded breathlessly.

'You don't have to decide anything now,' Miss Beedle

suggested over breakfast, but Valerie would, Valerie had. She wasn't going to go to the interview. She wasn't coming back to London. She was outraged at what had been uncovered. She had been made a fool of – and that was unforgivable.

She would take the job in Bristol instead; it mightn't be ideal, but she would excel at it. It would keep her in the area she loved, with the people she loved, and the people who loved and respected her enough to tell her the truth.

64

Jean

Jean didn't even realise anything was amiss until she went to work the next Monday morning.

An old man had moved into the Salts' flat, a constant reminder of the fact they were no longer there. There was tarpaulin over the upstairs windows. The doorstep was cracked and Jean couldn't do much about that, but she could prepare the flat to make it Valerie's home again. She had been given another chance and she wasn't going to blow it this time.

Jean stacked up the toys; they were memories rather than playthings now. The dominos with the missing bits, the Pinocchio book and the puppet. She got herself a second-hand dress from the market and took it in. She hadn't got herself anything for a while and she didn't want Valerie to think she'd let herself go. She would even get her hair done, nearer the time.

It was almost like preparing for a date.

All weekend she cleaned, rearranged and wiped. She organised. She had taken down the blackout curtains and hung up the old ones. The flat looked a treat even if she said so herself. Everything seemed to unite in saying 'welcome home'.

The only time she went out, she went to the old man's flat and told him, 'If anyone knocks, make sure you answer the door!'

He was playing patience. His hands were swimming in liver spots. Jean could see that he could put the red queen on the black king, but he was another one who hated to be told.

In town, she expected to see Valerie strolling along – and every young woman was Valerie until they drew closer and then they weren't. None were as lovely as her girl!

She prepared a cosy for the teapot and readied to bake currant buns as soon as she had notice. She wished Valerie had let her know exactly when the interview was – she would have liked to meet her at Paddington – but Valerie had laughed, *not to worry*. Jean supposed she had her reasons.

At the bus station, Mrs Peabody was wrapped in a big shawl like a secret, and her husband said, 'You'd better tell her' as he walked out of the office.

'What?' Jean's smile vanished fast. And then Mrs Peabody explained.

'It was Kenny,' she said helplessly. 'I don't know why he did it.'

Jean felt her heart sink into her boots. She could guess. She and Kenny had never got on.

'And how did she take it?'

'Badly,' Mrs Peabody said.

Jean had been found out. It was over. She was truly at Valerie's mercy now. She had never regretted anything so much in her life.

Mrs Peabody looked at her sympathetically before telling

her she was to go on the number 16, where Kenny was gloating
at her from behind the wheel.

65

Valerie

Morwenna was waiting for Valerie at Taunton railway station. Valerie waved and, although Morwenna returned the wave, it wasn't with that gap-between-her-teeth grin like usual. She looked subdued.

Valerie's first thought was to wonder who had died. Her second was that Morwenna had found out about her father and was going to declare Valerie a bastard or a liar.

Morwenna took her arm. 'I've got something to tell you...' she said, nerve-wracking words. Then she took a deep breath and out it poured.

'Paul tried to kiss me at the party.'

'What?'

This was hard to take in. It turned out that a friend, April Turner, had wanted to play a game called Spin the Bottle that American GIs had taught her older sister.

'So...?'

'And when it was Paul's turn, he spun it, and you had to choose who to take in the other room and he chose me.'

'What did you say?' Valerie asked, feeling her heart break at this news. How could Paul try to kiss her best friend?

Morwenna looked startled. 'I said no! I know how you feel about him!'

'Has he ever tried anything before?'

'Never,' Morwenna said fiercely. 'I swear on my mother's life.'

'Why did he do that?' wondered Valerie aloud. She couldn't understand it. They were so close to getting together, it was completely unreasonable and out of character and strange.

Morwenna shrugged. 'No idea!'

'Was he... had he been drinking?'

'Not that I'm aware of,' said Morwenna, blushing furiously. She was always so truthful – unlike everyone else in Valerie's life. 'I'm sorry, Val.'

I'll ask him, Valerie told herself. *I will.* She told herself it must be a misunderstanding – she had been certain they were moving in the same direction.

But Paul wasn't at home when she got back. And Mrs Howard – who presumably had no idea anything had happened – said this morning he had decided to join the celebrations at his school and would be away for at least another two weeks. She expected he would be having a whale of a time!

Valerie felt like she was going through motions; she felt like she was in shock. First the trauma of her mother's fabrications and now this.

She was so despondent Mrs Howard wondered if she was coming down with something and asked if she should wait until she felt better before going to Bristol. Valerie said no, she wanted to get started as soon as possible now, somewhere new, somewhere no one knew about any of this.

'I'm afraid you might be disappointed with the job,' Mrs

Howard admitted. She couldn't understand why Valerie hadn't even gone to the interview for the BBC job in London. 'You're capable of bigger things.'

'This will suit me better right now,' Valerie said, and, to reassure her, 'Anyway, I'll work my way up.'

She packed her pillowcase full of clothes, but when Mrs Howard saw it she insisted on giving her a suitcase of her own.

The phone kept ringing but Mrs Howard said she'd deal with it. Before she left though, she said, 'You will call your mother, won't you, Valerie? She sounds concerned.'

And Valerie lied and said she would, as soon as she'd settled in.

The wireless saved Valerie like it had many times before. It cut through her aching heart with noise, jokes and company. No matter what was going on with her, it took her away from her head into different stories, dramas, fiction, non-fiction. She joined people having good times, people having terrible times, and she joined in with the laughter.

She lost herself in other people's stories. The two people she loved most in the world had let her down: Paul and her mother. It was hard to believe.

Now that the war was over, some of the wartime broadcasts were replaced with what they called 'Light Entertainment' – programmes that were less intellectually demanding. There was a show called *Family Favourites* that was messages and music for those who were still apart. It appealed to Valerie in ways that surprised her. Whereas *It's That Man Again* made her fall about with laughter and *The Brains Trust* made her think, *Family Favourites* felt like an arrow through her heart.

She would hear about Prisoners of War and the people waiting for them to come home. Why hadn't Paul waited for her? Why on earth had he tried to kiss Morwenna? The time they spent together must have meant something, mustn't it? She had been convinced there was something beyond friendship between them.

Once she heard about a soldier in Italy who wanted to tell his mum, 'I'll be home soon, put the kettle on.'

And there was the time when a 'Jean in London' called, and Valerie held her breath that it was her Jean, but this Jean was calling out for her brother in Canada.

Valerie desperately wanted an explanation from her mother, but she still couldn't bear the idea of talking to her after so many lies.

66

Jean

They let Jean go as soon as the men came back from war. After all she'd done for them! All her efforts to keep London moving came to nothing. They threw out the lady clippies like half-eaten apples.

It wasn't that the demobbed chaps weren't nice fellas. In fact, some were lovely, with their pockmarked faces, hands so wobbly that you wondered if they'd be able to operate the intricacies of the clipper machine, you wanted to put them by a fireside and warm them up, but the military pension wasn't what it was.

Men had to work, so women had to shove over.

'Hope you don't mind, Mrs Hardman?' The man in the fur coat who had interviewed and employed her six years earlier told her. (It certainly looked like he had come through the war unscathed.)

Hope you don't mind stepping aside?

She did mind.

For five years, she had given her all. She had been in a bus that was sunk, a bus that broke down, a bus in the blackout. She had looked after drunk passengers, depressed passengers, young and old, rich and poor. She had been tripped up accidentally, kicked deliberately, provoked, teased, prized. She had made friends, made peace, made someone's day. She had sung 'Happy Birthday', cried at sad stories, told jokes, ruffled hair, helped a man with his tie, helped a woman with her wedding train, shaken paws with dogs... And now, she had been given her marching orders.

She was second choice, because she was female.

Iris had left as soon as she got married and, apparently, she was now pregnant. Mavis had left too.

'What about you, Mrs Peabody?'

'The only way they'll drag me out of the bus station is in a coffin.'

Jean wished she had thought to say something like that.

Mr Carrington Snr retired around the same time.

'What will you do all day?'

'I've got Richard.'

'Richard is back?' Jean gasped at the thought of the ginger-haired young man who had once asked her to be his girl. She collected herself. 'He didn't want to come in to say hello?'

'He didn't,' his father said curtly.

Jean had lots of questions, but he seemed reluctant to engage at first. Finally, he said Richard had been in the Middle East. He was wounded but he got off lightly. 'He felt awkward about you,' Carrington Snr said. 'He had such a crush but you turned him down.'

'I did *not* turn him down!' Jean protested, although maybe it looked that way from the outside. 'I wasn't ready...'

And she chose Tony. And Tony chose Pauline. And the bus station chose the men.

And Valerie chose some posh woman with a stick up her backside.

Try not to be bitter, Jean told herself. She remembered Mrs Penn whose house she used to clean talking about how being a nurse in the Great War was her greatest moment and nothing was ever the same after that. And at the time, Jean had thought how utterly sad that was – that she had only one moment that was great, and the rest of her life was grey mediocrity.

Now she understood. *Now* she empathised. It wasn't fair.

How easy it was to slip into that state of mind! She told herself not to. She mustn't. Try not to think it was the beginning of the end when it was only the end of the beginning. Try not to think everything was over for her now.

Indeed, they had a new government and some people – not Jean – were hopeful about that. Jean kept out of politics – whoever was in charge, they were all the same – but this lot were talking about a National Health Service and Jean did support that. Her heart check-ups didn't come cheap – imagine the relief if she didn't have that expense!

One day, there was a note from the Frouds on her doormat with an address. *Please forward the post* it said. That was all. They weren't coming back. Jean supposed them being there or not wouldn't make much difference to her.

Their street was part street, part bombsite. Many of the London streets were. The children clambered over old buildings like lizards in the sun; even the babies expertly crawled over rubble. Tiny Bobby Larke, whose widowed father drank day and night, was always up some scrap mountain shouting about Nazis.

Don't think about little Joe Salt, don't.

A month passed before Jean felt able to write to her daughter. Surely now the war was over, and they had both survived when so many people hadn't, Valerie wasn't going to hold this against her forever?

I'm so sorry. Please forgive me. I know I owe you an explanation. All I want is a second chance.

Valerie never replied.

67

WINTER 1945

Valerie

In Bristol, Valerie did occasional housekeeping duties in exchange for board. The duties were simple, and the elderly lady whose home it was was undemanding and nearly always out. She was also polite to the point of incurious about Valerie's background, which was helpful too. As a receptionist, men steamed past her and ignored her most of the time too. She kept busy with stamps on envelopes, trips to the post office, fixing the franking machine. Meeting and greeting visitors. Teas and coffees. Trying to eke out rations. Putting things in the right places.

The reception job didn't suit her, Mrs Howard was right, but she had expected that. Yet, as the song went, there was blue sky over the white cliffs of Dover. Slowly – and shyly – Valerie found that she was becoming someone people asked questions of. She kept the *Radio Times* on her desk and talked about programming – not about what was wrong but about how things might be better. Before long, the same men who had walked past her stopped to ask her opinions – what did you think? How? And not too long after that – why don't you have a go?

At first, Valerie was too wrapped up in her new job and her new house in a new city to miss Jean. Or rather she had missed her for so long, in her six years away, that this new breakdown in communication didn't feel very different.

Sometimes, though, Valerie went over what she had found out and it still struck her as absurd – if it had been a play on the wireless she might have complained it was unrealistic. How had she never realised previously? How long did her mother expect to hide it for? Her father was not a hero who saved two girls from a house fire; he lived with his wife and sons in Victoria Park.

The overwhelming emotion she had about it was humiliation. Sometimes, she felt like a child who believed in Father Christmas long after everyone else – even much younger children – knew he wasn't real. She was too embarrassed to tell Morwenna what she'd found out at first. For goodness' sake, they used to play 'rescuing girls from a fire'. Morwenna would pretend to climb ladders, slide down poles, while Valerie refused to be the girls but would shout out instructions.

Morwenna came to Bristol one Sunday afternoon, with a picnic of cakes and berries, and, nervously, Valerie did tell her. Morwenna understood that it was Jean who was the liar and not Valerie and there was something satisfying about her being appalled. Valerie was not wrong, Morwenna affirmed it; Jean was terrible to have told her such a huge untruth.

That was one good thing about not seeing Paul – she didn't have to tell him the story. It was the only good thing. When she thought of him her heart was full of splinters.

·   ·   ·

Every few weeks or so, Valerie went to visit Mrs Howard. It was expensive, but she felt obliged. No, it wasn't merely obligation; whatever snide comments Lydia made about Mrs H, Valerie loved her old friend and being in the delightful cottage with its arch of flowers at the gate, and those dusty musty books. They hunkered down to listen to their shows: *Family Favourites. The Brains Trust. It's That Man Again.* And then, they talked about books, art exhibitions and theatre, and it was wonderful – it was where she felt most at home.

However, the subject of Paul was less comfortable. He was an abysmal correspondent, Mrs Howard complained.

'You must have heard from him, Valerie dear?'

'No, actually, I haven't.'

'That's odd, you were always his favourite. Maybe it's the postal service.'

'Maybe.'

'You haven't had a falling-out?'

'*I* haven't fallen out with *him*...' she said, and Mrs Howard gave her a look.

68

Jean

Rich women will always need cleaners, the saying goes, and some of Jean's old clients got in touch after the war. A trickle not a flood, but it was better than nothing.

Mrs Cutler returned, with a tall, strapping polite lad. Jean remembered he was about the same age as Valerie. Mrs Cutler also seemed to have acquired another baby. Odd when her husband was still out in Burma.

'And how old is young Valerie – she must be sixteen now?' Mrs Cutler was defensive about her own business, nosy with others. 'Is she working?'

Jean flushed, but she had prepared a cover story.

'Valerie is staying on in the West Country. There are more opportunities for her there.'

Mrs Salt or Mrs Froud would have known straight away something was wrong. Since when were there more jobs for young girls outside of London?

Mrs Foley, who used to love dinner parties, had lost her son in Malta and was grief-stricken. She forgot to ask about Valerie the first two sessions. But on the third she asked Jean to stay for tea, and then she clasped her hands and said, 'I'm happy you didn't lose your precious girl.'

There was much to be thankful for.

She scrubbed their doorsteps. She fed their cats. It was like the last six years hadn't happened, and yet everything was changed. It was like taking the needle off the gramophone and putting it back – you expect it to be in the same place, but somehow it never is. The song has moved on.

Mrs Foley turned out to be a lovely listener. Perhaps listening to other people's stories was a chance for her to not be in her own grieving mind. And she complimented Jean too: 'How courageous to be in London during the Blitz – and then with all those doodlebugs!'

'I had no choice in the matter...'

'But still, you did more than your fair share.'

'Fair share' was a phrase from a different era. What was a fair share? The cost some people had paid was devastatingly enormous, while others had walked away unscathed. There was one thing Jean would never again believe in and that was that life was fair.

Only Mrs Foley asked about life on the buses. And this was a story that Jean could be effusive about. This was her specialist subject. She was no longer an expert on her daughter, but she was an expert on Routes 15, 29 and 4. One day, Mrs Foley asked Jean if she had ever seen that horrendous photograph of the bus that fell in a hole.

'It was in the newspapers,' she said. 'Made the hairs on the backs of my arms stand up on end!'

Jean looked up sharply. She had never seen any newspaper coverage of it.

'Those poor people,' Mrs Foley continued. 'There was a pregnant woman and she went into labour shortly afterwards – the baby was saved, thank goodness.'

Jean had not known that.

'What I don't get is why they drove into a hole.'

This Jean knew. 'I think the ground had been weakened, and the extra pressure of the bus made it open up while they were going along, and...'

'That explains it!' Mrs Foley said, then moved on to another topic, while Jean was left remembering that terrible day as though it were yesterday. And what had happened next. It wasn't only the ground had opened up that day; a deep chasm had also opened up between her and Valerie.

When she stopped working on the buses, Jean feared she would feel frantic in the way she used to before the war. She remembered how grateful she was to the bus for keeping her busy; now she was less busy, wouldn't she sink into the old panicky ways?

But no, she didn't.

Maybe it was the war that did it, that unnerving, can't-keep-still feeling; she couldn't say she missed it. It was nice to have space to think, to breathe. It was nice.

If only she wasn't so sad.

69

AUTUMN 1946

Valerie

Valerie arranged to meet Lydia at a tearoom near Bumble Cottage. She hadn't seen her for a while and she was surprised how ridiculously nervous she was. She kept checking her hair in the mirror.

She should try to make more of an effort with Lydia, she thought. Lydia was her childhood friend. Only a few people knew the real Valerie but Lydia was one of them. Perhaps that's why it was nerve-wracking.

Lydia was living about ten kilometres away with a family who ran kennels. She looked after the dogs. Mrs Howard had arranged it – not that Lydia displayed an ounce of gratitude towards Mrs H, as far as Valerie was aware.

For someone who worked with animals, Lydia always looked absurdly glamorous. Valerie felt ashamed of her speckiness and her shabbiness and resolved to step up her appearance next time – if there was going to be a next time. They talked about Francine.

'She never replies to my letters,' Lydia said.

'That's a shame.' Valerie was surprised to hear that Lydia wrote. She and Francine exchanged cards at Christmas and birthdays but nothing more.

'If she wants to be like that.' Lydia shrugged.

'I miss her,' Valerie confided, and Lydia made a face.

They still seemed to have little common ground. Valerie still found that surprising; their paths were similar, but their perspectives were as far apart as could be.

At work recently, Valerie had been allowed to sit in on a course about interview techniques –and one section she particularly enjoyed was 'how to draw out these people who are shut up like clams?' Here were basic questions: *What would you do with £100? When were you happiest?* That sort of thing. The instructor said Valerie might be good at it – if she got over her embarrassment.

It was slightly awkward, but Valerie launched in and was surprised that the questioning worked. Lydia responded immediately.

'Hundred pounds?' she pondered. 'I'd open a pet rescue centre in London.'

Favourite food? 'Marmalade – made from oranges, of course. None of that vile carrot stuff.'

'Happiest? Fishing with you and Paul.'

Valerie laughed. 'You only came a couple of times...'

'You asked, I answered,' she responded, pouting. Valerie apologised. She was breaking a basic rule. The instructor had told her never to tell the interviewee their answer was wrong. 'Do you want to know anything else?' Lydia said.

Something occurred to Valerie then too – in all their years at Bumble Cottage, Lydia had never cried to go home.

'Were you ever homesick?' she asked. She remembered how it was for her at Mrs Woods'. Maybe it wasn't homesick, maybe it was just agony. But Lydia had never experienced anywhere harsh like that. Lydia had been coddled her whole childhood.

'A little,' she said. 'But you got on with it.'

70

AUTUMN 1947

Valerie

In the end, it was Paul who got in touch first. Out the blue, two and a half years after she had last seen him, a telephone call.

The lady she lodged with left her a message.

Valerie was first dumbstruck and then suspicious: 'Has he ever called before?' Perhaps she had missed several calls?!

'No,' said her landlady indignantly. 'This is the first time.'

With trembling fingers, Valerie dialled the number back, and Paul answered. She'd recognise his voice anywhere. He would be back at home – Bumble Cottage – that weekend, did she want to see him?

'I don't know...'

He had let her down. He had chased her friend, *her best friend!* Yes, it sounded half-hearted. Yes, it sounded like a misunderstanding; but even so, could there be a greater insult?

'I'm off to New York next week,' he said. 'I'd like to see you before I go.'

. . .

Mrs Howard answered the door. First, she looked delighted, then concerned.

'You should have told me you were coming.'

'It was very last-minute,' Valerie admitted. She was working on a programme for the wireless – only on the final sequence, but she was actually involved! – yet she couldn't miss this chance to see Paul. She couldn't.

New York! New York, dammit. Paul had always wanted to go, but it had never sounded realistic, not during a war; not during peace either. How did this happen? Valerie knew it was something to do with his paintings. Something to do with his 'connections' too, no doubt, but still.

Paul walked into the drawing room. He was in a shirt and grey flannel shorts. His hair was longer than it used to be but his smile was exactly how she remembered. He hugged her and she felt herself melt into his arms. It had been a long time, although now he was in front of her, it felt like no time had passed at all.

She was still angry with him but seeing him made her soften. It was easier being angry with him when he was an idea in her head. In person, it was hard not to swoon.

Paul and Mrs Howard talked about what he would be doing in America, where he was staying, his expectations. They kept using the word 'opportunity' (five times) and 'once in a lifetime' (four). He would be working in a studio. Fully funded; the people – sponsors, tutors, patrons, Valerie wasn't sure which – were paying his passage.

She wouldn't get the chance to talk to him alone unless she created it herself. When Mrs Howard had finally gone to the kitchen to make tea, Valerie seized the moment.

'Why did you want to kiss Morwenna?'

'Woah,' he said, like he was talking to a horse. He looked startled. Well, he should have expected this.

'Tell me – you owe me that.'

'I didn't!' he insisted.

'You DID though! Everyone knows!'

'All right... It was because she was there and everyone was egging me on. I never had feelings for her though. And honestly, I was hurt and wanted to get back at you. I didn't think you were interested in me. I thought there was someone else you were interested in. There was, wasn't there?'

'No!' said Valerie, voice raised, shocked at this admission. 'There wasn't. But why on earth did you think that?'

Paul shifted uneasily. 'What does it matter now anyway? It was years ago.' He stared at her and his eyes were still piercing and the freckles still there on his nose. 'You've moved on, haven't you?'

'It matters because I haven't,' she said softly.

'There *was* someone though? I was sure there was.'

'There *wasn't*... Ever!' protested Valerie with emotion. 'I don't know why you thought that.'

They had wasted so much time. And why? She couldn't piece it together. Whatever had she done to make him feel that there was someone else?

He walked over to her. He was going to kiss her at long last—

'Paullll!' Mrs Howard called. 'Mr Cracknell is here to take you for a tennis lesson.'

Valerie had tea with Mrs Howard in the kitchen. For the first time, she noticed that Mrs Howard was looking tired and older. It seemed to have happened suddenly. Mrs Howard agreed she was exhausted. She blamed this year's Christmas play – a production of *The Importance of Being Earnest*.

'It's a comedy of errors and miscommunication. You'd like it, Valerie, but my goodness, it's hard work.'

'I'm sure,' Valerie said, although she could hardly think of anything but Paul and his arms when he hugged her, and his smile. She had a sudden intuition that he was covering up for someone, which was why he didn't want to say why he believed she was interested in someone else.

She tried to concentrate on Mrs Howard's conversation: the costumes, the props, the wonderful Algernon, the imperious Lady Bracknell – would the audience laugh? It was useless – her thoughts were jumping all over the place.

A couple of hours later Paul returned, hot and energised, twirling his racquet around like a drumstick.

'I thrashed Cracknell!' he called as he walked into the kitchen and peered into the cupboards.

'Really?' Mrs Howard and Valerie queried at the same time.

'No... he thrashed me!' Paul was laughing as he grabbed Valerie's hand. 'You don't mind if we go out, do you, Mum?'

Mrs Howard looked shocked. 'Don't you want to clean up first?'

'No time.' He winked at Valerie. 'She doesn't mind...'

They hadn't gone ten yards before he reached out, threw his arm round her shoulders the way they used to. She held her breath. It felt incredible. It was different to how it used to be, though – they were adults now.

He steered her fast.

'Where are we going?' Even the proximity of him made her skin hot with longing.

He took his arm from her shoulder – the disappointment! – then dug his hand in a pocket and pulled out a key to the barn where the land girls used to stay.

Goodness, this was what it was.

He slipped his hand back round her again and manoeuvred them there.

'Does anyone live here?' Valerie asked as they got closer.

'We've got it all to ourselves,' Paul said, grinning.

Valerie had never been inside before. There were two single beds, made up, and each with a bedside table next to it. There was a wardrobe and an ironing board and, most importantly, a wireless.

He sat on one of the beds. Valerie stood until she could stand no more. She thought she might die of embarrassment.

'You never told me how you felt about me,' Paul eventually said.

'What?' Valerie asked, shocked that they were finally being direct with each other.

'I never felt like you were interested,' said Paul as he smiled ruefully.

'But Paul, you must have known I was...' she said croakily.

'I knew you liked me, but you were determined not to love anyone. That's how you were, that's how it felt.'

That's how it was, she thought. But Paul was always the exception. How did he not realise that?

'Valerie,' he said, 'do you want me to stay?'

'Stay where?' She didn't know what he was asking her.

'I mean – do you want me to not go to America?'

She couldn't hold him back; she wouldn't want to do that. Not now, not ever.

'No, you have to go. It's an amazing opportunity.'

He had done boarding school, he had dutifully done his degree. Now it was time to do what he wanted.

'You do *want* to go, don't you?'

'I do and I don't,' he said. He often answered questions like that.

'We'll write.'

'Every month.'

She looked at his face, the planes of his cheeks. She knew his strengths – writing letters wasn't one of them. 'You won't, will you?'

'I will draw pictures for you.'

'I will make broadcasts for you.'

Paul grinned. 'This is Funf speaking!' he said in a funny imitation of the voice from the wireless they both loved.

Valerie was still laughing when he grabbed her hand. 'Does this mean I can kiss you?'

'Better late than never,' she whispered. The tension was unbearable.

He tilted his face towards hers. And gently pressed his lips on hers. She felt like she was liquid.

'Okay?'

'Mmm,' she said. Okay didn't cover it.

He did it again and again.

'Still okay?'

'More,' she said, and they tumbled back onto the bed.

As they went back to Bumble Cottage, Mrs Howard was in the garden shouting her hellos. Valerie could feel that her face was bright red.

'Did you have a nice walk?' asked Mrs Howard. 'I'm pruning the roses.'

Surely it was obvious that they hadn't just had a *nice walk*!

'*I* did,' said Paul emphatically. 'Did you, Valerie?'

'Yes, thank you, Paul,' she said. 'I will change for dinner.'

In her old bedroom, Valerie slipped into clean clothes. She smelled of desire and Paul.

At dinner, they talked theatre, art and wireless and everything in between. Mrs Howard imitated the woman playing Lady Bracknell. Paul, who knew the play (who knew everything), made jokes about handbags. And Valerie nodded and laughed but couldn't keep up.

They stayed downstairs drinking whisky and smoking. It felt like forever until Mrs Howard announced, 'I'm off to

Bedlington. Don't stay up late – it's an early start tomorrow, Paul, remember.'

Hovering at the doorway, she smiled over: 'I'll set the alarm.'

Valerie was nineteen and Paul was twenty-one. She was aching for them to spend more time alone together and she felt certain he was too. He threw another log on the fire, where it sizzled.

'Well,' he said, patting the cushion next to him. As she went over, she felt shy again, her heart thumping.

He kissed her. Then he got up and put the armchair against the door, its back wedged against the key, and pulled a face: 'In case Mother decides to remind us about the early start again.'

The fire kept on crackling.

She was asleep in her old room and her old bed when she heard voices downstairs. It was bright outside and she realised it was later than she expected. Pulling on her robe, she raced down to the hall, where Paul and Mrs Howard were marooned among the suitcases. Outside, a car hooted.

'I didn't want to wake you until the last minute.' Paul took her hand.

'Car is here, Paul,' Mrs Howard interrupted. 'Don't keep Mr Isaac waiting.' She was addressing Paul, but Valerie felt it was aimed at her too.

He hugged his mother with the unselfconscious ease of someone who hugs a lot.

And he hugged Valerie and kissed her, properly, lovingly, unashamedly, in front of his mother.

'I know you hate writing but...'

'I will,' she said breathlessly, 'I love you, Paul.'

'I love you, Valerie.'

And then he was gone.

It was nearly ten years since she'd first arrived here, and she was still the evacuee child in the house, not sure if she should be here now; a boundary had been crossed – or had it? Half at home, half not. The place that gave her sanctuary and, now, had given her something else entirely.

Valerie helped tidy the breakfast things away. She washed up. She wanted to be alone, and Mrs Howard let her be.

Later, though, they sat outside together in the garden on deckchairs making small talk. The vegetables were doing well. How pretty the lawn looked!

They didn't talk of Paul for a while until Mrs Howard said, 'He'll be at the port about midday,' and Valerie agreed.

Paul thought she wasn't interested in him. He thought she had someone else. And she suspected she knew why.

Mrs Howard was unfailingly pleasant to Valerie. It was more than politeness, it was genuine affection, Valerie was sure of it; but, when it came to a partner, she wanted more for her son than a girl like her.

It was only natural that Paul came first. Valerie understood that Mrs Howard didn't think she and Paul belonged together. She sympathised. She knew she was too London, too working class, too feeble, too bad at using a knife and fork. Too illegitimate, too like Jean.

Mrs Howard never said it outright, but Valerie supposed it was what lay beneath, it was in the mud, it was under the bed, it was between the lines. No one wanted their son and heir to fall in love with a dirty evacuee.

You didn't have to be a Lady Bracknell to think like that.

It took Paul six weeks to get to New York. His letters home took even longer.

Remind me never to go on a boat again!

Valerie didn't say that six weeks on a cruise ship where a big band played 'We'll Meet Again' three times a night and there were pools with five-metre diving boards sounded fantastic. Paul didn't write letters often; instead he wrote on the backs of cards with squiggle cartoons. Girls with big breasts and men with cigars – it wasn't Paul's style, but it was the fashion at the time.

'Come and see me,' he said. But there was no money for a transatlantic flight and certainly no time for a six-week journey over the Atlantic Ocean, diving boards or not. And the thought of hanging around him, shadowing him, while he chased his dreams was not appealing.

Valerie had ambitions of her own.

She did sometimes wish that, that morning at Bumble Cottage, she'd asked for more clarity – was he her boyfriend or not? – but clarity and Paul didn't seem to fit together.

They'd left it that he would give it a go in New York and she would continue to give it a go in Bristol. They weren't naive; they were going to be mature about this. Three, four years was a long time to ask someone to wait, but when you love someone, it's not waiting, insisted Paul, it's just being. She knew if she ever did ask him the boyfriend question, he'd probably answer, 'I adore you,' but then if it were the other way around, she probably would do the same. It wasn't that he was slippery, it was more that they were both realists.

71

SPRING 1948

Jean

One day the elderly man in the Salts' old flat was taken off. The flat stayed empty for about three months and then two women took it over. They drove a van and did the removal themselves. Jean watched from behind her lace curtains. They had a refrigerator and a gramophone. They must have been doing nicely. One of them was about fifty, the other maybe forty. They closed and opened the doors and windows gently so as not to disturb Jean, which she appreciated.

One evening they asked Jean round for a fish and chips supper. It was summer, but it was blowing a gale. The older one was Barb and the younger was Gwen. They turned out both to be forty-five – Barb had had a hard life.

In the flat, Valerie could only see one room, one large bed, messed up, but presumed that one of them slept in the other room that she couldn't see.

It wasn't until another six months later that the penny dropped – that's how slow Jean was. They'd been to see Alfred Hitchcock's *Rope* at the cinema and although Gwen and Barb held hands, she assumed it was because the film was so scary. She could have done with a hand-hold too.

She had seen Barb kiss Gwen on the cheek, but she herself had kissed Mrs Froud once when they had not seen each other for a while. Another time, Barb mentioned that she and Gwen shared a bath, but she knew money was tight.

'Is it... Are you...?' she finally asked one day.

She remembered Tony cracking jokes about lesbians. About comfortable shoes and about men who could 'turn them'. And it wasn't only Tony. It was men in the bus station. Men didn't like it, it suddenly occurred to her. That was why they made the jokes. Two ladies without men put their noses out of joint.

'Not interested in men?'

'Not in that way, no,' said Barb brightly.

Gwen said, 'I like them, I just prefer Barb.'

Jean didn't know what to do with this information. She went back to her flat with a headache. When she woke up in the morning, though, everything seemed clear and she couldn't understand her earlier confusion. Barb and Gwen had found love. Love, love, love. What a beautiful and special thing that was.

And anyway, Jean also preferred Barb to a lot of men. Barb made a mean beef and ale pie – and a terrible apple strudel. She was awful at pudding; no one could work out why. And Jean preferred Gwen to a lot of men too. She was funny, sarcastic and quick-witted. She was always having a moan about something but cheerfully; her complaints made Jean laugh.

They would have been great on the buses, she thought. They had the keep London moving spirit, that was for sure.

Jean realised she was in danger of becoming one of those people who only has one good era in their lives – one of those who can't resist bringing it into every single conversation. But then they were, if not *fun* times, then certainly exhilarating. You knew you were alive back then; now, sometimes, she wondered if she'd been born.

And Jean liked Barb and Gwen together too. They were great friends to her. What did it matter what they got up to in private?

To reciprocate, and in the spirit of honesty, Jean told Barb and Gwen about Valerie. They were having a cigarette on the doorstep while pigeons eyed them for leftovers and wasps spun around. Haltingly, Jean told them she had a daughter, that she lived far away and things between them were... she chose the word 'strained'. She remembered suddenly a pregnant Mrs Salt straining tea through a cloth for her and Mrs Froud and them all laughing at something or other the children had said.

'A lot of children had a difficult time when they were evacuated. It wasn't your fault,' Barb said.

'So many years far from home,' agreed Gwen. 'It can't have been easy for either of you.'

Jean couldn't explain. Valerie had both a horrendous time and a glorious time when she was evacuated. The problem wasn't the evacuation itself; it was Jean, stupid Jean.

'I didn't deal with it well. Any of it.'

From the moment Jean had told her the evacuation was a holiday, it had gone downhill. No – in fact it was going downhill long before that. Jean was always afraid of upsetting Valerie, yet she had ended up upsetting her even more. And that was the thing – she hadn't listened, she hadn't learned.

'Nobody dealt with it well,' Barb said. Her generous insistence that it wasn't Jean's fault actually had the opposite effect and Jean felt worse. Even if she accepted that it wasn't entirely her fault, it still was *half* her fault.

'I shouldn't have kept secrets.'

'We understand about secrets,' Barb said gently.

'Secrets *and* lies,' Jean said. She was filled to the brim with self-loathing, she couldn't see or hear anything but her own mistakes.

'We understand that too,' Gwen said, her eyes flickering over at Barb for a moment. 'I think you should go and see her,' Gwen went on, and Barb agreed.

'We could drive you.'

'No,' said Jean automatically, although part of her was thinking, gosh, the last few years would have been easier if she had people like this to lean on. Perhaps if she had real friends on her side – or for that matter hadn't wasted those years on Tony – she wouldn't have lost her daughter.

In the end, they couldn't go even if Jean had agreed. Barb and Gwen had to take Gwen's mother to the hospital. But the idea had been planted and the encouragement did not cease. Jean booked herself a train ticket.

72

SUMMER 1948

Valerie

In her continued efforts to be a better friend, Valerie had invited Lydia to Bristol. They arranged to meet at a Lyons Tea Rooms near the station. They only had an hour since Lydia couldn't be away from the dogs for long.

Before they'd even taken off their hats, Lydia had enquired, 'Are you courting anyone yet, Val?'

Valerie hated these discussions, *hated* them.

'Nope... How about you?'

'No one serious,' Lydia said glowering at the menu. 'Mum and Dad would love me to marry – but it's hard to find what they have.'

Valerie vaguely remembered that her own mother had been unimpressed with Mr Froud. 'My Neville', she used to call him.

'You know – they have such a strong marriage... Nothing compares.'

'Ah,' said Valerie, 'don't stop looking though.'

'I won't,' Lydia said, smiling to herself. 'The men I meet might not be princes, but frogs aren't too bad in the meantime.'

Valerie reached out and grabbed Lydia's hands, suddenly keen to make a confidence. 'You know Paul is in New York?'

Lydia looked up, more interested than she had been. 'Go on...'

'We-ll, before he went, we...'

Lydia squealed. 'Nooo! You went all the way?'

Valerie swallowed. 'Not... not *all* the way!'

'Oh.' Lydia sounded disappointed.

'But lots of kissing and cuddling.' Valerie couldn't stop beaming at the memory.

'Why didn't you have sex?'

Did she have to say 'sex'?

'Because we're not married!' Valerie said. *Obviously.* This was not the part she had expected to have to explain, although Lydia was perhaps the most unpredictable person she knew. As if Valerie would risk pregnancy and/or abandonment. She knew better than that, and she'd assumed Lydia did too. Perhaps she was wrong.

Lydia dabbed at her mouth with the serviette. 'I write to him,' she said from behind it.

'You do?' Now it was Valerie's turn to be shocked.

'About the dog,' Lydia said, as if it were obvious. 'He is his, after all.'

Funny, Valerie never thought of T.Rex as Paul's dog. T.Rex only answered to Lydia. He was indifferent to the rest of them, unless chicken was being offered and then he took an interest.

'Of course.'

She couldn't imagine what Lydia put in her letters to Paul: the crazy places T.Rex pooped, the other dogs he met on his walks, that sort of thing maybe?

It struck Valerie that Lydia was one of the only evacuees she knew who *didn't* feel torn between two worlds. Perhaps because, somehow, Lydia managed to carry both city and countryside within her. Whereas Valerie felt like she was the rope in a tug-of-war, being pulled in two directions. Lydia was more like a skipping rope, hopping, jumping, whirring around, doing exactly as she pleased.

'How is your mother?' Valerie asked in an attempt to change the subject.

'Same,' Lydia said vaguely. She never seemed to enjoy talking about Mrs Froud. 'How is Mrs H? What good deeds has she done now?'

This seemed such a cold way of talking about their benefactor – even for Lydia – that for a moment Valerie was speechless. If anyone was entitled to hold a grudge against Mrs Howard, it was Valerie herself, but she had forgiven her for the machinations around her and Paul's relationship. Actually, she hadn't blamed her for a moment. Mrs Howard had only ever had their interests at heart – even if she was wrong. So why was Lydia unrelentingly critical?

'How do you mean?'

'Nothing!' Lydia retracted quickly. 'She likes to be the saviour, doesn't she? She always favoured you.'

'She didn't!'

'You were the genius child. The one she would mould into a mini Mrs H. I was "pretty little Lyds".'

'I don't think that for—'

'It didn't matter, I had my own things going on. I'm surprised you didn't see it like that though. It reminded me of *Pygmalion* – you don't remember the terrible play?'

'Not really.'

Lydia shrugged. 'You were the perfect Eliza Doolittle to her Professor Higgins – flower girl made good!'

'Lydia!' Valerie scoffed. Sometimes her *not-actual-sister* did speak nonsense.

. . .

The next morning, Valerie had an even bigger surprise. She opened the door to find her mother standing nervously in front of her.

It was an older but a brighter, more healthy-looking version of Jean than she'd seen for years. She was wearing a hound-stooth coat and a colourful scarf. Her shoes were shiny. The morning was sunny and bright and, in an odd way, she matched it. She had a slick of lipstick over her mouth, and tiny red smears on her yellowy teeth.

'I don't want to intrude...' Jean's voice was submissive, but her eyes were hopeful.

'What are you doing here?' Valerie peered out into the street for a car – a Tony at the wheel perhaps – but saw nothing but the usual weekend traffic.

'I came to see you!' said her mother. 'It's been a while. Can I come in?'

'Not really,' said Valerie. 'I'm on my way to work.'

'But it's Saturday,' Jean pointed out.

'Yes, and I work on a Saturday,' Valerie said. She knew she was too old to roll her eyes, but she wanted to. 'How did you get my address?'

'Francine,' her mother said with eyes lowered. 'Sorry.'

'I see.' Valerie couldn't blame Francine for giving it to her, but she could blame Jean for putting Francine on the spot.

'Now I'm here, don't you have a lunch break?'

'Yes, but—'

'I could meet you then?' More hopefulness.

'If you like.'

'We have so much to catch up on,' Jean continued.

We're strangers, thought Valerie, but she acquiesced.

Throughout the morning, Valerie went over the questions she had. She decided this was her best opportunity to get to the bottom of the lies that had been told.

. . .

In the tea shop, Valerie had to convince Jean to take her coat off. Jean had never been to a café with table service before and she didn't know you didn't have to queue at the counter or what to do with the menu and Valerie was embarrassed for her.

Valerie wondered if the visit had something to do with Lydia's the day before, but her mother denied any connection – in fact, she had no idea Lydia had been.

'I'm glad you are still friends!' she said. 'I didn't think you'd stay in touch with her... Mind you, you three were inseparable when you were little.'

She kept her handbag on her knees as though readying for a fast escape.

'You see Francine, do you?' Valerie asked. 'Not just telephone calls?'

'Occasionally, yes.' Jean blushed as though caught out. 'She's getting on.'

This hurt. Even though it was Valerie's choice not to see her mother, it hurt that her mother met up with her old friend.

'She always asks after you.'

Valerie nodded. She couldn't think what to say.

When the waitress came, Valerie ordered them a pot of English tea and two slices of Madeira cake.

Her mother said she wasn't good with foreign food, and Valerie told her that fish and chips was foreign, and didn't she eat that every Friday?

Jean sat back in her chair, chastened. 'I have a photograph of Francine, if you wish to see...'

There she was, a serious-faced young woman in white sweater and dark trousers, leaning against a wall self-consciously. She could have been anyone. At the bottom of the photo, in Francine's sweet loopy handwriting, *Thanks for everything, Francine.*

'It's good you stay in touch,' Valerie said. She suspected

Jean was trying to tell her that she wasn't a completely bad person, or that at least not everyone thought so.

The cakes and the tea were set down with a clunk in front of them.

'What about my dad?' snapped Valerie, unable to keep it in for any longer. 'Still see him?'

She saw Jean was perspiring already; she should be glad Valerie had persuaded her to remove her coat.

'I don't have a photograph of—'

'You told me he died in a fire,' she hissed.

You told me he died in a fire saving two little girls!

The two women on the next table looked over at them with disapproving mouths. For once, Valerie didn't care. She couldn't get over this, she felt she never would... the enormity of the lie, the dastardly detail of it. It was indecent. It was mad. Why on earth had her mother done this? It erased everything good she had ever done.

'It didn't start like that.' Jean's fingers were shaking, and the cup made a clinking noise against the saucer.

Let her shake.

'You put two and two together and came up with five,' Jean continued.

'No, *you* did...'

'I did,' Jean said quietly, her face full of regret. 'You don't know how it was – at the school, in the street, everyone had someone – we didn't. No one understood.'

'But... *died in a fire?*'

There was something so corrupt about this detail.

'I thought it was better you thought that. I only said it once.'

'Once was too much!'

'You kept asking.'

'I kept asking? You're suggesting I'm the one to blame here?'

'No, I am,' Jean said. 'I am. Unreservedly. It was a terrible thing I did. It was untrue and it grew and grew and I didn't know how to stop it. I shouldn't have let it go on. I'm sorry, I regret it so much. If I could take it back, I would.'

They swallowed their tea and nibbled their cakes. Valerie had wanted a great Madeira sponge, to show off to her mother that she knew the best places and the best things to order, but in fact it was dry and rather mediocre.

She remembered poor Mrs Salt, buried in rubble; it was good her mother had been there for Francine – yet that made her heart ache too. Why couldn't her mother have been there for her when she needed it? Because that was another thing: Jean had had a merry time in London while Valerie was starving, not only for food but for affection too.

'I know you went to see him,' Jean said, laying down her fork.

Valerie was reminded first of the sweaty impatient man in her house and the way he stomped past her and then of the unpleasant man outside the public house.

'I've seen him twice in total – unimpressive both times.'

Jean laughed nervously. 'No one ever said I had good taste in men.'

'You can say that again!' Valerie said heartily, *too* heartily. 'What does he do – my dad – for a living?'

'He's a bookkeeper.'

'He keeps books?' Valerie asked, shocked. Maybe looks could be deceptive. Maybe beneath that sweaty exterior, underneath those enormous Y-fronts, there was the soul of a poet!

'Bookkeeping, numbers and things. He's great at adding up.'

'Right,' Valerie said, realising her mistake as she stacked up their cups. Lunch hour was over. 'You're with him now?'

Jean looked shocked. 'No, it was over years ago.' She paused. 'Honestly. It was madness – it was the war.'

How do I know that? thought Valerie. *How can I trust you? You, the person who I am supposed to trust most in the world?*

'Do you wish you were together?'

'I don't miss him.' Jean's voice was low and ashamed. 'But I suppose I do get lonely sometimes. That's why it happened. And I was frightened of the bombs and the gas.'

Wasn't that the truth! But rather than focus on the daughter who loved her, she'd turned to men. Valerie couldn't shake off this overwhelming sense of injustice. Half of her wanted to make up with her mother but the other half couldn't.

They walked together up the road, then Valerie had to go one way, Jean the other.

'Please forgive me,' Jean whispered.

Valerie couldn't find the words. The bitterness hadn't yet gone away, not yet. 'Can I trust you?' she asked uneasily.

'Yes!' Jean shot back unequivocally. 'You can.'

'There are no more secrets?'

'Absolutely no more secrets, Valerie. I promise you.'

The ice in Valerie's heart was melting. The apology she had received was more heart-felt than any she could have hoped for. The assurance that there would be no more secrets gave her great comfort. And Jean was her mother after all.

73

Jean

Gwen and Barb had forgotten about Jean's mission and were worrying about the coalman but later, as they were preparing tea, Gwen cried out, 'My word – how did it go with your Valerie?'

'I'm not entirely sure,' Jean admitted. Her neighbours looked at each other over the bread Barb was cutting into slices. She was far too generous with her portions – she was stuck in pre-war sizes.

'The important thing is you tried.'

'I tried.'

There were small shoots of hope. Jean had apologised, profusely, unreservedly, and she hoped Valerie realised that. Back outside her work, Valerie had kissed Jean on the cheek and said it had meant something that she'd come. And then Valerie said she would call – she actually said that – how about they called every week or so?

A call every week or so?

Jean knew better than to say, 'starting when?'

But Valerie had laughed suddenly and it was though she had read Jean's mind: 'How about you call me Sunday evening?'

'Yes,' Jean had said. 'Thank you!' She almost had her girl, her darling, back in her life.

She had to get a telephone installed, and quickly. In the meantime, she let herself dream. Valerie was going to come back to London some time, yes.

They might even take a holiday together one day!

She remembered the pictures Valerie had drawn at the Salts' place, the evening before the evacuation. That last evening before everything changed. Jean found the papers, still tucked away. There, one of her father, but also this one – how had she not seen this before? – it was of her and she had wings, no, they weren't wings, they were something else, and was that a broomstick? – was Valerie saying she was a witch? No, that was a basket and a bowl, those were sheets, Valerie had drawn her mother as she saw her – Jean was cleaning and smiling. At the bottom of the page, it said,

My Mummy.

74

Valerie

Valerie was also feeling optimistic.

She had mended things with Paul before he left for New York. Now she might mend things with her mother. The truth was, she had missed Jean. She mightn't see her much, but she missed having positive thoughts about her.

The weekend after her mum's visit, she went to Bumble Cottage. Mrs Howard had a new live-in housekeeper. She had moved to the village thirty years ago – 'I'm an outsider!' she said. She was a nice woman, but she seemed to think Valerie was royalty.

'Miss Valerie...'

'Please, just Valerie.'

'Of course, Miss Valerie, whatever you prefer.'

Valerie sat in the garden with Mrs Howard. The housekeeper poured the tea and carried out a plate of strawberry tarts, and Valerie tried not to feel awkward about being served. After all, Mrs Howard was perfectly relaxed.

'Any news from your mother, dear?'

'Actually, I saw her last week,' Valerie said. It was funny how Mrs Howard always enquired about Jean, whereas Jean could hardly bring herself to say Mrs Howard's name. Whenever she came up, or Bumble Cottage or even Somerset, she always looked like she was chewing wasps. Her animosity extended to the entire West Country.

'I imagine she was delighted to see you.'

'She was.'

'I'm pleased,' Mrs Howard said. 'It's awful to think that you have been estranged.'

Valerie didn't like the idea that Mrs Howard would think it was for trivial reasons – if Valerie and her mother were 'estranged', it wasn't Valerie's fault.

'There is a good reason for that...' Valerie took a deep breath.

'I wondered.'

Even she had wondered?! She made me stay at Mrs Woods'. She moved that man in. She kept my father a secret from me.

Valerie said out loud, 'I find it difficult.'

Mrs Howard nodded. 'Go on...'

'She doesn't understand anything about my life, what I do, who my friends are...'

It was not only that. 'I wish she hadn't lied to me – about my father.'

Mrs Howard was skilful at seeing things from Valerie's side, but this time she said, 'That's the way things were back then. I imagine she was only trying to protect you.'

Valerie gulped. 'It's worse than that. She told me he died saving two little girls in a fire. Instead, he is an adulterer who does bookkeeping in Victoria Park. My mother was a mistress for many years. His great talent is adding up.'

At this, Mrs Howard winced. 'That must have hurt.'

'It did,' Valerie said through gritted teeth. 'I can't seem to get over it.'

Mrs Howard patted her hand and they sat quietly for a moment, breathing in the stillness. And then Mrs Howard cut through the silence: 'I don't think I ever told you about Paul's father, did I?'

Valerie shook her head, suddenly nervous.

'Obviously, it was terrible that he died. We were in shock. Paul was only five.'

'How awful.'

'But you know he didn't live with us?'

'Didn't he?'

'No, I had asked him to leave some months earlier.'

'Oh...'

'He was a philanderer, you see.'

Mrs Howard said it slowly, but even so it was a word Valerie didn't recognise.

'I don't understand...'

'I put up with him for many years, for Paul's sake.' Mrs Howard passed a hand over her forehead and then her cheek. It was like she was checking she was all there. 'His other woman thought she was pregnant, you see... Paul doesn't know the full story. Fortunately, he never asked.'

Valerie nodded. She felt shocked yet relieved. She had thought a grubby provenance was unique to her. To find she was not alone was a revelation.

'I didn't see how it would be helpful for him to know. This is what we do for our children – we try to protect them. It doesn't always work out. Paul is like his father in many ways. And maybe sometimes protecting them is not always the right thing to do. Hindsight is a wonderful thing.'

'Isn't it?'

Valerie went up to bed early – to the room she had stayed in all those years – and thought about everything she had heard. It made her feel more tender towards Mrs Howard. She also thought she understood now why she hadn't wanted Paul and her to get together. She hadn't admitted it in so many words – but she may as well have.

The story made her feel more tender towards her mother too. People trapped in a corner will say anything to get out. She should have realised this. It was what motivated the lie that counted – and she couldn't think that her mother was motivated by anything bad.

75

Valerie

The next morning, Valerie went for a walk with Lydia and T.Rex and another dog, Bessie, that Lydia was looking after.

Lydia kept talking as though she were a dog. 'Can we have some meat, Mummy?' she said, and, 'I need wee-wee.'

Valerie had never confided in Lydia, and the talking-as-though-she-was-a-dog made it extra difficult. And even if she wasn't mind-reading a dog, Lydia, who had the perfect relationship with the perfect parents, wouldn't understand. Nevertheless, Valerie felt a powerful urge to confide in her old friend – Lydia knew Valerie well, but she was that rare person in that she also knew Jean well too.

'She kept a secret...'

Lydia pulled the dogs back to her. 'We've had enough, Mummy!' she said. Then she faced Valerie. Valerie could smell the powder on her cheeks.

'You did know, didn't you? You must have known all along...'

Lydia knew about my dad?

T.Rex barked at a fly. Lydia looked at Valerie with those disarming baby-blue eyes. Valerie blinked at her.

'I honestly had no idea...' Valerie admitted. *It doesn't matter*, she told herself.

'Mum told me ages ago. Apparently, she had a procedure and ended up in hospital...'

'A procedure?'

'You know, an abortion.'

Valerie kept very still. This wasn't what she was thinking about. This wasn't what she knew. She couldn't think of anything to say.

The dogs settled down, waiting for their treat. Lydia gave them something from her pocket. She patted them and coochy-cooed them. A man in a flat cap whistled at them. 'You can tickle my tummy!'

'I didn't think that was a secret. Everyone knew. She became rather ill apparently...'

Valerie didn't know what to say – she didn't want Lydia to know she didn't know. But she didn't know. She didn't.

So now there was that as well.

Absolutely no more secrets, Valerie. I promise you.

Liar.

76

Jean

The next Sunday evening Jean queued at the telephone box and called several times but Valerie didn't answer the telephone once.

They must need the engineers out, Jean told herself. Telephones in the home were a terrible idea – they raised hopes only to dash them.

Jean sent a letter. Then she decided you couldn't trust the postal service, so she sent a telegram.

How lovely to see you. Looking forward to meeting you in London.

She still felt positive but her nerves were jangling now too. Perhaps they had agreed to chat every other Sunday? Yes, that must have been it.

Gwen and Barb chorused – 'It's fine!'

'It will be, won't it?'

'You're her mum! Course it will be!'

She made plans for Valerie's visit. Gwen and Barb would want to meet her, of course. Maybe a trip to the cinema like they used to. Valerie might like *Hamlet*. Or even *Oliver Twist*. And anything else Valerie wanted to do: tea rooms, graveyards, books – *anything*.

The letter was garbled; Gwen said it was cruel but Jean couldn't go that far. She couldn't even bring herself to tell Gwen all of its contents – it made her too ashamed.

It said: Jean was a liar. It wasn't only the monstrous untruths about her father, it was everything, it was a litany of gross behaviour from the moment she was born until now. Valerie knew about the secret termination. She knew she could never trust a single word out of her mouth and what was a relationship without trust? It said, 'never come to my house again'.

Jean dropped the paper like it was on fire. She hadn't expected this, and yet, in a way, she had. Ever since she'd let Valerie leave. It was always going to come to this. She always knew it would be a battle to get her back. Just like in the village of Hamelin, there is a fate worse than rats.

77

SPRING 1949

Valerie

Valerie went to Weston-super-Mare with Morwenna and it was her first ever holiday.

It was only April and it was overcast but they swam in the cold, cold sea. Well, not 'swam' exactly, mostly she dipped and bobbed about in the shallows. Morwenna did the actual strokes, and leg-kicks. Morwenna even put her face right in *and* went out of her depth.

Morwenna was involved with Malachi, an Irish boy who was, like Morwenna, training to be a teacher. They both sang in a choir.

'Do you still like Paul?' she asked, floating on her back.

'He's my favourite person,' Valerie said helplessly. Morwenna splashed her in the face.

Valerie couldn't help insinuating that there'd been other men but no one matched up to Paul – but the truth was there hadn't been.

At work, she stuck with another girl, Anna, who did go

through the fellas, but Valerie kept her head down and dreamed of radio shows she'd make.

The girls dried off and wrapped up before stopping for cocoa at the ice cream kiosk. The man who served them said they should be arrested for swimming in the cold.

Morwenna wanted to see the fortune teller on the pier. While she was in the tent, Valerie admired the pier beams, the way you walked on water. The sudden flashes of blue in the cracks between the planks gave her a sea-sicky feeling.

Five minutes later, Morwenna emerged, beaming.

'Is it good? Should I warn Malachi?' joked Valerie.

There was sunlight over Morwenna's face. 'I'll tell you after your turn.'

In the tent, the fortune teller said, 'Hold out your palm,' which reminded Valerie of Mrs Woods readying to hit her. She flinched, but the woman grabbed her hand.

'This is your lifeline,' she said, tracing her palm. 'I see you've led many different lives in this one life.'

Valerie suddenly felt like she was ten years old again, on the train to a new home. Her heart was racing.

'I see conflict.'

Who doesn't have conflict? Valerie couldn't help being sceptical. The world wars, Iran, Berlin... It felt like it was never-ending. It was like being in a house where you expected to be safe but whichever room you turned to, there was a battle going on inside. These men, the colonels and the politicians, were having conflicts and the rest of them had to go along with it.

'And here,' the fortune teller said, pointing at another crease in Valerie's hand. 'Disconnect. Pain. Suffering.'

Should we do a radio show on fortune tellers? thought Valerie. *'Watch out, Scammers About?'*

'Your parents – are they dead?

You tell me, thought Valerie, folding her arms.

'No,' the woman decided. 'I see someone waiting for you.'

Paul? thought Valerie.

'Who?' she asked.

'A woman, and she's been waiting a long time.'

Valerie sighed. Jean had an uncanny talent for getting herself everywhere. No nook or cranny she wouldn't exploit. Well, Valerie wouldn't let her. Not any more.

'I see a baby.'

'Right.' Valerie shifted on the stool uneasily.

Her feelings about Jean's abortion were convoluted. If it were anyone else, she would be sympathetic; and she was mostly – she knew that money was tight, and how could you bring a baby into the world, in a war, without a husband again? – but other things were crowded into her head too: a. Valerie would have loved a brother or sister – it's hard to be an only child; b. It was illegal – Valerie didn't approve of law-breaking – c. it was dangerous – Jean might have died; and d. The big one. Jean didn't tell her. Even when she had a chance, she didn't tell her. Even when Valerie asked her for no more secrets, she didn't tell her.

And that of all the people in the world Lydia, bloody Lydia Froud, knew and she didn't was downright unforgivable.

'I see a husband. Yes. A loving marriage. You will have two children and they will look after you.'

Valerie supposed the fortune teller said this to everyone. Maybe it was what everyone wanted to hear. It wasn't the *only* thing Valerie wanted to hear.

'Does he have a name?' she asked tremulously. *Does it begin with P? Does it rhyme with 'All'? Is he the love of my life?*

'He has a name,' the fortune teller replied. Funny lady. She wouldn't say it though.

'What about my career?' Valerie enquired, and the fortune teller stared back at her open-mouthed, her fillings catching the light and glimmering.

'You will be what you will be.'

That seemed evasive. Valerie paid – an absolute rip-off, bloody Morwenna! But as she was about to leave, the fortune teller gave her a final prediction:

'If you can find it in your heart to forgive, you *will* find happiness.'

When she and Morwenna compared stories, Morwenna was annoyed: 'She didn't say I'd have children!'

'She didn't say I'd have a brilliant career.'

Morwenna slotted her arm through Valerie's and steered them back towards the beach. She wanted to collect stones for her Malachi.

'She must have got us muddled up.'

Valerie rolled her eyes. 'Must be that.'

78

SUMMER 1949

Jean

Mrs Penn's lovely daughter Shirley was working as a clerical assistant at the BBC and said they needed cleaners, but when Jean applied she found out it wasn't for cleaners, it was for in the canteen.

'I'm afraid I haven't done that before,' Jean admitted.

She'd lost confidence in the years since she'd stopped working on the buses. Sad how quickly it went.

I'm out of practice, that's all, she told herself, but it felt more significant than that.

She wondered if she'd ever be able to do new things. New things meant new problems. Best to stick to what you know.

But a few days passed, and Shirley was insistent: 'Course you can. They'll be in touch soon.'

She had got her hopes up and there was nothing worse than that. But they told Jean to come along anyway. At thirty-seven years old, Jean wasn't sure what other work she could do.

.   .   .

A mild-mannered man interviewed her. He was bald as a coot, and had no eyebrows or eyelashes either. Jean tried not to stare. His hands were trembly – ex-military, Jean deduced – but his smile was wide. She couldn't help comparing it to the interview she had had for the buses. This man talked a lot.

'We say "catering", but the role is for a glorified dinner lady.'

Glorified was a fancy word. Jean didn't think she'd ever been a glorified anything.

'Your years on the buses will stand you in excellent stead here. Can't think of a better recommendation.'

She blushed. Was he playing with her?

Broadcasting House in central London was further than she'd usually travel for a job, but this was full-time and good money, better than the buses, better than cleaning. And remarkably, the mild-mannered man was not a letch or a snob or a tittle-tattle.

The bomb damage in this part of London wasn't too great, which made Jean wonder how it was that some places got away with barely anything whereas others were destroyed. Like people, wasn't it? War did not discriminate – except when it did.

It was mostly men at the BBC. There were a few women, and these women wore the latest blouses with big collars and had no husbands, no children, no life outside of their work. They lived alone, probably on crumpets. At first, Jean felt sorry for them, but some of them reminded her of Valerie with their homely glasses and their narrowed eyes and she felt sorry for herself instead.

She liked the young men who were the majority of her— what were they? Not passengers! Not customers... people. And the older men and the girls from the typing pool. She didn't like the management, who tried too hard to be friendly.

Some of the young men winked at her. Jean knew she was hanging on to her looks by the edge of her fingertips. It took her a while before she realised they probably weren't winking at her in a *how's your father?* way – they were winking at her in a *hello, Mother* way.

The food wasn't slop, it wasn't *quite* school dinners, but Jean, who had never worked in a school, and couldn't remember much about the years she was in school herself, guessed it was probably similar. Like in school, there were great silver trays you had to swing around, and sometimes they were hot and sometimes they were heavy. Monday was spam. A bad day. Tuesday was sausage and mash and that ran out quickly, so there was always a scramble. Wednesday was pork. Thursday was mince. Friday was fish, typically cod but sometimes pollack.

There was talk about mixing it up. But it was just that, talk. Jean's heart still raced but the intervals between episodes grew longer. She still wondered if Tony would get in touch again; wouldn't he want to start something up? But he didn't and deep down she was glad.

She was one of the only ones there who'd stayed in London throughout the war.

'The entire time? Even during the Blitz?' people would ask, impressed.

'Absolutely...' She wasn't proud of that – she'd just done what had to be done – but she saw it roused some people. They said, 'Ask Jean what it was like!'

'Chaos. Horrendous. Busy...'

She occasionally heard from Mrs Froud, although it was familiarity rather than friendship – or maybe that was what friendship was. And although she felt like a mother without a daughter, she still had Francine Salt in her life, and that gave her joy. She thought about dying a lot. She thought about her heart giving out before she and Valerie were reconciled and that made her afraid.

She still thought about the woman who threw herself in
front of the bus.

A few of the people Jean served called themselves 'the
creatives'. These were the people who made the radio shows
that made the nation laugh. These were the people who were
going to try to cheer us up – to pack up our troubles in an old
kitbag, that kind of thing.

Sometimes, queueing with their trays, a creative wanted to
pick her brain. (That was what they said: 'Would you mind if I
pick your brain?')

'What is your favourite show on the wireless?'

'To be honest,' she said, leaning on her spoon, 'I don't listen
much.'

'What?'

'My daughter does though...' she said as though that would
compensate.

'Mrs Hardman, if you had to listen to a drama set in a
garage or a hairdresser's, which would you choose?'

'What about set in a canteen instead?' she said.

Oh, the hilarity. 'Good grief, no.'

If this was creativity, thought Jean, give her conformity any
day of the week!

79

WINTER 1949

Valerie

People always asked Valerie where she was from. They couldn't work it out. She had an accent that was neither London nor Somerset. And they asked her if she was married. And then, when she said no, they asked if she was walking out with anyone. That one always made her pause.

'Not exactly...'

Paul was too far away to do any walking out with. Besides, they'd never walked out, had they? They'd gone fishing, fought, laughed, argued, repeated dialogue they'd heard on the wireless and bared their souls, but no 'walking out'.

She couldn't help but think about the girlfriends Paul must have had. American girls in bobby socks and loafers. Who could say no? When in Rome etc... She guessed he would be unable to resist the temptations of other women, but she also believed he would come back to her one day.

He wrote less now, but she did too. It was always going to be hard without an end date in sight. She knew this. She feared he'd fallen out of love with her – perhaps he'd never been in love with her – but then, just as she was about to give up on him, there'd be another drawing, another sign.

Once he sent her a postcard that read:

I am at the Statue of Liberty and it's amazing but all I can think is: how much better it would be with you.

For days after that she found out everything she could about the Statue of Liberty; she read everything she could get her hands on about Emma Lazarus and the poem and the words.

Life was simpler without having to worry about her mother, Valerie rationalised. And the reason she no longer let herself worry about her was that Jean never told the truth – she was incapable of it. Honesty was the most important quality to Valerie. And the other reason was – Valerie could count on one hand the number of times she had said, 'I love you'.

Sometimes Valerie wondered if she had been too harsh – but the abortion, and especially Lydia knowing about the abortion when she didn't, was the final straw. There were too many things stacked up against Jean: Valerie already had a mother-figure in Mrs Howard, who held her in the highest esteem, and she had her own friends; she didn't need Jean as a friend. That wasn't to say she was still angry with Jean – no, she mostly felt sorry for her. But feeling sorry for someone is not a good enough reason to stay in touch.

Mr Fairweather was her boss at Bristol. His leg gave him pain and he avoided stairs, but he didn't complain. He had a framed photograph of a glamorous woman on his desk – Mrs Fairweather, presumably. And Valerie assumed it was this Mrs Fairweather who made him the excellent packed lunches he had every day.

Mr Fairweather thought Valerie was an ambitious young

lassy who was – his words – 'going places'. It turned out that Mr Fairweather was the master of sound effects too. Need a gun fired? Sounds of water? Sounds of rustling through the grass? There was something for everything. And sometimes the something that replaced the everything was more complex – need the sound of someone drinking a glass of milk? Don't have someone drinking a glass of milk, have an elaborate system of liquids falling through devices.

Valerie edited pieces. She learned to fade in and fade out and which jingles listeners liked and which they hated and which ones they hated but remembered. She also helped come up with new ideas.

There was talk of a comedy show about the volunteer army, but Mr Fairweather thought it was too soon. He thought people were fed up with the war. And Mr Fairweather had a theory that your first idea was not the best – everyone had that one – nor the second – it was probably too weird – but the third.

Valerie suggested a show about evacuation – it was her first, second and third idea.

He said, 'Dunkirk? That's been done plenty, don't you think?'

Valerie hesitated. It hadn't been done plenty, but that wasn't the story she was hoping to tell anyway.

'No, I mean children.'

'The Kindertransport? I think David Emery did a piece on that last year. You know the majority of those children never saw their parents again? Tragic.'

Valerie's heart sank. For what was the evacuation but another small story of the war, irrelevant, over, a glitch, a blip?

'The mass movement of city children to the countryside,' she said flatly. 'The biggest migration in history.'

'Nothing *happened* though, did it?' Mr Fairweather said.

She hesitated. *It did and it didn't*, she thought. Which was how Paul used to answer questions.

'That's what the programme could explore...'

'Not enough suffering though, was there?' he said. And Valerie thought it would take her weeks to answer that question – if she ever dared.

Valerie was doing well at work. She didn't like talking about it. Why couldn't the work she was doing speak for itself? But when Mr Fairweather invited her out for drinks to talk over her successes, she knew it was sensible to agree. She was surprised he didn't take her to the Lyons at the end of the street, where the team often went on a Friday, but to the 'railway hotel bar', which was a ten-minute walk away – on good legs. It took him fifteen. If she'd realised it was an occasion she would have dressed up.

'You're the only young lady in production at the station.'

'I am.'

Miss Klein, Anna, the other girl –had left. There had, of course, been a messy love affair, but Miss Klein had sworn that wasn't the only reason she was going. 'You have to move on,' she insisted. 'Otherwise, you get stale.' She was trying to get work in television.

'I think radio is finished,' she had announced on her last day.

'I think the two can coexist,' Valerie had retorted. People were quick to sound the wireless's death knell. As far as Valerie was concerned, a thing can struggle on dying for many, many years.

Anna had also promised to keep in touch but hadn't. They were friendly but, Valerie supposed, not *actual* friends although Valerie would have welcomed her friendship. Wireless could be quite lonely sometimes.

Mr Fairweather was keen on 'sticking power' – and, whenever he went on about that, she was reminded of Mrs

Howard's exhortation: 'I don't believe in shirking, do you, Valerie?'

'I like ambitious women,' Mr Fairweather said. 'We need more of them.'

Few men got what it was like to be an ambitious woman – what it felt like to know that you were capable, to know that you were equal, but to be treated as though you weren't. She found herself warming to him until, to her surprise, he talked about women's contributions to the war – including the often-under-estimated bus workers.

My mum made a notable contribution? It hardly seems likely.

'Are you with me, Miss Hardman?' he asked suddenly, clicking his fingers in front of her face.

'Oh absolutely,' she said. 'Lady clippies, underestimated. That's right.'

Over the drinks, Mr Fairweather continued with his flattery – she was a talent, an exception. Valerie found the compliments awkward, she was unused to them, but she knew Mrs Howard would tell her to accept them with good grace. She also saw that Mr Fairweather treated the barmaid like she was a human.

'You haven't been involved with anyone at work?' He cut into her thoughts.

Valerie looked up uncertainly, but he grinned at her: 'I always notice – that's good journalism.'

She wondered if he'd noticed Anna's gallivanting. It always came out; she thought again of her mother. Another reason she was glad to have stuck with Paul.

It was a jolly afternoon. Once they got on to *It's That Man Again*, Valerie was agog. Mr Fairweather's behind-the-scenes anecdotes were thrilling. Among most people, Valerie reined in her passion for the show – after all, it was *just* a radio show –

but with Mr Fairweather, she didn't have to. He instinctively understood what it represented to her.

It was a lifeboat in a tumultuous time. It took her out of herself. It spoke to her. Sometimes, a look behind the curtain can damage a fan's love affair. Sometimes, the Wizard of Oz is simply a selfish old man. 'Don't meet your idols' was the popular phrase. But nothing she had ever heard about the making of *It's That Man Again* made her feel like that; in fact, the anecdotes only increased her affection.

'And he was ill at this point.'

'Nooo...'

'Who do you think wrote that?'

'She was marvellous.'

He asked for the bill, then leaned forward and pulled off her glasses, only they snagged on one ear.

'Ow,' she cried.

In a low voice Mr Fairweather said, 'Can't I see how you look with them off?'

'Oh,' she said, removing them. 'I suppose.'

'Wow!' he said.

No one had ever 'wowed' Valerie before. Not even Paul.

'You have a beautiful face.'

And without her glasses, Mr Fairweather's looks had improved too, for he was blurry and if only the world was this fuzzy. Perhaps being ridiculously short-sighted was the way to go. It was very forgiving.

Valerie thanked him for paying and he was telling her more stories, or, as he said, 'giving away trade secrets', when she realised with horror that his hand was on her thigh.

At first she hoped it was a mistake – maybe it had dropped there, like a serviette – but he didn't lift it. Instead, his thumb started circling the hem of her skirt. It was deliberate!

Sometimes Valerie felt like she was behind in her social or rather her sexual development. The people five years older than her went racing around in the war having passionate liaisons, and the people a few years younger were unaffected by it. It was them, the middle lot – the odd ones out, who were shunted around the countryside like crown jewels. They were the inbetweeners.

She watched that thumb with its neat nail and she imagined Mr Fairweather sitting on the side of his bed in pyjamas and cutting them, and, even though she had been transfixed by the story he was telling of how the popular line: 'Don't forget the diver, sir. Every penny makes the water warmer!' came about, her attention was diverted.

He stopped speaking.

She waited. He had cleared his throat.

'Do you want to come to a hotel with me?'

She wasn't sure what he meant. Her cheeks were burning hot. Another bar? He must have meant that – hotels had bars.

'I've had enough to drink.'

How much clearing does a throat need? 'I don't mean to drink.'

'What do you mean?' Her question sounded bold, but it wasn't meant to be – it was just Valerie, straight down the line.

'To get a room.'

'I don't need a room,' Valerie explained.

She had never been propositioned before – was it a proposition? What if it wasn't? What if he was being boss-like and she was being prudish or unreasonable?

More throat-clearing. 'With me?'

Valerie gazed up at him, puzzled.

'What about your wife?'

Presumably there was a wife. The packed-lunch-maker? Oh God, what if he was a widower?

'What's that got to do with us?' he said.

Valerie couldn't believe her ears. 'Pardon?' she responded.

'You're a modern girl, a career woman, aren't you?' His hand was still there. 'You could meet them...'

'What? Who?'

'That cast of *It's That Man Again*. I could introduce you – it could be great experience for you. Personally, and professionally.'

It was excruciating! Valerie stood up. This was worse than a proposition, she realised. This was, this was, she didn't know what it was, but she was outraged. Who did he think she was? She was not like her mother – she would not be swayed.

She didn't usually see Mr Fairweather on a day-to-day basis, yet after that evening she bumped into him three times – what were the chances? – Monday, and twice on Tuesday.

At the end of the week, he pulled her aside and she knew he was going to tell her to clear her desk and leave – she'd heard this happened to women who turned their bosses down – but instead he apologised: 'I had too much to drink, I'm dreadfully sorry if I made a fool of myself.'

Valerie didn't think the problem was the too-much-to-drink, but she agreed she had no hard feelings. She realised that maybe she ought to look at moving on from the job, sooner rather than later. She had become rather comfortable and comfort was the antithesis of ambition. Anna had the right idea: not about television but about moving on.

If anything, this episode with her boss had made her judge Jean *more*. You could resist these things; you *could* turn men down. There were options. You didn't have to be a mistress. You didn't have to have bastards and terminations.

She wrote a furious letter to Paul – *how long can I wait?*, then ripped it up. She couldn't send that! Telling him about the sacrifices she had made in his name wouldn't bring him home – and was it all in his name anyway?

As to whether her future lay in wireless, Valerie was unde-terred. If ever she had doubts, she only had to remember that child far from home, a frightened girl in that shop crowded full of boxes with no prices, and a wireless set and the voices that were her friends.

She knew somewhere, someone out there would need her one day.

80

Jean

A tall man was waiting outside Broadcasting House. A tall man in the light grey pinstriped demob suit. It fitted him better than most. He also was in a raincoat and a felt hat, which was probably why she didn't recognise him at first.

'Evening, Mrs Hardman.'

'Evening,' Jean said in that brisk way you do when you're not sure who someone is.

'I'm afraid I have some sad news.'

Jean blanched. 'Valerie?' she squeaked.

'No, no,' he said quickly. 'Sorry to alarm you. It's my father.'

When Jean continued to look mystified, he added, 'Mr Carrington? From the buses?'

And then she knew who it was. It was Richard, the bus driver: Richard Carrington.

'He passed. Last week. I thought I should tell you. You were good to him during the war,' he said.

'He was good to me,' she said. She remembered a saucepan

she had taken round that she hadn't got back; she couldn't ask for it now, could she?

Somehow, Richard wasn't as lanky as he used to be. He was still red-headed under that hat, and still his pale skin flushed salmon pink, but now the combination seemed attractive. How had that happened?

She wondered if he remembered asking her to be his girl. Now she thought it had been the sweetest thing.

'So, he told me you worked here. He'd been ill for a long time and then went all of a sudden.'

'It's always a shock,' Jean said soothingly. 'Even when it's expected.'

'Exactly,' he said, like she'd said something revelatory. 'That's it.'

He twisted his hands. He looked like he was going to cry.

'I'm still in a daze.'

'Course you are,' she said. She wanted to be kind.

'He made it through the war and then... pfft.'

They went for a walk and the streets seemed bursting with vitality – in that shocking *life goes on way* that occurs to you after news of a death. Everything was louder and more colourful than it had been a few moments before; it felt like the cars were breathing fire, the pavement was swaying, the buildings were alive, the man selling newspapers was radiant.

There was a group of children in a walking crocodile, returning from a school trip maybe; there were some who couldn't stay in line, they couldn't keep still, and Jean empathised; how she empathised. Their teacher barked orders at them but still the children laughed and shouted. Life was everywhere.

They eventually sat on a bench not far from home and, after she'd asked him a few times, he relented and told her his story.

It was dusk and the streetlights glowed orange and the insects whirred frenetically in their light.

'Did I ever tell you that my mother left us?'

'I thought she was… you know, dead.'

'Yes,' he said. 'That's what people thought.' He paused. 'I guess I wanted people to think that.'

Jean nodded. That was a story she knew.

He told her he was working in insurance now. He went red again. And when he went red, he went scarlet to his tips.

'It's quiet but I'm not looking for excitement.'

'You never were, were you?' Jean asked, teasing slightly.

He smiled, contemplating his hands. 'Not especially. I'm after the quiet life. I was proud to serve though.'

'You should be!' said Jean with enthusiasm. 'Think what you did for your country!'

He grimaced. 'I did it to keep the people I cared about safe. Dad, and friends and – you. That's what was important to me. Not flag-waving or borders or the King or the stuffy military. It was so we could keep on our precious way of life.'

Jean realised she liked this man, she really did, and she wondered why she hadn't liked him first time round. Had he changed, or had she? She remembered he had told her he felt untethered. And she had thought about that word for a long time. *Tethered – attached by a rope, usually an animal.*

'I don't think you knew but I have a daughter…' Jean said after a moment of comfortable silence.

'Dad mentioned it to me not long ago.'

'Did he?' said Jean. Unbeknown to her, everyone had found out.

'Valerie, is it?'

'Yes – she doesn't live with me.'

'She doesn't?' He looked at her with gentle eyes and she wanted to cry. No one had been this gentle with her for years, if ever.

She took a deep breath. 'I don't see her at all. I mean, ever.'
There. That's it.

The world didn't stop spinning. He didn't think she was a witch. His face was sympathetic. 'That's tough for you.'

'It's my fault.' She sniffed.

She didn't think she could have borne it if he said something like *Hold on to your loved ones.* Or *Life is short.* She had heard all the homilies people liked to say and none did any good. Fortunately, he didn't. He sighed, and said, 'Life can be painful, can't it?'

'Do you remember you asked me to walk out with you?'

It was ten years ago. And she didn't know him any better now than she had then. But perhaps this was the beginning of knowing him.

Again, he blushed. No one did flaming cheeks like a redhead. 'I remember you said no.'

'Sorry,' she said. 'It was complicated.'

All the years she'd wasted on Tony, keeping secrets and secrets on top of secrets. She regretted getting pregnant during the war, but she didn't regret the termination even if it was unlawful. She was a practical person and she knew she was lucky she had survived it. It shouldn't have gone wrong; it shouldn't have been undignified.

She regretted not falling for kind Richard Carrington earlier. Not only at the beginning of the war, when he first asked her out and foolishly, she had only eyes for feckless Tony. She regretted not meeting him years before. If they had been childhood sweethearts, how different their lives might have been.

81

Valerie

Mrs Howard had lost weight, Valerie noticed with an ominous feeling, when she met her at the railway station at Bristol. Her cheekbones were even more prominent. She wore casual trousers and a sweater, yet as usual she wore them smartly – pearl necklace and earrings, expensive shoes; they did not look the way they would on most people. She had a new brooch too. She showed it to Valerie, saying, 'You'll like this one.' It was a treble clef and yes, Valerie thought it was lovely, although she would always like the frog brooch the most.

Valerie took her to her new lodgings, which were like her old lodgings but in a slightly more convenient location.

'Have you met anyone special?' Mrs Howard asked over tea.

Boyfriends? I find them disappointing compared to Paul.

Valerie didn't say that, of course. She said that she was concentrating on her work. That was far more palatable.

She missed Paul – she had begun referring to him as 'the love of my life', although only to herself. She wasn't sure if Mrs Howard realised. If she did, she was good at hiding it.

Mrs Howard told Valerie about her latest theatrical production: *All My Sons*, a new play by a young American playwright that she was sure Valerie would love. After she had talked at length on this subject, Mrs Howard told Valerie to brace herself – she had some sad news. Valerie was certain it would be about her own deteriorating health, so was doubly shocked when it wasn't.

'Mrs Woods has died,' Mrs Howard continued gently. 'An accident apparently, some boxes had fallen and knocked her off a stool... She wasn't discovered for days.'

What alarmed Valerie was that she couldn't find an ounce of sympathy for Beastly Woods, not any. She felt completely hollow about it. She pretended to though, because Mrs Howard was gazing at her with a concerned expression.

'How sad.'

'Tragic,' said Mrs Howard. 'I know your relationship was not what it should have been, but no one deserves an ending like that, do they?'

'Exactly,' said Valerie. 'More tea?'

Later, when Mrs Howard enquired whether Jean had visited Bristol again, Valerie told her no and moved the conversation on. As far as she was concerned, Mrs Howard was her mother, and a brilliant one at that. She'd been lucky.

They spent the rest of the day laughing about plays, books and, of course, shows on the wireless.

Valerie was promoted again at Bristol. The move ruffled a few feathers, but she was used to that. People were speculating that she was sleeping with Mr Fairweather, and she was glad – for all sorts of reasons – that she could look everyone in the eye and know that she was not.

There was constant talk about 'the power of wireless in a changing world' and Valerie always said – to anyone who asked

– that *It's That Man Again* had shaped a lot of her ideas. Gradually, she came to understand it wasn't the show itself; or rather it wasn't the show on its own, it was that rare combination – the perfect storm – the right programme reaching her at exactly the right point in her life: a voice in the darkness when she needed it most.

She had many ideas for new programmes. They crept up on her while she was sleeping or in the bath. They crept up on her while she was doing anything except when she was trying to think up new ideas! *You are not alone*, she wanted the programmes to say. Or *Have a listen to this. This'll interest you, cheer you, make you laugh.*

You could have all the ideas, of course, but ultimately, you had to settle on one or two. That was the rule, although Valerie, being Valerie, was now working on three.

The first was a series on piers. Best piers, great piers, did you know Southend Pier helped win the war? (Thank you, fortune teller! She may have been useless on telling fortunes, but she was brilliant inspiration.)

After two days of consideration and nail-biting on Valerie's part, Mr Fairweather gave it the thumbs-up.

The second was an emotional piece called *Thank You*. It was Valerie's most simple idea yet – you call in and thank someone for their kindness. For mending wirelesses, for sharing schoolwork, for opening up their home.

It was the sort of thing Anna would have told her to steer clear of – too sentimental, too ditsy. Anna had a mortal fear of labels or being pigeonholed. But it was also too good not to do, Valerie thought, so she pressed forwards with it anyway.

Mr Fairweather said he'd think about it. A few days later, he came back with a commission. 'My wife swayed it,' he said, blushing only slightly. 'She thinks it's genius.'

The Thank You show was another great success. Valerie was on a roll.

And then there was *The Woman on the Clapham Omnibus*.

It was a twist on the idea of the man on the Clapham Omnibus.

'Isn't that copying?' a member of the team asked.

'Not quite,' Valerie answered, thinking of a teacher in Somerset and a poetry competition. 'It's standing on the shoulder of giants.'

In these programmes, Valerie focused on the women. Women like her mother. She interviewed clippies, nurses, secretaries and grandmothers – all on the buses of Bristol.

The stories they heard! Women who had worked in the land army, the air raid patrol, the hospital. Mothers who had sent their children away, expecting never to see them again: 'I was sure he was lost...' Children who returned religious: 'They stayed with a vicar!' Children who came back two feet taller than when they'd gone away. It was an education. And yes, it made Valerie think of Jean.

One time, she even met a young woman who'd spent six months at Hedingway Hall. The name sounded familiar, although Valerie didn't know why at first. And then she remembered – it was where she might have been evacuated. 'It was there I learned croquet and badminton, and I still play,' the woman said, and for a moment Valerie felt like sobbing. Here was another path she might have travelled.

Valerie was out and about every day, lugging her equipment. And there were pieces in the newspaper about it and, yes, before too long she had caught the attention of the right people in London.

82

SPRING 1950

Jean

The head of the department came over to the dinner ladies with his tray and a query. Jean slopped the spam (it was Monday, obviously) onto a plate.

'Indulge me! I'm trying to find a normal woman.'

'I'm a normal woman,' volunteered Jean. Some people might be offended by the phrase 'normal woman' – for Jean, it felt like a promotion. 'How can I help?' More picking of brains, she supposed.

'We want to make our shows more appealing for lady listeners.'

'I see.'

'We don't know how to do that.'

Jean considered. 'Why not get a few more women on the creative team?'

'What? *Making* the shows, you mean?'

'Why not?'

He pondered before grinning at her. 'By Jove, that's an idea.'

So, you could say, indirectly, very indirectly, Jean was one of the reasons Valerie came back to London.

83

SUMMER 1950

Valerie

On Valerie's first day in the Department of Light Entertainment at Broadcasting House, an unexploded bomb was discovered in a nearby street. Everyone had to evacuate the building.

The morning had been stressful enough as it was. There was a kerfuffle about the lanyards and her name:

'Is that Valerie with a Y?'

'I don't think it's ever spelled with a Y...'

And exact job title. Eventually, she'd been sent, label round her neck, up to an office on the sixth floor, where three young men looked her over with matching quizzical expressions.

'I'm the new person,' she said, striding over to shake their hands.

'But you're a lady!' the first man said, and the other two could barely contain their laughter.

The BBC were looking for a female point of view. Their listeners were 50 per cent women, after all. They had *House-wives' Choice*, but they needed more – more dramas, more shows, more quizzes. Valerie was to help find and create content.

She had deliberated about the role for some time because, while it was her dream job, she didn't want to be in London. Ultimately though she accepted, and went back to the city she had been evacuated from ten and a half years earlier; but she was wary, wondering if it was a mistake.

There was no desk for her. Or there was, but it was covered with scripts and boxes and all sorts.

'You could try in there,' proposed one of the young men, hilariously pointing to a cupboard. He introduced himself as 'Bertie, like the abdicated king. Only even more fun.' 'We aren't formal in Light,' he added, which was why they addressed each other by their first names.

The one with the most boyish face but whose receding hair-line gave away that he was older said, 'I'm Boris. Like the Russian tsar – don't overthrow me.'

'Simmer down, boys,' said the last one, who also looked about fifteen at most.

This one explained what was already apparent – their manager was away, and no one knew what to do with her and wouldn't until he was back.

'I can do anything,' Valerie said.

At that, his cheeks coloured, and he leaned forward: 'Don't say that or they'll have you making tea.'

'You couldn't make us a brew, could you, darling?' inter-rupted Boris.

'No, of course she can't,' the one who hadn't yet told her his name retorted.

'Why don't you show me where the kitchen is, we'll do it together?'

Another misstep.

'Aye, aye,' Boris sniggered. 'I'm in there.'

The other man shook his head indulgently. 'It's her first day.' Then he grinned at her. 'We don't even know your name.'

'Valerie,' she said, holding out her lanyard for him to see. 'You can call me Val.'

'Godfrey,' he said in a rehearsed way, 'and you can call me God...'

Laughing, she shook her head. *Oh boy! This place is going to be interesting.* She sorted through the ashtrays, cups, pencils and jars of ink on the desk.

She was doing that when the alarm went off. It was tempting to sit it out, but her new colleagues got up, grumbling, so Valerie realised she was expected to as well.

'It's not a drill?'

''Fraid not,' said Godfrey. 'Nearly ten years after the Blitz, we're still having to evacuate.'

Another evacuation? thought Valerie. Story of her life.

Bertie and Boris dashed ahead, but the posh one – Godfrey – waited for her. She could imagine him in wellington boots with a shotgun. She knew men like that nowadays, but there would always be a corner of her heart that was incredulous that she did. She was a long way from Bethnal Green.

Between floors 3 and 2, she asked, 'Does this happen a lot?'

'Twelve odd times since I've been here, so I'd say around four a year.'

'Better safe than sorry,' she said, between the first floor and ground.

'Exactly.'

She could have told him she was evacuated during the war, only she didn't suppose he would be interested. Most people weren't. Out on the street, though, they got on to it in a round-about way.

'Do you know London well?' he asked.

'I wouldn't say "well". I lived here until I was ten though.'

Few weeks shy of her eleventh birthday. The worst birthday of all.

'You probably know it better than me. Where did you live after that?'

'Somerset.'

'Beautiful part of the world.'

If she had a guinea for every time someone said that...

'Very.'

Godfrey's jaw was heavy, and his eyes were green-brown. That phrase, 'he has a face for wireless', might have been made for him. He was wearing spectacles – like she did – and, although she was no expert, Valerie felt they were the wrong shape for his face. Maybe she was an expert – she felt like she had spent enough hours at the optician's to take it up as a career if wireless didn't work out.

'Evacuee?'

In a roundabout way was the only way people talked about it. As though those six years could only be approached from a slip lane. Why would people care? Worse things had happened.

'Got it in one.'

'I was at a boarding school, so my life hardly changed. Massive upheaval for you, I imagine.'

He had a caring way of speaking, which she hated. Not because it upset her but because she couldn't be pitied by a colleague. It would be as bad as making tea.

'Which boarding school was that?' Paul had been at boarding school.

Godfrey said it was St Johns in Scotland and she was relieved it wasn't Paul's school, although why it would matter she didn't know.

Valerie had moved back to London from Bristol only two weeks earlier, and counted herself lucky since she had found a bedsit to live in almost immediately and she could pay rent weekly. It was in a townhouse in Islington without lampshades and with lightbulbs that flickered. Her landlord said he would look into the wiring issue, but he hadn't yet and she didn't want to bother him.

On the positive side, she had her own indoor loo – it was a relief that she didn't have to share or go outside – and the neighbours on the same floor were an amenable middle-aged couple with a visiting black cat called Socks. The couple apologised about Socks' visits but, as Valerie waited to start working, those cat visits were a highlight of her day.

It was different from Bristol. The days were quicker, the streets more frantic. And the way people in London spoke with their 'excuse mes' and their 'mind how you goes' was different from the 'all right, my loves?' that she had grown used to.

Everyone was milling around the main road, awaiting further instructions. Except for Valerie, most were in groups, but she never minded being by herself.

Godfrey had raced back to help some older people who were wobbly on the stairs, which was good of him.

Out there on the pavement, it was as though the whole city was being presented for her, laid out like a great oil painting. In her eyeline, the historic buildings – and there wasn't one that wasn't darkened by soot, by ash, by filthy air – and, even on this street, this well-to-do avenue, there were the bombed-out sites, the cavities, the playgrounds of temptation.

The red telephone boxes, the pavement, the road signs, the traffic lights. The double-decker buses that said to the world, 'this is London', but which said something else entirely to Valerie Hardman.

After a while, some secretaries surrounded her.

They said, 'Are you new?' and 'Haven't seen *you* before...' but, when Valerie explained she was in Light Entertainment, in production, they lost interest, not in an impolite way but in a you're-no-good-for-us way. The men didn't talk to her at all. They were animatedly talking about communists. 'No one wants another war,' they said, and she thought, *I've heard that one before*.

Then, to her mortification, the actual head of the Light Entertainment department, Mr Copperthwaite, tapped her on the shoulder. Everyone looked over.

'Miss Hardman, our newest recruit? Here to shake things up, am I right?'

'I'll do my best, sir,' Valerie said, aware both of him and of their audience. The last thing she needed was to be singled out.

'I know your mother!'

'Sorry?'

'I saw her *Seagull* at the Old Vic. Fantastic director – one of the best of her generation. Do tell her I said hello.'

'Mrs Howard is my godmother,' was the word Valerie settled upon.

'Yes, yes,' he said impatiently as though she were the one missing the point, and then he stalked off before she could add anything else.

Everyone who had been listening stared back at the pavement.

An older woman in a patterned headscarf tied tightly under her chin made eye contact, so Valerie put on a pleasant expression and enquired, 'How long do you think we'll be out for?'

The woman shrugged like 'how long is a piece of string?' but offered Valerie a cigarette from a tin box.

'I don't think we should, should we?' asked Valerie, alarmed. She didn't want to turn down a friendly offer, but the prospect of setting off an almighty explosion was not how she had envisaged her first day.

'Suit yourself, doll,' said the woman. She strutted off, unlit cigarette dangling from her hand.

Valerie realised she wasn't doing a terrific job of making friends. And although she had a policy of not getting too close to colleagues – (that way lay all the horrors, thank you, Mr Fairweather!) – she knew she had better buck herself up. No girl is an island. If she wanted to make a splash in the Light Entertainment department, then she was going to have to make friends – otherwise it might as well be a repeat of all the other episodes of her life.

A man wearing an emergency-worker-style yellow vest over his suit clapped his hands for silence, which didn't work and then shouted that they needed to listen, which did.

'The Germans dropped tonnes of explosives on us in 1940,' he said. If Valerie had thought Godfrey and the head of Light had posh voices, this man sounded like a close relative of the King. 'And as you know, there are still some among us. This WAS a bomb, I repeat, a bomb, but it was a dud, and heroes from the army are removing it now.'

At this, everyone politely clapped like an unexpectedly good curtain call, and Godfrey whispered, 'I'm going down now, sir,' and Valerie beamed at him. It was a line from *It's That Man Again*, and hearing it gave her an inkling that, contrary to first impressions, they might get on after all.

As they walked back up, Boris sidled next to her: 'I knew a man in bomb disposal. Tough job.'

And Bertie said, 'It's bomb not-disposal that's tough.'

They both guffawed.

Over the next few days, Valerie developed a routine of arriving early at the office, leaving late and also working through lunch. Not only did you have to work hard, you had to be seen to be working hard. Men were allowed mistakes, women were not. They weren't even called mistakes when men made them. Wireless – or radio as it was called now – was a man's world and the Department of Light Entertainment even more so. Valerie had chosen this career despite the obstacles (there was an argument that Valerie had chosen it *because* of the obstacles) but the fact was: she loved it. She loved sending a message or story out there, into the world. Sometimes she thought that in a bizarre way, it was like catching then setting free a fish – watching it swim away, you couldn't be sure if it would make it home, but hopefully, you'd played your part.

And over the next few days Valerie grew to, if not like her co-workers, then certainly to enjoy their company. Godfrey was always willing to lend a hand. Boris always knew a man who'd done this and that. Bertie didn't say much but what he did say was with a big seedy grin on his face, so you were never sure if he was being serious or sardonic.

She got used to brushing off questions about her private life – Boris standing over her desk, tapping his teeth: 'Is there a special someone in your life, Miss Hardman?'

'There are lots of special someones, thank you, Boris.'

Bertie, with his pen tucked behind his ear; Valerie, willing it to leak.

'A little birdy told me...'

'I find little birdies to be unreliable sources...' Valerie chuckled to herself.

'That you're spoken for?'

'I prefer to speak for myself.'

'You're not engaged?'

Valerie laughed. 'I am not...'

'But you are not – as they say – looking for love?'

Valerie smiled at the thought of Paul. 'I most definitely am not.'

A postcard had been sent on to the new flat.

My darling girl, how long has it been now?

(one year, two months and five days, Paul.)

I haven't forgotten you. Have you forgotten me?

(never!)

Mother says your programmes are popular. That makes me proud. Did she tell you about my art shows?

(Yes.)

I can't believe people are coming to them! I can't believe people are buying my work. You're the talented one though. I tell everyone who goes to England to listen to 'The Woman on the Clacton omnibus'.

(He'd got the name wrong but okay.)

Love you, dear girl, always and forever.

Valerie's new colleagues were insistent that she join them for lunch in the canteen. They turned it into a joke: 'This canteen is a perk of the job! We owe everything to the dinner ladies.' But there were serious undertones too – it wouldn't reflect well on them if they were seen to leave her out.

Valerie was not keen on going, though. She prepared her cress sandwich at home under the flickering lightbulbs and ate at her desk.

'But the canteen is subsidised!' roared Boris.

'So is my sandwich!'

She wasn't particularly a lunch person, she explained to Bertie. Fruit cake was her only weakness. For a moment, she allowed herself to remember the most beautiful fruit cake she had ever seen: Lydia's one at Paddington station.

'They do fruit cake!' Bertie yelped.

She had so many proposals and scripts to get through, she told Godfrey.

'Thirty minutes won't make any difference,' he said.

Valerie held out for a couple more weeks, during which time there were no further evacuations. When finally, one Friday, she succumbed, they left before her; she didn't know where the canteen was and she ended up on the roof. Eventually she found it, on the first floor. She didn't know whether to push or pull the door, then she shoved it and ended up almost flying in. Godfrey, Boris and Bertie cheered. (You can take the boys out of boarding school but you can't take the boarding school out of the boy! Paul used to say that.)

Godfrey jumped up to assist: 'Do you need help?'

Valerie collected herself. 'Do I look like I need help?'

'With an entrance like that, I thought you might.'

Godfrey was fast becoming her favourite of the three stooges or the three musketeers or the three bears, which were all names she called them, depending on her mood and how aggravating they were being.

Picking up a wooden tray, Valerie joined the queue. She kept her eyes on the counter and the steaming metal trays of meat, potatoes and gravy. It smelled good.

Next to her, Godfrey was going on to the dinner ladies: 'Your gravy is second to none. It should win prizes.'

'Any sauces?' someone behind the counter asked. 'I haven't got all day.'

Finally, Valerie looked up.

There, under a paper hat and in overalls, with paper gloves on her hands, was her mother.

84

Valerie

Valerie's tray clattered onto the floor. Jean was staring at her, open-mouthed.

'Sorry,' she muttered. She went to put the tray back with the others and instead smacked into Godfrey, who was Godfreying, 'Ye gads, did you see, it's spotted dick today, Valerie? Lunch doesn't get any better than this.'

Muttering that she wasn't hungry, Valerie legged it to the door. Push or pull? Why did everything have to be so complicated? She shoved it, fell into the corridor, then dashed away into the street.

Her mother was working in the canteen!

Outside, Valerie lit a cigarette with trembling hands and consoled herself with smoke rings. Paul would have liked those. That was one thing she was expert at; Morwenna had taught her. She pulled her coat tightly around her. She mustn't look weak; she mustn't look emotional. The men at work – even the nice ones – were looking for any excuse to prove that women were useless. If she were spied sobbing in the street, it would be damaging not only for her but for every ambitious girl in every company.

A bus went by. A bloody bus. If it wasn't her mother, it was reminders of her mother. This one was advertising the film *The Blue Lagoon*, which Lydia had told Valerie she wanted to see. It was about two children marooned together on a desert island who grow up together and go on to have a baby. Lydia was a romantic and still believed in love stories, but Valerie had refused to go.

She stamped out the cigarette. *Be cool.*

Each time Valerie saw Jean, it felt like a graphic illustration of radio-waves – going up and down, hope then disappointment, up and down, down and up, disappointment then hope. She didn't want to play that again.

Back upstairs in the office, Godfrey was doing his surprisingly efficient two-finger typing. When Valerie came in he looked up, worried.

'Feeling poorly?' he asked. He could be patronising.

'I didn't fancy anything.'

Valerie squinted at him, dreading his response, but all he said was, 'Hard luck – let me know if I can get you anything.'

She resolved that she would continue to work through lunch in future.

They had a brainstorming session that afternoon, but after seeing Jean for the first time in years, Valerie was not in the mood.

'What about a comedy on the buses?' Boris proposed.

'What would be comic about that?' she snapped. Was he making a dig?

They had been allocated two scriptwriters, who were

waiting for them to advise them on topics. Apparently, they were side-splittingly funny and could make a show set on the head of a pin hilarious.

'We'll have a put-upon driver and a sex-mad clippie!' roared Bertie.

Valerie narrowed her eyes. 'And?'

'And...'

'I don't like it,' pronounced Valerie. 'What about a group of public school boys with no experience of the world who like to laugh at working-class people?'

Only Godfrey was amused. 'Touché,' he said.

'I still think we could do more with the war,' Valerie said. 'From the women's point of view.'

'People aren't ready yet. It's too close.'

Valerie exhaled. Could she be any more annoyed? 'When will they be ready?'

'I don't believe ever – not the next generation, maybe the one after that—'

'By which time,' she cut in, 'no one will be around to tell the tale.'

'What about Jack the Ripper?' said Bertie. Not a day went by without Bertie suggesting that.

Valerie had her monthlies too, and a massive headache. She was counting down the minutes until she could go home to process everything that had happened.

The next day, Mr Hogg, their manager, returned with fresh instructions from on high:

'We want you to create a new show for children.'

Valerie gulped. 'I thought I was here to increase our female listeners...'

'This first. If this succeeds, we'll have a little think about women.'

The way he said 'women' gave her goosebumps.

Mr Hogg had been polite the first time she met him, yet now he was sharp. She wondered if he had found out she had a mother working in the canteen. He was a snob; the old school tie network had got him his position rather than any passion for radio. Godfrey, bless him, got on famously with him, but no one else did.

'Children's programming is not as easy as people imagine.'

'I know, but I didn't think it was what I was here for.'

'You and the team will come up with some ideas.'

'We can do that, but...' They had assembled all these brilliant comedy writers, who were looking into all their brilliant ideas for Light Entertainment for *adults* not children.

'No buts...'

Valerie sighed. This move to London wasn't turning out how she had imagined. That thought struck her as amusing. Wasn't 'not turning out as she had imagined' the way it always was for her?

She told Godfrey, Boris and Bertie what they had to do and they stared around gloomily, and she couldn't help thinking that they were thinking it was because she was a woman and hadn't fought their corner hard enough.

'This is going to sound odd but are you avoiding the canteen?' Godfrey asked a few days later. They were finishing up a documentary series about modern houses and modern building materials – *Will They Stand the Test of Time?* – which would have been fascinating except for the presenter, who was one of those who liked to go on and on. It was so bad, Valerie said she preferred the minute pause *after* the programme to the programme itself. Godfrey declared that the most cutting criticism he'd ever heard.

She couldn't lie to Godfrey. He had the most guileless

expression. Boris suggested he was 'eminently punchable', which made them laugh, but there was some truth to it. 'I am,' he had conceded. 'Sorry!'

'You looked like you'd seen a ghost the other day.'

'Not a ghost, no...'

'The toad-in-the-hole can be dire and the spam pitiful but I'm guessing it's not that...'

'Correct,' she said.

He wrung his hands. 'Do you want to tell me the problem?'

If it was anyone else, she would have told them to sod off. But this was Godfrey, and sometimes he reminded her of a puppy – and you couldn't kick a puppy.

'It's a long story,' she said.

'I happen to like long stories,' he said, leaning against her now tidy desk.

'One of the dinner ladies is my mother.'

His face broke into a smile as though she were joking. And then he pressed his lips shut and then open again like one of Paul's fish.

'And you don't want to see her?'

'I don't,' Valerie replied quickly.

Mr Hogg was arriving – he always made a grand entrance – so Valerie and Godfrey quickly arranged to go for a drink later. Valerie considered cancelling – there was too much to do on *Will they Stand the Test of Time?* – but she was grateful for the chance to get it off her chest. She didn't have any friends in London yet and Godfrey – for all his faults – was a good listener.

They went to the Pied Piper public house, which overlooked the river. The Thames was looking grey and choppy today. Valerie relished its changeability. She missed Somerset but there was something majestic about the way the river made the city feel – like a lifeline winding through your palm. They watched a man fishing as Valerie attempted to explain her relationship with her mother.

'I spent the war away from her. Then, we met briefly and...'

'And what?'

'I found out more secrets,' she said. Everything they had was built on lies. And other people knew the truth; she was the only idiot who didn't. She felt a sense of exclusion, because it wasn't only that Jean was a great keeper of secrets – it was that she distributed them to the people she liked best, and that was never Valerie. Valerie the mushroom, always in the dark.

'I can't seem to forgive her...' Valerie said, biting her bottom lip to try to stop herself from crying.

'For keeping the secrets or what the secrets actually are?' Godfrey asked.

'You can't separate them like that...' Valerie laughed. He was being absurd.

'You can,' he said. 'Why not?'

'For both then,' she said, knowing her relationship with Jean was far too complicated for Godfrey to ever truly understand.

That evening, she dissected the conversation. She turned it upside down and examined it, the way she would a proposal or a script.

It *wasn't* just the secrets and lies. She and Jean might have managed to overcome them if the other mother-daughter things were in place. Fact was, they weren't. Her mother didn't understand her and she didn't understand her mother. There was no meeting of minds. There was very little common ground or shared history anymore. Perhaps that was neither of their faults.

Her mother made her feel like she was ten years old. It was as if Jean didn't realise she'd grown up. They had zipped past the teenage years and gone from ten to twenty without catching their breath. Was it any wonder their relationship was torturous?

Valerie also worried that her mother might affect her position at work. She knew that was heartless, ruthless even, but everyone knew you didn't bring your private life to work. Especially women. And you didn't get much more *bringing your private life to work* than having your mother serve soup in the canteen.

Everything she had achieved felt tenuous. She didn't have the confidence to shrug this off. Would people associate them?

Of course they would.

A few days later Valerie understood that Boris knew too.

'I haven't had a gooseberry tart like your mother served today since my grandmother, bless her soul, made one in 1935.'

Valerie blushed. She didn't think her mother had *made* the tart. Surely her role was merely to heat them up? Anyone could do that.

Godfrey swore on his life he hadn't said anything, but admitted Bertie suspected and Mr Hogg had queried it too: 'He asked me if you were sisters.'

'What did you say?'

'I said no.' Godfrey hesitated. 'But you do have the same name.'

It was all going to come out one way or another.

The next Monday, Valerie decided to face the canteen. Godfrey looked approving when she told him, even though she said, 'I don't know what I'm going to say yet...'

'You will.'

As her mother spooned the terrible spam onto her plate, she said in a low voice, 'It's good to see you, Val.'

Valerie nodded, momentarily speechless. Her actual mother, with her anxious eyes, was opposite her.

'I wonder if I could give you my new telephone number.'

'I don't mind,' Valerie managed to say.

Evidently, Jean had already prepared a note. There was something touching about that. She'd written the number, with 'Jean-Mum' under it. Valerie could imagine her labouring over that. Poor Jean-Mum.

'Call me, any time.'

Valerie waited until the weekend. Her mother answered breathlessly, and she kept saying she was delighted.

'Are you still in our old house?' Valerie asked.

'It would be lovely if you came, Val,' she said excitedly.

'I'm busy,' Valerie said. She nearly said 'Mum'. Force of habit, nothing else. 'But I will, soon.'

'How about Friday night?' Jean suggested, her voice full of hope. 'I'll get you a saveloy,' she added, remembering what Valerie liked from the fish and chips stand.

Her mother's hunger to see her was like a crow on a wire, stealthily watching her, hoping and waiting.

Back in the office, they got together to discuss where they had got so far with the children's show.

'Jack the Ripper!' cried Bertie.

'Robin Hood,' said Boris, even though they did him frequently.

'What about how the SS killed people?'

'We're making programmes for children,' Valerie reminded them. 'Has anyone here actually got any kids?'

Boris sarcastically said, 'Yeah, eight or nine. I've got so many, I've lost count.'

'Ha.'

'None of us have children,' Bertie sighed. 'What do we know about kids' programming?'

'Well,' Godfrey said, 'we were kids once, weren't we?'

It was endearing the way he always tried to look on the bright side.

'Hardly,' said Boris gloomily. 'I was an evacuee.'

Despite herself, Valerie laughed.

85

Jean

At the weekend Jean and Richard went to the cinema, where he bought her a packet of liquorice and she offered it by mistake to the man the other side of her.

Later, they went to the public house and he had an ale and she had one of their new cherryades. The bubbles went right up her nose, and she nearly spilled it in shock.

'You're not with it tonight, are you, Jean?' Richard said.

There were football fans filling up the bar, so perhaps it wasn't the best place for a serious conversation. She didn't mind them, but it would have been nice to go somewhere quiet. Richard was too softly spoken for this place.

'I saw Valerie this week.'

'Your Valerie?' he asked, his beautiful ginger eyebrows arched. This was how smitten Jean was – she adored the man's eyebrows!

Your Valerie, she thought; the girl is hardly mine.

'You'll never believe it. She's one of the bosses at work.'

She had a sudden memory of Valerie sitting on a stool in the street reading a book of rhymes to a doll and a sock. Jean had come back from work and had gone for her five minutes. When she came back, the dolls were smoking too.

Back in the present, Richard was saying, 'You must be proud.'

'It's nothing I've done,' she said, and he chewed his lip, went to the bar and ordered another round. This time she went for a gin. When she told them, Barb and Gwen had been diplomatic, but they'd made her feel worse. Richard was making her feel anxious too, although it wasn't his fault.

She's not going to like you, she thought.

He came back more sober than he had been. 'Is this... is this going to affect us, Jean?'

'Noooo,' she lied. Good grief; if Valerie knew she had 'yet another' boyfriend, then there'd be no hope of reconciliation, ever. The last thing she wanted was for her daughter to think, *here we go again – a man appears and whoosh, off she goes*. Jean didn't think that was what she did, but she knew Valerie thought she did. She'd twist it.

'It's great news,' he said, clinking his glass against hers. 'I'm here for you, Jean. Whatever you need.'

Her heart was going like the clappers – that old reminder of her mortality. If she had to put someone first, she thought, it would be her Val. It had to be.

'The only thing is we might need to slow things down.'

Jean used to tell Valerie that when you cut your hair, it grows back more quickly. The same with the plants she now collected on her window shelf. A trim of the leaves allows the plant to flourish.

But cutting back on Richard didn't seem to be working as well.

They – she – reduced the time they saw each other to once

a fortnight. Gone was the walk to work he used to do when he started late on Wednesdays. Gone was the night out at the pub. Gone was the cinema on Saturday. Gone was the park walk on Sunday.

'But we'll always have Friday fish and chips,' Jean said. She remembered the line in *Casablanca*: 'We'll always have Paris,' but it didn't have quite the same ring to it.

At first, Richard said he'd waited a long time for her already so 'what's a few more weeks?'

Weeks? thought Jean nervously. *It might be longer than that.*

Richard reorganised his routine as he had previously, only this time it was away from her. He saw the old crew from the buses, not Kenny, who he despised, but Albert and Perry. He watched cricket, he listened to his gramophone.

Gwen warned her, 'Richard won't wait for you forever, Jean. There aren't that many eligible men left.'

But Jean knew that, if she was to have any chance with Valerie, she couldn't be too involved with another man. Valerie would only retreat, and she couldn't go through that again.

86

AUTUMN 1950

Valerie

Perhaps it was because she was working in the same building now, perhaps it was a kind of osmosis, but Valerie couldn't stop dwelling on her mother. All thoughts led to Jean. It was a pleasure to stop obsessing about Paul, especially since the fortune teller's predictions – You will have *two children and they will look after you* – but it was also painful.

Valerie found herself unable to forgive her mum's secrecy even though she wanted to. All the things she hadn't told her. Her father wasn't dead, he was alive and well and living in Victoria Park. With his wife, might she add, and sons – her brothers. Why had Jean never been straight with her?

And yet Valerie couldn't address it with her; instead she would make snide comments that gave her a quick thrill of pleasure and then left her full of self-loathing.

Professionally, she grew more direct.

'Boris, that's the most ridiculous idea I've ever heard – it's genius!'

'Children don't want to be preached at, they want to be involved.'

But personally, she was unable to be clear.

And what of Paul? It still shocked Valerie that Paul had forged a career – more than a career, he was a doyen of the American art world – out of his twin passions: fishing and art. Sure, sometimes Paul now painted things that weren't fish, but these were greeted by his audience as his sideline or even as though he were being treacherous:

Sea creatures was what he was known for. The underwater world was what he was loved for. That's what they featured in the New York magazines. 'Paul Howard exhibits his latest "*Surf and Turf*"' – the turf were flowers, the surf were mackerel.

'I'll never get away from mackerel,' he wrote. 'And how are you, darling? Missing me?'

How am I? Still in love with you.

His fish paintings were everywhere: there was a pink curled prawn like a tiny curled-up baby in the womb; here, a herring on rye; there, a school of silver squid, like a metallic element. (Privately, Valerie preferred Miss Beedle's more emotional artworks, but she appreciated Paul's were more original.)

Near her birthday, she got a card, and he sounded fed up,

Help! They'll be wanting me to do octopuses next. Call me?

Their disjointed telephone calls were disappointing. There was always a long wait and sometimes a crackle. She'd say something then something else and he'd reply to the thing she'd said before that. It was a mess; it wasn't like in the films.

Besides, there was something magic in their raggedy written correspondence. She wrote to him about work, about her mother, about Lydia. She avoided the subject of Morwenna, naturally, and for some reason she avoided the subject of Godfrey too.

Paul was the love of her life. She remembered when he had taught her how to fish:

'Patience is key. There might be false alarms but when the real thing tugs, you'll know it.'

And she had a career; the job took up most, no, all of her time. She was determined to be a success. Paul Howard seemed to have walked effortlessly into glory, but she always knew the success of Valerie Hardman was going to be hard-won. But she wasn't a shirker; she knew her hard work would pay off – it had to.

Valerie's relationship with her mother still felt like a game of snakes and ladders. Sometimes, she moved up the board. Other times, she slithered back down to square one.

One evening, Jean met her after work with a bag of broken biscuits to share: 'Do you still like graveyards? I thought we could go and see the famous one at Highgate.'

Valerie knew her mother was trying, so although no, she didn't like graveyards in general, it was just the one in Somerset, they took the bus to North London. Her mother refrained from commenting on the clippie, although she laughed about him later – 'What terrible manners. Mrs Peabody wouldn't have let him get away with that!'

Those beautiful Victorian gravestones, full of tragedy and great love. Side by side, they ate the biscuits. Jean pointed out that Valerie had a clothes peg attached to her jacket, which made them laugh.

Valerie told her mother how she sometimes felt as though she was lost between two shores: 'I've tried to fit in wherever I was. I've experienced these different lives and sometimes I don't know which life is the real me.'

Jean opened her mouth slowly.

Please don't say anything silly, Valerie thought.

'The only time I felt like that,' said Jean slowly, 'was when I was with Tony during the war. I didn't know what I was doing.'

Valerie felt for her mother. She couldn't help it. How lonely she must have been during the war – and before the war too. No doubt about it, she was a survivor. She just wished it wasn't men – and especially married men – who she found solace in.

A while later, Valerie took a bottle of sweet German wine round to Romberg Road. Her mother had wanted to try it.

When Jean saw it, she covered her mouth. 'Oh my!'

'Someone left it in the office,' Valerie said and watched her mother's face fall. 'They send us things sometimes. I don't know why...'

Jean didn't have glasses. She got mugs from the cupboard and asked her about work.

'It's going well,' Valerie said, smiling.

'I'm proud of you. I know you've had a lot to overcome.'

'Not really,' Valerie said modestly. She knew she was contrary. With the men she worked with – with Godfrey, with Boris and Bertie – she wanted them to know how hard it had been. Yet with some people – her mother – she liked to pretend it was easy. 'Anyone could have done it.'

Valerie unscrewed the bottle and poured the wine. Jean was fussing because she didn't know what it was going to taste like.

'You don't have to have it,' said Valerie.

'I want to,' said Jean, like she was making a point.

'It should be chilled,' Valerie said but Jean interrupted smiling. 'I really don't mind.'

Valerie wanted to return to the conversation about work: 'You could have been someone too, if it weren't for... you know, Tony.'

Her mother screwed the cap back onto the bottle. She didn't

seem to know what to say. Finally, in a small voice, she said, 'I *am* someone, aren't I?'

It broke Valerie's heart a little but she wasn't ready to let go of her resentment, not yet. 'You're someone, but you could have been... you know... brilliant.'

'I don't know what you mean,' said Jean, swigging her wine. Valerie wanted to tell her not to gulp it like that, it wasn't juice, but Jean was wiping her mouth with the back of her wrist and insisting it was delicious. She said it reminded her of the summer before the war.

87

Jean

Jean couldn't sleep; that awful German alcohol had given her a bad stomach. She had drunk some horrid drinks in her time – she remembered the watered-down vodka they had had after a bad shift at the bus station – but this took the biscuit.

She couldn't help fretting that Valerie would find out about Richard Carrington. Which she did, of course she did.

A few days later, Valerie found her in the kitchens at work. It had been a busy Wednesday lunchtime (pork was popular) and Jean was washing up a tower of plates.

'Are you *living* with someone?' Valerie asked. Goodness she was blunt.

'Absolutely not.'

'You've got a new fella though?' she persisted.

Jean weighed up the odds of lying and getting away with it. There was no hiding from Valerie. She was forensic. She and Richard had been tiptoeing around each other but somehow Valerie must have caught wind of it.

'Yes,' she admitted. 'We've been walking out a while. We're taking it slowly. How did you find out?'

She knew how every word was grit on Valerie's wounds. Perhaps she could have made them sweeter, softer, but she didn't know how.

'You were seen,' Valerie said.

It was Gwen who had given them away, although it wasn't her fault. She'd heard someone arrive at the flat the other day and called out, 'Richard, is that you? Jean's doing her hair,' when it was Val.

'Taking it slowly, eh?'

'That's right. We met at the start of the war – he was a bus driver.' Jean paused. 'And he came back and found me.'

She couldn't get over it actually; it was the most romantic thing that had ever happened to her. But now poor Richard Carrington, who had been excited at their reunion, was in danger of fading into the background.

'Has my father been in touch?' Valerie asked brusquely. Like she didn't care, which meant she probably did.

'No, he's with his people,' Jean said, meaning to say, 'his family'. 'But if you want to see him...'

'I don't. I'm glad he's...' Valerie hesitated. 'Out of the picture.'

Jean sank her hand into the hot water, feeling for the cutlery. 'Please don't hate me.'

Her daughter's face was twisted. 'I don't hate you. I wish you had been honest with me.'

'I don't want to lose you, I only ever want to protect you. I got it wrong.'

Valerie didn't say anything, but she nodded.

Jean *wanted* to include Richard in her life though. She loved him. She had to be strong and push for this. She owed it to him. 'Would you like to meet him some time... my new chap?'

Valerie considered it. 'Okay. Maybe...'

Is this a thaw? Jean wondered. *Please let it be a thaw.* She knew though that it was probably too early to say.

88

Valerie

It was time for Valerie to pitch her idea for a children's wireless programme to her superiors. She was told to attend the board-room, where five inscrutable radio executives looked like they'd received some bad news. Valerie was introduced. When one of them said, 'Hardman? I know that name,' she thought she might die, but another man joked, 'Hardwoman!' and that made them chuckle.

'It's actually simple,' Valerie lied. She and the others had thought about how to approach this for ages and had decided the 'It's actually simple' approach was the best way.

'A doctor or a nurse to talk about growing up. I propose we call it *The Growing Up Show.*'

Valerie had wanted to call it *It's That Time of the Month Again!* in homage to her favourite wireless show. Godfrey found this hilarious, but his skin turned puce when she told him she was being serious.

She looked around the room; the radio executives looked even more miserable.

Someone's hearing aid whistled.

'*Growing Old Show*?'

'*Growing UP!*' corrected Valerie. 'Since many children are left in the dark about the facts of life.'

In the dark? She had been completely blind.

'You mean the birds and the bees?'

'Exactly. And we'll have a phone-in. It will be anonymous, which will embolden the children.'

Everyone stared.

And then one of them said, 'When I was a boy and my voice started breaking, I thought I was never going to sing again – but that's nothing compared to what I thought when I had my first wet dre—'

But the big boss had stood up: 'Over my dead body,' he roared.

Mr Hogg was looking at Valerie furiously. This was *not* what he'd had in mind. The meeting was over.

89

Jean

A few days later when Valerie was visiting the house at Romberg Road, Richard Carrington came by with some roses.

Both Jean and Valerie beseeched him to stay but Richard was resolute he was just popping by and he had to get home. He had acquired a new record for his gramophone and wanted to listen to it. He shook Valerie's hand and kissed Jean chastely. 'See you Friday.'

'I like him actually,' Valerie said when Jean returned from the front door touching her cheek.

After they'd settled at the kitchen table, Valerie talked about work, again. It was, Jean knew, her favourite subject, and it was better now that Jean could visualise some of the people and places she talked about.

'I wanted to make a series on the birds and the bees.'

Oof. Jean made a face. It was so typical of her daughter. What was it about her generation? They wanted to rummage through everyone's life stories, they wanted to shout from the rooftops, air their dirty laundry. It was like they couldn't resist swirling the soup. Sometimes it was best to let things settle.

She knew Valerie would come for the gritty details about the termination too, one day. Her generation wouldn't leave skeletons in the closet, they had to get them out and put them on the stage. Stiff upper lip might have been a nonsense for the upper classes, but my goodness, now it was gone she missed it. This generation was *Stick your tongue out.* And *Who cares?*

And then she thought what Barb and Gwen would say. They would say: step back, listen, don't jump in.

'Oh...' said Jean. 'Why is that?'

'Why what?' Valerie was always on the defensive, whatever Jean said.

'Why did you want to do that?' Jean asked.

Valerie smoothed down her skirt. 'I don't think I've ever told you this, but when I went away, on the very first day of the evacuation, I was bleeding. For the first few months I didn't know what it was. I was terrified.'

Jean's heart filled. It hadn't occurred to her. This was her fault; the poor, poor child. How could she have been so stupid? She'd neglected a most basic parental duty.

'I'm sorry.'

'It's fine,' Valerie said casually, but Jean knew it wasn't. 'Anyway, that's not why I'm telling you. I think it's remarkable not only that they said no but also how fervently they were against it.'

'Why?'

'They said it was undignified, unseemly and private.' Valerie snorted in disbelief.

Jean, whose thoughts had not been dissimilar, gulped. 'What will you do?'

'I'll drop it for now – but one day I WILL do it.'

Jean didn't doubt it, but her mind had started racing. 'But Val,' she said, 'didn't Mrs Woods help you?'

Valerie refused to look up.

'Vally?' Jean had a strange, agonised feeling in her chest. She needed something here and she didn't know what it was.

'Valerie, sweetheart. Why didn't Mrs Woods help you?'

Finally, Valerie looked up, and her expression was as hopeless and painful as a child's. 'Mrs Woods was awful,' she said. 'She hurt me.'

Jean would have done anything to hug her, but she knew Val didn't want that. Instead, she got down and knelt by her chair. 'I didn't know that,' Jean admitted. Her heart was sinking. She *should* have known. It was a mother's duty to know. It was agony and it was desperate, and she would have done anything for it not to be true – but it made sense. 'I'm sorry I didn't know.'

Valerie mechanically related how she was hardly fed. How she was hit. How she was called names.

And Jean understood. She understood why Valerie winced when she was offered apple dumplings 'like you used to have'. She understood why Valerie could be so stiff. She understood that it was the wireless had kept her going; that even the news in Norwegian was a comfort.

'Ha,' Valerie said weakly. 'Not many people know that I speak some Norwegian.'

Jean wouldn't let herself cry, she told herself. The time for crying was over.

'And then Mrs Howard took me in and things were better, it was like the time before was a nightmare... only it wasn't.'

'I didn't realise.'

Valerie seemed to shake herself out of it. She fiddled with her glasses, then smiled. 'Anyway, what were we talking about? Work, wasn't it? So yes, I need to come up with three ideas.'

She was professional again, explaining her world.

'We say three because the first will be the same as everyone's. The second will be daft but the third will be spot on...'

Jean got up suddenly. She walked over to the shelving unit and squinted at the few paperbacks there. Then she plucked at one: *Pinocchio.*

'You used to love this when you were little. You used to want to be him.'

Valerie looked at it, pulling a face. A father who was so desperate for a child that he created one out of wood – what possible appeal could that have had for little Valerie?

'Why not have readers doing a story? You could have famous people reading it. Like your friend the artist – Paul Howard, is it?'

Had she gone too far? Valerie was always prickly when she mentioned his name. Like a hedgehog rolling into a ball.

'Or not famous people, normal people,' Jean went on, praying Valerie wouldn't take it wrongly. 'The books are the thing...' She took the *Pinocchio* book from Valerie and put it back on the shelf. 'I'm afraid I don't think I'll be able to come up with two more ideas though. One's my limit!'

Unexpectedly, Valerie was looking thoughtful.

'Interesting,' she said, and she elongated the word, making it take up space. 'Very In-ter-rest-ing. Thanks...' She hesitated, but the next word came out quickly, short and taking up no space, 'Mum.'

90

WINTER 1950

Valerie

The next few weeks at work were some of Valerie's busiest ever. Repeatedly, she explained the project – Jean's idea – in meetings. She got better at deciphering which words made the radio executives' ears prick up and which phrases made their tails droop. And which radio executive couldn't seem to hear her voice at all.

She didn't trust Boris or Bertie not to claim her ideas for their own, as they did it so regularly that she wasn't sure if they were even aware they were doing it.

To the radio executives who didn't seem capable of hearing her speak, she sent Godfrey to explain it again.

She wasn't totally enamoured with the idea – 'readers reading a book' – but she had had to come up with something quickly and, more to the point, she had to find something that would be accepted.

One day, one of the more 'fiscally orientated' radio executive sidled up to her in the canteen.

'I asked my wife about your latest proposal,' he said, and, as

Valerie thought, *here we go again*, he looked up and his eyes weren't cynical. 'I couldn't believe it, but she said yes. My only worry is children want things faster and noisier nowadays. They don't have to wait, like we did through the war. Surely they don't have the wherewithal to listen quietly?'

'We mustn't underestimate them,' Valerie responded quickly.

'It's also not that original, is it?'

'It doesn't have to be,' Valerie was about to launch into her '*standing on the shoulders of giants*' speech but then he said something else surprising.

'When I was in Egypt in the war, I missed my boy terribly, and my wife. Sometimes I listened to *Music While You* Work. It made me happy to think they were out there listening too, some cosy fireside scene. It would be like that, wouldn't it? Except with stories.'

'That's exactly right,' said Valerie, thinking, *Jean is a genius.*

That wasn't the only remarkable thing to happen that lunchtime. Back at her desk, propped against her typewriter was a tired-looking postcard with the flamboyant writing that Valerie recognised instantly:

Water, water, everywhere, but none to fish in. This could drive a man insane. I thought I asked you to warn me off another Atlantic boat journey! So I'm at it again. Six weeks and counting. I see you in my dreams every night – will I see you in real life, darling girl?

Valerie read it and then folded it up so it fitted in her purse. She couldn't stop grinning.

91

Valerie

Lydia was back in London for a few days, and she came to meet Valerie one evening after work. Valerie always felt a mixture of excitement and trepidation on seeing her. It wasn't like meeting Morwenna, with whom she felt as comfortable as slipping on an old shoe. It wasn't like getting together with Mrs Howard to talk about the arts. She always hoped she'd get on with Lydia yet could never work out why they didn't quite click – it wasn't like they didn't have a zillion things in common.

Lydia talked about the dogs at the kennels and about her friends. When Valerie asked after her parents, she sighed. They were so happy, so in love, they set the bar for married life very high. Lydia wondered if she would ever find a Prince Charming of her own. She had always yearned for a wedding, and it seemed the years hadn't diminished that.

'It's not fair,' she continued, fluffing her hair. 'I have lots of male attention but none of them are exactly right.'

Valerie could feel Lydia was warming up to ask her about Paul, so she jumped in before she could.

'Paul's on his way back...' she said brightly, unsure whether Lydia would have heard or not.

'You've not been waiting for him?' Lydia asked, and her voice was incredulous, like: *you don't think they'll put a man on the moon?*

'Not *waiting* as such,' Valerie said. It was not like she was sitting on the platform of a railway station. She had plenty going on – more than plenty!

'What then?' Lydia asked.

'I mean – he'll be back soon.'

My darling girl, he'd written and *I see you in my dreams*.

Surely, these phrases were unequivocal.

'It's been such a long time,' Lydia said.

Did she have to sound so sneery? Not everyone changed partner every five minutes. Real life wasn't like country dancing. 'He always wanted to go to America,' Valerie said cheerfully. 'Good for him.'

Lydia appeared to shake herself. 'And he writes? Often?'

'Sometimes.' Valerie smiled.

Lydia picked up her glass and peered into it like she was expecting to see a fly. 'Here's to childhood sweethearts!'

92

SPRING 1951

Jean

Jean's idea about making a wireless programme of people reading books had, surprisingly, been accepted and would be a nationwide show soon. There had been some disagreement about the title. Valerie's suggestion to call it, *'It's That Book Again',* was predictably out-voted, but she didn't object to the eventual choice and the first book on *Read All About It* would be none other than *Pinocchio.*

When Valerie told her, Jean wasn't sure what it meant but she could see Valerie was thrilled.

'That calls for a saveloy!' she said.

'Even though it's not Friday,' teased Valerie, but it was in a friendly way, Jean hoped.

Jean sent Richard out to the fish shop. He spent most of the time at hers now and, if Valerie objected, she didn't say.

Jean was thinking about getting a television. It was another thing she was worried about; would Valerie – a wireless fan – see this as a betrayal too? But Valerie said it was a great idea and why not?

'Because I'm not sure when I'd have time to watch it,' Jean said.

Valerie said that Mrs Howard refused to get one because 'television is for shirkers'.

Jean laughed. She didn't mind it when Valerie mentioned Mrs Howard nowadays. It wasn't a competition, and she mentioned Barb, Gwen and Richard plenty too.

It was a lovely evening. For once, Valerie didn't only talk about work. They chatted about many things. Jean even told Valerie about the rat she used to have nightmares about.

'What do you think it signified?' Valerie asked, tapping her teeth.

'That I needed to put down rat poison?' speculated Jean and she was glad to see Valerie laugh.

Later, Richard, showing off the new house telephone, called the talking clock and then said, 'We'd better walk you to the underground.' The sky had turned dark suddenly, and the rain was making a loud pitter-patter sound on the roof.

'No need,' said Valerie heartily. 'I'm fine by myself.'

'We must,' said Jean. She loved an opportunity to look after Valerie.

Now they set off, the three of them. They only had one umbrella and they didn't all fit under it, so Richard insisted that Jean and Valerie huddled together and stayed dry. He did get wet – poor fella – his red hair was plastered over his forehead.

'It's almost as black as it was in the war,' said Jean, and then, 'Have you seen Lydia?'

'She's not often free...'

'She always thought she was better than you, didn't she?'

As soon as the words left her mouth, Jean knew this was a mistake. A shadow crossed her daughter's face. Jean had under-estimated how protective Val could be about people, *some* people. About Lydia. About Francine.

'What makes you say that?' Valerie enquired coolly, the old Valerie back with a vengeance.

'Her attitude – she always thought she was prettier than you... It's just an observation. Maybe I'm wrong.'

'You *are* wrong.' Valerie put her mother in her place. 'Lydia's not like that.'

'Sorry, I didn't mean anything by it.'

She was, Jean realised ruefully, in her daughter's bad books again. The more determined she was not to be, the more she found herself there. How easy it was for her to slip into them. Two steps forward, three steps back, it was a strange dance.

They arrived at the tube station and Valerie left, her glasses steamed up. No kiss, no hug this time, just a curt farewell.

'Come on, old girl,' Richard said gently. He saw Jean's pain. 'Let's get you back home.'

93

Valerie

A few days later, at the end of her shift, Valerie saw Mr Carrington outside Broadcasting house. Thinking of Jean's heart condition, she flung herself down the steps towards him, feeling sick: no, not Jean – not now. Why had she left her the other day with such animosity? By the time she got to him, she was figuring out how they would get to the hospital, who she would need to let know, and imagining all sorts of terrible scenarios.

'What's happened to Mum?'

He looked horrified. 'Nothing like that. Your mother is fine. I wanted to ask you something...'

Relief wiped out curiosity, but Valerie knew she was expected to say something. 'Go on.'

'I'm hoping to ask your mother to marry me...'

Valerie let out a long breath. Goodness, was that it? That was what he had come here for, dressed up in a suit and holding an umbrella even though today, there was no sign of rain?

'I wanted to ask your permission first.'

He looked like he realised he had misstepped. Valerie tried to recover. Everything was all right; her mother was in fine fettle. And it looked like her dreams were about to come true.

'I'm not her father.' Valerie managed to let out a laugh.

The whole asking-permission thing was archaic. It was something she would never understand. Her mother was an adult – she didn't need permission from anyone, and especially not from her.

'But,' persisted Mr Carrington, 'for me and Jean – your approval is important to us.'

'You have it,' she told him. Richard cared about her mother, and she knew Jean couldn't believe her luck. She couldn't resist asking, 'What would you have done if I said no?'

He tipped his hat at her and winked. He was a surprisingly handsome man, surprising because he was one of the non-showy invisible types, but when you did notice him he was lovely. Especially if you liked bright ginger hair, which her mother clearly did.

'I'd have gone ahead and asked her anyway,' he admitted, which Valerie considered was the correct answer.

'When are you going to do it?'

They started the walk up towards the railway station. There was rain in the air, grey clouds gathering overhead. Richard was not wrong to be prepared.

'We're going on a day trip next Saturday. Thought I'd ask her then.'

'Whereabouts?'

'West Country...'

She's going to hate that, thought Valerie. *She associates it with losing me.* But she didn't want to rain on Mr Carrington's parade.

Love was in the air, she thought after they parted ways. And maybe, for both of them. Her mother *and* her. Maybe they'd both had to not only meet the right person but also be at the right stage of their lives.

It was a nice thought and it followed her all the way home.

94

Jean

Richard had borrowed a Ford Popular for the day.

'Nice!' said Jean, who was unused to a shiny, privately owned car. He was looking handsome in his hat and suit. And he had packed a picnic.

'You shouldn't have,' she said, but she didn't mean it. She was bowled over by his thoughtfulness.

He wasn't a bad-tempered driver like Tony was, although the air did turn blue when the car got stuck behind some cyclists.

It took a long time to get out of London and an even longer time on the road west. Jean couldn't help imagining Valerie, Lydia and Francine heading off on the train that time. What must they have been thinking?

The Woods woman was dead apparently, and Jean was glad. When she had tearfully related Valerie's experiences to Richard by the fire a few days earlier, he held her hands and his face was golden in the firelight.

'Valerie has got over it, so you must too.'

'I don't know if she has...' Jean admitted.

He put her hands to his lips. 'She will.'

They went to Stonehenge. She remembered Tony laughing at her about calling it Stonehedge – and she remembered that he was determined not to go past. Richard was just so nice. They joined a line of people, lots of Americans and maybe some French people. They walked around the big ancient rocks in their mysterious circle and Jean was as impressed as she had known she would be. Then, Richard pulled her away from the queue and said, 'Jean,' in the same serious voice he used when he was talking about his late father.

'I don't know how they did it,' Jean mused. 'They must have been far cleverer than us, don't you think?'

'And stronger, Jean. The thing is I want to...'

'Do you think they had wheels back then?'

'I don't...'

'It's so fascinating.'

'Jean, I need to ask you something...'

Jean snapped to attention. She had a horrible feeling that Richard was splitting up with her. She had been confident recently that he loved her, but it might all have been a big joke. Or, if not a joke, a misunderstanding. She hadn't been the best girlfriend since Valerie was back on the scene, that was for certain. She hadn't *ever* been the best girlfriend, to be fair.

'What's the matter?'

'Jean, will you do me the honour... will you marry me?'

Oh! Jean was overcome with relief, and then pleasure, disbelief – and then joy!

'I've always thought you were lovely, Jean. Since the moment you first stepped foot on my bus.'

There was something about that last phrase that was funny

and, try as she might to be serious, Jean burst into laughter. Fortunately, after a moment, Richard did too.

'It doesn't get any more romantic than that!' she said.

'You still haven't answered,' he said, his face crinkled in the sunlight. He knew the answer though, he must have. She hadn't done a good job of concealing how much she adored him.

'Untethered,' she remembered him saying a long time ago, before the war had blown apart her certainties. And now, yes, she wanted nothing more than for them to be tethered together, always.

To be attached to someone you love is not to be restricted but to be free.

She threw her arms round him and planted kisses on his neck, his chin and his lips, right there at Stonehenge. His hat flipped off onto the ground and he ran to get it and, as he did, she shouted, 'The answer is yes, you silly sod!'

He came back, hat captured under his arm, and this time he knelt in front of her. He had a ring for her! He tried, he always tried hard to do everything right, and she would try too; it was the trying that mattered.

'A rock among the rocks,' he said. It was a diamond on a band, and she burst into tears.

She didn't know how she'd got here, she didn't know why she was here, but she knew he loved her.

What a feeling that was – it felt like it was the first time in her life she had been loved, comfortably loved. Jean remembered how she used to be able to stop buses with the press of a button, with a ding-ding. That moment, she felt so full of love she wished she could stop time.

95

Valerie

'You said what to her?' Godfrey said incredulously a few weeks later as they stood outside Broadcasting House. 'To your own mother?'

They were being evacuated again. It was the third time in six months. Valerie absently watched the policemen redirect the traffic. She remembered Somerset, where you could stand in the middle of the road for hours and the only traffic that would come upon you would be a lost sheep.

Most of the evening with her mother had been great. Jean was proudly wearing her new engagement ring – she called it her 'rock'. She and Mr Carrington would marry next year. 'A small do,' she had said, blushing, 'I'm too old for anything else.' Valerie got the idea that she wanted her to protest that she wasn't too old – and Valerie did. There was a sweetness about this relationship that Valerie approved of, and she was trying to be less fierce with Jean

But despite Valerie's intentions, the meeting hadn't ended

well. It often went like that with them – they had a good time together, then not so good, then good, then bad again.

Valerie had said, 'I hate the way everyone expects I will marry and leave work and stay at home with children... it's not fair.'

'I understand,' Jean had chipped in. 'Look at me, I always worked, I never stopped, even when you were tiny.'

Eyes narrowed, Valerie had looked at her. 'I didn't mean...'

'What?'

'I suppose I meant in a real profession or career, not your work.'

'Oh,' Jean had said. Valerie had registered the hurt but didn't know what to say, and Jean had left quickly after that.

Valerie tried not to think about it. Godfrey was being annoying. He was a white knight where her mother was concerned. She was an idiot to have told him anything.

She focused on the fact that Paul was on an ocean liner right now. Paul – the love of her life – was on his way. That would show everyone. How much quicker it would be if he didn't hate flying!

Godfrey pushed his glasses up his nose. He seemed irritated with her.

This time there was a bomb. There were the sounds of an explosion some way away.

'Jesus,' said Bertie.

They'd almost forgotten this was a possibility.

They weren't allowed back in yet and Godfrey wanted to continue the conversation. 'You seem harsh on Mrs Hardman, Valerie. It sounds like she tried her best.'

Valerie inhaled. She hadn't told him the half of it. She didn't expect Godfrey to disagree with her. He was the most agreeable person in the world. 'Cleaner to clippie to canteen – she loves all of them too.'

'Why say that? To hurt her?'

'No,' she said. It was awkward Godfrey taking her mother's side like this. If he could have seen the last ten years he'd understand. This didn't come from a place of nastiness. It was true. She felt like drawing him a diagram. Or a mathematical formula. Other people always equals greater than Valerie.

'You wanted to make your own mother feel like she was a nobody?' he persisted.

'Not a nobody, exactly.'

'What then?'

She was always surprised when Godfrey was this persistent. These people – privileged ones – they could afford to give people a break, couldn't they? And yet here he was, a dog with a bone, trying to get her to admit she was wrong.

Standing opposite the great lights of Piccadilly Circus and the signs for Coca-Cola and Guinness, she ground her cigarette beneath her shoe. Godfrey – Champion of the Dinner Ladies. Godfrey liked his causes, but she wouldn't have thought this would be his latest cause célèbre. She shouldn't have confided in him. Then she remembered that his own mother had died of a tumour when he was young. He probably had a thing for women of a certain age. Of course that must be it.

'She brought you up.' His tone was harsh, not like him at all. He was usually bright as a buttercup. She'd put a buttercup to his chin once, for fun, in the office, and it had showed yellow. He'd grabbed her wrist and said it always did.

'Hardly. I brought myself up – and Mrs Howard did too, of course.'

'But you were with your mother until...'

'Until I was eleven, I know, but...'

Her attitude may look horrible from the outside, but didn't Godfrey understand? This was how she felt and she couldn't get rid of it – she couldn't set it aside! She'd like to, but it wasn't as simple as that.

The memory of pleading with her to take her back to London.
The memory of waiting for her.
The memory of finding out about her father.

These wounds were still hot and fresh. They had done a documentary recently about people walking over hot coals in Guyana and not feeling a thing. That was not her. She *burned*.

She couldn't help that. She needed the wrongs to be acknowledged or atoned for. And Jean was incapable of it. Jean had walked off oblivious into her own happy ever after. She had found love and, though she didn't want it to, it gnawed at Valerie, it just did.

'She told me so many lies.'

'Why?'

'Why what?'

'Why do you think she lied to you?'

'Because that's how she deals with things – that's what she does.' Valerie felt tearful. And she didn't like being challenged on this because this was the version of her life that she was comfortable with. It fit her snugly now; she did not want to take it off.

'Or maybe because she thought it was for the best?'

Valerie tutted. They were going round in circles.

A few days later, Valerie was still waiting for Godfrey to apologise. It had occurred to her that the fact she never had told her mother how bad it was at Beastly Woods' was not actually Jean's fault – you might say she had been somewhat untruthful too. Valerie had dismissed this thought, though. She had been a child!

She decided that when Godfrey apologised she would accept it gracefully, and when they went over to the Pied Piper, she would buy him the lager shandy he liked, maybe even a large.

But Godfrey was bringing something over to her desk now. Not an apology but a scrapbook. There were several columns about buses during the war. If Valerie thought the BBC could be old-fashioned in tone (she did), they did nothing as nauseating as these articles: it was all: *ladies – bells – what a hoot!*

'There's a story about a bus in a crater,' Godfrey said, pointing another article out to Valerie, who scanned through it. 'Did you know your mum was involved?'

'Maybe. She had a busy war,' Valerie admitted grudgingly. She couldn't help herself thinking – *juggling all those secrets.*

'She was a heroine.' Godfrey said pointedly. He read: 'If it weren't for the brave conductress who acted with speed and alacrity, many lives might have been lost.'

As she read the date on the newspaper, Valerie realised it was the day she had come to London and been sent away again.

'That's nice,' she said coldly as she tried to process this new piece of information. At least Paul would be home soon, she thought. Paul was someone who would understand – he had always got her.

'I don't think you should say she's not a somebody, that's all,' Godfrey said defiantly. 'It's not true and it makes you sound bitter.'

'You've a cheek, son of the Right Honourable. Defender of the Canteen. *Mrs Hardman's gravy is second to none,*' Valerie said, mimicking his obsequious tone.

Godfrey slapped the pages shut. 'Be like that.'

He went off, probably to the pub without her. Men like him had the pick of everything and didn't even realise it. A girl called Shirley, a sweet, pink-cheeked thing in accounts, was always asking after him. Shirley wouldn't disagree with him even when he was wrong.

Godfrey was looking for a support person, Valerie thought

dismissively. Most men were. They wanted a home to come back to yet most of their lives would take place elsewhere. Men gave flowers to women – but what they were really saying was: *be my flower – be attractive for me, be my home.* That life wasn't for her.

96

Valerie

On the morning of the live recording of *Read All About It*, the new nationwide children's wireless programme, Valerie was at her desk at six. The reader was coming in at midday and for the recording at six p.m., they were going to have a live studio audience of under-sevens and their mothers. The team had reservations about this, but Valerie had overruled them.

Valerie probably hadn't needed to be in so early, but she wanted to be prepared for every eventuality. It didn't help that her monthlies were worse than ever. Her stomach was bloated and painful. She had worked until midnight the evening before – her mother had called to wish her luck, which was nice – and then taken a cab home, but she hadn't slept well because of the pain. Now Godfrey kept looking over sympathetically. She asked him why and he said because she kept making sad noises.

At nine in the morning there was a breathy phone call from the housekeeper at Bumble Cottage, which was one eventuality Valerie hadn't prepared for.

'Miss Valerie? Sorry to disturb you at work, I wasn't sure where to call.'

Valerie almost couldn't speak from fear.

'Mrs Howard had a stroke.'

She swallowed. She knew there were questions to ask, but she couldn't seem to find them.

The housekeeper told Valerie Mrs Howard was home, but her condition was deteriorating. Valerie thanked her and said she'd be there as soon as possible.

'I know a man who had a stroke, and he was fine,' piped up Boris when she told them, dazed.

'I'm really sorry, Miss Hardman, but we need to do the soundcheck,' Bertie said.

'I have to go to Somerset.' Valerie realised she didn't have anything she needed. There was no time to go to the chemist. She would wrap a sweater round her waist if need be, like in the bad old days. She would keep her fingers crossed and hope for the best.

Godfrey looked shocked. 'I don't see how you'll be back in time for the recording...'

'I simply must go, Godfrey.'

'I'll drive you,' he suggested. He had bought his car only two months previously, a Hillman; it was his pride and joy. Occasionally he talked about things other than the extortionate price of fuel – but not often.

'No, Godfrey, you need to be here.'

'You've been working hard on this—'

'It's all thanks to Mrs Howard. She set me on this path. I'll be back as soon as I can, I promise.'

She could make the ten o'clock train, she'd have a couple of hours there, then she could get the three o'clock back. She knew the Paddington—Taunton timetable inside out. She could do it;

she'd done similar before. It was tight, it would be unpleasant, but it would be doable.

She was leaving Taunton station when she saw a man she vaguely recognised, although he didn't seem to know her. It took her a good few moments before she worked out it was the Woods' son. It was a strange moment – once she had hated this person with all her might, but now she felt detached, and – goodness she was turning into Godfrey – more inclined to be generous. He had suffered too, no doubt, with a mother like that. She nodded at him and he tipped his hat.

The housekeeper made Valerie some tea and shook her head a lot, and said, 'doctor says...' and 'good of you to come'.

Valerie didn't ask about Paul but the other woman volunteered: 'Paul is devastated, as you can imagine. He only got back two days ago and now this...'

Valerie gulped. Paul had been home for two days yet hadn't called her? Did he not have her number? She wasn't sure what she thought about that, but she knew this wasn't the point. The point of this trip was Mrs Howard. She needed to focus on that.

Mrs Howard was asleep. Valerie sat on the armchair that someone had moved closer to the bed and willed her to open her eyes. She took the papers from her bag for the recording tonight – there was not much she could do about it if there was something wrong but, still, going over them eased her concerns.

Mrs Howard opened her eyes. When she saw Valerie, she smiled: 'To what do I owe the pleasure of all these visits?'

All these visits? Was she confused?

'You know what...' Valerie said, taking the hand of the woman who had done so much for her. 'You've been poorly, and we're worried about you.'

'Poorly,' Mrs Howard muttered. 'God, I hate that word.'

Valerie laughed. That was the Mrs Howard spirit. 'Ill then. Is that better?'

'I don't like any of them applied to me.' Mrs Howard pulled herself higher onto the pillow. 'Paul's back.'

'I heard...'

'Lydia is coming tonight.'

'Good... You deserve to be treated like a queen.'

'Piffle, I deserve peace and quiet.'

Opening the window, Valerie felt like she was letting the outside in. The first countryside she had loved. She felt an enormous gratitude that this world had been her platform, her diving board, and this person in the bed had been her guiding light.

She felt emotional.

Part of it was the stress of the job: having her ambitions come to fruition was incredible, but it was also frightening. So much depended on her. So much depended on her being right – and indeed staying right. And part of it was her deep affection for Mrs Howard. She remembered the terrible state she had been in when she was taken in. Her mother hadn't been there – Mrs Howard had.

'How will I ever thank you?'

'Valerie, we loved having you with us.'

'And I loved being here.'

'Did it upset your mother? I hate to think it did,' Mrs Howard said.

'I don't think that's the only reason things have been difficult between us. It probably didn't help, but there were other things.'

She nodded. 'I hope you make it up, Valerie. I do.'

'You made such a difference to my life. I wouldn't be where I am today without you.'

'I have written a will.'

Valerie gulped. *Must she talk like this?*

'Paul gets the house. Lydia, my jewellery.'

Valerie remembered how Mrs Howard's beautiful brooches had caught her eye, how they seemed gay and bright in a dull world. But Lydia, even more than she herself, had always been enthralled by a shiny thing. It was right that the jewellery was going to her.

'Not the brooches,' Mrs Howard said abruptly. It was like she read Valerie's mind sometimes. 'They're costume jewellery – not worth a lot – but I'd love you to have those. I remember you staring at them as a child.'

'Thank you,' whispered Valerie. She felt devastated. She would rather not have anything at all and instead to have Mrs Howard alive and healthy. She took off her glasses, wiped them on her blouse.

'You also get my book collection, dear, and the wireless, of course.'

'No, no! I couldn't possibly.' Those tears wouldn't hold back now. The library, where she had spent much of her teenage years, was wonderful. Through this woman she had found herself.

'If you need to sell, sell. There are some first editions that are worth a few bob.'

'Can we not talk about this now?'

The housekeeper bustled in and said Mrs Howard needed to rest and, although Valerie expected her to resist, Mrs Howard acquiesced. She must have been very poorly – no, ill. Just as Valerie stood to walk away, Mrs Howard grabbed her hand to pull her closer.

'I would like you and Paul to be together. I know you love each other.'

Her words gave Valerie a swooping, soaring feeling. 'You didn't always feel that way, did you?' she asked, because it felt as though the final pieces of the puzzle were coming together. Why Mrs Howard had wanted to keep them apart.

'You were both so young,' Mrs Howard said. 'You are similar, I saw that from the off. But I thought – he was like his father – I thought he needed to sow his wild oats. I didn't want you to hold him back' – she paused – 'or for him to hold *you* back.'

'It wasn't because I wasn't the right class?'

'Right class? What's the *right* class?'

'I assumed that was what you had against us being together.'

'You're a special girl,' Mrs Howard said. 'I don't think you realise – you've both got a lot of amazing things to do, and I admit I didn't think he would help you to achieve them. I know my Pauly. I thought you'd end up putting your ambitions aside to support him. He's self-centred like his father, like many men, you see. He always was.'

Shouldn't it have been our choice though? thought Valerie. Now that she couldn't be frustrated with Mrs Howard, for the first time she felt she was.

'I don't think that now,' Mrs Howard continued. 'You've both grown up. Paul will make an excellent partner. And' – she patted Valerie's hand – 'dear girl, you must know I hold you in the highest esteem.'

And Valerie knew that was true.

The housekeeper apologetically interrupted that it was time for her to go.

'He is here. In the barn, or fishing. His paintings sell all over the world.' Mrs Howard lay back, eyes closed.

Valerie felt proud too. 'He found what he was good at – and the world laps it up. You said that would happen.'

'Go to him.'

'I'm not sure...'

'Go and see him, now,' Mrs Howard commanded.

'I have to get back to London – it's my first big show tonight... Would you put the wireless on at six o'clock?'

'Of course.'

'And stay listening until after the end.'

'Always.' Mrs Hardman clasped Valerie's hands and they had never felt so frail and it broke Valerie's heart. 'Dear girl, you were never any trouble.'

It was only ten minutes to the barn. Unbelievable that Paul was back. This felt momentous – but what if it wasn't?

The barn was empty. After she knocked, Valerie peered through the window and it was clear someone had been in it recently: the teacup, the cloth, the half-drawn image on the canvas. A tan leather holdall on the floor. Paul was probably fishing at the lake. She could see some of his finished artwork too. Valerie remembered long ago thinking if he could see beauty in such plain creatures, there must be something very beautiful in Paul too. And another thought: 'He is the love of my life.'

There was a silver fish. Still, on a plate.

The flowers. Pansy against an orange background. Violet against a yellow. Did he just *know* what colours went with what or was this something studied? Both perhaps.

No portraits. She remembered asking him why not. He said he found them boring. 'What about a little one of me?' she had asked. Laughing, he said he could never do her justice.

She saw the bed where they had been together that time. It was unmade, of course.

She walked down towards the lake but couldn't see him there either. Time was ticking on. She had to get back for *Read All About It*. She and Paul had waited this long to be together – what difference would a few more days make?

By the time Valerie was on the train, she felt a regret so piercing it felt like something had punctured her heart. It wasn't just that she hadn't waited this time, it was that there had been so many missed opportunities. She spent the train journey obsessively going over and over them.

. . .

The switchboard at the BBC was lit up with callers that evening and the next day.

'My daughter loved it.'

'My son was transfixed!'

'My husband found it enchanting and clever.'

The review in that week's *Radio Times* said:

> *Who would have thought a programme having people simply reading books out on the wireless would have such nostalgic charm? What a comfort.* Read All About It *reminded me of sitting around the wireless during the early days of the war listening to Vera Lynn singing 'Goodnight Children Everywhere'.*

After the recording, Boris and Bertie congratulated themselves then went to their members' club to celebrate. Godfrey walked Valerie from the studio to the office. He'd changed his spectacles recently. Valerie guessed he was making an effort for sweet Shirley in accounts. They didn't stop him from looking shattered though. And his hair was all over the place.

'I didn't think you'd get back in time.'

'Neither did I.'

'It wouldn't have been a problem. It ran like clockwork – you'd done everything necessary.'

'I had to be here.'

She pictured Paul in that barn with its pictures and its bed, and what it represented to her. *We'll be together soon*, she told herself. *Patience.*

She looked up and realised Godfrey was gazing at her.

'Everything all right?' she asked.

'Fine,' he said. 'Well done.'

97

Jean

'Paul has an exhibition in a gallery in London,' Valerie told Jean.

'Of course he has,' Jean said.

Jean had only met Paul once, years ago, but she decided she didn't much like him. Where was he when her daughter needed him? Why had he spent so long in America? Art made her suspicious; America even more so. Nevertheless, she bit her tongue. It had taken her a while to learn that skill, but it was an important one, perhaps the most important one of her life.

'I wonder if you'll come with me,' Valerie said. 'As a thank-you,' she added. 'Everyone loved the show.'

'I don't need a thank-you,' began Jean.

'And I'll invite people from work...'

Jean had met Godfrey, who she adored. She disliked Boris with his endless anecdotes of stars, and she was undecided about Bertie, although she liked his saucy grin.

'And Richard, of course.'

'Sounds wonderful,' said Jean, wondering how she would

persuade Richard. Football? Yes. Outsized representations of carp? Not likely.

'I only hope Paul is happy to see me,' Valerie said nervously.

To Jean, Valerie was a force of nature, only Jean suspected she was not out of nature – she was not of this world. She was heaven-sent.

'Course he will be. He asked you to come, didn't he?'

'Oh yes,' Valerie said vaguely. 'He wants everyone to come.'

Jean heard the creatives talking about Miss Hardman as they queued for their lunches. She would whack them over the head with the frying pan if she heard anything nasty, but she only ever heard admiration, jealousy or irritation. A few said she'd be pretty without her spectacles, which wasn't entirely unfair. If they were saying bad things about Valerie behind her back, which they probably were, at least they were discreet enough not to do it in the canteen.

Jean knew she was not responsible for how Valerie had turned out – how did she create such a wonder? – but she couldn't help it: she was proud. *Pride comes before a fall*, she reminded herself, but much as she resisted it, it crept around her, tickling her heart.

Will Valerie ever realise how much she adored her?

And those missing ten years? Like one long and terrible day. Yes, she had mourned them, yes, she had grieved them, but she was ready to move on – if Valerie would let them.

Jean had loved Valerie's wireless show – and when Valerie had insisted it was down to her, she'd brushed it off. It was Valerie who had done the hard graft. Ideas were two a penny. She couldn't help imagining the Salt children gathering around to listen to it, little Joe cooing in her arms. They would have adored it – although, remembering Mrs Salt's alarm at *War of the Worlds*, perhaps she might have panicked at some parts of the story– *'Is it true his nose grew and grew?'*

Jean had been about to switch the wireless off when she remembered Valerie had told her not to. 'Keep listening,' she had said. 'Even after you think it's over.'

And so Jean did sit through the silence that she knew Valerie enjoyed. And then there was the continuity presenter (see, she knew the words now!) saying, 'And this, the first in a brand-new series, is dedicated to Mrs Hardman and Mrs Howard, trailblazers of two very different trails.'

Many years ago, if Jean had been told to share her daughter with another woman, she would have shrivelled up at the idea: you prepare to lose your child to a marriage partner, maybe, children of their own, but not to another woman. Right now though, Jean was delighted to be included. Valerie might never say such affectionate words to her face, she understood that, but she could say them to the world, and that was lovely.

98

Valerie

Outside the gallery, there were people standing around. They were people from the art world, and they all had a dandy twist about them, whether it was a swirly cravat or a beard or a fascinator. Valerie hoped that her mother wouldn't say anything silly. One fella looked the spit of van Gogh. He was in a smock and beret, yet he didn't seem embarrassed.

In her purse, Valerie had a precious handwritten invitation from Paul full of intimate phrasings and private doodles, which had arrived only the other day and had suffused her with hope.

Only Godfrey could come to the exhibition. Boris and Bertie were awfully sorry, but they were already going for drinks after work: 'cin-cin!' There were a lot of drinks after work – men only – in the clubs of Soho, and Valerie found it exasperating to be excluded. Godfrey told her what decisions and alliances were made over cigars and whiskies, but it wasn't the same.

It was good of Godfrey to come, she thought, although she had expected him to. He had a knack of being everywhere he was needed. Richard was going to meet them afterwards at the pub.

When they met at Leicester Square station, both Mum and Godfrey had looked approvingly at Valerie. Godfrey actually said, 'Wow!', which gave her a boost. 'That's the right reaction!' She was in a fitted dress with a tiny check print. Underneath, she was wearing her usual stockings and suspenders, but today she was wearing a corset too. Mum probably wished she was wearing bows in her hair, but she had gone for a single clip. She remembered Paul unclipping a clip, a long time ago. At work, she was as body-less as possible, as similar to the others – the men – as she could be, so as not to stand out. Today, she wanted to be the exact opposite. She *did* want to stand out, she wanted to be desirable to Paul, to show him she was attractive and that she'd grown up.

She didn't know whether to take off her spectacles. She might look better without them, but then it was possible she might never find Paul in a crowded room. There was no more room for misunderstandings.

'Are we ready to go in?' Jean asked enthusiastically. 'Show me those fish!'

'Do you mind if I go in first...' Valerie suggested. 'I need five minutes in there on my own. That's all right, isn't it?'

Godfrey and her mother smiled at each other and she sensed this was something they'd agreed anyway.

'Take as long as you like,' Godfrey said.

When she turned round at the gallery door she saw they were hunched over, lighting a cigarette between them, and it made her smile.

She saw him right away. Paul Howard surrounded by people, and he noticed her. He didn't hesitate; he left them and made a beeline for her. She was pleased about how ready she was, how calm.

They hugged and he didn't pull away like you would normally but, instead, pressed his lips to her ear, and his breath was hot. She was squeezed against his shoulder – and yes, her glasses frames did dig in a little.

'Why didn't you wait for me? Before? To see me, when you came to the house last month?'

'I had work...'

'But you could have,' he persisted.

'I didn't know,' Valerie said.

'You didn't know what?'

'How I'd be received.'

And she could feel him let out a deep breath, like a sigh of relief. And she felt the same. Relief like coming home.

'I'm here now,' she whispered. Into his soft hair, the hair over and around his ear, if she kissed that ear, if she...

'Mum sends her love,' he continued.

'And I to her,' she mumbled back. Mrs Howard's resilience, her rallying after the stroke, was the most surprising thing. It was a Shakespeare-year at the local theatre and Mrs Howard had told Valerie, 'I have to stay alive because I can't stand the thought of anyone else directing!' She was indomitable although Valerie didn't want to think about her now. Feeling the warmth of Paul's body – they were still entangled, pressed close – she thought about that time, that marvellous night they spent together in the barn. And Paul was making no effort to untwine himself... until he did.

'You hardly ever wrote,' she said. A part of her had always wondered if someone had intercepted their letters, like her mother's shilling in a birthday card all those years ago.

'I thought maybe you had someone else,' he said.

She shook her head. 'Who told you that?' Mrs Howard

again? She hadn't wanted them to get together, had she? She had forgiven her once, but...

He shook his head.

'I've not. There hasn't been...' she persisted. There had been half-opportunities, vague passes from men she hadn't wanted. She had turned them down willingly; she was never particularly tempted.

'All this time? You've been waiting for me?'

She nodded. This was excruciating; she got the impression he hadn't done the same. She got the impression he couldn't believe she had, that it was a failing of hers.

They were so close; he might have leaned in for a kiss.

But then Lydia was behind him, her hand on his shoulder.

Lydia?

Lydia's hair was in movie-star waves and her face shiny and clean. She looked like the Madonna, Valerie suddenly thought, and it was strange that it hadn't occurred to her before. There was something beatific about her – something above human. How could two people from the same town, the same house, turn out so differently?

Whatever Valerie put on, whatever title at work they gave her, deep down there was always part of her that would forever feel like a dirty evacuee, slum child.

But Lydia didn't seem to feel that way.

What is she doing here?

'You did tell her, didn't you?' Lydia was saying. Someone had put music on, too loud at first, and then they turned down the volume.

Tell her what?

Paul's expression was as unreadable as it ever was. 'Boarding school face', he'd called it. When you are living with a load of boys from the age of six, you learn quickly that to give anything away is weakness.

Somehow, he looked both surprised and not. Wary, that

was the word. Fearful even. She remembered something Mr Fairweather had once said about making good radio: 'When you can catch people at their moment of humanity – that's the story.'

This was Paul's story.

Had she not been at the heart of it, she would have wanted to record it, she would have wanted to broadcast it, add the sound of canned laughter. But this was her life.

'Not yet, no.' Paul's voice was soft. People were looking at them. Valerie knew they would be trying to place them. Trying to put a name to them.

Lydia was cool as a girl denying that she had a fruit cake in her borrowed suitcase.

'I will then. Valerie, we're engaged.'

Valerie stared at her friend's face, trying to take in the words: *We. Who is 'we'?*

'I told him to call you. I didn't want you to find out like this...' Her voice trailed off. 'But he wanted to tell you face to face.'

And now they were face to face, and Valerie tried to read whatever Paul's eyes were telling her, but her own were filled with tears.

'Gosh,' was all she could manage. 'I had no idea.'

That was true.

'That was quick?'

Was it quick? It didn't feel like the right word.

'Quick?' Lydia laughed. 'I've known Paul since I was nine.'

'Of course.'

Of course?

Was she really saying, 'I met him before you'? Valerie hadn't realised she was in a competition. More fool her. What would she have done if she had realised?

Behind them, there was one of his paintings: 'The Empire State Building in the distance–' and in the foreground, a koi carp. Did Paul get fed up putting fish everywhere, or did he like it?

Maybe whether he liked it or not wasn't the important thing: this was what Paul did.

'He needs someone to look after him.' The hand on his shoulder was ownership. As clear as a name tag round a neck.

'Don't we all?' she said lightly.

Oh, Paul.

She and Lydia stared at each other. Lydia, the prettiest evacuee in the village hall, and Paul, the man who could see beauty in everything. If an alien had landed in the gallery, she couldn't have been more surprised. In fact, she might have followed them up to their ship and asked them to 'Take me to your leader' like they did in the comics.

She suddenly wanted to snort.

Lydia and Paul. Paul and Lydia. She hadn't seen that coming. Perhaps Mrs Howard had. She had told her to go to the barn – she'd ordered her to. It said something about Valerie's emotions that she didn't wait, didn't it? Or perhaps it didn't. Perhaps, it said something about both of them.

Maybe this was how it was meant to be.

She hadn't got in touch sooner, she hadn't pushed enough. Maybe at a subconscious level she had known that the romantic dream that had sustained her for all these years was over: Paul was not hers.

Lydia was irresistible, she would allow that. And Paul was not built for resisting. She'd been warned about that – she couldn't say she was unaware.

'He's like his father,' Mrs Howard always said. For the first time, Valerie heard.

Paul put his arms round her again, but this time it felt short-term. He still smelled so... Pauly. She inhaled his hair. Her fisherman friend...

'I'll be in touch,' he mumbled.

'Marvellous.' She knew he wouldn't.

'Bye, Valerie,' Lydia said sweetly. 'You'll come to the wedding, say yes? Pinkie promise?'

Valerie swallowed. The art world sharks were gathering now, wanting to reclaim their boy. That was what he was here for.

'I wouldn't miss it for anything.'

Outside, the street was as grey and tired as any other London street that week, that month, that year. Despite the proximity to the centre, there were scrawny trees, blocked drains and shuttered shops. From up some stairs, a dog was howling at the moon, and someone shouted, 'There's absolutely no need for that racket, Samuel.'

Godfrey and Jean were still there, still smoking, at the bottom of the steps, wispy clouds appearing from their cigarettes and then dissipating. They didn't see her at first and again for a moment she watched them. They didn't know about the devastation that had occurred. She felt like one of those bombed buildings you see that are deemed safe and yet are death traps inside.

Jean had never seemed so beautiful to Valerie as she did then. It felt to Valerie that she had been waiting for her mother all her life: waiting at home, waiting at Mrs Woods', waiting at Mrs Howard's, waiting for an apology – but now for once her mother was waiting for her. It made her stop. It made her think it didn't matter who was waiting for whom.

At least she was here now. Thank God she was here now.

Paul was gone. He had never been hers. She understood that now. And yet, the way he had looked at her at the last? Like *he* was devastated… Like he did love her? Yet evidently, whatever it was, it was too late now.

99

Jean

Jean told Godfrey to go ahead to the pub, where Richard was waiting to meet them. She could see it at once; something had happened in the gallery that had pulverised her girl.

Godfrey prevaricated for a moment, and then said, 'If you're sure...'

'We're sure.'

He had that skill of hailing taxis that Jean always admired, and within seconds he was away, his cheeks flushed, his eyes worried.

Jean put her arm round her girl and, for the first time in years, Valerie let her.

'Mummy,' she sobbed.

What had he done to her girl? That Paul. That Howard boy. She'd kill him... She'd kill him and gladly be hanged for it.

'Mummy,' Val kept saying. 'It's all gone wrong... He doesn't want me.'

He wasn't going to get away with this, Jean thought.

They stayed hugging in the street. Jean didn't dare speak or move, but then Valerie untangled herself. She blew her nose on Jean's handkerchief so loudly that they both laughed. And Jean said, '*Jeg er stolt av deg.*'

'What was that?' Valerie sniffed.

'It's Norwegian,' Jean explained helpfully.

'I know that but why?'

'I thought to communicate with you. After you said about the wireless, in the war...'

Valerie's tears came again, and Jean hugged her close.

'I don't know what to do,' Valerie said.

'You'll pick yourself up,' said Jean. 'You'll face whatever it is.'

'I can't.'

'You will.'

'I feel stupid... and alone.'

'Never. And I'm here.'

'I wanted to be loved.'

'By the right person, Val. It has to be the right person. Believe me, it's something I know.'

'But he *is* the right person, I always thought he was...'

Jean clutched her girl tightly; it was what she had wanted to do for all these years, and for that, there was a tiny fraction of her that would always be shamefully grateful for the terrible heartache that Valerie was going through, if only because it was allowing her in. She could die happy.

Even after you think it's over, she thought, *listen on.*

'Mummy...'

'I'll take you home, my girl.'

'He's with Lydia, Paul is. They're engaged.'

'Lydia?' Jean nearly shrieked. Lydia butter-wouldn't-melt-in-her-mouth Froud? Prissy-in-pink. Jean had never trusted her, never.

She wanted to ask how that had happened, but she stopped

herself. The ways and means weren't important right now. Her girl's well-being was the only concern here.

'Oh, darling.'

'It's all right.' Valerie sniffed. 'Let's go to the Pied Piper.'

'What?' gasped Jean.

'The pub? Where we're meeting the others.'

Jean looped her arm through her daughter's, Tweedledum and Tweedledee again. 'If you're sure? Let's go.'

As they marched down the street (no taxis flew to their attention the way they had to Godfrey), Jean was once again filled with love and admiration for her daughter, her Val. What an astonishing young woman she had become.

100

Valerie

London was coming back to life. There were revellers everywhere, packed buses, steamed-up taxis and bold bell-ringing cyclists. Godfrey and Richard were sitting side by side in a leather banquette inside the public house.

'Who wants a drink?' Valerie said in her professional voice, the voice that did not brook dissent. Her tone said no one was going to feel sorry for her ever again.

'I'll go,' said Godfrey quietly.

Richard reached over to take her mum's hand.

All the way there, Valerie's mind had been whirring nineteen to the dozen. She couldn't stop herself. Godfrey jokingly diagnosed her with *wireless producer's disease*. Even heartbroken, she couldn't help coming up with ideas for shows: a documentary on reunions? What about places where you fell in and out of love? A comedy set in the art world? A programme on fish? *'It's that mackerel again'*?

What *was* wrong with her?

Godfrey got wine for Valerie and himself. Jean had sworn

off alcohol, so she and Richard had colas. Was it only the thick lenses that made Godfrey's eyes look desperately concerned?

Valerie's mind was whirring about something else as well. It seemed to her that Godfrey too was one of the invisible ones who, when you took the time to notice, was quite attractive in his own way. And he was definitely kind. Intelligent. Funny. A connoisseur of great radio. Maybe that was another thing she had in common with her mother – she too didn't see what she had until it was right in front of her nose.

'I propose a toast,' she said. 'Here's to my mum and my soon-to-be-stepfather, Mr Carrington, and to...'

Maybe she shouldn't dismiss the man now sitting opposite her. There were things to explore there, definitely, she knew, if she would only let herself. She tried to remember if the fortune teller had actually said Paul's name, or if she'd assumed she was referring to him. *Two children*, she thought. The prospect made her heady suddenly.

If she had children she would never let them out of her sight.

But maybe she'd have to. That was the way of the world and beyond her control.

'Valerie?' Jean prompted her. 'You were saying?'

Valerie looked around wildly; for a moment she couldn't find the words, and then she pulled herself together. 'Sorry, Mum. *Jeg elsker deg.*' She flushed as she explained to the others. 'That means "I love you".'

She softly clinked her mother's glass. 'Here's to finding your way home.'

A LETTER FROM LIZZIE

Dear reader,

Thank you so much for reading *A Child Far from Home*. This is the first book in the Wartime Evacuee series and I do hope you enjoyed it. I loved writing it.

If you want to be kept up to date with all my latest releases, just sign up at the following link. Your email address will never be shared and you can unsubscribe at any time. You'll hear about the subsequent books, see the covers and read the blurbs before anyone else.

www.bookouture.com/lizzie-page

During the Second World War, my dad was evacuated from East London to Hinckley in Leicestershire. He had a terrible time, while his sister had a brilliant time. From a young age, I was aware of the different experiences evacuated children had. For some children, evacuation was life-changing in many marvellous ways, for others, not so much.

I have already written about the experiences of a woman, Phyllis, who looks after an evacuated child, in my third novel, *When I Was Yours*. The arrival of Pearl, a small girl from London, in Phyllis's orderly home, changes everything. This time round, I wanted to focus on the children who were evacuated and the mothers who let them go. I wanted to look at their lives and the effect evacuation may have on that special relationship both in the short and long term.

I hope this story rings true to you and that you loved Valerie and Jean as much as I came to. The next story in the series will focus on Lydia and Mrs Froud – and I can't wait to hear what you think!

If you have enjoyed *A Child Far from Home*, do consider leaving a review, or letting your friends know about it.

With huge thanks,

Lizzie

facebook.com/LizziePage

x.com/LizziePagewrite

instagram.com/lizziepagewriter

amazon.com/stores/Lizzie-Page/author/B079KSR8PZ

ACKNOWLEDGEMENTS

Firstly, thank you to you, dear reader. I appreciate you getting all the way here. It's a real honour and privilege to have my books read and I will always be grateful that you picked up mine.

I am thrilled to be working with the best publishers again. This is my eleventh book with Bookouture, yet each time feels fresh, exciting and it always feels like my book-babies are in safe hands. I don't know how they do it but they do.

My editor on this book has been the wonderful Claire Simmonds. She gets what I'm trying to say and helps me say it better. What more could you want in an editor?! She's brilliant.

Thank you to copy-editor, Jacqui Lewis, and proofreader, Jane Donovan. It's reassuring how professional you consistently are. You always see the things I have lost sight of. Thank you.

Thanks must go to the entire team, from cover designers to the data people – and the marketeers and EVERYBODY! Bookouture has a reputation for being a happy company to be involved with – deservedly so.

To write this book, I chatted with a lot of people who were children during the war. Three wonderful women who were evacuated/with an association with evacuation were a particular help. And those are Rachelle's nan – Elizabeth (Betty) Vine, Rachelle's nan's great friend, Jean Saunders, and my in-laws' neighbour, Janet Smart. Thank you so much, you wonderful, wonderful ladies, for giving me so much flavour and colour. Your honest recollections were invaluable to me.

And finally, thank you once again to friends and family for facilitating my writing. It's the weekend before Christmas. Youngest daughter is out shopping for presents, middle son is at the football with husband, oldest son is getting ready to fly back home for the holidays – and Lenny the dog is sitting in his usual place at the window, howling at ambulances.

And here I am, at the keyboard, one of my favourite places, writing this. It's a good life. Thank you.

PUBLISHING TEAM

Turning a manuscript into a book requires the efforts of many people. The publishing team at Bookouture would like to acknowledge everyone who contributed to this publication.

Audio
Alba Proko
Sinead O'Connor
Melissa Tran

Commercial
Lauren Morrissette
Hannah Richmond
Imogen Allport

Contracts
Peta Nightingale

Cover design
Debbie Clement

Data and analysis
Mark Alder
Mohamed Bussuri

Printed in Great Britain
by Amazon

58018248R00260